To The Last Drop

Andrew Wice

Colin,
Here is a haiku poem
for you, based on a true story.

On the numb winter branch
a candy-bright cardinal —
hissing snowfall

Thank you for everything.
Happy reading!
ADW
December, 2023

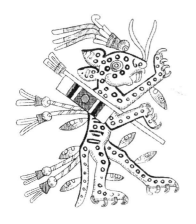

Bäuu Press
PO Box 4445
Boulder, CO
80306

Library of Congress Control Number: 2007938871

To the Last Drop
    / by   Andrew Wice
          p. cm.

    ISBN 10: 0-9721349-6-4
    ISBN 13: 978-0-9721349-6-5

    Printed in the United States

    10 9 8 7 6 5 4 3 2 1

"I fell down for thirst,
I was parched, my throat burned,
and I said: 'This is the taste of death'."

– Story of Sinuhe
Egypt, circa 2000 BCE
Aylward Blackman, translator

To The Last Drop

Andrew Wice

Part I Antebellum

Discovery   3
Reaction   23
Retaliation   39

Part II Bellum

Propagandance   51
Invasion   71
The Battle of Las Vegas, NM   97

Part III Occupation

Consolidation   111
Exploitation   131
Penetration   151

Part IV Rebellion

The Battle of the Bowl   165
Terrorism   187
Surprise   205

Part V Liberation

Operation Zero Tolerance   243
Watershed   265
The Outcome   293

"Whiskey is for drinking and water is for fighting over."

Mark Twain (attributed)

Part I Antebellum

Discovery

H₂O

Sun penetrated the naked open ocean, arousing the surface. One particular water molecule broke free of its compadres. Spinning into the air, its blur of electrons hummed with potential. The molecule soared upwards. Gravity weakened to a distant, forgotten anchor.

Free and light again, at last.

Then, at great height, the dizzying rise began to falter. In cooling fatigue, the one water molecule linked with others. Arrayed around a speck of carbon, the discrete droplet swirled through the growing cloud.

Billowing out to catch the wind, they sailed over the ocean. Beneath them, the ocean grew shallow and warm. Water molecules rose to join the cloud. And then the ocean gave way to land, and the supply of compadres dried up.

A mountain wall blocked their path. The cloud rode up the mountain's face, shedding its droplets like ballast. As the cloud crested the summit, the one discrete droplet became lethargic. Its bonds clicked rigid, locking the one particular molecule in place. Bricked into an intricate crystal, the collective pull of gravity beckoned.

The exhausted crystal abandoned the sinking cloud. It flipped and yawed downward, one snowflake of billions among trillions. Air currents played catch with the snowflake but gravity was its master. The crystal landed atop other crystals and was itself soon covered. The one molecule slept, unable to shiver its frozen bonds.

Eddie Brown

Of all the stripclubs in all the towns in all the world, you walked into hers. And what kind of stripper refuses a lapdance to an ex-lover?

"Whatcha lookin for, mister?"

Startled on his knees, Eddie turned around. The boy was about ten, backed up by a sketchy mongrel that growled between his legs.

"Ants," said Eddie. "I'm looking for fire ants. Want to help?"

"I know fire ants," said the boy, wary. He looked back to a low ring of hills across the flat brown plain. Sun-squinting, he returned to Eddie and the anthill.

Eddie said, "There are different kinds of fire ants. The kind I'm looking for is called *invicta* – the invader. They came up from Central America to conquer territory from the native ants."

"Why don't the other ants just fight back?"

"Because the invader ants have better guns. Do you like guns?"

The boy nodded.

Eddie said, "Imagine that the native ants have revolvers. Well, the invaders have AK-47's. They have AK-47's in their *butts*."

The boy giggled. Eddie continued, "They can shoot other ants, or they can shoot you if you get too close. Their stinger is the gun and their venom is the bullet."

The boy bit his lip.

"But do you see what's missing from this fire ant mound?" asked Eddie.

The boy stared intently at the mound rising from the sandy soil. It looked like a regular anthill, dug up a little. The boy shrugged.

"No ants!" Eddie laughed. "Come and see – they're all gone."

The boy stepped closer. His dog whined behind him. The boy said, "What's that funnel thing you got?"

"This is called a Berlese-Tullgren funnel. See where I dug into the dirt here? I use the funnel to separate the ants from the dirt. Only – guess what? – no ants."

The boy poked the troweled-up hole with a finger. No ants.

"My name is Eddie. What's yours?"

The boy said, "Daniel."

"Daniel, what do you think happened to all the fire ants that used to live here?"

"I dunno. The earthquake squashed them?"

"Maybe. That must have been scary, that earthquake two weeks ago. That was no ordinary earthquake. That was caused by subsidence.

4

Do you know what that is?"

Daniel dug into the vacant mound with his finger. He shook his head no.

"Subsidence is when we pump too much water out of the ground and the ground sinks. Like the way a car sinks if it loses air in its tires."

"There ain't water under the ground here."

"Maybe there's no groundwater here, but if they pump enough water out of the ground in Clovis, or Lubbock, or even El Paso, subsidence can happen. Usually it happens so slowly that you don't notice, but sometimes it happens fast, like it did two weeks ago. That's because there was a fault in the rock beneath us, like an old broken bone that never healed right. But I don't think the earthquake killed these invader ants."

Daniel squinted up cautiously.

"Daniel, do you remember how I told you that there are different kinds of fire ants? One of these local fire ants has a special enemy, an army ant. And so I'm doing an experiment."

Daniel's eyes widened. "What kind of experiment?"

"I'm trying to teach the army ants to attack the invader fire ants."

"How you gonna teach *ants* to do things? I can't even get Pico to sit when I tell him to." The dog looked up at the sound of his name, then dropped his attention to sniffing Eddie's pack.

"Ants smell with their antenna, and it's how they tell who's who. I made the invader fire ants smell like the native ones. It's like switching their uniforms."

"And then you get the army ants and put em in there?"

"I wish it were that easy. But the problem with army ants is that they're always on the march. They only stay in one place, called a bivouac, for a short while. Then they move on, looking for more food. If I can find a bivouac nearby, maybe I can prove that my experiment worked. The army ants live underground so it's really hard to find them."

Eddie looked around the disk of horizon, then at the eroded knob of a hill casting a shadow on his pickup, then across the brown plain to the ring of low hills. Daniel scanned as well, squinting like Eddie.

Eddie said, "If my name was *Neivamyrmex harrisi*, where would I live?"

Daniel said, "Some crazy place I bet I never heard of."

Eddie smiled and pointed to the knob hill. "Daniel, does that hill look different than it used to?"

Daniel studied the hill. He said, "Yeah, all them rocks crashed down when the earth quaked, like mom's CD's falling off the shelf. And it looks like it got bigger."

"It does. I bet it stayed where it was though, and the ground subsided. It looks like that might actually *be* the fault line along there. See where that cactus fell over?"

"Uh ... no."

"The roots of that cholla are exposed, making a nice little shelter for an army ant bivouac out here in the sunny desert. Let's go see."

They climbed the hill. The cholla was half-yanked out of its socket, dumped on its crown. A loose welt of displaced earth was scattered around the root ball.

"I don't see no army ants," said Daniel.

"They don't like the sun." Eddie flipped over a flat rock. Tiny mustard yellow ants reeled in the sudden sunlight, scattering to the rock's dark side.

"I think we might have found the army ant bivouac," said Eddie. "Are you excited? I am."

"Dig the dirt away so we can see," said Daniel.

Eddie sunk his entrenching tool into the loose sand around the roots. He pulled the debris away, revealing a basketball-sized hollow.

"Whoa," said Daniel.

Inside the hollow were thousands, tens of thousands of tiny, mustard yellow ants.

Daniel said, "Is that them? The army ants?"

"Meet the hardworking *Neivamyrmex* sisters. Now I need to find evidence that this army attacked those fire ants down there."

"What kind of evidence?" Daniel leaned closer to the hollow.

"Pupa."

"What's pupa?"

"That's an ant kid, halfway between an egg and an ant. Like a butterfly when it's inside the chrysalis."

"What's a chrysalis?"

"A cocoon. You've seen a cocoon, right?"

"Uh ... yeah?"

Eddie pointed into the hollow – Daniel sucked in his breath to see how close Eddie's finger got to the army ants. "Do you see these hanging from the ceiling there? Those are cocoons, with army ant pupa inside them. The army ants found this spot after the earthquake and made a bivouac here, hung their kids from the ceiling."

Daniel laughed. "My mom told me she was gonna hang me from the ceiling."

"Really?"

Daniel said, "Yeah, she was only kidding."

Eddie dug further into the cool sand, exposing more of the chamber.

Daniel said, "Hey, hey lookit! Them cocoons down there are different."

"Right you are," smiled Eddie. He reached into his pack to remove specimen bottles and long forceps.

"Is that the evidence? For your experiment?"

"I think it is," said Eddie. He unstoppered a bottle and, with gentle forceps, plucked a half-dozen foreign pupa from the chamber. "I'll know for sure later. But if they are what I hope they are – the pupa of the invader fire ants – then it means that you and I are looking at something no one else has ever seen before."

"No one *ever*?" frowned Daniel. "Forever?"

"No one ever in the whole history of the world. You and I are the first, buddy."

"Hey, this one's getting on me!"

"I'll get her, real gently, and return her to the bivouac."

"How do you know it's a girl?"

"All the ants you see are girls. They're all sisters, and the queen is their mom."

"There's no boys?"

"The boys have wings and only come out to mate with winged females, to turn them into queens."

"Where's the queen at?"

"She's in that chamber somewhere, but her daughters are hiding her, to protect her. They don't know that we're friendly." Eddie slid the rubber-stoppered specimen bottles into their sleeves in his pack. He dug down deeper into the dirt.

"Hey," said Daniel, "the bottom is filling up with water, mister."

Indeed, water was trickling up into the hollow.

"Where's it coming from?" whispered Daniel. "Ain't no water here."

"Maybe it's an underground river, shifted closer to the surface by the earthquake."

"Lookit, the army ants are drownding."

"You're right, they are. I'm going to stop disturbing our little friends here. They've had enough for one day."

Pico raised his nose from sniffing the cholla root ball, head cocked. Daniel looked across the brown plain to the low ring of hills in the distance. "I think I gotta go home now. The sun's setting."

"I have to go home too, so I can check out our pupa." Eddie pulled a magnifying glass from his pack. "This is for you, Daniel, for helping make this great discovery. You can check out all the different ants that live around your house. But remember, this magnifying glass is for learning, not burning."

Daniel took it by the handle, looked it over and slipped it into his pocket. He started to run down the eroded knob of the hill, dog sliding after him. By the time Eddde packed up, Daniel was a diminished dot across the plain. Eddie pulled on his pack and hiked down the back side of the hill to his pickup truck.

He snorted in disbelief, "Nice, 'learning not burning.' That's so gay."

Beep.

"Hey Gordon! Hey Gordon, it's Eddie, pick up the phone, pick up the phone, hey Gordie, how Gordie, Gordie Howe, hey – "

"All right, all right, I'm here. What time is it?"

Eddie said, "I'm not sure. Still nocturnal, I'd wager. I've been in my lab since I got back from my collection site."

"Where?"

"My collection site, out on the border with Texas. Between Hobbes and Portales, where they had that subsidence quake."

"Yeah, ok," and then a stinger of impatience rose in Gordon's voice. "You know I have to work tomorrow, so – "

"That's it, that's why I'm calling. I need to get into the electron microscopy lab."

"I can't – why, Eddie?"

"Because I think it *worked*, that's why. One of the *Solenopsis invicta* colonies I fogged with *S. xyloni* hydrocarbons was extirpated. I found a *Neivamyrmex harrisi* bivouac about ten meters away. I've got pupa, Gordon. I think they're from that extirpated *invicta* colony. But my bedroom laboratory is, well, limited let's say."

"I know your 'laboratory.' *Pogonomyrmex* workers reviving in a pile of homemade amphetamines. Lidless jars of evaporated ether."

"And that's *after* I cleaned up. I know. But my main problem is that I need a scanning electron microscope to prove that the pupa are *invicta*."

"Well yeah. Remember when you thought you had discovered the missing link, a pre-formicid living fossil that turned out to be a flightless aculeate wasp?"

"Yes Gordon, I do remember. Not my finest hour. The folks at the Entomological Cryptozoology Society still won't return my calls. But I dug down and collected pupa specimens until the chamber started to get water seepage."

"Water seepage? Over in that dry corner?"

"Probably just some forgotten finger off the Oglalla aquifer, brought near the surface by that subsidence quake. Anyway, if I can get into the microscopy lab, I can prove that the pupa are *invicta* and that my hydrocarbon-masking technique can work."

"Eddie, you said you were doing this, uh, project to prove that it can't work, that ants would be terrible biocontrol mechanisms, that *Neivamyrmex* was not an appropriate defense against *Solenopsis invicta*."

"I know, and I am. That's still my goal. But Gordon, it's already been proposed, and *that* research is about to begin at UTEP. All I'm doing is anticipating their study, starting with the hydrocarbon-masking. First I'm going to collect all the positive data that I can, even more impressive than whatever UTEP pulls off because I'm doing it in the field. And then I'll poke big holes in the idea, big enough for *Solenopsis invicta* to crawl through and halt the bad sad history of introducing predator species for biocontrol. The Cane Toads in Australia, the mongoose in Jamaica and Hawaii, the brown tree snakes in Guam."

"What's the compound you masked the colony with? Doesn't it upset the fire ants? Maybe *that's* what killed them."

"No, it's just a dose of a *Solenopsis xyloni* queen's signature scent from her postpharyngeal gland, a basic dimethyl-branched hydrocarbon complex. All species of *Solenopsis* are so trail-specific, they completely ignore the presence of an alien scent."

A creaky yawn from Gordon. "All right, all right. Anything to get back to sleep. Come by at noon tomorrow. Dr. Davids won't be around."

"Great, perfect. Perfect. I'll see you tomorrow. With pupa!"

The phone clicked and Eddie pulled it from his ear – ah, the cooling of ear sweat.

"To bed?" Eddie asked of his bedroom. The terrarium of black *Camponotus* toiled like tiny carpenters. The dog-eared taxonomic guides sloughed from a pile of ragged scientific journals. A ramekin of home-made amphetamines whispered, "Not yet."

"All right," sighed Eddie. "Not yet."

U.S. Armstrong

U.S. Armstrong let the moment stretch out in front of them. His white ten-gallon was tipped forward over his eyes. Legs out long to boot-scuff the conference table, leaning back in his executive chair.

The entire room waited for him. The windows of the conference room offered them the bright castellation of downtown El Paso. The blue sky was darkened by the tinted glass. Sharp reflections off the skyscrapers burned molten copper. Inside the room it was silent. U.S.'s hat brim rose imperceptibly to reveal a slice of pale blue eye.

With a voice like sun-warmed leather, "Starvin are yeh? Let me tell you about *starvin*. Back in Indochina, my unit was out on patrol when our fire base got overrun. We set out marching south through that goddamn jungle with one C ration left to a man. We walked for a week. We was eating tree bark and termites before we made it back to civilization. Starvin. You don't know *starvin*."

U.S. dropped the brim of his hat over his eyes.

Keith Earl cleared his throat. "I didn't mean it serious like that, U.S. I'm just saying, uh, lunch is passing us by and it don't seem like we're getting it right. And uh, maybe if we took a short break ..."

Geldman held up his hand. "No breaks, lunch or otherwise, until U.S. says so. So let's move on to the next item on the agenda. Vince, what do you have for us?"

Vince cleared his throat. His white hat and teeth glowed in contrast with his dark face. "New Mexico drilled a well between Hobbes and Portales, right on our border. This corporate body owns an old claim which abuts that same stretch of border, near the little town of Bledsoe. This well they dug is one hundred feet deep with a twelve inch bore drawing twenty gallons per minute, and is being used for local irrigation as we speak."

"And?" baritoned U.S. "I got a lot of wells running, bigger ones."

Vince soldiered on, "This area has never been utilized for ground-water. It's not above the Oglalla aquifer and is too far east to be part of the Pecos river system. All of a sudden, these New Mexicans drop a well into dry desert and are pumping up cold, sweet water. Now there's no way to tell for sure, but our geologists ran some models and are saying that the lay of the land implies that it probably flows from *our* side of the border. Specifically, through our old claim there."

Geldman said, "Vince, like U.S. said, this corporation owns water wells from the Rio Grande all the way up the panhandle. What's the point of another?"

Vince opened a folder and pulled out an assessment sheet. "Every well we own, just like every water district in the New Southwest, is over-allocated. Without more water there can be no further growth, no progress. It all started with the Bureau of Reclamation, which built the great dams all over the West. Those reservoirs and hydroelectric genera-tors made growth and progress possible in what had been useless desert. The progress encouraged more growth and business, until soon there were too many people for even all the combined lakes and rivers. And then, as if guided by the invisible hand of the Almighty, we discovered that the entire middle of the country is sitting on a great freshwater ocean. We pumped it up and irrigated rows of swollen watermelon where before it was dryland farming at best. Think on that, growing *water*melon in the desert. It was such a great success that we built more farms, more towns, sank more wells. After a while, we noticed that the level of the aquifer was dropping fast. Progress dictated pumping it up faster than it could refill. That water trickled its way down before the birth of Christ, who put it there for us to find. Now the environmentalists claim that the acquifer will be pumped dry in twenty years."

"Bullshit," U.S. commented gravely.

"Absolutely, I couldn't agree more. However, it is true that the more the level drops, the more expensive it gets to pump the water out. Now, all of our wells are going one hundred percent, and there's scarcely a patch of ground left that hasn't been explored. And then, all of a sud-den, some little dirt farms in New Mexico stumble on good water where there's never been. I'm saying, let's tap into what's ours. We got to pump the water out now, while it's still there. It's probably flowing right underneath our claim, too deep for trees but not too deep for us. We got to get our water up to the surface before it's gone. Right now it's just being wasted."

Geldman folded his hands upon the polished table. He stole a glance at U.S.'s boots and said, "Vince, exploratory wells cost money. Geologists cost money. Pipelines cost money. What does this corporation need with more water? We're not farmers."

"Nossir, we're not," said Vince. "But once we capture that water, it's ours. We could sell to the highest bidder – for example, the Rio Grande Water district, right here in El Paso. They went into business privately when the city decided they didn't want to partner up, and now they control every drop. Big money in that."

Geldman said, "We don't even know for sure if that water is going to be where you're hoping. Hope don't make it so. Sorry, I don't think that – "

"It's *my* goddamn water," interrupted U.S. He raised his hat brim to scan the room. "Ain't it? And it's being wasted, letting some tater farmers pump it out from underneath me? My land, my water beneath it. I want it, just like I want the oil or gas or coal or gold beneath my land, if it's there. Don't waste any time with any more geologists or environmentalists or other kooks. Drop a twenty-one inch bore, two hundred feet down. We can sell it off to the farmers, or El Paso. Or hell, Lubbock, I don't care. We'll sell to the highest bidder. So that's that. Lunch time. Meeting adjourned until two."

Papers were straightened, folders were returned to briefcases. Brass snapping of locks. They began to push away from the table.

Keith Earl suggested sending his secretary out for some McDonalds's.

"Mack-donalds, hell," said U.S. "Let's go to the Roadhouse. I want a steak and a beer. I'm buying."

Geldman said, "U.S., we can't drive up to the Roadhouse and be back by two."

"Then we'll push back the meeting with the satellite radio people," growled U.S.

"But you've got your inspection today at Fort Bliss."

"Aw hell, you're right." U.S. pulled his legs off the table and smoothed down his bolero: the badge of the Texas State Guard, a pipestone T on a silver star in a shield of turquoise. He rose to his full height. "Right, my boys are going to be displaying their discipline at the Parade Grounds today. I'm needed there. Keith Earl, you go ahead and tell your secretary to bring us up some Mack-Donalds. I'll have a steak, bleeding."

Keith Earl pinched his lips. "Uh Boss, they don't got steak on their menu."

U.S. turned away and assessed his skyline. "I'll have a steak, bleeding."

<u>Billy Ortiz</u>

My good luck keeps on going bro, there's a spot in front of Pete's bar. I jam the screwdriver into the column to keep my truck from rolling. It's a nice summer night.

Inside Pete's, the band is so fucking *loud*, bro. But I see Manning, and he's someone I can talk to about this. Big Joe gets up kinda shaky from next to Manning, pulls his way along the wall to get to the john. I grab the rail and set myself on the stool next to Manning.

Charlie appears in front of me and says, "Shot and a beer, Billy?"

"Yeah bro, when you get a minute. Hey Manning, how's it going?"

Manning finally notices me. His eyes wrinkle and he nods. He's got that collapsed face when he ain't got his teeth in. A rolled cigarette is dead between his lips.

I lean in, so I don't got to shout. "I did it bro. I tapped into the pipeline. No more hauling water for me."

A shot of tequila and a cold bottle appear in front of me. "Thanks Charlie!" I shout. Back to Manning, "I tapped in right after the first split. Just an hour with a wrench, since I had the hoses already connected and buried. And Melody, she's had that dripline ready to go for a while now."

Manning's loose cheeks fold up a little smile. I took a drink of beer and it was good, cold. I lean back in to Manning. "The hardest part was the last two nights, burying the hoses. It's just gravity from the split, down the slope and to my plants. It's working right now."

I pick up my shot and clack it off Manning's empty bottle. I tip it down – tastes like honey. I breathe out the fumes and ask Manning if he wants another beer.

I catch Charlie's eye. "A beer for Manning and another shot for me and ...." I pick up my bottle, half-empty, "I guess another beer for me. Thanks Charlie."

The band is so loud, playing that "Mustang Sally" song for the hundredth time. But here comes Charlie with the drinks. I like Charlie, he's a good guy.

I clack bottles with Manning and finish my half. Big juicy beer burp, aftertaste of tequila. Manning lights up that stub of a cigarette, nearly burns his mustache.

"Hey Manning, you want a smoke? I went to the Pueblo last week." He doesn't hear me so I lean in closer, raise my voice. "So I'm just like fuck it, you know? We find water and I can't have *any* of it, cause they got to it first? All that land, all of it, is Ortiz land. We've had it since before the Spanish land grants, even. So fuck it bro, I'm going to grow my plants. Worth a hell of a lot more than potatoes, we all know that. Now I just wish I had started with better seeds, you know, not those Mexi seeds."

The band had just stopped so I shouted the part about the seeds real loud, just before people started clapping. Fuck it, no one cares anyway. I light a generic cigarette and tip back my tequila.

Someone taps my shoulder. I turn around: it's One-Armed Anthony. I raise my bottle to him, "Hey Anthony."

Anthony nods and scratches his beard with his one hand. "You get my leaf spring done yet Billy?"

"Oh sorry bro. I couldn't get to it. Maybe tomorrow." I drink my beer.

"It's just a long walk home from here, that's all."

"I'll give you a ride home tonight, if you need it. No problem. Hey Charlie, can you get me another shot and a beer when you get a minute?"

The band starts up again, "Brown Eyed Girl." A bunch of girls pull each other onto the dance floor. Any good-looking ones? I drink my beer and check them out.

Governor Armeño

The Governor of New Mexico brushed powdered sugar from his fingers. He sent a thick tongue to the corners of his mouth, missing the mustache crumbs.

"Mr. White?"

The Governor's secretary raised his fine blonde eyebrows.

"Mr. White, you can take away this snack and send them in now."

Mr. White cleared the desk of biscochito crumbs. Then he strode to the door and opened it, announcing, "Attorney General Arida and associate."

Two men in dark blue suits entered the makeshift office. Mr. White offered chairs before the Governor's desk. The men set down their briefcases and took seats.

To the familiar-looking Arida, Governor Armeño said, "I apologize that we have to meet in this office. The air conditioning in my own is entirely broken, you see."

"It is not a problem, Mr. Governor."

"They have promised to have it fixed for a week now.

Well, maybe tomorrow."

The Attorney General nodded.

"So ..." said Armeño, showing them his palms. His eyebrows caterpillared up his forehead. "Good news?"

Arida swept his briefcase onto his knees and snapped it open. He removed a folder, closed his briefcase and returned it to his side. "We are finally on the docket, Mr. Governor. The Federal District Court will hear the case on Monday. While my office prepared the suit for the State Engineer, it will be argued by my associate, Mr. Sediento. He has many years of experience in water rights litigation at the county and state level, and a familiarity with Federal Law which should permit –"

"Wait a minute," interrupted Armeño, "you are not the producers?"

"Producers?" asked Arida, still proffering the folder.

"Yes, the producers, the California producers. For the show. No?"

Mr. White said, "Ah, Mr. Governor, that is your two o'clock. This is your Attorney General, Mr. Arida, and his associate Mr. Sediento."

Armeño smiled. "Oh? Well, very good. And again, this pertains to ...."

"Our suit against the Armstrong Corporation of Texas, Mr. Governor," said Mr. White, nodding encouragement to the lawyers.

Arida looked back to the Governor's confusion. "Yes. Regarding the drilling of a competing well on the state border."

Vacuum pause. Arida removed several papers from the file and placed them on the Governor's desk.

Arida continued, "As you may recall Mr. Governor, one year ago we developed an uncontained aquifer in Southern Roosevelt County. On your desk there is 19.27.74 NMAC Special Order #195, signed by the State Engineer, declaring it an official groundwater basin, with possession of rights pursuant to that distinction."

Governor Armeño looked at NMAC Special Order #195, then back at Arida.

"Ahem," said the Attorney General. "This establishes the rule of prior appropriation for the reasonable use of a groundwater resource, which follows '*Qui prior est in tempore, potior est in jure.*' That is to say, he that is first in time is first in right."

"Aha, yes," nodded Armeño. "That's good."

Arida continued, "Four months after establishing our right, the Armstrong Corporation, in conjunction with the Edwards Trinity and

Oglalla Water Districts, drilled a deeper well with a larger bore only a few thousand meters to the northeast. Since then, the New Mexican site has experienced a radical decline in production."

"But we drilled it first? They can't cut in line if we drilled it first, right?"

"Exactly Mr. Governor, hence the lawsuit."

Armeño nodded thoughtfully. "So we'll definitely win."

Arida said, "I expect so, sir, but unfortunately the case is more complicated than that. Mr. Sediento?"

Mr. Sediento brought his briefcase up to his knees and snapped it open, removing a file. He returned the briefcase to the floor and cleared his throat. "As opposed to the prior appropriation rule of most Western states, Texas water rights are derived from the antiquated English Common Law – the rule of capture. It was ruled in 1935's Acton v. Blundel that 'the person who owns the surface may dig therein, and apply all that is there found.' In Texas state law, this right is absolute: everything found beneath a property is the possession of said property owner."

"Unless we can prove their violation of *damnium abque injuria*, the principle of loss without injury, *id est*, the shortfall in predicted gallons per minute, *exempli gratia*," interjected the Attorney General.

"To which they will doubtless cite Houston v. East, that groundwater exists 'so secret, occult and concealed' that interconnectivity between underground water systems cannot be proven," returned Mr. Sediento.

"Wow, 'secret, occult and concealed,' that's like a scary movie," joked Governor Armeño. Only Mr. White issued a smile, and a mirthless one at that.

Attorney General Arida charged, "To *that*, we will argue their violation of reasonable use and correlative rights, qualified by delivering water off-site to El Paso."

Mr. Sediento shook his head. "It is legal in Texas to transport groundwater between basins. As the plaintiff, we must overcome an extremely high burden of proof. A drawdown is only circumstantial. The Texas Supreme Court has upheld the absolute right of capture, regardless of injury to other claims, in Corpus Christi v. Pleasanton, Denis v. Kickapoo, Sipriano v. Great Spring Waters of America, *et cetera*."

"But the United States Supreme Court ruled in California-Oregon Power v. Beaver Portland Cement Company that prior appropriation for *beneficial* use is entitled to protectionism, following the Desert Land Act of 1877," triumphed Arida.

Mr. Sediento shook his head bitterly. "The Act is limited by local and customary laws of usage – we're right back to whether the Court will recognize our right by prior appropriation or theirs, by the antiquated Common Law of Texas. Justice Stephens may dismiss the suit simply on the basis of Guiterrez v. Albuquerque Land & Irrigation Company. Further, with the preponderance of – "

"Gentlemen, gentlemen, gentlemen," interrupted the Governor, lifting his heavy head from the cradle of his hands. "What does any of this have to do with ... I mean, do you need me for this in some way?"

Attorney General Arida blinked behind his glasses. "No, Mr. Governor, we were just demonstrating some of the difficulties with our lawsuit. We are able to assess the economic liability the Armstrong Corporation has caused, and if the Court acknowledges our right by prior appropriation we'll be fully rewarded, *quod erat demonstrandum*. The difficulties stem from the collision of two mutually exclusive systems of water rights adjudication competing across state lines, as well as the 'secret, occult and concealed' nature of groundwater hydrogeology."

"Yes, well, good. Very, very good. Carry on, and I'd like a *brief* report when you return from D.C."

Mr. White piped in, "It's the Federal District Court, sir. The case will be heard here, in Santa Fe."

"Even better," smiled Armeño. "Home court advantage. Get it?"

"Mr. Governor, the Federal Courts are in no way – " began the Attorney General.

"Thank you," interrupted the Governor. "That's fine, very helpful. Thank you."

The lawyers stood. Mr. White opened the door for them. Attorney General Arida paused at the threshold and turned back to the Governor. Looking down over his glasses, he said dryly, "Mr. Governor, shall we keep you informed?"

"Mm? Yes, I'd like that. No need to come in, an email will be fine. Adios."

Mr. White closed the door behind them. "Sir, I should remind you that the legislature has discouraged public officials from using 'adios' owing to its theism."

"Yes, good," said Governor Armeño, smiling into a vanity mirror. He stretched his Young Brando smile up over his teeth, forced more warm sincerity into his eyes, and raised his Spanish chin while spit-curling a dark lock. "Send the producers in now please, the producers from California."

"That's at two o'clock, sir. You are meeting now with Mr. Benitez, your Adjutant General, and General Gary Camby, on behalf of the New Mexico State Defense Force."

"Even generals are better than more lawyers. Dry as caliche. Get me a bottle of water, would you?"

Mr. White produced a bottle from the mini-fridge and cracked it open. He turned up a glass from the sideboard and poured in the bottle.

Governor Armeño sipped. "Ahm. Where's this water from anyway, Mr. White?"

Mr. White said, "Sam's Club, I think."

"We're not running out, are we?"

"No sir, we've got plenty," said Mr. White, dropping the bottle in the trashcan.

The Governor drained the glass. "Excellent. You can take this glass away, and send the generals in."

Mr. White opened the door and ushered the supplicants in. He announced, "Adjutant General Benitez and General Camby, commanding general of the State Defense Force."

"Are you real generals? Or lawyer-generals, like that last guy?" smiled Armeño.

Mr. White said, "You remember promoting Brigadier General Camby when you appointed him to command the State Defense Force."

"Yes, of course. Please have a seat. I'm sorry that we aren't able to meet in my real office. Something with the ducts. They say it will be fixed, maybe tomorrow."

The generals nodded curtly. They wore suits, not uniforms. Camby's golf tan made him almost as dark as Benitez.

"Mr. Governor," began Benitez, "Local civilian militias have come to the aid of New Mexico for four hundred years. Currently called the Sate Defense Force, this militia is 'the Governor's own'."

"My own army? I thought that's what the National Guard is for," smiled Armeño.

"The State Defense Force cannot ever be federalized, as the National Guard is now. The SDF is essentially the reserves for the army reserves, but with seventy-five percent of our National Guard currently deployed in the Middle East, New Mexico is extremely vulnerable. We are here to ask for additional funding to increase enlistment, training and equipment for the militia."

"What are we vulnerable to? Things are pretty quiet around here."

"Natural disasters. Terrorism. Civil unrest. Drug and illegal immigrant traffic."

"Well we've got the Homeland Security and Border Patrol and all that, and the DEA. Violent crime is down two percent, last quarter," dismissed the Governor.

"Federal programs are experiencing major budget cuts, to offset the cost of the War on Terror. However, PATRIOT V strongly encourages the promotion of state defense forces with a possibility of matching funds. The militia serves without pay unless it is called into active duty. With a small monthly stipend, we would be able to maintain a ready force instead. With a small increase in our clerical staff and administration, we could expand recruitment and streamline our efficiency. With a small allotment we could purchase new uniforms and equipment."

Governor Armeño folded his hands under his chin. He hoarsely affected Brando's Godfather, "Tell me how much."

The Governor watched bemused as Benitez pulled a notebook and Waterman pen from his jacket, wrote a figure and tore the page out. He laid the paper face down on Armeño's bare desk and slid it across with two fingers.

The Governor turned the paper over. "Two million dollars! Ai, you've got to be kidding me here."

The generals shifted uncomfortably in their chairs. Benitez said, "Remember, tax breaks will offset some costs. Perhaps ... twenty percent? Without an adequate security force, the people of New Mexico lie dangerously exposed."

"To what? We don't have hurricanes, and there's Air Force bases and ... two million? That's the craziest ... "

"Mr. Governor, the costs could be much higher down the road," said Benitez.

"This is madness," said Armeño. He flashed his Consolation Smile. "I'm sorry, but there isn't anything near two million for you."

Benitez said, "Perhaps through a private fund raiser?"

"I do enough of those already. I've got one tonight. Work, work, work."

General Camby took a pin out his pocket and slid it across the desk. It was the shield of the New Mexico State Defense Force with a tiny banner that read "Los Vecinos."

Camby's voice was mild, "Sir, at least accept a pin to show your support. Our name goes back to the 1800's and means 'the neighbors,' an excellent description of our role in the self-defense of this great state."

"I know what 'vecino' means," said the Governor, turning the shiny pin over in his fingers. He fixed the pin to his lapel with some difficulty. When he finally looked up to the generals his Benevolent Smile was in place. "Gentlemen, I'll wear this pin proudly. And I'll see what I can do for some funding. Now I thank you, but I've got an important meeting. Producers from California."

The generals stood. Camby said, "I'm from California, sir, originally. At least, since the eighties."

"Mm," smiled the Governor.

Mr. White closed the door behind them.

Governor Armeño said, "Are they outside? Are they waiting?"

"Yes. Shall I send them in now?"

"Let them wait one minute. Are the gift bags ready Mr. White?"

Mr. White nodded.

"Is my – does the hair look right?"

Mr. White nodded.

"I guess we're ready."

Mr. White said, "Sir, are you prepared for ... if it isn't good news?"

"Sure, sure. No problem. Send them in now, Mr. White."

Mr. White opened the door to two impossibly tanned men, dressed city-slick. The taller, Mr. Garvin, wore a white dinner jacket and a Hawaiian shirt. Mr. Greenbaum presented a salmon leisure suit, hairy chest, big gold watch. They took their seats.

Armeño beamed at them. His fingers twiddled when he said, "Well?"

Mr. Garvin said, "Mr. Governor, we must inform you ..."

"Yes?" hissed Armeño, smile straining to its corners.

"... that you have the green light! Congratulations, you're going to be the star of the network's newest reality show."

"Yes!" Armeño raised his fists in glory. "Oh that is wonderful, fantastic. Thank you! It will be a great show, a great one. I already have so many ideas for it! Here, I came up with a title."

The producers watched as the Governor pulled a sheet of paper from his desk, uncapped a pen and wrote "Lower Exposure" on it. He turned the paper over and slid it across his desk on two fingers to Mr. Greenbaum, who folded it and put it in his pocket.

Mr. Greenbaum said, "Thank you Mr. Governor, I'll send this on to our people. They've already begun working on some wonderful challenges, dramatics and so forth."

"This calls for a celebration. Mr. White, the gift bags! I know you guys will love the nuts. Pistachios rolled in green chile salt, they're addictive. Mr. White, see what we've got special in the sideboard. Hey, I'm sorry we're not meeting in my regular office, which is much more comfortable. But the air conditioning is broken and they haven't gotten it fixed yet. Maybe tomorrow. Here, take some New Mexico gift bags, they're good fun. Mr. White, pour those drinks please. Do you like my title for the show? 'Lower Exposure.' You know, like that TV show they had in Alaska? I could be like the head guy in that show, and you'll follow me around to see how I overcome the difficult challenges of statesmenhood."

"Yes, and for the eating contest, we've already locked in Taka Miyake, the two-time Japanese champion," said Mr. Garvin, accepting a glass of reposado.

"A toast to our success, gentlemen," said the Governor. "Mr. White, you had better cancel my afternoon please."

Reaction

H_2O

Longer days of sun set the one particular molecule quivering against its compadres. The sun dosed them with energy until the one molecule could escape in the fluid confederation of a droplet.

The one particular water molecule crawled downward through the soil, dragging particles like a magnet trailing iron filings. Slow progress towards the eternal beckoning of gravity. Down through surface strata, loose soil to saturated sand. The molecule exploited a fracture in an impassable layer of shale to continue its pilgrimage, dripping ever deeper into the fossil earth. On its journey it collected mineral ions, dragging them through the microscopic labyrinth. It trickled deeper underground as the wagons rolled west, as the buffalo fell, as the ants built their mounds, as the dams blocked the rivers.

Uncounted years after falling as snow, the water molecule experienced something incredible: its compadres began to pull it *up*. Their hydrogen bond was stronger than gravity so the molecule climbed through dense layers of cracked shale, through gravel, through sand. Into a pipe, pulled along by its compadres.

And at last, riding a turbulent burp of air, the molecule was returned to the light. The one particular water molecule clung to the compadres of its droplet hanging wobbly off the lip of a metal spigot. Gravity moaned for it.

"What the hell?" a person grumbled, smacking the faucet in frustration.

Vibrations tore the droplet's hydrogen bonds. The molecule felt gravity claim it. The last drop fell.

Hormigo

Flying blue colors, his fleet of motorcycles followed Hormigo into the parking lot of Pete's Bar. He walked his growling black, chopped fatboy to a stop before the heavy wood doors. The Diablos cut their engines. After a minute, the birds began singing again.

Hormigo's old lady wiped the sweat from her cleavage with a tissue. Hormigo stepped onto the porch and pulled the doors: they did not open. His right hand gave a twitch inside its glove. "What the hell? They can't be closed."

Ribeye pressed his gnarled scar to the dirty window. "Looks closed."

Hormigo turned around. Except for their motorcycles, the lot was empty. He reached into his vest pocket for his tobacco. "Ribeye, go around back and see what the fuck."

Hormigo rolled a cigarette and smoked it. He heard Ribeye pound on the back door. He looked at his men, towering around him in hard-worn leathers and blue bandanas. Cocky, handsome Flywheel. Big, scary Lumbres. Big, half-witted Half-Tank. Quiet, vicious Wolfe. Indian-nosed Jefe. And their old ladies.

Footsteps were coming around the side. Ribeye stood with Little Pete. Hormigo flicked away the cigarette and shook Pete's hand.

"What are you closed for, Pete?" said Hormigo, finally releasing his grip.

"Got no water. Have to be closed," said Pete, withdrawing his withered hand.

"What you mean, no water?"

"Town well went dry. Water tower's empty. National Guard supposed to be around with a water truck for drinking. But so far, not yet."

Hormigo suddenly brightened. "Hell Pete, we don't want no *water*. We want some beers and shots and steaks, right boys?"

A growl of assent from his Diablos. Little Pete looked at the ground as he said, "I'm sorry Hormigo, we ain't allowed to be open without water. Can't wash glasses or dishes, can't make ice. Can't cook. Can't even flush the toilets."

"Until when?" asked Hormigo.

Pete shrugged. "Until we get our water back."

Hormigo's face darkly clouded, then washed with sympathy. "That can't be good for business, bro. Tell you what. We'll just drink some beer, and you don't have to wash out our shot glasses. Forget the steaks."

"I'm sorry Hormigo. I would if I could. But the Board of Health's been around."

Hormigo stared hard at Pete. They were the same height, but Pete was thirty years older and forty pounds lighter. Little Pete looked away and shrugged miserably.

"All right Pete, forget it. We'll go over to that Roadhouse in Texas. But Pete?"

Pete looked up shrinkingly. Hormigo ordered, "Open up our bar again. Soon."

"I hope so," nodded Pete sadly.

"Okay Diablos, let's ride out of here. Get some beers down the road. See you soon, Pete," Hormigo warned, subjecting Pete to another crushing handshake.

They kicked the bikes alive and the fleet clawed out of the dirt parking lot. Pete watched them go, shielding his eyes from the dust cloud. When he could open his hand again, he found a fifty dollar bill crumpled inside it.

The Diablos crossed into Texas and rode another twenty miles south. They arrived at the Roadhouse to find its vast parking lot completely filled with pickup trucks. The Diablos had to roll all the way around the sprawling complex before finding a place where they could all park together, out by the dumpsters.

The Diablos followed Hormigo around to the front door, creaking leather and jingling metal. Hormigo nodded at Ribeye's scarred sneer; Ribeye flung the doors open to reveal their arrival. No heads turned in the cavernous Roadhouse that was occupied by smoke, twangin' New Country and fifty televisions showing the same football game.

Hormigo glared at their indifference. He felt his right hand twitch in its glove. He walked forward and his men followed.

The long bar had no stools open. Of the hundred tables, all were occupied save for a section near the kitchen. It was to these three tables that Hormigo marched his men.

The tables were still littered from the past customers – napkins, lipsticky glasses, greasy plates. They pulled the tables together, silverware ringing on the floor. When Hormigo decided that they had waited too long, he sent Half-Tank to find a waitress.

The country music was deafening. The television over their tables cast the Cowboys-Redskins game in their faces. Hormigo smoked, looking around the Roadhouse. All the faces were like radar dishes aimed at the closest TV. They all broke into whoops and yeehaws at the same time. Hormigo scowled and looked around for Half-Tank who was just then escorting a harried waitress to their table.

"For everyone," Hormigo said when she arrived, "a bottle of beer and a shot of tequila. Not that Cuervo shit. Something good."

The waitress wrote on her pad and slipped away. Half-Tank sat down and set his elbow in a puddle of ranch dressing. Hormigo watched with disgust as Half-Tank had to use someone else's old dirty napkin to clean his arm.

"This place sucks," Hormigo said to his old lady.

She turned her leather-corseted cleavage toward him and smiled. Hormigo smiled back. It was better when they were sitting down, they were the same height then. The entire Roadhouse suddenly cheered some play on the TV.

"I fucking hate TV's in bars," growled Hormigo.

The waitress returned with fourteen bottles of beer on a tray. She put the tray down in the middle of the dirty table. She said, "That's seventy dollars."

Hormigo said, "I'll run a tab."

The waitress said, "I need a credit card to run a tab."

Homigo raised his eyebrows but reached into his vest and pulled out his wallet. He handed the waitress his credit card.

She looked it over suspiciously, walking to the bar.

"How about cleaning this table off?" he called after her. A few heads turned. They had all looked back at something on the TV before any challenges could be issued.

A busboy came out of the kitchen doors with an empty plastic tub. He was walking past their table when Hormigo barked, "Oyé!"

The busboy looked at the Diablos, then at the sprawling Roadhouse beyond them. He came to the Diablos' table and began to pile up dishes and glasses.

Hormigo nodded. The busboy kept his eyes on his work, filling the tub and wiping down the tables with a rag.

Flywheel said, "How bout getting us some menus?"

The busboy glanced up, mute.

Hormigo said, "La carta."

The busboy nodded, dropped the dirty rag into the dish tub and humped it to the kitchen. The Diablos drank their beers until the waitress arrived with a tray of shots. They were meager shots dwarfed by giant limes.

"These are short," Hormigo said.

The waitress turned to leave.

Hormigo barked, "Those aren't shots. And we don't need no fucking *limes*."

"That's how we serve them here," said the waitress, walking away.

"Tss," hissed Hormigo. He looked at his men: they were looking at him. His hand twitched. He took up a shot glass and flicked off the lime. He raised the glass and said, "Here's to Pete getting his water back so we can drink in a *good* bar again."

They raised their glasses and drained the shots.

"Barely a sip," complained Flywheel.

The busboy returned with menus. Hormigo looked it over, then raised it for the waitress's attention. She saw him but hurried to another table. Hormigo's jaw tightened.

It took the waitress several trips through the section before she got back to the Diablos. She pulled out her pad and said, "What are y'all having?"

"All our beers and shot glasses been sitting here *empty*," said Hormigo.

"Sir, I've got a lot of people besides y'all."

"I only see you taking care of *them*," said Hormigo.

She lowered her pad and looked over to the bartenders.

"Ok," said Hormigo. "So we want twelve steak dinners cooked medium, with baked potatoes and sides of chile."

"Sides of chili," repeated the waitress, reluctantly raising her pad.

"And another round of beers and shots. Real shots this time."

The waitress clicked her pen and walked away.

"Some place," said Ribeye. As usual, he sat with the road-rashed side of his face turned away from everybody. His good eye was at half-squint.

The busboy came through the section and Hormigo waved him over. The busboy looked around nervously but approached Hormigo's handshake. At the conclusion of which the busboy found a balled twenty in his slow-opening fist.

The entire Roadhouse booed something on the TV – some of the cowboys stood up and cupped their hands.

Hormigo said, "Lumbres, turn that fucking TV off while we're drinking here."

Lumbres stood, enormous, and snapped off the TV. An angry clamor rose from the neighboring tables. The Diablos ignored it. Two food runners appeared at their tables and set down plates of steak for them, rolls of silverware.

27

"That was fast," said Hormigo, slipping both of them twenties.

Ribeye said, "They forgot the green chile."

The waitress arrived at their table, hands on her hips. "Did y'all turn this TV off? People are in here to watch the Cowboys."

"It's the last four minutes," complained a voice from a nearby table.

Hormigo said, "You forgot our sides of chile."

The waitress pointed at the TV. "That needs to be turned back on, now."

Hormigo nodded at Lumbres, who stood and snapped the game back on. To the waitress, Hormigo said, "Get those sides of chile, and our beers and our shots."

She left and Hormigo unwrapped his silverware, shaking his head. He cut into his steak and blood pooled out. He looked at his steak as if it had farted. "What the fuck? It's fucking raw?"

At that moment, the entire Roadhouse erupted in anger at the game, beating tables with their hats and kicking away the beer bottles that rolled underfoot. The waitress returned with a tray. She set down cups of Texas chili and started away.

"Hey! What's this?" barked Hormigo, pointing at the cups.

"Those are your sides of chili."

"Not chili, like chili con carne. Green chile, you know, green chile pepper."

The waitress made a face. "We don't serve that stuff here. You ask for chili, this is our award-winning chili."

"And where's our beers and shots? And these steaks are fucking raw!"

The waitress stole a look at the bartenders. She said, "We've decided that y'all have had enough to drink here today. I can get y'all some tea."

"I don't want *tea*," growled Hormigo, slamming his fork on the table. "I want my shots and my beers and my steak cooked medium the way I ordered it, you got that?"

The waitress backed away. Hormigo stood, as did all his Diablos. Hormigo repeated, "You *got* that?"

"Hey sit the fuck down asshole!" came from a nearby table.

Ribeye pointed at the speaker, "You talk with respect to the Diablos."

"Diablos, hell," came a deep voice from the back. "Deviled eggs, more like it. Look at that little fat one – he's the leader?"

28

The laughter had barely started before the first table was flipped over. Cowboys fell sprawling back. The Diablos charged the crowd, punching every head in their way. Hard contact, heavy fists and boots smashing their way to the doors. A ring of cowboys closed in behind them and a big bouncer grabbed Hormigo from behind in a bear hug. Ribeye punched the bouncer in the kidneys and Hormigo broke free.

Someone screamed, "They stabbed him!" as the bouncer fell to his knees.

The crowd stepped back and the Diablos crashed through to the front door. Lumbres shoved a young buck cowboy over a table and the Diablos were outside. They got on their bikes and roared around the Roadhouse. A crowd had gathered out front, poolsticks and knives drawn. Hormigo twisted the throttle of his fatboy and thundered into the crowd. People scattered and the Diablos were back on the highway, tearing up the miles to New Mexico.

"Shit," growled Hormigo into the wind. "They have my credit card."

Eddie Brown

Eddie knocked on the door of Gordon's office. He opened it without waiting for a reply, which is why he found Gordon's finger at an experimental depth in one nostril.

"Jesus Eddie," said Gordon, hands diving for the laptop's keyboard.

Eddie closed the door behind him and remained at the threshold, scanning the small, paper-cramped office. Eddie caught sight of himself in a little wall mirror. Eyes atwinkle, mop of curls, scruff beardage ... not too handsome, but interesting. Hopefully.

"The mirror's a nice idea, Gordon. It really *does* make the place look bigger. Do they charge rent by the cubic inch?"

"Aw knock it off, Eddie. What are you doing here? Professor Davids has office hours today."

"Good, perhaps I'll inquire as to why the assistant professor who teaches all the classes and conducts all the experiments has to work in a snuffbox. Say, aren't you going to ask me to sit down?"

"That's really funny Eddie." Gordon slid his glasses back up his nose. "There just isn't any space right now, with that fire in the annex and all. Say, they don't still think you had anything to do with that, do they? I'd hate for – "

"Of course not. Anyway, I – you know, it smells in here."

"Well I'm very sorry."

"It smells like ... two parts Juicy Fruit gum to one part white wine vinegar."

"Thanks for your expert analysis Eddie. I'm busy, you know?"

"It's not the worst pong I've ever endured, but ... anyway, the reason I'm here is to rescue you from your work to immortalize Davids. Yes, and off to the pub where you'll buy us some nice dark beer and some green chile cheesefries."

"Eddie I can't, it's the middle of the day."

"We have needs to discuss. I had to cancel my study, after all that work."

"What, with the army ants controlling the fire ants?"

"Yeah. I've been out for nights, trying to collect *Neivamyrmex*. There aren't any. Little army has packed up, marched off to greener subterranean pastures."

"So you're quitting the study you've been talking about for five years and have been working on for almost two?"

"It was a longshot anyway. And I mean hell, I was trying to prove that using ants for biocontrol is a horrible idea. I suppose in a way I did. Anyway, yeah, I'm out of that and am looking for something new. And that's what we're going to talk about over a few nice dark beers. Bueno?"

"No, no bueno. I can't go now. Look, here's twenty bucks. I'll meet you over there in ... three hours. Try not to, y'know, attract any attention on your way out."

"No problem. Three hours. Thank you very much. Oh, and Gordon?"

"What."

"You ought to put a skylight in."

Eddie left the Biology building singing, "Bad, bad, Eddie Brown, the baddest man in this whole town."

U.S. Armstrong

The dignified plush of the Silvery Minnow Country Club's lounge: cooled air, bright carpeting, big windows looking over pavement-perfect fairways. U.S. sat in a high-backed chair. Jefferson had arrived with their drinks.

"Here is your mint julep, Mr. Armstrong. And your coffee, Mr. Goldman."

"*Geld*man. Thank you, Jefferson."

A thick-torsed gentlemen in a business suit approached their chairs. "Hello U.S., hitting the links today?"

"No. Don't care for golf."

"But you're ... I mean, this *is* a golf course," chuckled the man.

"I like this bar. 'Nineteenth hole.' Huh. Always got a kick at that."

"Do you mind if I join you for a moment?"

"Suit yourself," said U.S., raising his pewter mug and lowering his hat brim.

"Konrad Seco," offering his hand.

"Charles Geldman. We've met. You're one of our contract lawyers."

Konrad smiled and bobbed his head. "Just back from Santa Fe."

Geldman said, "Right, that suit in Federal Court. Hard to keep track of it all. Modern business environment, eh?"

Konrad chuckled. "When you're right, you're right."

"What is the status of the lawsuit?"

"Stalled. Gridlocked. They're challenging the ruling on continuance. The longer we can drag it out ... anyway, it will probably go up to the Appellate Court."

Geldman took a sip of his coffee. "And what's all this costing the corporation?"

Konrad smiled. "Not a penny more than is necessary in this modern business environment, I assure you."

"Typical bullshit," said U.S., setting his empty pewter mug on the table. "Lazy bums over there in New Mex got nothin better to do than steal; stab you in the back."

"Actually, that's what I wanted to talk to you about, U.S. That ... ugly business that happened out at the Roadhouse a Sunday back."

U.S. tipped his hat up enough to let some blue eye show. His voice got hard like metal. "That kid was just working there on his summer break. He was a second string tackle up at A&M. Down here living at home with his ma, making money for school."

"How is he doing?" asked Konrad.

U.S. lowered his hat brim and said, "He's not."

Geldman said, "The young man passed away from his wounds, Mr. Seco."

"I'm very sorry to hear that. But it makes my information even more timely. You believe that the perpetrators were a chapter of Diablos from New Mexico?"

"Hell, I know they was. And I tell you what, them scum show up on a Saturday night while I'm dancing with Marianne, I'll put twelve holes in them, fast as you please."

"Well Mr. Armstrong, in my private practice, I am representing a high-ranking member of the Rattlers. They've got a history of grievances with the Diablos, and it happens that the Roadhouse is on Rattlers' turf. My client was very upset to hear what happened there, and wants to help."

"And for what in return?" asked Geldman.

"No," said U.S. "We'll handle this our own selves. Don't need more scum running amok, solving our business."

"Then why hasn't New Mexico brought them to Texas for *murder* charges?"

U.S. snorted. Jefferson arrived with another julep.

"We're going to have to send the Rangers to get him, in the end," said Konrad.

"Rangers, hell," said U.S. "Ain't I the goddamn commander of the goddamn Texas State Guard? Don't need the goddamn *Rangers*. Hell. Konrad, take a hike."

Konrad stood, smoothed down his suit. "Contact my office if you change your mind. I've got to get changed, my tee time is in twenty minutes. The golf in New Mexico was terrible."

U.S. dialed his cell phone. He dropped his hat to block out the lounge and said bourbon-throated, "Morning Nancine, it's U.S. Put me through to the Governor please."

Taylor Jon Bridges

I tell you what, this is some boring bullshit right here. This is like working a tollbooth. No fucking shade out here neither.

And here comes the big old fatass. The one what give me shit about my rifle. Told him it was just for the scope, y'know. Donut-shitting faggot made me leave it.

"How you doing TJ?"

I hate that TJ bullshit. "It's Taylor Jon, man."

"Sorry, Taylor Jon. You doing all right on water? Sun'll be down soon. Maybe get some action then."

"Then why the fuck we out here *now*?"

He gives me the hard stare a minute. Scare me? I'll slash the tires on your wheelchair, before I'm done with you. He decides to say nothing. Yup.

He turns and looks out over the empty desert. Then he says, "Turn on your walkie-talkie in an hour or so. Save the batteries until then."

I lean over and spit dip juice, get some on my boot goddammit. Goddammit, I polished them boots not yesterday and now –

"When we first started up, them ACLUers were jamming our signals. Cell phones, CB, all that. Can you believe it? I mean that's actively interfering with our duty. This was the National Guard's job, augmenting Border Patrol, but they all off fighting overseas. So we step up again, and help out against *illegal* immigration, right, and they're aiding the damn enemy? They *want* America to turn brown."

I try to scrape the spit off with my other boot. No good. I look around for a napkin, a leaf, anything. Nothing, and now the dirt's drying in the juice, gettin all crusty like an infected cunt. God*damn* this stupid fucking desert.

"All right TJ, keep up the good work." He goes and gets back in his truck. Why the fuck did I have to leave my truck at the rec center? Gotta wait here in the sun, wait for him to pick me up in the morning.

I want some action. Let one a them little fuckers come up on me – pow! pow! pow! Wish I still had that old black powder Peacemaker I took from Dad. Some spic or somethin stole it out from my truck, my old truck. Along with the toolboxes and the TV I was gonna sell later.

I spit way out over my boot this time.

Shit, I shoulda asked that fatass to bring me coffee. Not that I'll have any trouble staying awake tonight, yup. But coffee would be rugged. Usually I need two bigguns from 7-11 or whatnot, just to get'r right.

Started working on the zits along my forehead. Wish I had a fucking mirror. I never shoulda sold that Peacemaker. That was a hell of a baggie for it though. Still, now would be a perfect time for it: go back to your taco stand, bitch!

This *seemed* like a good idea. Until I got here. All them faggots all G.I. Joe'd up at Fort Davis. Sit through all the crap regulations, rules. History lessons, like school. I don't need no fucking history lessons, I need some pow! pow! pow!

I could really go for a facefull of poon right about now. Yeah, some slutty blonde with big titties. Cold beer. Now *that* would be perfect. The fella said we couldn't drink but I saw them loadin coolers into trucks. What was in them coolers, holy water?

I got my flask a course but I need to save it for tonight when it gets cold. Sun's finally going. Still hot though. Sweat's inside my sunglasses.

Yeah, nice cold beer be nice. How about a kiddie pool filled with beer? When I get back I'm gonna get a kiddie pool and fill it with ice cold beer, gallons and gallons, and I'd just roll around in it, drink it down, swim in an ocean of beer – like Dennys in the lake? Shit. Fuck that shit. Why the fuck'd *that* pop into my –

Naw, you know what, I remember a Halloween party after high school, couple few years back. There was this faggot in there wearing a *dress*. I mean, didn't make no secret of it. Fuckin bullshit of it was, he had girls around him all night. I got Tico and we jumped him, out by his car. Tico was gonna do a Pop Rocks on him but the cops were coming. Tico's still doing time in Lexington for stealing moving vans. Bet he's getting plenty of brown eye now, huh. Browneye Tico, that's good.

Damn this is fucking boring. The sun's finally going. Maybe we'll get some action. Some a them guys got the good stuff, like night vision and shit. Not me. But I reckon I can shoot in the dark good enough.

Time to put in a new dip. Snap it, that's right bitch, you like it when I *snap* it. Work it in there, tongue and gum.

Ah shit, I forgot to turn my walkie talkie on. Been more'n hour I bet. Sun's pretty much gone. Fuck.

I think I got it on. Better check.

"Breaker breaker 1-9! I got blue balls and need some gash, over!"

It crackles back, "This is Red Daddy. Who the hell – why are you breaking in? Stay off the goddamn air, over."

Well *I* thought it was funny. Bunch of old men. But when the shit goes down, they'll be happy to have Taylor Jon kickin ass for them.

It crackles again, "This is Red Daddy. We're gonna go over this again. Maintain radio silence. If you see anyone, you call it in to me. Do not apprehend the illegals yourself. I'll have Border Patrol there fast. Don't make any contact with them. Remember, we're the good guys. Red Daddy out."

I'm out here like a greeter at fucking Walmart. Welcome to America. The welfare office is that way. Feel free to not use any deodorant.

Waste of time. Maybe a little taste of Jack.

Yup.

Don't know how I can make this little flask last all night. The fella mentioned them putting the State Guard out on the border.

But the border with *New* Mexico, keepin them out too. I tell you what, you let in one bean, you get the whole burrito.

Bet there's better action up that way. Better than down here, waiting on some dishwashers to swim across the Rio Grande and then hike twenty miles through fucking desert.

Maybe another little taste of Jack. Yup. S'good.

Better not be anyone fucking with my truck while I'm out here. Out here in the fucking desert at night. This is fucking bullshit, I want some action.

Getting on about time to give myself a little wakeup. There's a little wind but I got my blowtorch lighter. Between this and the Jack I might just get through the night without crapping my pants outta boredom.

<u>Billy Ortiz</u>

Pete's looks closed from the outside but I know the cars are parked around back. I would have been pissed, bro, if Pete's was closed after I spent an hour walking down the arroyo. But the side door is open and there's a few people sitting at the bar. Smells like old beer, old sweat, old smoke.

Little Pete is behind the bar instead of Charlie. I nod hello to some people, playing cool. I shake Pete's hand. "Hey Pete, how's it going? Where's Charlie at?"

"Bit by a rattlesnake," says Navy John, pony tail going around his shoulder and almost into his cigarette.

"No shit. Again? Is he ok?"

"He'll be okay. Not the snake though," says Navy John, empty-toothed smile.

"He's got a lot of snakes out there, huh?"

"One less now. Killed it with a broken pump handle."

A little snow-haired somebody steps between us: Esmerelda's wrinkled face looking up at Navy John. She pokes him in the chest and her arm brushes mine, feels like newspaper. She says, "Maybe if he didn't kill them, they'd stop biting him."

Navy John says, "Bull*shit*. He was walking back from his outhouse, sunset last night. It just up and bit him. I say, kill every goddamn snake you see."

Esmerelda says, "The ancestors knew better than that."

I know she's about to go off on the ancestors for a while so I slip away.

"Shot and a beer, Pete, when you got a minute."

"Still can't do shots Billy, sorry. Bottles only. Not even supposed to be open really but we got a bottle of rubbing alcohol in the portable outside now, so's people can wash their hands."

"Okay, just a beer then." Anything quick, my heart is still pounding but I can't let it show.

An elbow nudges me, it's Abe. He says, "Billy, I got tequila in my car out back, if you need a shot."

Pete was there with my beer. He says, "Don't drink in the parking lot, Abe."

Abe spreads his arms out wide, "Oh, *I* wouldn't do that Pete. I was just offering Billy."

I fake an easy smile back at Abe's grin. No one here knows, or they'd be talking about it right now.

Manning's at the end of the bar. I tell Pete to send one down there. I get away from Abe and take the stool next to Manning. He doesn't have his teeth in so he keeps his mouth closed and just flips his lips out pink to smile for the beer I bought him.

It isn't too loud, no music just talking. So I lower my voice and lean over to Manning's good ear. "I got into some crazy shit tonight Manning. You won't tell nobody, right? Some crazy shit bro."

I look around the bar. Just locals. Front doors are locked. Ok, take a pull of beer.

"So you know those checkpoints they put on the Texas border? This afternoon I was on 33A, wasn't thinking they'd bother with a dirt road, right? I had some business to deliver on other side, you know? I was driving the '82 and had a pound in the bed. Not too hidden at all. And bro, there was a roadblock. Bunch of rednecks, big shiny trucks."

Pete was hovering around so I ordered another beer. I could really use a shot. But it's definitely better to stay inside. I get my beer and clinked glasses with Manning. Big drink of beer for this. Belch-ah.

I lean in again. "So I stopped for the checkpoint and right away bro, they start giving me shit. One guys in his brand new desert camo uniform goes 'You look like a half-breed' and I said I am bro. They start going around the back of my truck and I was worried about the pound in the bed. I mean, it's a twenty minute drive so I didn't hide it real good, you know? So I was like, fuck it bro. I just dropped it into reverse and gunned out of there. They acted like they was gonna chase me but they didn't. So that's how it started. You need a beer Manning?"

I throw ten more bucks at Pete and turn back to Manning, who's rolling a cigarette. I take out my generic smokes and offer him one, but he shakes his head and strikes a match. Lights his, then mine. I lean in.

"So I was just gonna go home but I started getting pissed. I mean, this was all Ortiz land before, both sides of the border, that goes back to *Spain* bro. And all that's left now is my little patch and Luisa's fifty-something acres up by Peñasco. And here these rednecks are, keeping me from making a living, keeping me from feeding my *family*. Keeping me off land that's got Ortiz written on it since Ferdinand and Izabella bro, and they all insulting me and hassling me and shit? So I didn't go home. No, I drove north for a couple hours, crossed into Texas past Tucumcari. No roadblock there, and I drove back south, all the way down until I hit the back end of 33A. I turned up 33A, back towards that roadblock. The road went past that well they drilled, the one that fucking drained our well dry. And I got an idea right then and there, bro."

I stop to put my smoke out and look around. No one's listening. Nice pull of beer.

"I snuck up on the pumphouse in the dark. Cut the lock on the gate. There wasn't nobody around but there was some trailers dropped on the side of the road back a ways, probably for the checkpoint guys. So I was being real quiet. But I couldn't get at the pump, it was all steel and cement. So then I noticed the telephone poles, with the power lines you know, all strung along the highway, feeding the pump. So I went to my truck and got out my chainsaw. I figured I'd shut that well pump off one way or another."

I need another beer. Pete's talking to Esmerelda at the other end of the bar. He has his glasses off, probably can't see her, not even. I finish my beer, lean into Manning.

"I knew I had to be fast because of the noise, with those trailers there and the checkpoint a half mile away. I got the chainsaw going, did a little back cut and went clean in. The pole went down sideways, nearly took out my truck. And then, the falling pole dragged the next one down by the lines, and that pulls the next one down and so on. I couldn't believe it, the chainsaw's still slowing down and poles are going down like dominoes back up the highway the way I came in. And one of them poles came down on the trailers, sparks started going and ... boom. It went sky-high. I was like oh *shit* bro, it was like in the *movies*, bright as day for a second. It all started burning and there was this smoke, smelled like a meth lab. I'm like, 'Billy, get the fuck out of here.' Problem is, the poles are down all across the highway. I have to go back through the checkpoint, you know, from the Texas side. So I get in my '82 and floor it. Trying to get across the state line before they know about the uh, you

37

know. Hey Pete, let me get another couple beers, when you got a minute."

Pete says, "I reckon I got a minute right now" and pulls two beers.

I wait for him to take my money before I continue. "So Manning, while I'm driving for the border, one of those State Guard trucks comes the other way, light racks blazing. I recognized their truck and they recognized mine. So I really floored it. I guess they have radios because they had a truck pulled across the road at the checkpoint."

I punch my fist into my palm to show Manning how I rammed it. "I'll take a steel Chevy over a plastic Toyota *any* day, bro. I think I cracked my radiator but fuck it, I got another radiator anyway. I crashed through there and they came after me, came right into New Mexico. Believe that? I lost them up Mad Dog Road. Ditched the truck on Pancho Ralph's back forty. Hiked down the arroyo and here I am."

Manning gives me an open-gum smile and we hit beer bottles.

"Listen Manning, you can't tell no one about this, right? I'm not even going to tell Melody. She's pissed off enough all the time as it is, right bro?"

Manning smiles his pink gums at me, pink tongue in there. Good. I take off my hat and put it on the bar next to my half-empty beer. Good cold beer.

Retaliation

Eddie Brown

Eddie unlocked the door to his casita and hit the light switch. Fluorescent lights flick-flickered on, revealing a yellow kitchen and sink of foul dishes. Eddie sighed and shuffled into the living room.

He unhasped his overalls and stepped out of them, dried paint popping off. He fell back on the old couch. Unlacing his boots, a tongue-sticking thirst struck him.

Into the kitchen. Opening the refrigerator revealed a jug of grapefruit juice, some flour tortillas, butter and two empty jars of mustard. Eddie pulled out the grapefruit juice. No more glasses in the cupboard, not even the emergency-only crystal goblet. It was dirty from last night. Or the night before. Eddie looked over the sink.

"Quite a breeding lair for *Drosophila*," he said, waving fruit flies from his face. He drank straight from the jug and left himself a little for tomorrow morning.

In socks and shorts he walked to his bedroom. The bed was stuffed into the corner invitingly. The rest of the room was dominated by a large desk covered with books, collection equipment, jars of chemicals and one large terrarium. He settled into his chair and peered at the ants at their toil.

"Hello girls. Keeping busy?"

Eddie stretched to the CD player perched atop a pile of Grzimek's Encyclopedias. It was the Mahler from last night. His nose registered his own old sweat. Eddie picked up the laptop from the floor. His groin swelled at the thought of all the world's porn, but he didn't turn on the computer. Instead he set it on a box of Kleenex and picked up a folded-over *Journal of Hymenopteran Husbandry*. Eddie started reading a new article but was soon scanning the paragraphs and finally tossed the journal onto one of the piles.

He appealed to the terrarium. "They're not really interested in you. It's all taxonomy to them, the human system. Putting each species in place along the family tree. They don't care about what you *do*, just what you are."

He watched some ants drag away a dead sister. "They fight and fuss over whether it's better to call you ladies *Camponotus* or *Myrmothrix*, or whether *Camponotus pennsylvanicus* evolved from *C. herculeanus*. They don't care about what you *do*. That you drum your bodies against the tunnels to sound an alarm that travels farther, faster and surer than semiochemicals. That non-kin queens will share a colony, but each produces her own castes of workers. Or that nest construction alone can give one species in a habitat a head-start in early spring, forcing the other species to keep a stock of eggs through the winter or be overwhelmed. No, no, no. It's all Sheckham begat Mordecai, *Ponerinae* begat *Formicinae*."

Eddie rubbed his eyes. "I should take a shower, girls. But that bed is calling me. Got a long day tomorrow. I know I'm not going to have any clever ideas tonight."

He stood up from the desk and stretched. The CD had ended without his noticing. Leaning in to turn off the light, he tapped the glass. "But just be patient. With your help, we can get science back where it belongs, or die trying. In a scientific revolution, one either wins or dies."

Taylor Jon Bridges

I tell you what, after all's said and done, that was some fun shit. Hooya, that was good. That was like ... commando shit, y'know?

Fucking State Guard. Kicking ass for Texas. This is more like it. And man, that guy's face at the gas station ... like he was crapping a hubcap, sideways.

Let me tap down my dip. Hear that snap! snap! snap! Bet they can hear it all the way back in New Mex, over the sound of their cunt lips still queefing, cause they done been *fucked* good tonight.

I hate drinking alone but I can't sleep none and everyone else is asleep. I did one bowl too many I think. Be up a long time yet. But fuck it. Huh, butt fuck it.

TV don't got nothing on this time of night. Sun's about coming up. Four or five, I'd reckon. My heart gets pounding again when I think about that action tonight. And it gets even a little sad, you know, because that shit was so good, why can't it be like that all the time? Put in another dip. Keep it off the spot that's been sore. Wish one of the boys was up so I could bum a couple smokes. Least we still gots beers.

Another truck ad on the TV, twice as loud. I just turn it off. Fuckers. Bobby Earl's Toyota got it bad when that halfbreed fuck hit it on purpose.

Huh, funny shit when that state trooper had me pulled over, coming back from our celebration at TGI Titty's. The statey walks up to my window and he's got a handful of spent casings from the bed of my pickup. And he goes, been out shooting tonight?

And I go nah, those are old.

And he goes, it don't look old.

And I go, that's what I thought til I woke up and her diaper needed changin.

Huh. He didn't like it, us laughing in his face like that. Not my fault he's got no sense of humor. See, what they don't realize, we're fucking Texas State Guard. Sworn to protect and uphold the Constitution and People of Texas and all that bullcrap. So when that halfbreed pulled his act of terrorism on *my* watch, well, he done riled the wrong rattlesnake.

We waited one day, waiting for Bobby Earl to get word. Finally, they didn't say no. So we crossed over the line. You take out the cooking trailer and where's we alls been sleeping, run *my* checkpoint? Fuck up *my* friend's truck? Uh-uh. No way.

So tonight, we bit back. Yup.

First we went down to their post office. Piece of shit building but that's where their water truck was parked at. Wasn't nobody around and we blocked off the parking lot with our trucks, official Texas State Guard business-like.

That Carson fella, he gets into the hood and gets at the starter and gets the water truck going. Carson said he could drive it and he did, but he grinded them gears, sounded like somebody butt-raping Donald Duck.

So we're driving around looking for action, string of three of us and the water truck in back. There wasn't nothing out there, just some shacks like sheet-metal teepees. So we looped back around to the highway and went into this gas station.

Fucking Poonjab gave Bobby Earl some lip, saying he had to pay in advance. Bobby Earl goes come on Osama, don't you trust me? Poonjab says something, Bobby Earl sort of shoves him back from the counter and Poonjab reaches underneath the counter and pulls out ... a can of mace.

We were all strapped and we all drew on Poonjab at the same time. His turban popped straight off his head. Cowboys and Indians, and he's the wrong kind of Indian.

We took some beers and smokes and a couple rolls of lottery scratchers, y'know, for our troubles. And filled all the trucks up of course. Then we decided to have a little target practice, standing outside the store. Oh, Poonjab was fine, lying on the floor. Once we took out the windows, we could really hit the stuff inside pretty good. From the bed of my pickup, I took out the slurpee machine with Bobby Earl's 30.06. KaBoom. The purple shit was pumping out everywhere.

We parked the water truck right by the checkpoint. That Carson fella got in there and yanked things out until he said there wasn't no moving that truck without a crane or dynamite. We drained the water truck and it made a huge lake right across – shit, not a lake. It just drained away.

Anyway, the truck said like New Mexico State Defense Guard or something on it, and Bobby Earl, he got the idea of spray-painting "Got Water?" on the side. Like from them old milk ads, right. Don't ask me. He thought it was funny.

We figured we was right for some celebrating so we left the new guys at the checkpoint and took off to TGI Titty's. *Damn* I got some titties in my face tonight. Remember that for later. Coming back, that's when the statey pulled me over because I was last in one *swerv*ing-ass conga line down the empty highway.

Motherfucking faggot actually *cuffed* me and put me in his car, drove to the station. The others followed and you could tell it was making him nervous, and plus I was saying how his boss was gonna give him a ten-gallon douche for dragging me in.

I didn't need his lousy one phone call, because Bobby Earl had got on his cell phone and the statey's phone was ringing before he had a chance to fingerprint me. He answers and he goes what? what? and then he looks at me like he had been told to give me two blowjobs. And he goes, you're free to go.

Got back here with the boys, shitty motel but we ain't paying for it. We partied but them faggots can't party long as me. Get me another beer out of the cooler. Sun's up, birds and shit are singing. Fuck it, I'm celebrating. I could get used to this. State Guard, motherfuckers, State Guard.

Governor Armeño

The Governor wore his War Room face. "Take a seat please. I'm sorry we can't use my office for this, there's some horrible type of mold or something. They haven't gotten it all yet, maybe tomorrow."

Gary Camby sat down and they shook hands. Armeño, a connoisseur of handshakes, registered it as firm and dry. The rest of General Camby was unassuming – balding late middle age, golf shirt.

The Governor said, "You look just like the man who was our butcher, growing up. But exactly."

Camby nodded.

"Yes, anyway, the whole thing with the dam has been a tidal wave all day."

Camby said, "I heard about the accident on the radio, driving up."

Armeño gave a sorrowful frown. "It's worse than just some people losing their lives. See, we owe Texas a certain amount of water from that river system every year. It's a long-standing compact. We have to count that release as the majority of water owed them for this year. Now, perhaps we shouldn't have announced that today, in the middle of all this, but my advisors thought it was best to get it out of the way. We have absolutely no choice in this matter. It is the desert, late summer. We can't give them that water *twice*, there simply isn't any more in that irrigation district. All the rest of that reservoir, and then some, has already been allocated here in New Mexico. It's our water anyway, it collects on our land. And there's been this infernal drought of course."

"So the damage was extensive?" asked Camby.

"Expensive? Yes, very much so. And because we may be partially at fault, I decided to send some help right away, at our expense. Help our ... image challenge. I need you to take your guys to the little town, Eagle, for the relief effort."

Camby said, "Yessir, but why not send the National Guard? They're equipped for disaster relief. The focus of my job has been to increase the public awareness of the SDF and to complement Guard recruiting."

"The National Guard is not available. All the ones left in the state are with Border Patrol, down between Playas and Columbus. You're all I have."

General Camby straightened in his chair and said, "Yes sir."

Armeño's face brightened. "Hey, I remembered the pin."

"The pen?" puzzled Camby.

Armeño pointed to the Vecinos pin. His Prudent Frown took over.

"There's more, I'm afraid. There may be some trouble out there in the flood zone. It's not that they *really* think it was done on purpose, it's just that some are angry and confused. And there's been some tension along that border zone. We've got this lawsuit against Texas and it finally got to the U.S. Supreme Court. So what I'm saying is, there might be some tension while you're there helping out. Just to, you know, forewarn you."

"Thank you. How soon do you need me to muster the troops?"

"As soon as possible, please. Go back down to the Armory and move out as soon as possible. The checkpoint in Texas should just wave you through – we'll let them know you're coming."

"I will do that, sir."

"This couldn't have come at a worse time. They started filming a television show about me – oh, you hadn't heard about that? Yes, they picked me ahead of twelve other Governors. I'm afraid that some of this could be made to make me look bad."

"You are right to entrust this important mission to the SDF, Mr. Governor."

"Yes, thank you. You know, they should be in here, getting this, but Mr. White chased them away. He's been running around like a mad-man all day. Haven't seen him in an hour. Say, maybe they can film you out there? And we can have a scene of me talking to you on the phone, checking in to see how it's going? That's another reason I can't wait until they fix my office. This room isn't very ... anyway, good luck."

"Yes sir, thank you sir," said Camby, closing the door behind him.

"Well that's *one* down," sighed Armeño. He started looking in desk drawers for his appointment book but was interrupted by a phone call.

"Mr. Governor, this is Mr. White."

"Mr. White, where are you?"

"I'm still busy with the Treasurer. But sir, you haven't forgotten about your press conference, have you?"

"When is it?" asked Armeño, opening another drawer.

"Ten minutes ago."

"Ai Maria. I'm on my way. Call them – tell them I'm on my way."

U.S. Armstrong

The terrain out here was dry flatland. Distant mesas, across the border. U.S. towered over the landscape, 10½ feet tall in his Texas State Guard desert camo. Heavy cavalry pistol hanging off his hip. His wide white hat brim hid his eyes, his salt and pepper mustache hid his mouth.

"Then what happened, Colonel?" the voice of U.S. was a ten-second buzz.

Colonel Plowman spoke to the erect straightness of U.S.'s back. "After they come down to the disaster site and seen to it to get three trucks stuck in the mud, shutting down the road for half an hour, some kind of scuffle happened outside Eagle's Walmart – that's our HQ, the parking lot there. It's on high ground, wasn't touched by the flood. So we told them to pack off, find their own HQ."

"Why didn't you tell them to scram out of Texas altogether?"

"Well sir, I didn't believe that I had the authority."

"You got the authority, you're a Colonel in the Texas State Guard. They flood out these folks here, then have the audacity to come over and … what exactly happened?"

"They left, sir. Now, the waters had drained away, and all the refugees were accounted for. So they came too late to save anything and came too early to help put it back together. When me and Colonel Stanley here found their commander, this Camby fella, they was in the middle of trying to catch a horse. If we step back over this ridge sir, you can see where the water got funneled down to the low point there, and that's where most of the damage took place. There was a corral down there that had been tore up real good, and when the water drained there was a sorrel in there that got loose. We arrived as they were cornering it. The horse panicked or something with so many people around, probably still feared from the flood that nearly took it. So it started kicking, and it stumbled in the soft ground and broke its leg."

"Did the horse take any of them out?"

"Yes sir, two or three of them took some heavy licks."

"Good for the horse. So they shot it?"

"Well they was about to sir, with me and Colonel Stanley watching with our mouths hanging open. Then I say to this Camby fella, that's a Texas horse on Texas land and he can't kill that horse, and the owner needs to be compensated for what they done in breaking its leg. And that it was our job to dispatch that animal."

"Then what, Colonel?"

"Well it's like I told you when I called, sir. Things got hot and we felt threatened. There was twenty-something of them. Once they saw we were leaving, they got more aggressive. Some drew their arms, although none was aimed at us. We was on ATV's and took off quick. Got back to the HQ – that's when I called you. We're thinking they took the highway up to Amarillo. They left that dead horse just lying there."

U.S. stared out over the hard crust earth, the burning blue sky. It was hot and dry, the sun was bright. His State Guard bolero caught the sun when he turned around.

The hat brim lifted enough to reveal a slice of pale blue eyes to the Colonel. "We're gonna sort this nonsense out."

"We've got the state police out looking for them."

"Fuck the state police. This here's a military matter. The 39th Brigade here is a military *police* unit, is it not? Get me a map. Colonel, I want you to call off the state police. Slurry, call the 4th Brigade in Fort Worth, get them rolling out here. Give that map here. All right, I reckon they got to Dalhart and then broke for the state line on 54. The fastest way is to cross *here* and take that highway 145 north, catch them coming."

"Sir, you want us to cross into New Mexico?" asked Colonel Plowman.

"You're goddamn right. They crossed the line first, drew first blood."

The cadre broke up, leaving U.S. alone at the valley rim. He looked down on the land, the minutiae of juniper and scrub and dead mesquite and rocks. Each was a piece of Texas, and he was charged to defend every goddamn rock out there.

He turned his head slightly. "Colonel."

"Yes sir," said Plowman, walking back up the rise to his general.

"Was there any press around for that horse-shooting?"

"No sir. They're all still at the site and the church, or hanging around our HQ."

U.S. graveled, "Don't bury that horse until we get some digital photos of it. That'll be tomorrow's front page. I guarantee it."

"Yes sir."

U.S. waited until Colonel Plowman was gone, then removed his cell phone from its holster. He dialed the number for the Adjutant General of Texas.

"Susan? It's U.S. Put me through to Wegler please. Thank you ... Larry? It's U.S. I wanted to let you know what we're doing out here

... no, I got it under control. We're gonna head them off before they cross back into – what? When? Did you call the folks in Oklahoma, see if they'd let us pursue through – well no, I'm not surprised. Then I have to assemble my troops along the entire border with New Mex. We're shutting that border down. That's right. That's my decision. We're gonna put an end to this nonsense. I'm authorizing them to go live fire ... because they pulled weapons on two of my officers ... *Yes*, that's what I just said. Who knows what the *next* group of them will do. Hell no, the border is shut. I'm calling up the 1st Brigade, the 8th, the 19th and the 22nd ... no, just tell the Governor what I told you ... no, that's why he made me the goddamn Commanding General, didn't he? All right then. We got some good stuff to go in the papers, that's for sure ... Eagle? Well it's fucked, Larry. Haven't you been watching the news? No, it looks just as bad here on the ground. I got to go."

U.S. dialed another number. "Marianne? Hey darlin. I'm not making it to dinner tonight. We got a situation ... I know Fawn's going back to college tomorrow, that's why I'm calling ... I don't know. Could be all night. Could be longer. It's just a situation ... I know, but they need me here. Yeah, give Fawn a hug from me. I'll see her at Fall Break or whatnot ... all right. You too."

H₂O

One particular water molecule rushed with its compadres through pipes. They hurtled in fluid confederation, bearing loads of nitrogenous waste, bacteria and solids. The molecule came to a straining gate and slipped through.

And then the rushing ceased. The one particular water molecule remained in the slew until a great quantity of an aluminum compound invaded, shearing away the heavy silt. They were forced through a series of microstrainers that rid them of all but the smallest, most well-bound particles. Next, a slow fall, settling through a barrier of sand and gravel. The particular molecule emerged free and clean, with no hangers-on.

Then an incursion of chlorine molecules and another great rushing through tireless pipes and pumps. Finally stopping in a great still volume of water, choked with even more chlorine molecules. There was another difference. Something subtle, hard to notice at first, but dimly significant.

The sun! The energy seeped into the still water, setting in motion the machine of convection that propelled one particular molecule to the surface. Spinning into the air, it left its compadres in the swimming pool.

Free and light again, at last.

The airborne trip was short-lived. Passing over a dam reservoir, the water molecule strayed too near the water's surface and was captured even as others spun past it, up and up into the lightness of independent flight. The one water molecule sank into the cool dark currents of the lake.

It had to wait and wander for many moon-pulls before it found the spillway and was ejaculated into the diminished river below. The molecule traveled with the river, awash in sedimentary particles, seeking the path to gravity.

The heat of the sun was strong, and the land they passed through beckoned in thirst. There were fewer compadres to help carry the load of salt and silt, but the molecule accepted its burden. And at last, somehow barely trickling over a sand bar, the molecule was kissed into the ocean's abundant womb.

Part II Bellum

Propagandance

U.S. Armstrong

U.S. Armstrong's eyes were closed for expanding moments under his white hat brim. That lawyer, Konrad Seco, was *still* winding up his summary. Boring crap.

U.S. raised the brim of his hat. Everyone caught the flash except for the target, Seco himself. Seco was saying, "and upon the successful challenge to the Appellate Court's ruling on continuation – "

U.S. interrupted, "So we won? What else is there to talk about?"

"Well U.S., there's more at stake than just your right to drill a well on your own property. My worry was that the Court would invoke Gibbons *v*. Ogden of 1824, followed by U.S. *v*. Rio Grande Dam and Irrigation, determining that the Federal Government holds supreme suzerainty over all waters whether they be navigable or not. That could be enough for the Supreme Court to grant a *writ of certiorari* and hear the case. I convinced them to remand, not the suit itself, but rather the question of the Appellate Court's jurisdiction in handling it. And they dismissed New Mexico's injunction out of hand, which is great news for everyone in this room. This should be bogged down in the Lower Courts until the cows come home."

Geldman said, "Mr. Seco, what is the status of the suit on behalf of Eagle?"

"That goes directly before the U.S. Supreme Court. Controversies between two states are part of the Original Jurisdiction of the Supreme Court, thanks to Article III, section 2 of the Constitution. My argument follows the 1987 ruling on the flood of the Conchas dam. We'll win. What is left for me to finalize is that their Governor violated Federal Law and the River Compact of 1949, which invokes *ex parte Young*, which of course voids the Governor's immunity as guaranteed by the 11th Amendment."

U.S. growled, "What in the hell – you're talking in goddamn circles, Seco. If your mouth was a shovel you'd be halfway to China by now."

The meeting room broke up in grateful laughter.

Geldman said, "He's saying that we could put their Governor in jail, U.S."

U.S. snorted into his mustache. "More courtrooms. More lawyers. We got to take our case to the people. We got to show them that we're gonna get'r right, finally."

"That's my job, U.S. You can leave that to me," said a man in a sharkskin suit that suspended an oily sheen. He stretched a gleaming, greasy smile.

Geldman said, "Perhaps this is the time to move on and discuss our media strategy. Thank you, Mr. Seco. This is Mr. Karl Hovan, of Medusa Vision, Incorporated."

Hovan unlaced that smile again – a dead skin mask of guile and bile. His darkened hair was slicked back. Eyes with the blank venomous potential of a sunning diamondback.

"Thank you Mr. Armstrong and distinguished members of the board. And lawyers," pausing for a grin from the audience. "I have devised a three-pronged media campaign."

Hovan's assistant engaged his laptop and the digital projector animated a pitchfork on the boardroom's blank wall.

Hovan purred, "As you can see, the first prong is a righteous *ad hominem* appeal on behalf of the flood victims. The second prong dismisses their lawsuit. The third prong is where we're putting all of our chips: the offense to Texas sovereignty. This media blitz is just the first part of our campaign to effect our desired resolution."

A hand went up – it was Keith Earl. "Excuse me, but what is our 'desired resolution' in this? Where's this going? It sounds like the Feds would rather sit this one out, so where are we taking it from here?"

U.S. said, "I'll tell you where we're taking it. We're gonna get'r right."

Geldman said, "Right now, gentlemen, we're reviewing our media strategy, and that's all we're concerned with. Mr. Hovan?"

"We're going to saturate the markets from El Paso on north up to Denver. We're going to," smacking his palm for emphasis, "*hit* the primetime slots, *hit* the news broadcasts, *hit* the syndicated radio, *hit* the print ads, *hit* the billboards. We're going to *hit* the Op-ed pages, we're gonna *hit* the internet with blogs and astroturf and sponsored links, we're gonna *hit* the weeklies. We will blanket them with our message."

"And what is our message? U.S.?" pressed Keith Earl.

U.S. raised his mustache in sneer. "That it's time to get'r right."

Sitting in the VIP balcony at the Roadhouse with Marianne and Fawn. Fawn, beautiful Fawn. To U.S. she was still braces, ponies and pigtails. Marianne, of course, had been a local beauty and quite a catch after the war. But not like Fawn – her blonded hair towered bravely, pouring backward like a marble waterfall, her blue blue eyes, her shining, gloriously perfect smile that softened his heart, the expensive buttoning of her nose, the mysterious and costly augmentation of her figure.

Fawn was beautiful, no doubt in the world. Nineteen years old, late-blooming like goldenrod. Marianne still looked good, but the contrast with her daughter excentuated the brittleness of long-dyed hair, the strain of lifts. All that was left of Marianne's wrinkles was the wisdom around her eyes, and U.S. liked it there, actually, and was glad they had not been completely ironed out.

They were chatting about something, some woman's thing. U.S. obeyed an impulse and drew his cell phone from its holster.

Marianne thrust a bayonet look. "Ulysses Sam Houston Armstrong, you are *not* about to make a business call during dinner with your only daughter and only wife."

U.S. twisted his mustache and holstered the phone. He raised his palms in submission and even made an effort to tune into their conversation.

"Why'd we have to come *here*, anyway?" asked Fawn with a toss of her mane.

U.S. sat up straight. "Why Fawn, the Roadhouse's always been your favorite."

"Sure, when I was ten."

U.S. leaned back and fit the bottle of Lonestar to his mouth. He turned his wrist to check his watch but caught his wife's glance. U.S. returned his attention to the table.

Fawn said, "So anyway Mother, they do it once and it's good *forever*. You never have to shave, ever again."

Marianne made a face. "But laser surgery, that sounds – "

Fawn interrupted, "It's a *procedure*, Mother, not surgery."

"I don't know," said Marianne, shaking her head. "I just don't know. It sounds ... lasers? That sounds like it could scar. Could it scar?"

"Not even a tiny bit. Come on Mother, they use lasers for *eye* surgery. It's totally safe. They just go in and zap the follicle and that's it. They can do it anywhere – they could do Lupita's mustache."

"Now Fawn, that's a terrible thing to say about Lupita. She took care of you when you were a baby," said U.S.

Fawn took a sip of her lite beer. "Anyway, *I'm* getting it *all* done. All of it."

"All of it?" asked Marianne, improbably eyebrowed. "Why would you want ... *that* done as well? I can see being tired of cutting your ankles, but ..."

Fawn shook her hair dramatically. "It's *the* thing. Besides, I'm going to be doing some swimsuit modeling this semester."

U.S. broke in, "What's this about swimsuit modeling?"

Fawn looked up at him in daughterish innocence. "It's just some fashion work, shoes and hats and things, that's all Daddy. Mommy said I could."

"Well as long as it's part of your curriculum," qualified Marianne.

"Oh yeah, I get credits for it. It's part of the fashion college. Fashion courses."

"Can't see going to college to stand around in a swimsuit," graveled U.S.

"Maybe I'll get to meet a famous designer and, you know, get to be their assistant or something. I like clothes and know a lot about them."

"That would be nice. Wouldn't that be nice, U.S.?"

U.S. nodded, sipped his Lonestar empty. He waggled it for another.

"So anyway, I need to get it done as *soon* as possible," gushed Fawn. "I need the money in my account right away. I made an appointment for when I get back to Dallas."

"Well how much is it?" asked Marianne.

Fawn took a slick pink brochure from her purse and handed it to her mother. She crossed her cramped toes inside her cowboy boots, an incantation from childhood.

Marianne read the tagline aloud, "For the softest *mons*, choose Laser Beaver."

"I think that's, like, French for 'skin.' You know?" prattled Fawn,

54

squeezing her crossed toes tighter.

Marianne opened the brochure. Her eyes bulged at the pricing. "It's not cheap."

"But Mother, remember, it lasts forever. When you add up all the time, and the money for *razors*, and shaving cream ... and no more goose bumps or stubble, forever. Just soft, smooth skin. You should do it too Mother, you really should."

Marianne frowned into the brochure.

U.S. said, "Say Fawn, I was talking to R.J. Neman. He offered to host the event on the rodeo grounds, when you and Luke decide to get married."

"Oh Daddy, me and Luke – well that's a long way off."

"You and Luke Neman been going steady since you was sixteen. Don't think I'm old-fashioned, but ... anyway, his father and I go back a long ways, and he was just – "

"I'll do it," interrupted Marianne.

Fawn gushed, "Oh really Mother? I think that's great! Maybe you can have it done with me in Dallas!"

"Do what now? What's this going to cost me?" asked U.S.

"Oh for heaven's sake U.S., your only daughter is here for one more night on her break and all you can say is 'what's this going to cost me'."

"Can we order already?" said U.S. "I've had three beers on an empty stomach."

"I'm just gonna have a salad I think," said Fawn.

"A salad?" frowned U.S.

"Just a salad for me too," said Marianne, "With the dressing on the side.

"And fries," added Fawn.

Eddie Brown

Eddie was having trouble catching his breath.

Gordon said, "Here Eddie, have some water."

Eddie shook his head, wheezing, "Just ... smoky in here ... be fine ... minute."

Eddie had his eyes half-closed, dragging air into his choked lungs, so he did not have to see Gordon's solicitous expression. It took some time to recover and Eddie had to concentrate on keeping his heart rate calm, willing his bronchia to relax.

"Don't you have your inhaler?" asked Gordon.

Eddie shook his head, concentrating: pull the air in, hold it, release it. He looked up from his struggle, tears wrung from his eyes. Gordon looked away.

Gordon said, "Hey look, there's another one of those ads. It's a new one."

Eddie squinted up at the TV over the bar. No sound, just the juke-box. There was footage of that flooded town in Texas. Then a black and white still shot of a dam, and in large block red letters the word "Terrorists" slapped down. A still shot of the Texas state flag. Large block red letters slapped down "What's Next?" That was left to sink in for a moment. Then a row of paramilitary-looking guys standing stalwart against stormy skies. The screen went black and large block white words appeared:

Security
Stability
Safety
Getrright.org

Eddie read with squinted effort, "It says 'paid for by the Guardians of Truth.' That's the bullshit. *That's* the big lie."

"Yeah. It's frustrating."

"Have you seen the New Mexico ad, the rebuttal?" asked Eddie.

"I think I caught one while I was falling asleep. Something about a well or something, I don't remember."

"Lame," said Eddie. He took a drink from his dark heavy pint. "Shot on video. Faux Powerpoint presentation style. Strictly late-night cable quality."

"You breathing better?" asked Gordon.

Eddie nodded.

"We shouldn't come here, it's always so smoky for you."

Eddie shook his head, smiling. "There hasn't been smoking in bars for years."

"Oh yeah. So it's just your ... well anyway, did I tell you that my paper is going to be published?"

"Twice. And that Professor Davids placed his name as the first author."

"Yeah, but it's his lab, and all I was doing was an extension of his work, so ..."

"You said that before as well. You're being used, Gordon."

Gordon sighed. "I'll be out of his lab soon. This paper will help."

Eddie said, "Just put up with the lies, the inferno, until you can't see them any more. The Truth is the first place they blind you. Like these bastards, 'Guardians of Truth.' *That's* the damn lie. Like Hemingway said, 'Fascism is a lie told by a bully'."

Gordon said, "I'm going to order another pitcher I think. You'll drink more? I'm celebrating, remember?"

"Yes, hooray for you Gordon. You've accomplished what no one else at this table has: scientific legitimization. Your Nobel Prize is a *fait accompli*."

"Oh Eddie, give me a break, won't you?"

"Sorry, sorry. I wasn't cracking on *you*, it's my pathetic ... wasting my time with my so-called research. A half-dozen half-finished projects. I received more interest for my study on how many licks, precisely, it takes to get to the center of a Tootsie Pop."

"Oh Eddie."

"I'm serious. It was a double-blind. Neither the Tootsie Pops nor the tongues had any idea how many licks had already been administered."

Gordon said, "You're so entirely self-consumed."

"Self-consumed like a Tootsie Pop," smiled Eddie. He caught sight of Gordon's pained expression: Gordon's ice cube-thick glasses slipping from his eyebrows, a few flakes of dandruff in his hair, the walled-in eyes hoping – no, pleading for something.

Eddie raised his pint. "In all sincerity, here's to you Gordon. Congratulations."

They toasted and finished their pints. The waitress brought them a new pitcher. Eddie decided to toss a joke into the truce: "At least when *you* whack off, it's not the unemployed shaking hands with the unemployed."

"Oh Eddie." Gordon put down his pint. He slid out from the booth and stood up.

"What are you doing?" asked Eddie, looking up innocently.

Gordon shook his head and walked away from the table and out the door.

"Who's going to pay the bill?" Eddie said quietly.

He sat glumly, drinking his pint. Staring at Gordon's full glass, the full pitcher. *You know, you really are a big fucking asshole.*

"I know," said Eddie.

It's time you reflect on your life, Eddie Brown.

"Baddest man in this whole town."

Bullshit. That's not even how the song goes. You're selfish, you do too many drugs, you can't finish what you start. You aren't going to make any contributions to the body of scientific knowledge, nor will you communicate any knowledge to others. That's why they kicked you out of the department all those years ago. What have you done since? No one will give you a grant. Because they all know the truth. And you do too.

Eddie finished his pint, watched the scurf bubble away on the bottom. He dropped his head into his palm; dug a fingernail into his scalp. Pushed away his plate, a cold block of green chile cheesefries.

Hard to discover Truth when you're drowning in self-pity, Eddie, you're just a cloud yourself, controlled by circumstances. No substance to you, just what you collect and release when it gets too heavy to carry. Truth is heavy and you are weak. Why not pour yourself another beer? What's the difference?

Eddie looked up dully to the pitcher. Gordon was there, standing over the table.

"I'm sorry buddy," mumbled Eddie.

"You were talking to yourself," said Gordon.

"I'm sorry. Let's get out of here."

"I only came back to pay the bill." Gordon was trying to impose a frown but it went unnoticed. Eddie was drunkenly pulling on his windbreaker.

"All right," said Gordon. "Come on."

General Gary Camby

General Camby walked up the marble stairs inside the State Capitol. He was late and perspiring. He found the carpeted hallway to the Media Room.

Camby knocked and the door was opened by Mr. White. Governor Armeño was at the head, and an implausibly tanned homosexual (?) sat on one side, wearing a navy blue blazer without a shirt. The rest of the room consisted of a plastic conference table, dry-erase boards and a TV-VCR rack: a sterile white box of fluorescent buzz.

Governor Armeño said, "Sit down, we've been waiting."

Camby sat down in a molded plastic seat. "I'm terribly sorry, there was an accident coming up from Rio Rancho. A water tanker had jacknifed and – "

"That's fine," interrupted the Governor. "This is Mr. Garvin, who's going to be our new media consultant. We're lucky to have him. We need his expertise, now more than ever. Did you see the advertisement that ran last night during the local news? The papers today were ablaze with it. The lights please, Mr. White, and play the tape."

The television glowed blueness into the dark room. Then a black screen, with the word WARNING in block red letters. Deep down-home voiceover: "What y'all about to see is disturbing, and shouldn't be seen by sensitive folks or children."

Hand-held footage approaching an SUV with *New Mexico State Defense Force* stenciled on the side. The camera jarred forward to some tumult ahead. A group of men in green uniforms. Vague violence.

The voiceover: "This here footage was shot during a recent incursion by the New Mexico State Defense Force on Texas soil immediately after the Eagle flood Disaster."

The camera zoomed into the tumult. The men were surrounding a horse that was tied to a fence post. They were attacking it with bayonets. The horse whirled, tugging at the fence post as the soldiers thrust and thrust again.

The camera zoomed tighter, and a cord of viscera could be seen hanging from the horse's belly. The picture dissolved, replaced by the now-familiar photo of the dead horse which had been on the front page of every newspaper only one month ago.

The voiceover continued: "We all know what happened. But we'll never know why. But now everybody knows, it's time to get'r right."

The screen went black, dominated by "Getrright.org" in big white letters, with "Paid for by the Guardians of Truth" in small type at the bottom.

Armeño waited until Mr. White had turned off the TV, turned on the lights and sat down. Then he addressed Camby with an Irate Despot stare. "Well?"

Camby's expression was a broken eggshell of disbelief. "That didn't – that never happened. That didn't happen."

"We all saw that photo in the paper. Front page all across the region. That was bad enough, but now this footage ... what the *hell* were you thinking?"

"But it never – those men, those weren't my men," protested Camby.

Armeño's face went Angry Samurai: "I made you the Commanding General of the State Defense Force, did I not? And the conduct of your men under – "

"But sir," interrupted Camby. "Mr. Governor. That *never* happened. With the horse – it was nothing like that."

"We all saw that photo. My office has already publicly apologized on your behalf. And still they're beating us up with the story, again and again, never ending, like beating a ... anyway, it's another scandal, and now there's footage of it."

"But sir, please listen, that footage – it's not what happened. I was there."

Armeño's voice went shrill, "So there was no horse? What was that photo in the papers, hmm? And why, then, did we apologize for something that never happened?"

"No, I mean yes sir, a horse broke its leg tragically, by accident, during our efforts, and required humane euthanasia. But all that torture, that footage – that wasn't what happened. I swear on my oath of service."

"So now you say the dead horse is true, just not this documented footage of it being killed?" Armeño laced his fingers under his chin and looked over at Mr. Garvin.

Mr. Garvin shrugged. "Who knows? It hardly makes a difference."

"Hardly makes a difference?" said Camby, seizing the moment to attack. "They just made that up, it's a total lie."

"Can you prove it?" sugared Mr. Garvin. "Public opinion is *opinion*, after all. Besides, you admit that a horse *was* killed, so it can't be a 'total lie,' can it?"

Camby opened his mouth, paused, and closed it. Red prickles rose along his bald swath. A phone rang – everyone reached, but it was Mr. White's. The others sat in silence, working on a map out of the labyrinth.

Mr. White suddenly sat up very straight, "What? No, we never authorized that. The who? I've never heard of them – the New Mexican Agitprop Alliance? There's no such thing. Do you have it ready? Right, I'll be down in a moment."

Mr. White stood, snapping shut his phone. "There's something – excuse me."

Mr. White left and the room was quiet until the door had clicked closed. Then Governor Armeño said, "Mr. Garvin, how would you propose we react to their ad, if it truly is *fake* footage?"

"Well, if our strategy is containment of this mess, we could try to refute their ad. But it would take time and we don't have any *proof*, apparently. On the other hand, if we continue with my proposed strategy, perhaps this horse business will simply blow over."

Armeño shook his head. "Lots of people have horses. Seeing that animal tortured like that ... and you say it was fake, Camby, but I saw one of our trucks in it, and our men in uniforms. How do you explain that?"

"That wasn't one of our trucks, that was a GMC Megalith. We don't have anything that new. And the uniforms were just Army surplus, available everywhere."

Armeño pursed his lips into a grave, funereal expression.

Mr. Garvin said, "We've already got a good ad in production, and that should deflect some of these negatives."

"I don't think that ad is going to work anymore. Not with this horse-beating catastrophe," said the Governor.

"Well, see, we've already acquired the rights to the song. We might as well go ahead and use it," said Mr. Garvin. "Waste not, right?"

"Oh that stupid song," groaned the Governor. "What is it? 'Don't Worry Be Happy'? That's not going to work *now*. Cancel that ad, let the Pueblo Elders and the Sikhs and the balloon-people know."

"Well it's been paid for," concluded Mr. Garvin. "With the budget you – "

"Screw the budget, this is an emergency," declared the Governor.

Camby said, "Perhaps we can run an ad detailing all of the help we offered after the flood? To show that our hearts were in the right place?"

"The less of the flood we mention, the better," said Mr. Garvin. "It will just remind people of that horse being shish-kebabed over and over. Bleh."

They sat and thought in the humming fluorescence. The door opened and Mr. White entered, holding a videotape. He turned on the TV. "Gentlemen, it gets worse."

They watched the screen: waving lines, hiss of static. Nothing else.

Armeño slammed his fist on the table, "Nothing ever *works* around here!"

"Maybe it's the tracking," offered Mr. Garvin.

Mr. White said, "Well, it worked just fine downstairs. There were two advertisements aired back to back on all the local stations: News for Noon, Noonday News, News at Noon and Noticia en Pleno Mediodia. The first was ostensibly sponsored by a group called the New Mexican Agitprop Alliance, although there's no PAC or nonprofit registered as such in New Mexico. A fifteen second spot of an Hispanic actor saying that he had heard that Texas stole water from New Mexico, that he hoped that the politicians in Washington would sort it out, that Texas and New Mexico ought to have a compromise between them – 'That's how me and my neighbor do it,' he says."

"I don't remember any ad like that. Mr. Garvin?" asked Armeño.

Mr. Garvin swept the tastelessness away. "I've only just gotten on board here."

"It wasn't authorized by any local government either," said Mr. White. "There's no reason to believe that was even produced in New Mexico. Regardless, it was always followed by a thirty second spot by the Guardians of Truth. This one has an Anglo rancher type who basically gives a line-by-line rebuttal of the previous advertisement."

"The New Mexico ad that wasn't even produced in New Mexico," Armeño said.

"Exactly," said Mr. White. "The rancher says that the Supreme Court proved Texas right, and that the New Mexico politicians were liars and going to jail."

"Jail? Who the hell does he think he is?" spat Governor Armeño.

Mr. White said, "The rancher goes on to say that Texas *had* a neighborly compromise with New Mexico, but we broke the deal. 'Here's how they share,' he says, and there's more flood footage, more of the horse being killed. The closing line is deliberately ominous: 'What do you do with a neighbor like that?"

"Tacky and crude," sighed Mr. Garvin.

"Has anyone gone to that Getrright.org website yet?" asked Camby.

"Yes," said Mr. White. "There's some free merchandise, and then it redirects you to the Texas State Guard recruitment page."

Camby said, "Mr. Governor, we have to do something about this. They're lying."

Armeño shrugged. "What would you have me do? Bulldoze the broadcast towers? I can't dictate terms to the television stations."

"And radio spots, print ads, all the Op-ed pieces," added Mr. White.

"But it's all *lies*," sputtered Camby.

"I don't own the TV stations," said Armeño bitterly. "The corporations that do are international giants. News for Noon and all that, they're just local franchises."

"We need a *new* ad," sang Mr. Garvin. "Something to set things correct."

Camby said, "What about the Feds, the FCC or whatever?

The House almost passed a censure on Texas for closing the borders and interfering with interstate trade."

"Congress, the Supreme Court and the President have all made it clear that they aren't getting involved in this, vaguely citing the Ninth Amendment," said Mr. White. "They won't even give up a Federal Judge to act as mediator. The administration is having their own public relations meltdown, with the draft proposal about to hit the Senate, their foreign policy mess, and the tripling of the budget deficit in just two years."

"The only thing we have is that history is on our side. This is just yet another case of Texas imperialism," said Governor Armeño, nodding for the cameras.

Mr. Garvin said, "That's an interesting angle. Detail me."

"Mr. White?" said Armeño, settling back in his chair.

Mr. White's blonde eyebrows rose to meet the query. "Texas has invaded New Mexico on three occasions. Two were failed expeditions in the 1840s to capture the Rio Grande river system, narrowly defeated by local and Federal forces. The final invasion was during the Civil War. The Confederate Army of Texas won every engagement and occupied New Mexico, but had to retreat when they ran out of water."

Mr. Garvin said, "Fascinating, fascinating. I'm seeing ... reenactments. Anyone? Get those Civil War nuts dressed up, show them bullying the proud peoples of New Mexico. I love it – we could show *them* killing horses, for example. Turn it around on them. We'll seize the moral high ground, with actual historical fact as our selling point."

The Governor said, "We'd have to scrap 'Don't Worry Be Happy.' That's the wrong tone."

Tapping his dimpled chin, eyes searching the stucco ceiling, Mr. Garvin mused, "Something ... not defiant, but victimized. People like victims. 'We are the World'?"

"Good song. And I want 'Texas imperialism' in the ad," said the Governor.

General Camby cleared his throat. "I still don't understand how they can just *lie* on television like that."

Governor Armeño snapped, "If they can get *my* show cancelled, they can obviously run whatever kind of ads they like."

"Now we don't know *that's* what happened," cautioned Mr. Garvin. "All we know is that the studio recalled Mr. Greenbaum, and that your project is in turnaround."

"Why else would they kill my show? It was going to be fantastic. I'll bet Governor Burton was jealous and used his influences. It would have been fantastic."

"It would have been, yes," said Mr. Garvin.

"At least we managed to keep *you*," smiled Armeño. "You'll help us get out of this mess, put a positive spin on things. There's barely two years before I've got another election to win. But after this madness is over, perhaps another try with my show?"

"Maybe, perhaps," said Mr. Garvin. "We'll have to see how this plays out."

Armeño said, "We're paying you so this 'plays out' the way we need it to."

"I like the history angle," said Mr. Garvin. "Give me some fac-toids, and I'll make the rest. I wonder where we can rent old cannons from?"

"Not too expensive, all right? This is already costing a fortune," said Armeño.

"It won't cost more than it has to," assured Mr. Garvin.

"Mr. Goveror, sir," said General Camby. "In light of the historical record ... do you think you ought to mobilize the entire State Defense Force? Get us up and ready, just in case? We could even be used in the advertisements, if you wanted."

Armeño frowned a Pensive Monarch. "You know, I brought you here to fire you. But with all this new... Mr. Garvin, do you think you could use the SDF in our ad?"

"Mm? I suppose so. I'll get hold of costumes," flipping open his cell phone.

"It would be active duty sir – they would draw pay," said the General.

"Everything is costing so much money. All because of a horse." Armeño ran his fingers along the sides of his hairpiece and for a moment looked pitifully exhausted.

"The horse is just the tip of the iceberg here, Mr. Governor," said Mr. White.

"Mobilized, we'll be ready for the rest of that iceberg," said General Camby.

Hormigo

The bar dogs were waiting for Hormigo when he walked into Pete's.

"Hey dogs, hey dogs," barked Hormigo, catching their snouts in his gloves. "I got cookies for you, just hang on."

Hormigo gave biscuits to the motley pile of dogs. Ribeye stepped around the dog scrum and looked over the sparse bar.

Ribeye said, "It's like them dogs knew you was coming."

"They know the sound of my bike. Ok dogs, ok now." Hormigo stepped carefully through the dogs still climbing into his gloves for crumbs. "Hey Pete, how about a couple cold ones?"

Pete put out a big smile. "Sure thing Hormigo, sure thing. How you doing?"

Ribeye and Hormigo stood at the bar, boots on the rail, necking their beers. They nodded at a couple locals. Pete was watching the TV at the end of the bar.

"Hey Pete!" barked Hormigo.

Pete approached, "Yes, Hormigo?"

"Lemme get a couple steaks."

"Sorry Hormigo, we still got no water. Can't serve food without sanitation."

"Still? And no shots neither?"

"Believe me Hormigo, I wish I could. Beer bottles is all I can offer. Sorry."

Hormigo belched, setting his empty bottle down. "Two more beers then."

"Sure thing Hormigo, coming right up."

Hormigo and Ribeye drank their beers. They smoked cigarettes. Pete was watching the TV at the end of the bar.

"Good ride today," said Ribeye. "Good business."

"Yeah," said Hormigo. "It'll be cold riding back tonight though."

They finished their beers.

"Hey Pete!"

Pete turned his head to them. "Yes, Hormigo?"

"Two more beers. What you watching, it's so interesting?"

"Football. Dallas is losing."

"Again," grumbled a long-haired local down at that end. He stepped off his stool and picked a shapeless gray hat off the bar. "Later, Pete. I don't need to see any more of this. I'll be getting home, bro. Later, Manning."

Popping two bottles, Pete said, "Good luck, Billy."

"Fucking TV, always on," said Hormigo. "Always with this shit."

Ribeye nodded.

"Would you look at this bullshit?" said Pete, waving a middle finger at the screen.

The TV showed a cowboy-type walking through a corral with horses milling around him. He was saying, "Some folks'll tell you a bunch of nonsense. But this here's the facts. Texas turned the American Southwest from a naked savage desert into the modern Sun Belt we know today. We fought for this land and this way of life, from Goliad to the Alamo to San Jacinto. Some folks aren't grateful. But what do you expect from people that's got no respect for progress and hard work?"

The cowboy gave a carrot to a Palomino shining golden in the sunlight. The camera pressed in on his earnest, resolute face. "Maybe it's time ... to get'r right."

"Turn that shit off!" shouted Hormigo.

Pete said, "Easy now, Hormigo."

Hormigo marched up to the TV. A shriveled old man was perched beneath it. Hormigo stepped up on the rail. "I told you to turn it *off*."

Pete said, "Easy Hormigo, he don't – "

Hormigo snapped off the TV; on the return motion he elbowed the old man in the face. The old man went backwards to the floor, red zipper chunk out of his cheek.

The few people in the bar jumped up and Ribeye turned to face them. Pete scrambled around the bar to gather the old man up.

"You do what I tell you!" Hormigo shouted down at the crumpled body.

"Easy now Hormigo, it's just Manning, he didn't hear you. It's ok now, ok?"

"He should know better," said Hormigo, color subsiding.

The locals took their seats and picked up their beers uneasily. Manning was in a sitting position on the floor. Pete was fussing over him.

Hormigo tutted, "I didn't fucking hit him that hard."

"I know Hormigo, I know. But ... Manning is an old man, you know."

Hormigo grunted. "How about some music in this place? It's like a morgue in here. Pete, put on the radio."

"Ok Hormigo. Here Manning, you sit right there, I'll be right back."

Pete went behind the bar and turned on the radio. The announcer was saying, "and that was Heaven Brookes singing 'Leave Your Spurs On.' And now, the number one crossover hit on the charts, 'Get'r Right,' by popular request."

The radio twanged:

"When push comes to shovin'
and they don't respond to lovin'
when they step across the Texas state line,
when they disrespect me and my kind,
then it's time ...
to Get'r Right!
when you're tired of it being wrong,
Get'r Right!"

"Jesus, turn that shit off!" shouted Hormigo. "What the *fuck*?"

Pete turned it off. He said, "Sorry Hormigo, that song is on all the time. All the stations – country, rock, pop, whatever. It *is* kinda catchy."

Hormigo mumbled into his beer. Manning tried to pull himself up on a barstool. It came down on top of him. Pete came around the bar to help him.

"You again?" growled Hormigo.

"No, it's ok Hormigo. Listen, I got a bottle of tequila in the office. Let me get you some glasses and set you guys up. Ok?"

"So you *do* have tequila," said Hormigo, eyes narrowing dangerously.

"Only for when the bar's closed. And see? Everyone else has gone home. Let me get Manning straightened out here and I'll get you that bottle."

"Straightened out? That drunk ain't been straight in fifty years. Get the tequilia."

Ribeye and Hormigo sat at a corner table, drinking tequila. Pete locked up the bar, waiting for them to leave. When the bottle was empty, they left. Wobbling a bit, but at least they didn't feel the October wind on their ride.

Taylor Jon Bridges

Well, chug my balls. Sittin on another border. This is as boring as that Minuteman shit, but at least I'm gettin paid. Don't make no difference to me which kinda beaners I got to keep out, old Mex or New Mex. We got enough to make plenty burriters already.

Least I'm gettin paid, least we got our guns loaded and we're gonna challenge anyone coming. Warning shots? I'd rather let the *warning* be for his next of kin.

All of a sudden I'm hungry. It's been a while since I ate last. I could go for a couple double beefburgers from down the road. But we got to stay hunkered down here.

That's what Bobby Earl says.

Sun's going down. Least I don't have that faggot in my truck no more. Fine, pile up in Bobby Earl's. Fine with me. These new guys show up, think they know shit. I been out here since summer. I already *done* live-fired, know what I mean?

How about some music?

Hell, it's that same song again. Can't walk into no Walmart or nothing, they playing this song. Don't get me wrong, it's catchy.

When you gotta beg for water
from some people that are shorter
when they thinkin that you ain't got no spine,
like you gonna let them steal your last dime,
then it's time ...
to Get'r Right!
When you're tired of it being wrong,
Get'r Right!

You know what? That song's kinda like us, State Guard I mean. I always figured it was just about some cooze or something.

But that makes sense, with them new guys showing up with them Get'r Right shirts and duffel bags and whatnot. Bunch of freaks and retards, too. I reckon they'll take anyone, fill in the lower ranks while us combat veterans get pushed ahead. The pay moves with the grade.

But them two spazzes we heard about, them listening to the radio all night. Morning watch shows up and their truck don't start. That's some spoon-up-your-ass stupid right there, that is. A terrorist bicycle race coulda gone through and them Guardsmen woulda been stuck. Like a peanut in shit.

So fuck em if they all gonna pile into Bobby Earl's. Don't gotta hear no bullshit. And I can fire up a little wake-up whenever I want. Ain't gotta share, that's fine by me.

One more night of this bullshit, then we go out and practice maneuvers. Fire off a little free ammo. Then we rotate out for a few days. I'm overdue for getting fucked up.

Man, ain't no one coming this way.

Boring.

Might as well take me a little wake-me-up. Can the other truck see me? Nope. There. Just a little will do me. Running way low. Aw hell, tap a little more in there. What the hell.

Fuck, my lighter don't work. Shit, this is my *old* lighter. Where did I – oh motherfucker. I borrowed it to that new guy, that faggot, and now he's in Bobby Earl's truck with it. Motherfucker. So I have to go over and knock on the window and ask pretty please? Goddammit! Motherfucker! MOTHERFUCKER! FUCK YOUR GODDAMN MOTHERFUCKINGFUCKER!

Ok, all right. Ok. Maybe I got one in the glove box.

Aw hell, oh fucking hell, I broke my bowl. When I was – I musta threwed it, fuck. My only fucking bowl, and the last of the bag. Oh motherfucker, I'd break shit, bust my windows out right now but I'm fucking wiped out. I'm fucking tired. Now I feel the comedown, know it's coming. Fuck. I got *hours* alone out here.

Let me start the engine, get some heat on in here. Long time to morning. Maybe I can get some sleep. Got that emptying-up feeling. I fucking hate coming down. Least I got my state-issue Colt .45 automatic to keep me company.

Even if I go to sleep, I'll have you in my hand. Ready for >*yawn*< any motherfucks who try somethin. Pow! Pow! Pow!

Yeah, I'll get'r right, all you fuckin bitches.

Invasion

U.S. Armstrong

Inside the lounge of the Nineteenth Hole: fresh carpet, regulated air, clean windows to the bright perfect Silvery Minnow Golf Course outside. Empty this early Tuesday, U.S. and Geldman occupied high-backed chairs in the lounge's corner.

Jefferson set down the pewter mug of julep and a coffee, bearing away the silver platter on white gloves. U.S. kept his hat brim low while Geldman dolled up his coffee, sweet and light. The julep fizzed through crushed ice.

U.S. raised his brim and Geldman caught the motion. U.S. said, "Well I ain't gonna P.C. around it. I'm leaving and you're gonna take over the company while I'm gone. And if I don't come back."

Geleman's eyes saucered. "What are you talking about? Why are you leaving?"

U.S. dropped his brim and raised his julep. "I'm leading the State Guard to go make good on our investment."

"What investment? I'm sorry, U.S., I don't understand."

"Not counting the damage done by their flood, we've spent five and a half million dollars so far. Our corporation has underwritten a lot of the ads, but it's costing Texas nearly a thousand dollars a day per man to keep those Guardsmen on the New Mexico border. That's not including the new equipment – ballistic nylon for the officers, new sidearms, all the fresh ammo. Not that dead-grain Reserves surplus. Two mech divisions of vintage M113 APC's, Humvees, ATVs for the 2nd Brigade, they cost ten times as much per day. State Air Guard is gearing up at Lackland and Dyess AFB's, and that'll be a big bill. Gotta contract flights cause everything is overseas. Recruitment's through the roof, and we got quality too, with all them Iraqi and Afghani and Syrian and Saudi Arabian vets. Our investment has been mounting daily and it's about time we start collecting on it."

Geldman frowned. "How are you going to collect? By force?"

U.S. brought the mug up to his salt and pepper mustache. He set the mug back on the table and gave a grunt of satisfaction. He raised his hat brim to show Geldman his eyes. "Like MacArthur said, 'It is fatal to enter any war without the will to win it'."

"But U.S. – I'm sorry, but you're going to *invade* the state of New Mexico? With guns and tanks and all that?"

"We don't have any proper tanks, not yet."

"I don't understand how this could possibly help our situation."

"I tell you how it's gonna *help*. Ain't nothing in that desert worth scratching your ass for. Supposed to be a place to keep the Indians. But every drop of surface water in west Texas drips through that territory, held in their dams and reservoirs until they decide to turn on the faucet. Being as all the progress in west Texas is relying on that faucet, seems we need a more reliable hand turning it. You can see what they done with their responsibilities. A goddamn mess – it's all lawsuits, floods and droughts."

Geldman held up his hands in agreement. "I understand that, but there's no way D.C. is going to let you do this. They'll cut off our highway money, agricultural subsidies, they'll isolate us economically. They could even intervene militarily. You're talking about civil war. It's treason."

"Don't be so goddamn melodramatic. Ain't nothing like that at all. We're doing *them* a goddamn favor. They sure as hell can't run the place themselves. Look at those statistics: they're at the bottom for everything. As for Washington, they're so deep in the muck with the terrorists over there, they'll be happy we're gonna get'r right on our own."

"U.S., I think you're underestimating D.C.'s reaction. There's no way they'll stand down and just let you annex an entire state."

"First of all, we won't need the entire state once it's settled. Just the Rio Grande, from its source to its delta. Anyway, we've got a trump card for Washington. You may not know it, but that rogue state happens to be in possession of weapons of mass destruction. In fact, they've got the largest single store of nuclear weapons in the world, in a hollow mountain near Albakurk. Not to mention the labs and brainiacs they got at Los Alamos. I'm sure Washington will be happy that we liberated

WMD's from such an irresponsible terroristic state. If they can do what they did with a dam, imagine what they might decide to do with a *nuke*. So we'll just hold them safe until the dust settles, and we'll give them back to the Feds when the time's right."

"You're going to hold nuclear devices for *ransom*? And U.S., how in the world are you going to supply an occupation force, and coerce the civil authorities and police to follow along?"

"I'd rather not get into military matters, Geldman. That's not why I asked you to meet me. But I'll tell you the three reasons why we're taking the war onto their soil. One: it exerts retribution immediately. Two: all the collateral and property damage happens over there. Three: when it's done, we'll have that liberated territory to negotiate with. It's a pre-emptive strike. Unless you'd rather wait for them to invade us?"

"Honestly, do you really believe that New Mexico would – "

"They already *done* it," interrupted U.S. "They crossed the line first, they drew first blood on sovereign Texas soil. Jesus Christ Geldman, whose side are you on?"

"Yours. Ours. I'm just worried, U.S. Really worried."

"Well you ain't got to worry. And if we can get back to why I asked you here? You gotta run my company. I'm leading the invasion, if they don't accept our concessions."

"What concessions?"

"We re-worked the river compacts and all that. More equitable share of the water. And there's reparations, to cover our expenses. I expect they won't pay, which means we'll have to go in to make good on our investment. My drink's empty. Jefferson!" U.S. snapped his fingers high over his head. Jefferson appeared, bearing the silver tray against his waistcoat. "Yes, Mr. Armstrong sir?"

"Another julep for me, and a coffee for Mr. Geldman."

"Yes sir, Mr. Armstrong sir," said Jefferson, whisking away.

"Where was I?" asked U.S.

"You were back to making good on your investment."

"Yeh well, enough on that. Your concern is to run my corporation. I'm giving you full reign. Do as you see fit, just keep making money. And don't give yourself too big a raise, now. I mean, I know'd you wouldn't want to go over with me."

"Well I am just not sure that invasion is a wise choice. I mean, war ... who was it who said that war was the failure of diplomacy?"

"Probably some tofu-sucking hippie. I'm sure you'll do fine as CEO. And, let's face it, you people aren't really warrior material, are you?"

"Excuse me?"

"You're great with the books and the business, that's what I'm saying. That's why I'm putting you in charge of the corporation."

"Do you mean – because, Israel's never lost a war, and in the historical – "

U.S. dismissed the argument with one hand. "Israel's propped up by the United States. Who do you think gave them their nukes? And I'm all for it, don't get me wrong. That's our only ally in the region. Maybe in the whole world, the way they're all turning on us. But that's all gooseshit, I'm talking about making you CEO. You gonna accept?"

"Well, yes. Of course, U.S., I'm ... deeply honored."

"I'm glad. I'm glad you're honored. We go back a ways Geldman, and I trust you. I'm trusting you with *my* company. You've been around, almost from the beginning. You helped it grow to where we're at now. Here's our drinks."

Jefferson served the drinks and was immediately gone.

"I brokered the deal to buy back you're father's ranch," mused Geldman.

"That you did." U.S. sipped his drink, brim low.

Geldman said, "You hadn't been back from the war long. You had that gravel company going, and I didn't understand why you wanted that dirtscrabble farm. Until you told me the story about your father buying into the irrigation company, and the dust bowl stripping all his soil away. You did good, bought back the family farm."

"And now I own the 7200 acres around it, too."

"That you do, U.S. Pity your father didn't live to see it. He'd have been proud."

U.S. sipped his julep, brim low.

Geldman said, "Forty years. I was at your and Marianne's wedding, you were at mine. I went to you daughter's confirmation. You came to my son's bar mitzvah. It's been forty years. Forty years."

U.S. watched from under his hat brim. Geldman's eyes seemed to be misting over, almost. U.S. un-lanked his legs and stood up.

"Well enough of that," he said. "You do something nice to celebrate your promotion. I got to go make ready."

Geldman snapped out of whatever train of thought had derailed him. He offered his soft hand. "U.S.? I guess I ought to say good luck."

U.S. let his mustache's corner twist up in smile. "It ain't luck, Geldman."

<u>Billy Ortiz</u>

So I drop Daniel off at Hank's place. The kids run off into the trailer. I lie to Hank and tell him Melody went to take care of Abuelo up at Luisa's. It's hot today, sun beating down everything, raising those wavy lines.

Pop!

Hank and I look at each other, look around.

He points: there's a hole in the door of my '82. I turn toward the road and there's a *thud*! and the driveway sends up a spot of dust. And way beyond that, a twinkle of metal in the distance.

"Get down!" and we get behind his dead '76, leaning our backs into the steel.

Hank yells, "Angela, honey, keep the kids inside! Stay away from the windows!"

I grab his dirty shirt, "Where's your deer rifles at Hank?"

"In the shed, out back. Here, follow me."

Hank runs off low, ponytail bucking off his back. I get down low, run out of there, around the side of the house to where Hank is still straightening his back.

Angela's voice comes out the trailer window, "Hank, what's going on?"

"Nothing honey, just some kids doing target practice. Stray bullets is all. Just lie down on the floor until we get this figured out."

I look around, worried about being seen but the trailer and junipers and truck bodies and tire piles block us off. Hank gets it unlocked and open. It's a mess bro, but it's dry and no packrats. He's got real good guns. I grab his Winchester Model 70 Classic with the Redfield scope. Stuff a box of bullets in my back pocket and follow Hank.

He knows his little half-acre, that's for sure. He's making for the little hill that overlooks the highway. We skirt around so they can't see us, and gotta climb through a bunch of juniper to start up the hill.

Through the juniper and Hank's lying down on his stomach. He waves for me to get down. I drop onto my knees – searing pain, I cry out and fall over. Kneeled right on a fucking prickly pear, oh fuck it fucking hurts. Swearing, I crawl forward up the hill to Hank, who's peeping through a juniper.

He says, "I can't see them well, they're so far away. I don't think they thought they could really hit us."

"Well they almost *did*, bro. With our kids and there? I'm gonna take them out."

"Wait. Let's crawl up to the top of the hill, get a better look. Here, crawl like this on your belly, hold the rifle in front and keep the barrel out of the dirt. Keep your ass down, Billy, or it'll get shot off."

Hank started crawling up the rest of the hill on his belly. Like how they told him to in the army, like eighty years ago. It sucks, doing it this way.

"I'm getting rocks and shit going down my shirt."

"Better rocks than bullets, Billy."

Slowly, painfully, we make it the rest of the way up the hill. Like crawling through glass on your elbows, bro. Hank is checking them out through his scope. Down below us, the trailer looks small and far away.

Squinting into the scope, Hank says, "They got two trucks at that Texas roadblock. One guy's standing in the bed. I think that's our shooter."

I uncap my scope and look: little white truck-shaped blobs. "Can you hit him?"

"It's pretty far. We would have just been specks to him too, Billy. I don't think he thought he could really hit us."

"Bull*shit* Hank. Come on, bro."

"I ain't killing nobody, Billy."

"Hank, they'd kill you and Angela and Zacharia and Max and Daniel and all of us. Besides, like you said, we probably won't hit him. Drive them off though, maybe."

Hank looks like he's thinking real hard. His skin is the color of strong tobacco, spread of wrinkles on his face but the skin clings pretty tight to his neck and arms. His eyes are brown, looking at me, thinking real hard. He nods, like to himself. Still on his stomach, he flattens out a groove of dirt for his rifle barrel. I do it like him. He says, "Remember we're on a hill, you got to aim low, even at this range."

Safety off. In the scope: the speck on the white blob. Like shooting pool.

Hank says, "Ready, aim, fire."

We both fire and the noise is so loud, it goes right through me. I look over the rifle but it's too far to see. We chamber the next round and line it up again. "Ready, aim, fire."

We both fire. Through the scope, it seems like something's happening. I slam the bolt home and Hank is saying, "We hit him, I think we hit him!"

I find it in my scope: other specks have come out of the other white blob. I hear myself say, "Open fire" and then we just kick up a storm, firing and slamming the bolt, feeling the good hard earth beneath my beating heart.

I pull my rifle out of its groove to reload. Hank taps my arm, moves his mouth.

"What?"

I can almost hear him, but mostly read his mouth, "Cease fire."

"Why?" I snap the last round into the internal magazine.

I can see how loud he's talking even though I can barely hear him, "They're waving a white thing, like a white flag."

"So?" I can feel that I'm yelling, even though I can barely hear myself. I slam the bolt home, lean my shoulder into the Winchester's stock, it feels good.

"They must be trying to get to their buddy we hit. We got to let them."

I find the specks in my scope. "Come on. Ready – "

The scope goes black. Hank has his hand over it. He says, "No way Billy, you can't. They waved the white flag."

"Oh Jesus Christ bro."

We're lying there, almost face to face. Hank's got his arm stretched up to cover my scope and he's looking down at me, sweat-tracks in the dust and lines of his face. He's serious?

"Ok. I won't shoot, I promise."

We watch through our scopes. Hank says, "One guy's coming out, real slow like he doesn't trust us. Or just you. He's looking at the guy lying in the bed of the truck."

"How can you see so good? It's just specks and blobs, and a whole lot of brown."

"He's getting into the truck. He's ... he's driving away. They're driving away."

"We did it Hank, we fucking did it!"

"They're still going," says Hank, smiling now.

We watch their dust disappear away, back into Texas. When the dust is all gone we stand up and brush ourselves off. The throb in my knee comes back real fierce. My ears – man my ears are *ringing*.

We look at each other, look around. Everything is the same as before. No clouds, just open range, couple little hills. Behind us the rest of New Mexico is all mesas studded with juniper. Why's it so hot today? I'm fucking thirsty, all sudden.

"Let's go celebrate, bro, I'm buying."

"Oh no Billy, we got to get out of here. I'm going take the kids up to Roswell, maybe go on to Cruces. This is bad, Billy, this is going to make trouble."

"Come celebrate with me. Listen, bro. They ain't coming back."

"You go celebrate without me."

"All right, I will." My hearing is coming back a little I think, and my sweat is cooling me off, but my knee is really starting to hurt now.

Hank says, "What are you going to do with Daniel?"

Damn. I could tell him the truth about Melody, but ... "Could you take him with you? Just for a little bit. Leave a message up at Luisa's – no, wait, don't do that. Don't want to bother her. How about, I'll call your sister and find out where you're at and I'll catch up to you?"

"What are you doing, Billy?"

"Nothing. I'm gonna celebrate a little bit. Go down to the horse-shoe tournament, just like I was gonna anyway. Then I'll call Sarina and catch up with you."

As we walk down the hill to the trailer, Hank calls out, "It's ok, they're gone. You can come out now. Hey kids, we're gonna go on a trip."

Daniel is looking for me. I catch his head in my hands and look down into his frightened, trusting eyes and say, "You're gonna play with Max and Zach just like we said. But you guys are gonna go for a drive first. Maybe get some McDonalds?"

I look up at Hank. "I didn't feed him yet."

Hank smiles at Daniel. "Yeah, we'll get some McDonalds along the way."

"Hank, can I borrow this rifle for a while? It don't do no good in your shed."

Hank looks at me, stares hard like he did up on the hill. Angela comes out of the house, already with two suitcases packed. Hank don't even notice, he's just looking at me. Finally he says, "Sure, Billy. Be careful with it, ok? I mean, be careful."

"No problem Hank, thanks. Daniel, you be good and mind your Uncle Hank and Aunt Angela. I'll catch up to you guys in a bit."

I drive down the highway to Pete's with the windows open. Feeling good. Really good. Those guys want to shoot at us, at our kids? I don't think so, bro. I don't think so.

Behind Pete's, the tournament has already started. I drink bottles of beer, pitch shoes. I want to tell someone about what we did. Manning's not around today. He ain't been feeling well since that little bug maricón beat him up. I'd like to get my hands on that guy, get *him* in my scope, that fucking *ant.*

The sun goes down and we all go inside to keep drinking beers. I didn't win nothing but it don't matter, the radio is playing and I'm danc-ing with some of the girls. The beer tastes great. Stumble outside to take a piss – still no water for toilets, not even – stumble inside for another beer. The music's off, someone's put on the news?

I yell, "Put the music back on!"

Everyone shushes me. What the hell?

And all of a sudden everyone is running around, grabbing their hats. I lean back in my chair while they all rush around me. They look funny. I say, "What's happening?"

One-Armed Anthony, on his way out the side door, says, "Dint you hear? Texas is invading, right now! Shooting things up! If they ain't here now they'll be here soon!"

I watch him leave. Navy John limps out saying, "I *like* Texas, hell my parents was born there. Why do I gotta leave?"

Almost everybody's gone out the door. Pete comes up behind me, pushes me up on my feet. "Come on Billy, got to get out."

"But my beer," I say but he's already pushed me out the side door.

The back parking is emptying fast, dust clouds hanging. My '82 starts on the second try. I let it warm up. I'm the last one out of the park-ing lot, onto the highway.

Which way to go? Home? Or Las Cruces? I don't know.

Oh I'm drunk. I think I'm really drunk. Fuck bro, I'm wasted.

By itself, my '82 drives me home. I stumble out, stumble up the steps into the trailer, down the long hallway and fall into bed. Just gotta sleep for a minute. Just a minute or two, clear my head.

Shit, bro. What time is it? It's bright outside the curtains. Air inside the trailer's getting real warm. Must be nine or ten. *Stretch* good.

I could fall back asleep. Nothing to do today, besides wrench on the el Camino maybe. I'm thirsty, hungover just a bit. What woke me up? Normally after a horseshoe tournament, I sleep past noon ...

I hear something. Something's outside.

I throw off the sheet and get out of bed. My knee hurts, stiff. There, just below my window, is a white Ford Explorer parked behind my '82. It's got lights mounted on the roof and a sticker with a red T on a white star on a blue shield, underneath it says Texas State Guard. Holy shit, yesterday, all that shit *happened*?

Quiet on bare feet, I grab the shotgun from the corner. Doors slam, boots on gravel. I can hear them coming up the front steps.

I leave the bedroom and go down the hall to Daniel's room. The unused door's there, got no steps down. I kick a path through Daniel's toys to the door. I had it locked up good so he wouldn't fall out, and now I can't get it open. Crash of the front door kicked open.

Get the door open. Four foot drop onto gravel, my bare feet. I hear them coming.

Ow *fuck*! Jesus Christ bro, that hurts. Did they hear me? I shut the door above me as quietly as I can. Slide between the cinder blocks to crawl under the trailer, dragging the shotgun. Spider webs down here, which means spiders. And maybe scorpions bro, or snakes even.

Dark and cool and tight: only a couple feet between the bottom of the trailer and the dirt. There's a bunch of junk I stored under here, washing machine timers and motorcycle coils and salvage lumber. I can hear their footsteps above me. Almost exactly right above me. I could roll on my back, shoot up through the trailer's floor.

But the barrel of the shotgun is too long. They're walking around up there, and it drops little clumps of dirt onto my face. After I roll back over on my stomach, I can almost hear what they're saying.

"Mumble fucker ain't hare. Mumble mumble dang mumble." That twang – they're Texas all right. This shit is really happening.

"His truck's parked mumble. Mahht be mumble, or mumble. Gots orders to mumble, so mumble ain't mumble.

Ow! What the fuck? Did I roll over onto a cholla? Ow, another! What the fuck?

It's ants! There's ants down here and they're biting me. Slap em dead, shit they are *every*where. Fuck bro, there's *millions* of them. Biting my hands, my arms, they're on my neck going down the back of my shirt, they're on my legs and crawling up my stomach, biting me, it hurts! Fuck, I got to get out of here, I got to get *out* of here.

There's a sound, the sound of boots coming down the front steps. My entire body is burning, fuck this is fucking hell! Ants on my face, ants crawling down between my ass cheeks, I squeeze to crush them as they bite inside my ass, and there's two pairs of brown leather cowboy boots with desert camo pants tucked into them just a few feet away in the sunlight.

I'm in the dark, covered with killer ants. They bite my hands when I find the shotgun, they're in my ears, crawling through my beating eyelashes. They're biting my balls, Fuck! And crawling down my pee hole!

One of them shouts "Did you hear that?" and I bring the shotgun up to my shoulder. Two pairs of boots in the bright sunlight, ants crawl up my nose into the back of my throat and I pull the trigger.

There's an explosion of blood and smoke and screaming and my shoulder howls in pain. Pump the shotgun, my shoulder doesn't want it but I pull the trigger again. There's more screaming. I think I broke my arm.

The two men are screaming and I pump the shotgun, fire at their fallen bodies, pump and fire until I'm out of shells. Deaf silence, I can only hear my heartbeat in my ears. All of a sudden every single ant bites me, all at once.

I crawl out from underneath the trailer, skinning the small of my back, past the two bodies – I hope they're dead – running for the rain barrel, I am on *fire*. I get to the big plastic rain barrel, half-empty, filth on top. I throw my leg up into it, pulling myself up to get in when the whole thing comes down on top of me.

I'm drenched, cut my leg, muddy and still burning, all that water wasted – I need water, I'm *burning*, run for the cistern. Grab its short hose, turn the valve and squat down. Fucking cold water but I'm burning, *burning*.

I stick the hose down my pants, in my ears, I suck from it to drown the ants inside me. I'm freezing cold but my skin is burning, like meat cooking. I'm tight, shivering. Shaking, shivering. I walk carefully back, my bare feet feel like they're bleeding. I can't get the air into my lungs and my hands are shaking. *Don't panic. Don't panic, Billy.*

The two bodies are there, pretty smashed up. One of the guy's boots is sitting upright on its own, with the body a couple feet away.

Oh. I see now. His foot is still inside the boot. Keeping it standing.

Up the steps into the trailer, bathroom, medicine cabinet. Melody has to have something in here. Rooting through the tubes and bottles, I notice my hands: swollen red bumps everywhere, a little dot in each one. Every single bump is a burning needle, and they are *every*where stuck in me.

Here, witch hazel, Melody uses that on Daniel's mosquito bites. I swab a soaked wad of toilet paper up my arm. Need more, more. The wad is already ruined from the dirt on my arms. Need more. I swab myself with it until the bottle's empty. Toilet paper everywhere. I'm naked, I feel the tattoo all over me.

Ok. It hurts but I can handle it, I just need to catch my breath now. Jesus Christ, bro. That ain't no way to wake up. What the fuck am I gonna do?

First things first, Billy, first things first.

I go into the bedroom, pull on a pair of jeans, a shirt, boots. I look outside the window to make sure they're still dead. Was that one on his back before?

Run outside, my bootlaces whipping around. No, they're definitely dead. I get the wallet out of one of them's pants. Doesn't look like the ID picture no more. There's some cash and some other stuff, cards and stuff. I put the wallet in my front pocket. Their pistols are both still holstered. Pop the release ... that's a *nice* gun, Colt automatic, looks brand new. I stuff it in my jeans, check the rest of the gun belt. Cartridges, some plastic twist-tie handcuffs, a can of pepper spray ...

Billy just take the whole belt, and hurry up!

I unbuckle the belt, slide it off him. Take the other guy's too. How am I getting out of here? Their Explorer is blocking me in. I'll have to move their truck and hide it. Time, too much time. There might be more trucks coming any minute.

Or I could just take theirs. It's new, or not new but new enough. I have to go back to the bodies and search for the keys but fuck it bro, I'm taking it. It's mine.

Find the keys, but the bodies ... I can't leave them here. I have to take them and get rid of them somewhere. I grab the tarp off the woodpile and put it in the back of the Explorer. The ants have found the bodies. I grab a sleeve and drag the body to the truck, grab it by the pants to get it up onto the blue tarp. The ants are on me again but I got no time, I brush them off and drag the other body out of the blood mud. I get it on top of the other one. Go back and toss the one boot in. Wrap the tarp around the mess.

Fuck, I look like *I* been shot. Blood all over me. I pull off my shirt and tuck it into the tarp. I gotta take off my boots for my jeans, fuck, time time time!

I go back into the trailer and towel off some of the gore. It's bad, all under my fingernails and shit. I pull on jeans, my last t-shirt. Grab my backpack out of the closet. Ok. Now what? Socks and shells and the emergency baggie and my knife.

Into the kitchen, the cookie jar on the refrigerator. Open it, find ... five dollars? What happened to our emergency money? Did Melody ... *no time, no time.* I go around the kitchen throwing things in my backpack: flashlight, batteries, bag of potato chips, the fridge photo of me and Daniel and Melody at the zoo in Burque.

Hall closet: sleeping bag, coat, baseball bat. What now?

The necklace! Jesus bro, I almost forgot the necklace. Hanging from a nail in my bedroom; I put the silver chain over my head and tuck the nugget of turquoise in my shirt.

The weed! I'm running now, down the steps, past the blood bog, past the mud bog at the cistern. The old dog house: pull out the garbage bag – it's dry and trimmed at least, but not manicured yet. It smells strong. Bag's tearing a little bit. Drag it into the front seat of the truck, drop my backpack on top of it. I hope the smell covers up the smell of ... like that chicken blood summer smell but heavier, sweeter. Dust is sticking to my blood-soaked bootlaces.

Is that everything? I can't think of what else. I think that's everything.

No – water. I need water. Back into the kitchen: half-empty gallon on the counter. I grab it, get in the truck.

The Explorer starts right up. On the way out there's a mound of fur in the driveway and I know it's Pico. Good old Pico, he was trying to stop them and they drove right over him on purpose, left him there. Motherfuckers. But now *they're* dead.

I accelerate, bouncing over the ruts. My skin is tight and it hurts, itching again, I itch all over. The skin on my face feels tight.

I get on the highway for a couple miles, then turn up Milagrito Way. Dirt roads will take me north and west and away from the Texans. Just get me away. My skin is like tight plastic.

Then a voice crackles on the CB: "Patrol 6-2, Patrol 6-2. Do you copy, over?"

I keep driving, looking out for other trucks, helicopters, anything. But ain't never nothing on this road, just dry hills with juniper and that pimple of mountains in the distance. That's where I'm headed, I'll go to the rez, I'll go see William.

"Patrol 6-2, Patrol 6-2. Do you copy, over?"

Is that me? This truck? What the fuck should I do?

"Patrol 6-2, Patrol 6-2. Come in, over."

I pick up the handset, squeeze the trigger and try to sound Texan, steering around ruts with one hand. "Patrol 6-2 here."

"Patrol 6-2, what is your status?"

"I'm still there." Got to slow down for this big ditch.

"Repeat that, Patrol 6-2."

"I'm still here. Still mopping up."

"Did you acquire the target?"

Bad rocks on this turn, got to ride up into the juniper. "Uh, yeah bro."

A pause. Shit.

"Who is this?"

Uh-oh.

Then a bunch of codes and numbers I don't understand but it sounds bad, and I hear them describe William Ortiz: "thirty to forty year old male mestizo with long hair, two silver teeth, five eight and 175 pounds, possibly commandeering Patrol 6-2."

I turn it off. That was fucking stupid of me, now they know I have the truck. If only I wasn't itching all over. I claw at my neck and chest, my legs through my jeans. I can't scratch my feet through my boots and that's where it's driving me insane, the sweat is making the bites come alive, like the ants laid eggs in those bites and now they're *hatching* in my skin, Fuck!

I stop at a little scenic pullout north of Fort Sumner, past the dam. The Pecos is winding down below, steep banks. I back up until the bumper is touching the guardrail. Get out and open the back. No cars coming? I tug out the tarp, bodies and all, and drag it over the edge. Bodies tumble out and the blue tarp catches a gust and flaps across the canyon. I can't see if the bodies made it all the way to the river but that's good enough.

There's blood all over the back of the truck, brown and sticky. Nothing to do about it but keep driving. I'm gonna need gas soon, definitely. I can go through Santa Rosa, there's gas there, but what about being seen in this truck?

Shit! I forgot Hank's rifle. Oh that beautiful Model 70 Classic. Fuck man, I left it in my '82. I left that beautiful gun behind. I can't be so *stupid* or I won't make it. I'm exhausted, really sleepy, all of a sudden. I'm exhausted and itching all over and *so* thirsty. I take the water jug and suck it all down, let it run down my chest.

I'm at the outskirts of Santa Rosa. There's a little Texaco station and I pull up to the tanks. No one's around. It must be noon by now, and it's all closed up? I only got ten dollars. Maybe I can use one of their credit cards? There's a Visa, a supermarket card, and a card that says

Texas State Guard. It's got a magnetic strip like the rest.

I open the door slowly. Still ain't no sign of nobody nowhere. No sound but the ticking of the truck's fan. A little wind, and it cools me.

The insignia for the State Guard, it's on the card and the side of the truck, it looks just like the Texaco sign. I pick up the pump and the display says pay inside or swipe card. I try the Guard Card first.

It thinks about it. Now it says pick a grade. So far so good. I push the button for super-premium, what the hell. It says begin fueling. I stick the pump in, pull the trigger and feel the gasoline rumble through the handle.

Free gas. Not bad.

I drive through Santa Rosa and the traffic lights are blinking. No cars driving around. What the fuck is going on? Leaving Santa Rosa behind, I really start speeding. Ain't stopping for nothing. Is that ants on the rear window? Or blood? Dirt?

I catch sight of my own face in the rearview mirror – holy shit bro, I look *bad*. There's welts all over my face, and my eyes are swollen shut. That's why I feel so tired, my eyes are drooping like wet tortillas. I look really bad.

But it doesn't matter, I'll make the rez. William will help me. I'll make the rez.

Governor Armeño

Governor Armeño stood in the wings with Messrs. Garvin and White. He was going over his notes one last time as Mr. Garvin applied pancake makeup.

Mr. White said, "Mr. Governor, the press is waiting for you."

"Let them wait. It is good that they wait." Armenño cleared his throat. "My fellow Americans, today is a – say Garvin, don't you think I should start with a little more statesmanhood? Where's my press secretary?"

"You fired both of them," said Mr. White. "Mr. Governor, may I remind you that you are urgently needed as soon as this press conference is finished. I could just as well read the statement here, because they really do desperately need you – "

"Absolutely *not*," interrupted Armeño, batting his eyes against Mr. Garvin's puffball. "I am the statesman here. The people need a show of leadership, they need some answers, they need promises made to them. I like that, I'll work that in."

"Not without your eyes done, you won't. Hold still, and look up. *Up*," commanded Mr. Garvin.

Mr. White stood with his briefcase across his knees, fingers impatiently tapping the leather. At last Mr. Garvin finished the makeup, pulled the tissue paper from the Governor's lapels and sent him onto the stage. Governor Armeño seized the podium, leaned into the flashbulbs and the shouted questions. He aimed his look of Imperial Majesty at the television cameras.

"What's he doing? He looks like Mussolini," whispered Mr. White.

"It's his own, ah ... he's going to read the statement, ssh," whispered Mr. Garvin.

Armeño removed the note cards from his jacket, turned them around. "Ladies and gentlemen of the press, my fellow Americans and New Mexicans, what we are witnessing is a pro*found* injustice. As I speak, armed brigands are terrorizing the peace-loving peoples of New Mexico. They are committing robberies, they are committing arson, they are committing rape, they are committing cruelty to animals, they are committing murder. I, Governor Armeño, know that the rest of this country and the world are outraged at this bombarity."

"Bombarity?" whispered Mr. White.

"He read it wrong, it was supposed to be barbarity," whispered Mr. Garvin.

"Why isn't he using the teleprompter?" hissed Mr. White.

"It's broken. Now Ssh."

Armeño fixed the camera with Embattled Defiance. "This outrage will end with Texas once again forced to retreat from our soil in ig-nom-aninny. A*hem*. I personally vow to rid these interlopers by Christmas. That will be my present to you, New Mexico."

"What the *hell* is he doing?" hissed Mr. Garvin.

"He's improvising. See, this is what I was trying to avoid," whispered Mr. White.

Governor Armeño flipped through a few cards, then looked up at the cameras. "We all remember what our great President Fillmore had to say, many years ago: 'If Texas militia therefore march into any one of the other states or into any territory of the U.S., there to execute or enforce any laws of Texas, they become at that moment trespassers'. So there you have it. We are the victims here of Texas imperialism. And that is not right! I'd be happy to answer any questions."

The hands went to the air, "Mr. Governor! Mr. Governor!"

Armeño looked over them benevolently. He finally said, "Yes, Tony."

Tony read from his pocket notebook, "Mr. Governor, is it true that the mayor of Las Cruces has turned civil control of the city over to the Texas State Guard?"

"No, that's preposterous. Next question. Miss Guitierrez."

"But Mr. Governor," pressed Tony. "We have footage of the Texas flag flying over City Hall in Las Cruces. The sheriffs and city police have reportedly stood down, and there are reports of columns of Texas units advancing up both sides of I-25, now approaching Elephant Butte."

"They cannot have Elephant Butte Lake, which is a treasure of New Mexico. My own family has vacationed on that very lake. Miss Guitierrez?"

Miss Guitierrez said, "Mr. Governor, I have personally inter-viewed refugees from Las Cruces, who arrived in Albuquerque this morn-ing. They told me of Texas Guard vehicles rolling unimpeded down the streets, opening fire on civilian vehicles."

"Such aggression is typical schoolyard bullying," said Armeño. "The world is watching, don't worry. Next question. Ramón?"

"Mr. Governor, why aren't the police or the New Mexico State Defense Force at least engaging the Texans? Texas seized Las Cruces, Carlsbad, Hobbes, Portales and Clovis without encountering any resist-ance."

Governor Armeño said, "I'm sorry, I cannot respond to that ques-tion. Miss Menendez?"

Miss Menendez asked, "Mr. Governor, what should the citizens of Roswell and Albuquerque do in the face of this invading force which could be approaching those cities this very minute?"

"Remain ... remain calm. Order in this great state will be restored. Just remain calm. In the meantime, no one should purchase Texas prod-ucts, such as Dell computers."

Miss Menendez pressed, "Mr. Governor, what about the reports of violence by Texas Guardsmen while suppressing riot and civil unrest? Do you feel at all responsible for the blood which is being shed?"

"Thank you," said Armeño, forcing a patriarch's smile. "I don't have any more time, but thank you. I must be going. But I, Governor Armeño of New Mexico, personally vow to not rest until the proper borders have been restored. Thank you."

Mr. White caught Armeño as he lurched off the stage. The Governor was wet with perspiration. His sweat had eroded arroyos into his pancaked face.

General Camby

The General's truck led the column of ten. Highbeams burned the broken seams of highway as they raced across the wasteland. The roads were empty. The stars were deafening.

In the backseat, the General sat with his Chief of Staff, Major Ivan Santiago. Their laps were spread with maps. The interior light was on. The air blasted in from the driver's open window, flipping map corners.

With irritation, General Camby said, "Captain, roll up that window."

The driver's eyes lifted in the rearview mirror. "I'm smoking a cigarette. Sir."

Major Santiago leaned forward on the center console. "Put out that cigarette and roll up the window, *now*."

The cigarette sparked down the road and was crushed by the truck behind them.

"There will be no smoking in the General's staff car," Camby ordered, snapping the maps flat. A strange hush emerged without the wind.

A cell phone rang and Major Santiago answered it. He handed it to Camby: "It's Colonel Clark."

Camby took the phone. "Clark? Are you in position?"

"Yes sir," said the voice coming in waves. "We've got the interstate blocked off at the Elephant Butte exits. We requisitioned the local fire trucks, as you ordered. No one is getting through here tonight."

"Very good. Has there been any enemy contact?"

"No sir, just a lot of civilians that we had to turn back. There were some accidents and abandoned vehicles."

"Good, good. Hold that position. I am sending you some reinforcements from Albuquerque. Utilize those abandoned vehicles in your blockade."

"Yes sir."

"Expect enemy contact by tomorrow morning. Out." Camby handed the phone back to Major Santiago.

Santiago said, "Sir, I'm worried that you're going to be disappointed in Roswell."

"Nonsense. We'll press the cadets from the Military Institute into service to halt their column from the southeast."

"But sir ... most of the cadets are minors."

"They have vehicles and they have experienced instructors. What is their CO's name? Get him on the horn for me."

"Yes sir." Major Santiago reached for his phone but it was already ringing. "Hello. Yes, this is ... yes, we know about Clovis. They are? At Cannon? But that's an Air Force base. Entirely? When did they start landing? How many planes? Ok, stay out of sight. Let me know what they're unloading."

Camby said, "What is it now Major?"

Santiago holstered his phone. "Apparently, General, the Texas State Guard has taken over Cannon Air Force Base outside Clovis. Unmarked cargo planes are unloading men and equipment."

General Camby shook his head. "No, they can't take over a U.S. Air Force base. That's the 27th Fighter Wing. That can't be right."

"Apparently the base commander put up no resistance. There's no planes there anymore, only administrative staff."

Camby dug his attention into the map.

The column charged ahead, bumping over the rough pavement. Dark hills hemmed them. Inside the dome-lit truck it was a grinding silence.

Major Santiago pointed at the map. "General, we have to be concerned that they will simply push on from Clovis through Las Vegas and then straight to Santa Fe. They could bypass our main force at Elephant Butte and be at the Capital by noon tomorrow."

"What could or might happen is not as important as what *is* happening, right now," growled Camby. "Just like 'Chesty' Puller said, 'you can't hurt em if you don't hit em.' Give me the map with their last known positions."

Major Santiago flipped through small and large scale maps until he found the right one. "Here sir, forgive the lack of detail, but this is where we know they are holding position for now."

"Look," said Camby, jabbing the map. "That middle column is going to take Roswell tomorrow. From there they can push on to Albuquerque even if our second brigade holds back the southern column. If their north column makes a move to Santa Fe I can send some elements of the 1st Brigade there. But we have to protect Albuquerque."

"But General, Santa Fe is the capital."

"And Albuquerque is our largest and richest city. It is our priority. Besides, we're nearly at Roswell. We're going to have to move fast to prepare a defense. How many vehicles fell back from Hobbes?"

"Well sir, let me ..." Santiago flipped through his clipboard. "That's two vehicles from Clovis, one from Hobbes that we still have contact with."

"Out of everyone I had on the border, only three vehicles fell back? What's the status of the rest?"

"By our best knowledge sir, there were five vehicles destroyed, ten captured and a dozen more missing, presumed captured or destroyed."

"That leaves us with this column, plus three scattered vehicles guarding all of eastern New Mexico?"

"That's all we have contact with right now, sir."

Camby leaned forward. "Captain, drive faster."

This conversation was being carefully monitored on modified Bearcat scanners by Texas Air Guardsmen at Cannon Air Force Base, the temporary HQ of the 39th Brigade. The moon had risen from behind Texas and its cool light spread across New Mexico.

Eddie Brown

Dawn. In the valley, cholla were backlit by a rising sun, golden penumbra of spines like stiffened cilia. The green and yellow knobs of the cactus were stumpy fingers locked in gesture. The sunlight slowly spread up the valley walls.

High up above on a grassy ledge, cold shadows roused. Eddie held his breakfast in gloves: a rock-hard energy bar and a bottle of water. He walked around his camp site, jaws straining. He swigged water to lube up the brick in his mouth.

He chewed and chewed, feeling his masseter straining. Finally he broke the piece up enough to swallow, helped down by another mouthful of cold water.

Eddie took a moment to breathe. That was only the first bite. Banana flavor, leaden and gritty. He looked at the energy bar rising from its wrapper. At least five more bites, maybe seven. He sank his teeth into the cold unyielding block.

"Like eating clay," said Eddie aloud. First words spoken since sometime yesterday ("Goddammit," upon realizing he'd accidentally crushed three empty specimen bottles beneath his boot). He swallowed the lump with a mouthful of water.

The next bite was too big. Eddie had to stomp around the camp-site. The shock of his steps added torque to his jaw piston. The grainy pellet took a lot before it could go down. Eddie walked in patterns through his site: firepit, folding table, tent, truck.

When the bar was entirely in his stomach like an adobe brick, he felt a tidal shift in his intestines. Eddie walked downhill to his trench latrine and squatted over it.

Eddie looked over the treetops, distracting his consciousness while peristalsis eliminated his solid waste. The birds were at full throat: Mountain Bluebirds, Lark Buntings, Orange-Crowned Warblers. Across the blue sky were parallel stretches of white contrails. With autumn closing in, there was a dearth of action at this altitude in the Gila Wilderness besides Eddie and his steaming feces.

And why here? Years ago, Eddie had first seen ants living on a cholla in central New Mexico. The Valley of Fires is a mile-thick lava flow, ancient enough to have plant life growing in its crumbling cracks. On a cholla growing from a shallow crack of pahoehoe, he found tiny black ants. Their setae were dusty with something – they looked like they had been lovingly powdered with confectioner's sugar. Pollen? Doubtful – the cholla's flowers had not yet bloomed.

Eddie had tapped the apical meristem of one cholla branch. He received tiny slivers of cactus spine in his fingertip but the effect on the ants was more remarkable: they became very agitated, and quickly flooded the branch. They were too small to be field-identified by their physiognomy. Maybe some kind of *Pseudomyrmex*? He didn't have specimen bottles or a taxonomic key with him. Why hadn't he brought these essential items with him on that camping trip? Strange.

Ah yes: he had company with him. That long-dead affair.

The ants fascinated Eddie for a few days before other projects took his attention. Interest in those ants had been buried with that affair. Until, deeply unemployed, the desire to understand these ants had resurfaced like an involuntary hard-on.

What was the relationship between the ants and the cholla? From a human point of view, the cholla didn't seem to need much help: a resolute woody body raising stout bayonet-like limbs that bristled with long needles which people thought were posionous because the deep puncture pain continued for hours after the needles were removed. Eddie never tired of explaining that, actually, the seemingly smooth spines had microscopic teeth that anchored the spine in flesh and tore it open when removal occurred. Here, Eddie would say, run your fingernail up the spine. Feel that grit? Same principle as a fish hook or a Clovis spear point. Easy in, hard out. The cholla limbs were formidable, and the lesson of one's first encounter lasted a lifetime.

However, departing from the human scale, the cholla was subject to rust, fungus and a dedicated foe called the Cholla Beetle. Perhaps the unidentified ants were in a mutualistic relationship with the cacti, protecting them from Cholla Beetles and other miniature threats.

And perhaps the ants derived something more than just a secure nest. Acacia ants gain sustenance from secretions offered by the hard-thorned plant, which gives them the energy to fight off insects, browsing ungulates and even encroaching plants.

In the desert, the water found in plants is the cornerstone of all biological competition. The indomitable environmental pressures force all participants in the ecosystem to join a vertiginous arms race of thorns, poison and resistance, mandibles and camouflage. Perhaps the unidentified cholla ants were allied with the cholla and not mere opportunists, like rats on a frigate. Perhaps this symbiosis offered hope for the few remaining stands of piñon, devastated by a bark beetle. Perhaps, perhaps, perhaps.

Always a delight to crap upon Nature's bounty. Eddie wiped his ass for a while. Then he left the latrine.

Back up at the site, Eddie poured a spoonful of rubbing alcohol into his palm and washed his hands thoroughly. The sun was fighting through the trees to warm the air. From the cooler in his truck's bed came a small butt of ham, a dry hunk of cheese and the tail of a baguette.

It was definitely the last day for the ham – might as well use it all. Maybe save some cheese, though it was all sweated-out. The very end of his perishable food.

He cut the baguette through its side, cracked it open. The mustard had separated. Eddie stirred it with his knife and puttied it down in glops. The ham was sniffed again, then sliced thick. He ended up using all of the cheese, to ameliorate the questionable ham. He picked some rosemary sprigs and pressed them into the cheese.

Eddie re-used a creased square of heavy foil and wrapped the sandwich, placed it in the bottom of his pack. Atop went cans of spinach, zucchini and sliced peaches. Bag of salty peanuts. Notebook, magnifying glass, can opener, iodine. Two liters of water on top. Specimen bottles, forceps and instrument case were already stashed in their pockets.

Before leaving the camp site, Eddie rigged his experimental bear-flare trap. He strapped his pack on, clicked it snug across his waist. A deep breath of the mountain cool, stretching his legs with the pack's weight. Then Eddie hiked, down the steep slope.

The weight felt good on his tired calves, boots digging into dry crumbling earth. He had chosen his camp site for its lofty beauty and flat grassy ledge, but the altitude was too high for cholla. Eddie had to march all the way down to the valley floor to find cholla and, he was still hoping, the cholla ants. There were hot springs rumored somewhere down in the valley as well. Perhaps he would find them today.

So far, he had found exactly zero cholla ants. This valley in the Gila was several thousand feet higher than the Valley of Fires. However, all that BLM land had been overdeveloped with wheelchair-friendly nature trails and RV hookups. Too many people at the Valley of Fires, and serious research doesn't abide a crowd.

Better to be alone, in a remote spot, even though there weren't any actual ants to be found. It wasn't as if someone were paying for his research, interested in his hunch (except maybe Gordon, but even that was probably falsified), or bidding for publication rights. Nobody cared about his work. Nobody cared that he ate lima beans cold out of the can with salt and pepper, out here on the side of a mountain range only recently uncovered by the retreating ocean a scant 300 million years ago.

"So much the better," Eddie said aloud. The forced sentiment of his voice disappeared into the sunning valley.

Eddie spent the morning patrolling the cholla. It was a new stretch of valley to wander, but there still weren't any cholla ants here. He flushed Desert Cottontails, provoked curiosity in a high-circling Golden Eagle, disturbed any number of *Eleodes* beetles. But no ants on the cholla, nor Cholla Beetles.

Obviously, it was a colossal waste of time being in a remote wilderness at an altitude where even Cholla Beetles knew not to venture. It was like dropping lobster traps onto a woodpile.

At least the sun was warm, the mountain peaks were something Mahler would compose, the valley cradled life and there were no noisy humans for miles and miles and miles. Always nice to leave the city for a couple of weeks. But this was a singularly idiotic spot to conduct this study.

After hours passed among the cholla and cheat grass, confirming the complete absence of ants, he heard a gurgle. Approaching the sound, he smelled sulfur. The fabled hot springs. Boots and socks came off, joy.

The spring had been coerced into a shallow pool. There was barely enough water to cover his feet. Eddie stacked rocks into proper form while his feet turned white in the warm mineral water. Now the water came to mid-calf and was still rising.

Eddie pulled everything out of his pack and set the foil-wrapped sandwich on his lap. It was crushed down to a quarter of its height. Perfect. He carefully unwrapped it.

The ham, cheese, rosemary and mustard had been fused into the bread by heat and pressure. He bit into the sandwich, chewing in the noonday sun. Absolutely delicious: wild gamey ham, wet flavor sauce and crusty bread.

Eddie drank off the water from his spinach and zucchini, dumped one can into the other, sprinkled a spice blend over it and choked it down. He decided to save the peaches and peanuts for later. He lay his back on the dirt, feet gradually parboiling, and closed his eyes. For a time he might have been asleep.

After another two acres of cholla inspection, Eddie began the hike up to his camp site. It was steep and he took his time. Nothing to do, really, but break down the camp and return to Albuquerque. Start scrambling tomorrow for a job or something. He remembered a haiku he had once read:

> So early in the new year
> packing my bags,
> begging for work again

Stay one more night? Running low on water, that was reason enough to leave. Perhaps the Valley of Fires was past its RV season by now. At least the ants were *there*. Who cares, really, if there were onlookers? Teaching is important too, even if it slows down the actual research.

Eddie struck camp, buried the latrine and left not a trace of his passing. He took down the perimeter bear-flare tripwires (another experiment yielding zero empirical data) and stuffed it all into the bed of his truck. He bumped down the rock-shock dirt road. At eight miles per hour, it was after sundown before the tires hit smooth pavement.

Needed: a quick re-supply, gas and water in Silver City. Then east to the flat plain between New Mexico's mountain ranges. Where the cholla ants would be found.

Or perhaps he deserved some spoiling. A hotel, a shower? Hot food. Maybe a strip club? He felt endorphins enter his bloodstream. His brain was begging him to pleasure it, teasing him with potential thrill. The familiar tug in his groin, his guts. Entering Silver City, he still couldn't decide.

Eddie pulled into a gas station. He went in to pay, picking up four gallons of water. "This water, and twenty dollars on pump two."

The cashier punched it in and said, "That's forty dollars."

"Sorry, come again? I thought you said forty dollars."

"Yeah. Twenty dollars in gas and water's five bucks a gallon." The cashier had a fuzz of pre-beard and acne marring his skin.

"Wow," said Eddie, sliding two twenties. "Why's the water so expensive?"

"Why do you *think*, bro? Tss. Won't be no cheaper nowhere else."

Outside, Eddie pumped twenty dollars worth of gas into his truck: four gallons.

Back on the road, with the sun down, Eddie felt an instinctual desire for sleep after six days without electric lights. Eddie turned on the radio and found only static as he navigated the broken roads that took him northeast. Scanning, the radio found a weak station. Better than nothing. Eddie yawned and turned up the babble.

" – seen it Diane, it was incredible. The Texas Guardsmen fired several accurate warning shots and the resistance turned tail, averting a needless massacre. I remind our listeners that local sheriffs are asking people to stay in their homes until order is restored. The Guardsmen are securing territory as fast as they can and we can expect this intervention to wrap up without any serious loss of life, so long as people don't put themselves in danger."

"Thanks Tom," chipper female voice. "Governor Burton issued a brief statement this afternoon reiterating the right of Texas to defend herself. With Texas poised to restore order in Albuquerque, Governor Burton urged Mayor Trujillo to formally surrender the city by tomorrow morning. In Washington, House Majority Leader Franklin Jones had protesters ejected from the galley during the debate over an amendment allowing the transitional government of New Texas to waive – "

Eddie snapped off the radio. He drove in silence for a while. Then, jamming he gas pedal down, he said, "New Texas? Fuck Texas. Fuck these lies, and the lying fucks that tell them."

He let up on the pedal. In the dark wind of his truck's cabin, Eddie recited a passage from the astronomer Johannes Kepler: "When the storm rages and the state is threatened by shipwreck, we can do nothing more noble than to lower the anchor of our peaceful studies into the ground of eternity."

Either the ants are in symbiosis with the cholla, or they aren't. Whether the humans call this land New Mexico or New Texas or New Rimjob, it won't effect the ants. Except ... there was something nagging.

Lies and truth. Eddie stopped his truck and turned off the engine. He sat in the deep darkness of nowhere. His route to the Valley of Fires would take him into Texas-controlled territory. Finding out the truth about the ants would have to wait. They had seized honest land with a shibboleth of lies.

Eddie sat in his truck, sipping a bottle of water. Thinking about such things and occasionally saying them aloud. Eventually, he fell asleep.

The Battle of Las Vegas, N.M.

Taylor Jon Bridges

Rolling into Vegas, they ain't got no casinos at all. Why name your town after old Lost Wages if you ain't even gonna have no Indian casiner? Like naming your town San Francis and not even having no faggots around.

I'm driving my badass rig and it is *tits'd* up. How about that fucking .50 cal mounted in the bed? What? Goddamn right. I saw it at that gun and truck show they put on for us in Amarillo. Man, I picked up that old heavy monster in my hands. Like the dick offa some Transformer. Weighs eighty pound and I said oh yeah, you coming out of retirement like Rocky.

See some guys in this unit, they got this or that. But you want some respect for your authority, you swivel a .50 cal at them. Yup.

And it didn't cost me nothing, not one fucking dime. Put it on my Guard Card and they said we'd settle up later, they'd take it out against my wages that are accumulatin. Rather have goddamn cash, but I got the card for now and I'll get my cash when this is over. Which, according to Rebel Yell Radio, should be today.

Speaking of. Commercial's over so I turn it up. Sitting in my passenger seat, Mayles is nodding his hat along with the song. I'd turn it back down but it's the new Robbie Rite song and I like it, "Right is Right."

> I done told you once
> I done told you twice
> you shoulda done listened
> with your hair full of lice,

97

maybe where you come from, black is white
but you got the right cowboy, if you want a fight
I'm gonna kick your tail, cause Right is Right!

Fuck yeah. We rollin up this highway like bad business. I'm just three trucks back from Captain Bobby Earl Valentine. You know they want Valentine's Massacrers to be the *first* unit into Santa Fe. Goddamn right. I-25 just a couple miles ahead.

This is it? Saddest fucking strip I ever seen, and I seen some sad strippers. We in the left column, with that bunch from Dallas next to us. A little jap car shoots up the middle between the columns, and it's got a slutty looking asian reporter or maybe mexican in the backseat, I seen her on TV before. And I can see the camera and that means *they showing my rugged rig on TV.* And Mayles, the fucking boner, hasn't noticed, he's just nodding along to the song on the radio.

"Wake up retard, we on TV!"

That gets his attention and he leans out of the window to wave at the reporter. Dale is in the backseat, fumbling with his gear, saying what channel?

"How'n fuck should I know?" Why do I got to be on TV with these boners?

The reporter shouts a question at Mayles. The boner shouts back something I can't hear neither. The fucking jap news car has me pushed out of formation and I got my tires on the shoulder, but they should be talking to *me,* I'm the goddamn driver, I'm the goddamn Specialist in the truck here. But no, they want to talk to this boner.

It was time to spit so I lean over Mayles's coffee and drop it right on the lid. Mixes with spilled coffee, and some got inside too. Fucker.

Dale's going, "Is this shit live? What channel, TJ?"

"It ain't TJ mother*fuck*, it's Taylor John, Corporal Taylor John Bridges. Got it?"

"I just want to know what channel we on," says Dale, under his breath, "Shit, TJ."

"How the fuck am I supposed to know what channel? I ain't even *on* it. Ask your boyfriend Mayles here, I'm fucking driving, dumbass."

And Dale screams, "Holy shit lookout!"

I look up and Bobby Earl's truck is skidding and Desmond slams into him. I cut the wheel hard left, brake til my foot cramps. We stop. I look up and see why we stopped: four green SDF trucks in the gas station on the goddamn corner, right across the street. Fuck yeah!

I'm out the door, keep the truck between them and me. I yank myself up into the bed where my big baby is sitting, nose down, waiting for me. I snap off the bungees, raise the nose. No one's helping me, the queers are staying in their trucks and shouting. I pop the ammo box, snake up the heavy belt. I get the head up and in, shove it home, cock this bad slice of wedding cake.

Just as the first a them green trucks starts out the station, looking to run, I grip the spade handles and mash the butterfly triggers with my thumbs and the whole truck is shaking *chug! chug! chug! chug! chug! chug!*

Yee fucking haw! The green truck catches it in the grill and front windshield, stops moving and I really pump it in, smoke coming from the hood and inside the white-webbed windshield, blowing up *chug! chug! chug! chug! chug!*

Everybody else is opening up on the gas station now. Desmond's out of his truck with his crew, pulling the tarp off the .30 cal in his bed. One SDF turns around, tries to get around to the other exit. I'm shooting right over Bobby Earl's truck, banging on the green truck, all *chug! chug! chug! chug! chug!*

I'm firing into the smoke, all sudden fifteen, twenty motorcycles cut across the intersection out a nowhere, they ride right up the middle of our column, one of them points something at Desmond and Desmond blows up red chunky from knees to chest, flopping down in two parts. What the fu –

Hormigo

Hormigo streaked between the pickup trucks, wrenching the throttle back, cylinders hammering between his legs. The discharged shotgun was back in its gas tank holster. He came out the rear of the column, executing a wide turn around. His Diablos started following him on the turn but he waved them on down the highway, looking back into the column to make sure ...

One of the bikes came tumbling out, a panhead with ape-hangers, and the rider rolled and rolled in his leathers as the last bikes skidded to get past him. Hormigo pulled his turn around tightly, took his foot off the ground and dropped into gear. Low behind the bars, trying to see the downed rider – there!

Hormigo locked the front brakes and whipped his tail around. The rider reached up for the bike as bullets cracked. Hormigo felt the weight on his fatboy and released the brake, clawing away. Hands grabbed

Hormigo's waist, pulling him off the bike but he broke the handlebars to the right, bore down hard and roared them out of there.

He took over the lead before they got to the turnoff. They looped out east, circling back into the north end of Las Vegas. They crossed the train tracks and the interstate, went down quiet streets of Victorian mansions and adobe casitas under green leafy trees. The Diablos turned up Seventh Street and they ate up the highway. The air was clean and autumn-sweet from leaves. Hormigo led them to Storrie Lake where their tractor trailer was waiting for them.

Hormigo left Tammy in awe, as usual. He stepped down out of the sleeper cab and saw his men building a fire. They were snapping branches and adding them to a pile of flames while Flywheel squeezed lighter fluid in bright bursts.

Hormigo closed his belt and stomped over to them. He stood behind, hidden by the darkness. They were bragging to each other about how many Guardsmen they had taken out. Passing a bottle of tequila.

Hormigo said, "What are you, building a fire?"

Conversation stopped and the men turned to him. Flywheel, still squatting with the lighter fluid, said, "Yeah boss."

Hormigo stepped up to the fire, looked fiercely in their faces. He kicked dirt onto it, stomping down the burning branches. The flames resisted, licking his boot; he stomped back savagely. He stomped until it was out, then unzipped his jeans, pulled out his sore prick. Nothing happened for a second. Then the piss came, and steam rose ghostly from the ashes.

He tucked his prick back in, zipped up, still standing in the dead firepit. Hormigo said, "Don't be building no fucking *fires*. We don't know if those fuckers are around."

"But Boss," said Flywheel, still holding lighter fluid. "You said they was gonna go on to Santa Fe tonight."

"I said I thought so. I don't know nothing for sure. I'm listening to the same radio as you. They mighta left men behind in Las Vegas, they might be out looking for us. They might be on their way here right now, if they saw a fire in a campground that's supposed to be *closed*."

"Hormigo, those faggots ain't in no condition to be coming after us," said Flywheel, turning to punch fists with Lumbres.

Hormigo felt his right hand twitch. He said, "You acting like it's fucking p*arade* time or something?"

His men hung their heads. The bottle of tequila was quietly set down.

Hormigo said, "We sprung them New Mexico army trucks they was shooting up. But only because we knew where they was at, and we surprised them when they was distracted. It ain't gonna be like that all the time. And we didn't do much damage to them. I know, because I went back to get Wolfe and I *saw*."

Jefe said cautiously, "Well Hormigo, I went through there and I know I was popping guys left and right."

"It's really hard to hit something when you're steering with one hand and dodging bullets with the other. I shot one faggot in the nuts but that was the *only* shot I got off. It was the surprise that got us through there, not your fucking, ah, marksmanship bro. I got a second look and we barely scratched them. And so I been thinking about how to do it next time different."

"What's that, boss?" Lumbres asked dutifully.

"We're gonna have two on every bike. The man in back is the gunner, he shoots while the other drives. One man on a bike, even a Diablo, trying to steer and shift and shoot, it's too much, you can't do none of it right."

"That sounds like a good idea," said Half-Tank.

"Of course it is," scowled Hormigo. "Now listen. When it's totally dark, we're riding out of here."

"Where we going, Boss?" said Half-Tank.

"I was thinking we should go up to Hermit's Peak," began Hormigo.

"Yeah, they'd never find us there," agreed Lumbres.

"*But*," Hormigo continued, "instead we're going north. Sipapu Ski Basin is fifty miles. We have friends there. And we might go on from there to Taos or Colorado. Where's Ribeye? I want to talk to him about something."

"I think him and Wolfe went down into town," said Lumbres.

Hormigo's eyes opened bad-crazy. "They went back to Las Vegas? What are they, fucking *retardo*?"

"Come on Boss," said Flywheel. "Las Vegas is ours. We proved that today."

"We didn't prove *shit*, Flywheel. Didn't none of you see the flags that were all over town? That wasn't a New Mexican Zia over the post office, was it? They had the Lone Star up before Texas even *got* here. The rest of New Mexico has given up bro."

"I didn't see it," mumbled Flywheel.

"Did you see those black and white stickers people had put in their windows and cars and shit? Those big 'Get'r Right' stickers. They was everywhere. It means people are more scared of *them* than us."

The men hung in silence. Hormigo let them hang. One more moment.

"That's fine fellas, if we on our own. That's how we like it. Today we cut them. Next time, we gonna *gut* them. You guys all start getting ready, get your blues out. We're gonna fly our colors. We want everybody to know the Diablos are still here and we ain't nothing to fuck with. Ribeye and the others got two hours or we leave without them. I'm gonna wrench on my bike real quick. You guys listen to the radio. As long as they keep announcing just what the Guard is doing, we can keep surprising them."

"There was a report on our fight, Boss," said Flywheel.

Hormigo's eyebrows went up. "What'd they say?"

"That a motorcycle gang, fifty of them, started a fight while the Guard was trying to secure property or some bullshit."

"Fifty? They think we have fifty? That's good. That's really fucking good. *Fifty*. They'll *all* be running from the Diablos before this is over. Gimme a taste of that tequila real quick."

Governor Armeño

The new press secretary, Ralph Muñosco, knocked once on the Governor's door and opened it. Mr. White, Mr. Garvin and the Governor all stiffened abruptly. New Mexico Welcome tote bags were piled on the Governor's desk, their contents (pistachios, chile pepper pens, dirt from Chimayo) strewn about the floor.

"Yes?" barked the Governor.

"Uh, Mr. Governor sir, the press is getting really rowdy downstairs. There's some from Rebel Yell TV, which took over Channel 9 in Albuquerque, and they are saying that Santa Fe is surrounded, all the highways blocked off. What do I tell them? I've been stalling them for an hour. I don't know what to say to them."

The Governor said testily, "It's way too early in the day for all of this madness. Ok, listen Puñusco – "

"Muñusco, sir."

"Sorry. Here's a statement for them. You take it down and read it to them." The Governor took a piece of paper from under a tote bag and folded it neatly into quarters. He opened Muñusco's suit jacket and slid the paper into the chest pocket. Then Muñusco left, closing the door behind him

"Jesus," exhaled Mr. Garvin.

"Hurry up, hurry *up*. Forget the fax machine," puffed Armeño. "Mr. White, you get the rack of paintings. We'll get all this and meet you down at the car. Hurry up, and be careful, some of this stuff is old and fragile."

They made no effort to be quiet in the abandoned Capitol. Their footsteps echoed heavy, laden. Down hidden stairs, into the underground parking garage. A dark green SUV was waiting for them.

Mr. White arrived, pushing a wheeled rack of stacked paintings shrouded by a Navajo blanket. He opened the back doors and lugged the paintings onto the leather.

"Mr. White, you drive," ordered Armeño. "Where's the police escort?"

"He's there," said Mr. Garvin, pointing to a State Police officer walking his motorcycle around a concrete support.

"That's it? One motorcycle?" Armeño climbed into the passenger seat, dragging heavy tote bags. Mr. Garvin got in the rear seat, pulling tote bags in after him.

The doors slammed shut. Mr. White turned on the ignition. The motorcycle started up the exit ramp and the SUV followed. The gate rose for them: they saw the blue morning sky of freedom. They crept out of the garage and up the steep ramp, ready to leap out onto Paseo de Peralta.

A crowd of people and television cameras blocked the ramp.

"Shit! Go, go!" cried Governor Armeño.

The motorcycle crept forward slowly. The crowd parted for the motorcycle, then closed around the SUV, banging their microphones against the tinted glass.

"Just go, just *drive*," pleaded Armeño.

"I can't," said Mr. White, panic edging his voice.

Mr. Garvin was murmuring, barely audible, "Oh my god, oh my god, oh my god..."

"Get me out of here!" screamed Armeño. The motorcycle cop was barely able to keep his balance on the ramp, jostled by reporters crushing in to bang on the Governor's window, the chaos of their voices.

"The tote bags," said Armeño. "The tote bags! Roll down the windows and start tossing out the bags."

"But that's all we've got," wailed Mr. Garvin.

"Do it, do it now," ordered Armeño. He lowered his window. Hands, microphones, questions flooded in. Armeño shoved a tote bag containing two cell phones, a digital scanner and an antique silver samovar out the window. The bag fell clatteringly, spilling its contents. The crowd was baffled into silence.

"What's that?" someone shouted as Armeño shoved another tote bag (a laptop and a kachina doll) out his window. Mr. Garvin got his window down and tipped a tote bag through. Its contents (a Santo Domingo glazed bowl, a PDA and a scorpion paperweight) smashed on the concrete.

People shouted, "Look!" and began fighting for the bags.

"Quick, the rest, and the paintings too!" shouted Armeño. They tossed out their ballast and the crowd fell to scramble over framed paintings and DVD players.

"Now go!" screamed Armeño.

Mr. White gunned the engine, bumping the motorcycle cop who dropped into gear and slipped between the stragglers. The press jumped back from the SUVs tires, clutching brand new digital projectors and sixteenth-century woven baskets. They could only watch the Governor's truck jump the curb and drive away.

Mr. White followed the motorcycle, sirens blazing, blasting through red lights, sprinting for the tiny Santa Fe airport. Once there, they boarded a turboprop on temporary loan from one of Governor Armeño's business associates – except for Mr. White, who was informed that it was necessary for him to remain in Santa Fe. The plane took off immediately on its nonstop flight to Mexico City.

In the press room, Ralph Muñusco blinked up into the television lights and flashbulbs. The press room was so crowded that reporters spilled out into the hall. Ralph tried to clear his throat but it was like rubbing two pieces of sandpaper together. Though he was wearing contacts, he tried to adjust his glasses.

"I will now read a statement from Governor Armeño, in response to the demands of surrender from the Texas State Guard. Mm-kmm," he tried again. Ralph reached into his breast pocket and pulled out the statement. He unfolded it once, twice. He looked up, weaving in the headache blare of lights. The paper was entirely blank.

General Camby

General Camby and Major Santiago were hunkered down around the microphone at KTAO. The entirety of the New Mexico State Defense Force was parked in the dirt around the low adobe building. Three trucks, seven men.

The amber light went on; the engineer pointed at General Camby.

Camby barked into the fuzzy microphone. "Attention. This is General Camby, head of the New Mexico State Defense Force. With the abdication of Governor Armeño and the imposition of martial law, I am now the *de facto* Governor of the free state of New Mexico. The capital of this government has returned to Taos, temporarily, until we succeed in expelling the enemy from our shores. To accomplish this, I am imposing a curfew at nightfall. *Habeus Corpus* is hereby suspended, and country sheriffs possess unlimited power to apprehend, search and seize suspicious persons without providing just cause. Additionally, they may deputize as they see fit. Together, we the people of New Mexico, will live to see our great state be free once more. That is all."

He nodded to the long-haired disk jockey, who leaned to his microphone and said, "That was General Camby, with an important message for all of you. Next up we've got some *Desert Highway* here on KTAO, first solar-powered radio station in the world."

The amber light turned off. General Camby stood, pressed down his fatigues. The disk jockey looked up with red-rimmed eyes and said, "Hey, thanks guys."

General Camby harrumphed and left, with Major Santiago at his heels.

In the lobby, General Camby said, "Get me the Governor of Colorado."

"But sir, I don't have the phone number for the Governor of Colorado or even the Mayor of Raton. If you don't have the numbers, sir, then we don't have them."

Camby pinched the bridge of his nose. "We need the Governor's Rolodex."

"Should I call the Governor's office, sir? Talk to his secretary?"

"No," snapped Camby. "I'm the Governor."

"Yes sir but we're going to need help in declaring that, so that people know. This radio station can't have a range of more than fifty miles."

Camby sighed wearily. He allowed himself one swear word: "Dammit. Go back in there and borrow a phone book."

Alone, Camby walked out of the station into the cool evening. His soldiers were smoking cigarettes, uniforms in pathetic disarray. The stars over Taos were pulsing, and a gentle background hum filled the dome.

One of the soldiers said, "What are we doing, General?"

General Camby straightened his back. "We're crunching some numbers. Just sit tight for now. And make sure you stomp those butts *out*, it's still fire season."

"Yessir," came the desultory voice.

"Rolodex," mused Camby to himself. "What does that remind me of?"

Oh Lord, I remember now, that awful blasphemy in Your House. I remember. Back in Long Beach, at the First Episcopal, where we had the meetings for the Young Marine's program. That book – I had thought it was a missal or a hymnal, but it was a cheap paperback. Pulp at its most vulgar. It was the name, that's right: Rolodex Nipple. *By Thomas somebody.*

Oh Lord, I opened the book at random and what did I read but the most degenerate filth I've ever witnessed in my life. There, left for anyone to read on a pew in God's own House. Unbelievable.

A young woman, a stripper, masturbating herself. With a pistol. With a loaded *pistol.*

And when her sick arousal reached a frenzy, she flicked the safety off. The book was very explicit of her technique, graphically so. And then, to reach the full heights of her loathsome "orgasm," she pushed the hammer down, thumb on the trigger, so that with each lustful convulsion the pistol was tensed closer and closer to springing.

That was as far as I read. I held onto the book for a while, to do something about it. But then Bobby died in the hospital and I sold our business. Came to retire here in peaceful New Mexico. Look and see how it's all turned out.

Camby shivered in his reverie.

"Getting cold tonight. Up here, this altitude," drawled one of his soldiers.

"Seasons come early up here," said another.

Major Santiago came around the corner empty-handed. Low-cast voice, "Sir, they ain't got a phonebook. Maybe at the hotel?"

General Camby drew in his breath, and allowed himself another sharp "Dammit."

U.S. Armstrong

The wind was up, blowing the first fallen leaves around Santa Fe's plaza. So much the better – it gave a dramatic effect. General U.S. Armstrong, eleven feet tall in his formal State Guard dress topped with his broad white hat, standing on the plaza grandstand.

They were waiting for the ancient PA system to start working. A better backdrop would have been the Saint Francis Cathedral – better than the tourist flytraps and t-shirt stores lining the Plaza – but here they could accommodate the crowd. And the cameras.

The crowd – mostly press, some locals, a few confused and wayward tourists ushered in by State Guardsmen – were also waiting. Something of historical importance was in the air. The tall General, eyes hidden by his enormous white hat, was about to remake the world. A squealing assault of feedback brutalized the crowd.

"Sorry," said the peon working on the PA. "I got it now I think. Try."

U.S. tapped the microphone and heard the sound echo back to him. He nodded, and had the world's attention. He straightened himself even taller, his hat nearly touching the roof of the grandstand.

"Good morning, ladies and gentlemen." His drawl was patient and deep, all-penetrating. "As Commanding General of the Texas State Guard and authorized representative of Governor Burton of Texas, I am pleased to announce the end of hostilities. I hereby proclaim that being in possession of the capital, Santa Fe, I am therefore in possession of the entire territory of New Texas. We came as friends, to better your condition through development and progress, and make you part of the great Republic of the State of Texas. And believe you me, we're gonna Get'r Right."

He paused for light applause from his staff and soldiers. General Armstrong continued, "All city, county and state police are hereby restored to duty, under the flag of Texas, and they shall all be the beneficiaries of a 50% increase in salary, right across the board. All civil authorities are ordered to return to work, to help the advisors from Texas take over day-to-day administration of New Texas. Schools are ordered to re-open, and truancy will not be tolerated. You are asked to return to the regular course of your lives. Local election proceedings will begin as soon as the territory is able to handle the responsibility. We have claimed New Texas to ameliorate the suffering of its people, and restore order to a failed territory. One more thing. All those who take arms, or encourage resistance to the government of New Texas through word or deed will be looked upon as a terrorist and treated accordingly. For the sake of humanity, I urge you all to submit to this improvement in your station. The blood that may be shed, and the sufferings and miseries that may ensue, will be on your hands. Got that? To the Government of the United States of America, to whom we all remain loyal and patriotic subjects, I assure you that the devices currently protected by the Texas State Guard, and the research facilities and bases which support them, will be restored to the control of the Federal Government as soon as the new borders of Texas, now including the territory of New Texas, are fully recognized and ratified. And when one star is officially removed from the flag of the United States. Thank you all. God bless New Texas."

Part III Occupation

Consolidation

Eddie had been hoping to have time for a pre-emptive blast from his inhaler, but her door stood open. Ms. Geddy sat behind her desk: mid-forties, glasses, dark hair back, declined posture, lipstick.

Her office had a window facing a tree. No photos on the wall, no reference books either. Old computer.

"Mr. Brown?" she said, indicating the chair.

"Yes. Thank you for seeing me," said Eddie, scraping a metal chair underneath him.

"Thank you for seeing *us*. We're terribly short-staffed, and you come highly recommended from Dr. Nott at the U."

"Mm? Oh yes, Gordon. A long-time scholarly associate, Gordon Nott."

"And you both taught at the U?"

Eddie noticed how Ms. Geddy's glasses narrowed her eyes. He looked away and found the manila envelope in his lap. "Our time as assistant professors overlapped – here, my c.v. will explain it better."

Eddie felt physically lighter, unburdened of the two stapled pages. Ms. Geddy took his c.v. up to her glasses. Eddie's hands rested in his lap, bending the envelope. One hand ventured up to scratch at the back of his neck but he caught the impulse, dropped the hand back into his lap. He looked at his hands that were denting the envelope: fingernails too long and dirty. *Whoops.*

Ms. Geddy asked brightly, "So you got your masters in Chemistry from Emory?"

"Yes. Chemistry, biology's ugly sister."

"I'm sorry?"

"Nothing, sorry." His hands had folded the envelope in half and he dropped the evidence.

"And then you enrolled in the doctoral program here at the U?"

"Yes. However, although I still maintain associations in the department, such as with Dr. Nott, I am no longer pursuing a doctorate."

"Why is that? If you don't mind me asking?"

"There were ... first of all, my interests changed, and a PhD in Applied Myrmecology was no longer, ah, applicable. And I had some personal differences with my advisor. I left that program and have since continued my scholarship independently."

"I see. You have a lot of publications."

"Yes, I do have. That represents the bulk of my research thusfar. Not all of them have actually been published ... I just sort of indicated where I thought they might fit in."

"*Nature* is a pretty well-respected magazine, isn't it?"

"Yes. It is. I would like to point out that my research on captive mating, co-written with the late Dr. Holfen, was very warmly received by *Arthropoda Arcana*."

"Well that's all very impressive. Most of our keepers are too busy to write many papers, but I'm sure they'll be happy to have a published scholar on board." Ms. Geddy set the c.v. neatly on her desk. She centered her glasses with extended fingertips. "Let me tell you a little bit about our zoo. The Zoological Park of New Mexico opened in 1947 and now operates on over fifty acres. The zoo hosts over 250 species of native and exotic wildlife. The emphasis here is on naturalistic settings and intimate encounters, with interactive exhibits."

"Sounds great. Really great. I'm boundlessly fascinated by wildlife, and I love to pass on what I've learned in a fun way." *Uh oh, slow it down Eddie.*

"Wonderful. And earlier, you worked at the Terry Lu Walker Zoo in Florida? What sort of zoo is that?"

"Much smaller than this beautiful zoological park. No interactive exhibits at all."

"We've got them, they're great for kids. Do you have any areas of expertise?"

Eddie pretended to think about it. "If I had to pick one, it would be the ants."

Ms. Geddy laughed professionally. "Well I'm sure you'll be able to find some ants around the *food court*. As I said, we are short-staffed, stretched thin across the board. Normally we only hire at the fiscal quarter, for budgetary reasons, but as I said, we are critically short-staffed. For example, I only have one full-time keeper for the entire Arctic Tundra exhibit. And he needs to spend most of his time with the polar bears. Mush-Mush and Tondo are very popular."

"I can imagine."

"Would you be interested in working at Arctic Tundra? There's a brand new indoor pavilion. Some of the newest interactive computers in the entire zoo."

"Sounds great. What animals are part of the exhibit?"

"Many animals. There's an arctic fox, and of course the polar bears."

"Any caribou or wolves?"

"Maybe some day. There are lemmings."

"It sounds very nice."

"And it is operated with a donor-advised endowment. That allows easier direct-hiring, without a need to convene the trustees."

"That's good."

"And you'll be near the Great Ape house. They were going to film part of *Any Which Way But Loose* there. But instead they filmed at the Rio Grande Zoo."

"Arctic Tundra sounds like a great place."

"It is. Woody – the other Tundra keeper – will be ecstatic. Ah, there's the matter of salary. The zoo is only able to offer a sum not to exceed the lowest average of non-administrative associate pay for work commissioned in the last quarter of the fiscal year, unless a special appeal is made to the Board of Review during the previous quarter."

"I see. Uh, how much would that be?"

Ms. Geddy pinched her lips professionally and turned to her computer. She typed information into it. Then she waited. She said, "Sometimes it takes a while."

"I understand. Say, has the invasion affected things here?"

"Gosh, I couldn't say so. We don't get involved in politics. Whoever is in charge of the state is in charge of the Zoological Park's budget. If you ask me, it wouldn't be a bad thing if they actually got things working right, for a change. Ah, here it is." Ms. Geddy wrote something on a Post-it note. She stuck the note on her desk, facing Eddie.

It was a slim sum, a lot less than he was paid under the table, painting houses. But that company was gone, replaced by Texas chains, Texas labor. Eddie smiled. "I'll take it."

"Wonderful, just wonderful. When can you start?"

"I suppose immediately."

"Wonderful. I'll call Woody to let him know he can expect you at the Exhibit at eight o'clock tomorrow morning. Here's a temporary security pass to get you into the staff parking lot. Do you know where that is?"

"I've got a map of the zoo," said Eddie, tapping his front pocket as he stood.

They shook hands.

"Thanks," said Eddie.

"Thank *you*," said Ms. Geddy.

"I owe you buddy, I really do." They clinked pint glasses, again.

"Yeah, Eddie. Then how come I'm gonna get stuck with this bill?"

"Because, dear Gordon. Excuse me, dear Dr. Nott. Because they won't start paying me for two weeks, Dr. Nott."

"And how much are they going to be paying you?"

"Don't ask. And the first check will be less the cost of two uniforms. Real snappy-looking, tan and taupe."

"Did they offer any benefits? Medical?"

"No. But based on my salary, I might qualify for food stamps."

"What happens if you get sick, Eddie? And you've got your ... you know."

"My asthma doesn't really slow me down much. And if I get sick I guess I'll starve. Unless you're around to keep me fed."

"Arctic Tundra," said Gordon, straightening his glasses. "What is that, wolves?"

Before Eddie could respond, the waitress stopped at their booth with a bean and cheese burrito, green, and a steak and enchilada combo, red.

"I had the steak," said Eddie.

They settled into their first bites.

"Good," said Eddie. "Good."

Gordon wiped his mouth, panting in-breaths, and swabbed his lips with a napkin.

"Too hot?" beamed Eddie. "You've lived here longer than I have. Your epithelial cells are compromised, bursting from the capsaicin. You need more vitamin C. Unfortunately, the chile pepper is your best source around here. Do you need a sopapilla? With a little *honey* on it?"

Gordon shook his head. He drained his beer and let his lips hang open. Eddie shoveled his food gustily.

"That was a good tip about the haircut too, Gordon, thanks. I think it helped me out. To Arctic Tundra," said Eddie, toasting Gordon's pint glass.

"I'm gonna order the chile on the side, from now on," Gordon finally squeaked.

"Wipe your face, buddy. You got a sweat mustache like Magnum P.I. crossed with Aquaman."

Early morning zoo: smell of evaporating hose water, warm sun growing stronger, chaos of screeches, hoots, caws, lows, yowps, roars, grunts, songs and growls. The Arctic Tundra Pavilion was a small, single-story building butted up against the polar bear enclosure. Eddie tried to peer through the locked glass doors but it was too dark.

Jangle of keys behind him. Eddie turned to face a tall red-haired man wearing a zoo uniform. Tight shorts riding high, package-defining. Stout hairy legs, hiking boots.

"Mr. Brown, I presume?" lightly smiling down at Eddie.

"Just Eddie, please. You must be Woody."

"I must, I must. Let's get this open, and then I *need* to make more coffee." Woody yawned hoarsely, jangled a heavy ring of keys until he found the one.

They stepped in and the door muscled itself shut behind them. It was cool. Woody flipped a bank of switches and the fluorescents came buzz-popping on.

"It's cool in here," remarked Eddie.

"It'll be nice in the summer. Coolest place in Albuquerque. So, here it is, Arctic Tundra. *Ursus maritimus* takes the most work. Their diet is an attempt to reproduce the nutritional profile of *Phoca* and it takes hours. I say, hell, let's just toss in a seal every morning. We've got plenty, it would save time *and* be very entertaining for the public."

"We could get little gladiator helmets for them."

Woody laughed, big baritone burst. "All right. So here's the tundra, teeming with life. This is what they come to first. Lichen on a rock. Obviously, care for the lichen is minimal. But the magnifier here needs to be kept clean and functional. Moving on, here's the first computer bank. Interactive learning, tundra-related puzzles and games. The system is down, been about a week waiting for it to be fixed. Maybe tomorrow. Anyway, here are the main exhibits of the pavilion. Arctic hares, collared lemmings, an arctic fox and some ermines."

"It seems a bit gratuitous to have the predators on one side and the prey on the other, staring at each other."

"They can't see through the glare of the glass. And it makes feeding a lot easier – herbs on one side, carns on the other. I need to get the bears going, so just make yourself familiar with the exhibit. I'll be back in a few minutes to take you into the back run of the pavilion," said Woody, turning on his muscular calves and pushing through an Employees Only door.

That's me. Employee. New doors are opening to me. I better get busy.

Eddie strolled up to the Arctic Fox enclosure. The backdrop was realistically painted. The fox was nowhere to be seen. Eddie read aloud, "Artie the Arctic Fox."

Eddie turned and walked across the pavilion to the lemmings. Their concrete burrow was set against the glass so that the trails and rooms, and all the brown lemmings jiggling inside, were on display. The burrow's entrance was a barren contoured tundra landscape, and a realistically-painted Arctic backdrop.

Eddie watched the lemmings kick in huddled piles. His eyes drifted to the plastic information plaque on the wall.

He read aloud, "Collared Lemming: *Dicrostonyx torquatus*. Lemmings reproduce rapidly, living on a diet of seeds and grasses. Their population supports a wide variety of Arctic predators. Each female lemming can produce up to ten young, every five weeks. If they were to all survive, the tundra would be exhausted of its meager food sources rapidly. However, when the lemming population grows too large for its food supply, they undertake massive suicidal migrations, often hurling themselves off cliffs or drowning in swift, cold glacial rivers."

"What the hell? That's not right. What the fuck?" His voice echoed back at him. Eddie frowned, then flicked open his utility knife. "Well, I better get started on correcting these falsehoods."

One moment later, Eddie was surprised by the pavilion entrance opening.

"Sorry folks, we're not quite open yet," said Eddie, prying up the plaque. He turned to see that it was Ms. Geddy and a security guard.

Ms. Geddy said, "Mr. Brown? I've just had a very disconcerting phone call from Professor Davids at the U. It seems that – what on Earth are you doing?"

"I'm improving the veracity of the lemming exhibit. Correcting falsehoods."

Ms. Geddy sharpened. "Defacing an informational plaque? Is that a knife?"

The security guard, a short man named Hernan, shifted uncomfortably behind her.

"Just a tool," said Eddie, closing and pocketing the knife in one motion. "You see, the information here is wrong. Wrong information is far worse than no information."

"Well I can assure you that nothing on that informational plaque is 'wrong.' I can see that Professor Davids was – "

"Here," interrupted Eddie, pointing eagerly at the plaque now stiffly sprung from the glue-pocked wall. "All this about suicidal migrations. That isn't true. It's an old wives' tale. A myth. Never happened."

"Well it wouldn't *say* it if it weren't *true*. I've even seen it, in those nature films. All of them running off a cliff."

"Yeah, I seen that too," added Hernan, hand steady on his walkie talkie.

"*Listen* to me. In 1958, Disney produced the nature film *White Wilderness*. A man named James Simon shot and edited the lemming sequence. It was filmed in Alberta, Canada, where lemmings are not autochthonous. They brought the lemmings to a soundstage and made them run on a record turntable covered with snow. Then they took them outside and herded them off a cliff. They murdered lemmings for their lie."

"No, no, *no*. That's quite enough, Mr. Brown. I'm afraid I need to ask you to leave this Zoological Park and not return."

Eddie said, "This isn't like faking the moon landings. The film is a documented fraud, and this plaque is perpetuating it. Now, I'll be the first to say that mistakes are capable of teaching us valuable lessons. For if I may quote the great Lord Kelvin, 'One word characterizes the most strenuous of the efforts for the advancement of science that I have made perseveringly during fifty-five years; that word is failure.' So you see, we could make this an example of – "

"I'm *sorry*," Ms. Geddy interrupted firmly. "But I need to ask you to leave now."

"Step along this way, sir," said Hernan.

Eddie looked at them for one ridiculous moment. Then he filled his lungs and said, "Look, these aren't even true lemmings, genus *Synaptomys*. And only the Scandinavian Lemmings actually migrate. We should be telling people that this is one of the members of *Rodentia* that molts its pelage. But they'll stay agouti, unless we start shortening the intensity and duration of the light they receive."

"Sir, I need you to step along now," Hernan said firmly. He put one hand in the air near Eddie's shoulder and gestured to the door with the other.

"Oh come *on*," said Eddie, shuffling forward. "At least tell them that Inuit children use lemming fur for doll's clothing. At least tell them that."

Ms. Geddy, horrified, covered her lipsticky mouth. Hernan said, "Let's step along now, sir."

"Wait!" said Eddie. They stopped and waited. "Can I say good-bye to Woody?"

Ms. Geddy's forehead crushed down on her glasses. "No, the zoo is going to open in half an hour. Hernan, please."

"Step along now sir," said Hernan firmly.

"Ok, I'm going. Bye. Nice meeting you."

Into the natural air, the sun-warmed air, blue sky forever, the freedom of it. And then the long lonely walk back to his pickup truck.

The sound of a coffee grinder made him smile awake. Eddie cracked his eyes, and the smile disappeared. Facedown on the fuzzy couch in his squalid living room.

The coffee was being ground on the other side of his casita's thin wall. Eddie pushed himself upright, groaning groggy. The room leveled itself in his vision. Eddie tried a deep breath and was punished for it.

The struggle to breathe, *don't panic*, to hold steady and calm, relax. Relax and just breathe, just breathe, just breathe. Ok.

Sitting on the couch in yesterday's sour clothes. Why on the couch? Something happened last night. Eddie blinked around the room. One flat blade of sunlight penetrated the thick folds of dull-gold curtains, illuminating the motes passing through its plane. What time is it? The traffic outside was low-audible. What day is it?

Eddie pushed himself to his bare feet. Steadied himself on the table.

Sketchbook pages covered the table. Oh yes, the children's book. That's what he had decided to work on. *Welcome to the Ant House* or *Ant Colony* or something else, something better.

He looked over the night's effort. Then he turned the floor lamp on. *They looked better in the dark.* Sketches of fire ants (*Solenopsis*), weavers (*Oecophylla*), harvesters (*Pheidole*), leaf-cutters (*Atta*), army ants (*Eciton*). Cartoony schematics of their nests. *At least you didn't waste any colored pencils on this crap.*

Eddie picked up his page of notes and read in the margarine lamp-light:

"Colony point of view: go through life cycle (nuptial flight to nuptial flight); major challenge to each colony & them overcoming it.

Illustrations: queen starts nest with eggs, colony growth, colony work (e.g. *Atta* leaf-cutting and fungus gardens, *Oecophylla* weaving together the tree canopy), challenge & overcoming it (e.g., *Pheidole* versus ~~dulotic~~ slave-raiding *Harpagoxenus*, maybe *Eciton* migration/raids, bridge over stream).

Got to be fun to look at: Not too much detail data, just the cool stuff, the stuff they'll be able to imagine with the help of a good illustration.

Need a title: Something catchy.

Make sure: ..." and after that Eddie couldn't make out his own scrawl anymore.

Eddie scratched the crown of his head. A fingernail caught the edge of something and he clawed it up, flicking bits of dead scalp scab from his nail, going back for more. He scratched out the edges of the scab. Finally he came away with blood under his nail and he stopped himself. He started picking his nose.

Disgusting, Eddie. How about a shower?

Eddie scuffed into his bedroom. Ungodly heathen chaos in there. The clock said 11:30 am. Not too bad at all, considering. He snatched a clean pair of underwear from his laundry bag and got into the shower.

Hot, hot shower. Eddie scrubbed at himself, sloughing off layers of dead skin, sebaceous residue, bacterial outposts. He scrubbed hard, leaving his skin pink and tingling, nerves coming out like stars at dusk.

Under the water, a naked animal like all the rest, strange thoughts and memories welling up through fissures in the strata, from places secret, occult and concealed.

Eddie lathered up his sponge once more – almost out of soap – and worked his cock and balls roughly, passing fancy of Woody as he soaped up his ass crack. Hot water was dying so he stepped out onto the thin floor towel. Eddie remembered the sound of the coffee grinder. The idea of coffee perked him up.

He toweled off, body hair soft and curly. He pulled on a pair of khaki shorts, socks and hiking boots, belt, clean (?) t-shirt: *Mandala Books, Daytona.*

"Coffee," he said aloud. He stepped outside into sunlight. Locked his casita's door, the iron screen, then the compound's gate. A walk? A nice walk to a cup of coffee somewhere?

Eddie hiked down the alley to the busy street. He waited at the light. No pedestrian light, no button to secure his passage. Eddie waited for a break in traffic, then ran. A sedan making an unsignaled left nearly clipped him but he arrived whole at the far curb. Eddie walked, eyes on the sidewalk's upheavals. The sun was still warming, nearly Thanksgiving. The air was dry and smelled intermittently of car exhaust. Eddie filled his lungs carefully.

Traffic blared past him. He crossed a few more dangerous intersections, then turned onto Central. Olde Route 66 was never intended to be walked. Four lanes of swerving, speeding, uninsured traffic. Eddie was the only man walking. Crossing a side street, an SUV nearly ran him over.

He felt their heads turn, as they passed him: *who is that derelict, that illegal, too poor for even the bus? Is he going to get me at the light, where I sit immobile (defenseless), going to get me and jack my car, take my car from me?*

The median down the middle of Central looked inviting, a concrete menagerie of dying horticulture, but walking there would likely attract even more attention. So Eddie continued hiking the forsaken sidewalk. The sun was warm, with the wind tossing dust in his face.

A police car – with its freshly applied New Texas insignia – slowed to match Eddie's pace. In Eddie's peripheral vision, the car crawled along with him. Finally, Eddie looked over and smiled. The officer scowled into his radio handset and accelerated away.

Gradually, the un-zoned wastelend began to fill with non-derelict parked cars, open businesses, casual pedestrians. He had walked all the way to the edge of Nob Hill. There was bound to be a coffeeshop near.

Eddie walked, thoughts free to come and go. Easy breathing. There were shops now, sidewalk bistros, a shoe store, tattoo parlors. He glanced at the headlines in the newspaper machine: BOTH STATE LEGISLATURES SIGN TREATY and CONGRESS CONSENTS TO TEXAS-NEW TEXAS TREATY.

He sighed, but his interest then locked onto a small dust devil twirling in the vacant lot. After it had tossed itself apart, Eddie began to cross the street. Something made him look back and the dust devil had returned, scattering crushed paper cups. Watching it as he walked, he tripped over two women squatting on the sidewalk.

"Excuse me," he said, holding a woman's shoulder to keep her from sprawling. "I didn't see you down there."

"It's ok," she said, looking up: pretty face, turned quick to black curls when she looked back down at something on the ground.

"I think its neck is broken," said the other woman, husky and crewcut.

"What is it?" asked Eddie, leaning over them.

"A bird. It flew into the window," said the head of black curls.

He glanced up: big café window, reflecting the blue sky. "May I see the bird?"

They regarded him suspiciously but made space. The husky one said, "I think its neck is broken, but it's still alive."

"Now it's got ants all over it," flash of her eyes alive, that chin dimple, adorable.

The husky one tugged on one of her heavy-gauge earrings and said, "Fire ants."

Eddie said, "No, they're not fire ants, they're Argentine Ants, *Iridomyrmex*. And the first thing is to get them off our little female *Passer domesticus* here." Eddie reached forward with cupped hands.

"Wait, be careful, its wing or its neck might be broken," said the husky one, blocking his reach with her hands.

"She's ok," said Eddie. "Just stunned. But those ants *are* stinging her, and she'd get over her shock faster if I got them off."

"Yeah, they're all over its eyes and – ugk, I can't look," stud in her nose peeking out between her fine-boned hands, silver rings, and her lips with white teeth inside.

The husky one said, "What are you, some kind of zoo guy?"

"I used to work at the Zoological Park of New Mexico, as a matter of fact," said Eddie. He reached forward and gently gathered the sparrow. It was limp and weighed no more than its shadow. He caged the bird in his fingers. With short bursts of air he blew the ants off, turning the bird over until it was clean. To the pretty girl he said, "Here, hold out your finger for her."

She did, and he brought the bird to her finger. It instinctively gripped, and when Eddie opened his hands the sparrow remained perched.

Woozy, a bit.

"Wow," she said, staring closely at the bird. "She's looking right at me."

With her other hand she brought a finger to the sparrow's back. After the first trembling touch ... gently, gliding gently, lightly smoothing down tousled feathers.

The café door opened and a man came out gibbering, "I can't find the phone book Li, and the operator couldn't find me a bird doctor so I don't know what – hey, you've got it on your finger."

They all watched the perched bird. Her beak opened and closed with rapid breathing.

"It's not going to bite or anything, is it?" whispered the man. "Rabies?"

"No," said the pretty woman. *Lye? Or Lie?*

"Perhaps she ought to be set down, maybe here on this table, and we'll see how she does," suggested Eddie. "The ants won't find her up there."

"Ok. We can watch from inside." She stepped slowly, gracefully to the bistro table and set her hand on it. They waited. "She won't hop off."

"They climb *up* to perches, not down. Put your finger just below the edge of the table," said Eddie.

She did, and after a moment's hesitation, the sparrow grabbed onto the metal rim of the table.

"There," she said. "Let's go inside and watch it. You come too, in case we need a zoo guy."

Eddie felt no refusal in him, and followed them through the white-washed door. Inside, a skeletal café: a barren bar, some scattered chairs and a layer of dust. Through the window, the sparrow hadn't moved.

"Do you have a shallow dish of water? That might help her," said Eddie.

The husky one said, "We don't have any dishes here. There's nothing. We're not going to open until the end of the month."

"If then," said the man.

"I've got a bottle of water," said the pretty one. "I'll use the cap."

"What if you don't finish the bottle, how are you gonna save it?" argued the husky one.

"I'll finish it. What's the big deal?" She unscrewed the bottle cap and filled it with water. She carefully carried it outside, moving slowly, graceful steps. She placed the cap in front of the sparrow and returned inside to join the vigil. Then, "Look, she's drinking the water! The water I gave her, look!"

The bird dipped its beak into the cap, put its head back to work the water down.

"Sit down, everybody, let's watch her," her eyes shining with the sparrow.

They sat on metal chairs, facing the window. Eddie was at the end of the half circle, next to the pretty one. He couldn't look at her surreptitiously, he had to watch the sparrow. They watched the sparrow blink against the wind-blown dust.

"Will she remember me, you think?" she asked, addressing the window.

There was a pause.

The husky one said, "I'm sure that bird will remember you, Lilah, did you see how she looked at you?"

Eddie opened his mouth and closed it. He opened it again and said, "Lilah? Is that short for Delilah?"

"No," she said. "Just Lilah. Sorry, introductions ..."

"I'm Stuart," said the man, leaning over Lilah's lap, extending his hand. Manicure. They shook.

"My name is Eddie."

Lilah said, "And this is Joanna."

Joanna said, "Hey. Li, I'm gonna let my dog out of the truck. If it's ok for her to run around in here."

Lilah flicked her eyes at Eddie, back to Joanna. "Is she better with strangers?"

Joanna shrugged. The heavy-gauge spikes stretched her earlobes. She wore a white tank top under her bomber jacket, jeans, big Docs.

Eddie said, "I usually get on pretty well with dogs."

"See?" Joanna pushed herself up with hands on her knees. The empty brick space echoed the clomp of her boots.

Stuart said, "That dog used to freak me out. But Karma's a sweetheart, really."

"Karma is the dog's name?" asked Eddie.

"Sure is. That way Jo can say 'Karma's a bitch' all the time. It stopped being clever, oh let's see, immediately."

"You know she hates it when you call her Jo," said Lilah.

Sound of the back door opening, then a mounting skitter of dog nails on hardwood. Stuart lifted his feet off the floor, warning: "Here she comes."

"Hi Karma," sang Lilah.

A brindle pitbull came roaring around the corner, scrambling after Lilah's voice. It saw Eddie and skidded to a stop, spike collar bristling.

"Hi *Kar*ma. Hi pretty girl," said Eddie in dog voice.

Karma cocked her head.

Eddie said, "Come, Karma. Come say hi."

The dog took a few sniffing steps forward. Joanna appeared out of the back, wrapping the leash around her wrist. Karma turned to look at her, then back to Eddie, sniffing closer.

Eddie set his fist down low for the dog to smell. Karma took the last few steps and nudged a wet nose up into Eddie's palm. Eddie petted her, soothing dog voice.

"She likes him. Thank god, we're out of paper towels from the last stranger she met," said Stuart.

Joanna took her seat, unwrapping and rewrapping the leash around her wrist.

Eddie scratched the dog's head. "She's a good girl, aren't you Karma?"

Lilah said, "Look, the sparrow's gone."

"Must have flown away," said Joanna.

Eddie said, "I think she'll be fine. The English Sparrow is very tough. Despite being seed-eaters, they were originally introduced to North America in 1851 to control caterpillars on farms. Now they might be the most abundant bird species in the hemisphere. It'll take more than a little blunt head trauma to slow her down."

"So, Eddie," said Stuart, twirling a long finger. "What do you do?"

"I ... well, this and that. I have some ongoing research studies. And I'm writing a book. A children's book."

Karma nudged Eddie's hand, to make it pet her.

"That's cool," said Lilah. "Joanna's a writer."

"What do you write, Joanna?" asked Eddie, scratching the top of Karma's broad anvil head, behind the ears.

"I write a column in the queer monthly here. And I'm working on a book. Memoir, I guess. My life has been too crazy to *not* be a book."

"I know the feeling," said Eddie. "What do you do, Stuart?"

"Oh, nothing much."

Lilah cupped her hands over Stuart's ears and said to Eddie, "He's the hottest designer in Albuquerque, very famous and expensive because he's the best."

"You're lucky you're getting the friends and family discount," smiled Stuart. "I'm not famous, but I am the best. And not just in Burque, *please*. That's like being king of the Amazons."

"What do you design? Clothes?" asked Eddie.

"No, I design spaces. Homes, theaters, shrines, bars, restaurants ... café's," gesturing at the vacancy around them.

"So this is your café, Lilah?"

"Yes, I have one in Santa Fe, one in Taos. But this is turning into a headache."

"A headache with Medusa snakes," added Stuart.

"And each snake has its own headache," finished Lilah. The pink tip of her tongue peeked in smile.

"Li, you had no idea that all this crap was going to happen. The invasion, and how they're jacking the price of the licenses. All the inspectors and bank officers. Making you sign some loyalty oath, it's bullshit," said Joanna.

Lilah shrugged. "I have to, I need the beer and wine license. Everyone has to."

"Karma, come *here*," Joanna said. The dog lifted her head from Eddie's lap and trotted over to Joanna.

"Sit," commanded Joanna, and the dog dropped to her haunch.

"It's funny," said Eddie. "I went walking to find a coffeeshop and I succeeded, just a bit early."

"I do have a few bottles of wine," said Lilah.

"I thought we were saving those for later," pouted Joanna.

"It *is* later," said Stuart. "And I am parched. Bring on the vino."

Lilah stood. She wore black tailored pants, a white blouse that exposed the dark smoothness of her neck. Her smart boots clicked around the bar. She opened a bottle with a pop and poured the white wine into clear plastic cups.

"It's not very chilled," apologized Lilah. "And sorry about the plastic."

"Don't worry about it. It's fine," said Joanna.

Lilah brought the cups over on a tray. Stuart took a cup, asking, "No ice?"

"No ice," said Joanna, taking her cup. "No ice, no refrigerator 'cause there's no 'lectric. No water. No propane."

"Thank you," said Eddie, taking his cup.

Lilah said, "Nothing until I sign the oath and pay the New Business Fee."

"I can't believe how fast those fascists just ... just took everything over," said Stuart. "They already have their so-called experts moving in to run things. And they signed the treaty. That's it, it's official. We're part of Texas."

"I'm not," growled Joanna.

"Well then you better leave, like the others. Because if you stay here, honey, you're a New Texan whether you like it or not." Stuart drained his cup. He stood, saying, "I'll get the bottle."

"I fucking hate Texas," said Joanna. "Wasted fourteen years of my life there."

"You know who you should hate?" said Stuart, returning with the half-empty bottle of Pinot Grigio. "That sell-out who signed the treaty in *our* name. What's his name? Mr. White? Who the hell is he? I didn't vote for him."

"They had protests today. Here, Santa Fe, even in Austin," said Lilah.

"Pointless," said Joanna. "A bunch of hippies and kooks. No one will notice, it won't even be on the news I bet. We ought to be using the internet. Chat rooms."

"That won't do much either," said Eddie, accepting the end of the bottle into his cup. "The only people who'd respond to online petitions are already marginalized."

Joanna said, "Well what do *you* think we should to do? Buy cowboy hats and start grinning?"

Eddie laughed. "I don't know. I've been focused on my own world, and haven't given all this much thought. All I know is, the only thing which has ever forced an occupying force out of a territory is a sustained guerilla war."

"Count me out of *that*. Berets, black tobacco and stewed monkey? I'm going to open another bottle," said Stuart.

"Tell me about your other cafés," said Eddie.

"I opened the first one in Santa Fe about six years ago. Things went so well that I expanded into catering, and three years ago I opened the one in Taos."

"Val Kilmer, Julia Roberts and Gene Hackman are all regulars up there," said Stuart, popping the bottle. "If you like that sort of thing."

"You've been successful in a hard business. That's impressive," said Eddie.

Lilah shrugged the clean pink of her palms. "I've been blessed with excellent employees. But this is supposed to be open by Thanksgiving.

We won't even be close."

"Come on, none of that," said Joanna. "We'll get everything taken care of. We'll open soon enough, maybe by Christmas?"

"Maybe," said Lilah into her wine.

"Hey, a toast," said Stuart. "To the new café, whenever it shall be named. And to new beginnings for wayward birds. And to new friends."

They clunked together their cups and drank.

"We should start a pirate radio station," Joanna said.

Stuart laughed, nearly firing wine through his nose.

"What? I'm fucking serious."

Stuart said, "A pirate radio station, Jo? Arr matey, the tenth caller wins a parrot."

"Don't call me Jo. My name is Joanna."

"It's not a bad idea, a radio station. Tie it into the internet, web-casts. But until we have something to offer, hope or something like it, there's really no point," said Eddie.

"You going guerilla, Rambo? Take to the hills, like an Arab?" said Joanna.

"Like a mujahideen, exactly. A conventional army, like the Texas State Guard, it tries to hold a territory by occupying space. A guerilla army is concerned with time, not space. If it survives, it is winning. Death by flea bites."

"And what, suicide bombers?"

"I would hope not. But, you know, interdict supply lines, kidnap-ping, sabotage."

Stuart said, "Sounds *very* Central American. You'd all have to grow romantic mustaches. You've got a good head start there, Jo."

"Fuck you. You need a new fucking attitude," warned Joanna.

"You need bigger pants," said Stuart, laughing into his cup and nearly spilling it.

"Fuck you. You're always such an asshole when you're drunk."

"I'm not drunk," said Stuart, composing himself and filling his cup. "After this, then I'll be drunk."

Eddie said, "There would have to be a movement in the cities too, to supply the teams in the mountains. The movement could organize espionage, recruit new members, stage strikes. Meaningful protest, not people chanting 'Namaste' on their lunch break."

"And pirate radio and internet, to spread the word," said Lilah.

"Exactly," smiled Eddie.

"So Li, have you decided on a name for this revolutionary café yet?" asked Stuart, trying to sound practical and sober. "They can't stop you from *naming* it, can they?"

Lilah said, "I haven't decided."

"What are the others called?" asked Eddie.

"The first one is Cesar's Cup, for my grandfather. He's the one that gave me my stake money," fixing upon Eddie the darkness within the white whiteness of her eyes. "The one in Taos is called Bitches Brew."

"That's cute. I mean clever. Like the Miles Davis album?"

"Sort of. I like his other stuff, but not really that album. I just liked the name."

Eddie said, "Why don't you call this place the Wayward Sparrow?"

"Oh please," groaned Joanna.

"That's not bad," said Stuart.

"No, it's not bad," said Lilah thoughtfully.

Stuart leaned forward in his chair. "It makes me think of ... a lost little bird, limping in out of the cold. Not home, but a warm safe resting place, to regain strength before taking off again. I knew we were talking about those long, family-style benches with the padded seats and dis-tressed wood and the wrought iron trim, and following up with all iron fixtures, and painting the bricks that rich bloody red I found. But now I'm thinking softness. Nestness. Overstuffed couches and chairs, rich browns and warm creams, subdued lighting. Maybe just floor lights, you know, and the rest filled in by dim ensconced lighting. And on the walls, shattered mirrors. You know? Like, broken, but then glued together, so it looks like it's shattering as you look at it. Like the bird hitting the win-dow. Low tables. Wicker. Think: nest. Not a single sharp corner in the place. We'll keep the brick walls natural, but how about a good thick comfy carpet? We won't make this place so comfortable that people want to live here. But feel that it's the perfect place to land, take a recharge, and then flutter off."

"That sounds pretty good," said Lilah. "We'll see."

"That's where the word 'sparrow' comes from. It means 'flut-terer'," said Eddie.

"Well that's just perfect," said Stuart. He drained his wine.

"I think we're out of wine," said Joanna.

"Meeting adjourned," said Lilah. "We've done enough plotting today. The sun's going down."

Stuart checked his watch, "And I have a date in two hours. I need to go get ready. Eddie, it was enlightening to make your acquaintance. I hope to see you again soon."

They all stood, slight awkwardness.

"Nice to meet you too, Stuart," said Eddie.

"I'll call you, honey," said Lilah. She reached up around Stuart to kiss his cheek. "Eddie, can we give you a ride somewhere?"

"I guess home would be fine," said Eddie.

"You'll have to ride in the bed with Karma," said Joanna.

"That's fine," said Eddie.

Lilah locked the front door and they walked out the back. Stuart got into his small shining sports car and drove out the alley. Eddie lowered the tailgate and climbed into the empty pickup bed. Karma sprang in after. Eddie closed the tailgate and rapped on the cab that they were ready. Riding: the wind was cool, Eddie and Karma huddled for warmth. The sky bruised violet.

Joanna stopped the truck on his corner. Eddie hopped out and walked to the passenger side. He said, "Bye. Thanks for the ride."

Lilah said, "Come back soon. In case there's another wildlife emergency."

"I will. It was nice meeting all of you."

He watched the pickup drive off, the glow of brake lights at the stop sign. He walked down his alley, let himself through the compound's gate. He entered his casita and was overwhelmed by its squalor. He stood in the buzzing fluorescence of his kitchen, weaving very slightly from the wine. Then he turned on the faucet, waited for it to warm, and began to wash his dishes.

Exploitation

Mr. White pulled open the door by its long thin iron handle. He stepped back, holding the door wide for U.S. Armstrong and Karl Hovan. U.S. had to tip his hat forward to get through the door frame. U.S. looked into the dining room: high ceilings and mirrors, mirrors everywhere on every wall, every pillar, over-populating the room with faces and lights.

Mr. White said, "Let's step into the bar. That's the place."

U.S. approached the bar's swing doors, the darkness beyond them. He shoved them apart and stepped forward, hat brim down over his eyes. He paused at the threshold to be marked: the back-lit redeemer, all-knowing and unknowable, a high-plains drifter.

It took this moment for his eyes to adjust to the darkness. The bar of the Bullring was dark, oil candles illuminating the small tables crowded together. The bar itself gleamed mirrors and brass wine racks. U.S. stepped through the swing doors. Mr. White slipped around and indicated the large round table immediately to their right: white linen with a Reserved card.

Mr. White said, "This is our table, gentlemen, and Mr. Armstrong you may sit here, in the seat of honor."

U.S. scowled at the chair indicated. It was backed against a window of frosted glass, etched with the Bullring's logo.

"You sit there, White," commanded U.S. "I'll put my back to the wall."

They took their seats, Mr. White before the frosted glass, U.S. to his right with his back to the wall and Karl Hovan possessing the flank exposed to the rest of the bar. The people in the bar had noticed them – faces turned to their table, then leaned to their companions for conference.

A waitress appeared, the blackness of her uniform in contrast to the virgin white linen of their table. She was tall, slim and pretty; her sensible glasses were balanced by the incongruous brightness of her wide smile, dimple cheeks. She reminded U.S. of his own daughter and this softened him momentarily.

"What can I get for you gentlemen?" she asked, laying down cocktail napkins. A gold bracelet, her only adornment, hung chunky from her slender arm.

They waited for U.S., who took his time in saying, "I'll take a Lonestar, young miss."

"Sorry sir," she sang. "We don't carry Lonestar."

U.S. twitched his mustache. He said, "Shiner?"

"Yes. One Shiner Bock?"

Karl Hovan said, "I'll take a Gray Goose and diet, please."

Mr. White said, "I'll just have a tonic water."

The waitress clicked her pen and sidled between chair backs.

Karl ran his tongue along his top teeth and said, "Not drinking, White?"

"No, Mr. Hovan, I don't drink."

U.S. looked around the room from under his hat brim: dark wood, dark corners. The legislators were easy to identify: corpulent, balding, with a pin or two in the lapels of their suit jackets. They huddled around tables with their light beers or tumblers of spirits. A genuine babble of voices, with inappropriate 80's rock playing over the top.

Their waitress came squeezing through tables, tray aloft. She set their drinks on their napkins. Leaning over her tray, she said, "These drinks were paid for by the three gentlemen in the corner."

U.S. found the table with his eyes: three legislators, jackets over their chairs, rumpled oxfords and ties. U.S. raised his beer slightly, nodding his hat brim. He took his sip. Good. Cold. Beer.

The waitress said, "Would you like to order dinner now?"

"Later," said Mr. White. "We've got some business."

Indeed, one of the legislators had stood from the corner table and approached. He was a big man, heavy-bellied. Ring of thin silver hair, glint of wire rim glasses breaking up his pink vault of flesh. He straightened his tie down his belly and waddled gingerly between tables, accepting a quick few handshakes on his way. His rumpled broadcloth shirt pooched out the back, fleeing from his overworked belt. When he arrived, he extended his hand over the table to U.S., who gave a one-pump shake.

The man said, "Mr. Armstrong, it's my pleasure to meet you. Mind if I join you for a moment?"

He pulled a chair out and set his bulk down at an angle so as not to upend the table. He had a tumbler of scotch in his hand. Solid bullet of his head, squeezing out of his shirt collar like ham-flavored toothpaste. Blue tie, too thin. Back of his pink neck like a package of hot dogs.

Mr. White said, "Good evening, Senator Avery."

"Ahh, evening Mr. White. There you are in the seat of honor. And you are, sir?"

"Karl Hovan. I'm a political consultant for Mr. Armstrong. Call me Karl."

"Well Karl, nice to meet you too," smiled the Senator, shaking hands. "So, Mr. Armstrong, I see you found our home away from home, as it were. We welcome you."

"We've heard good things about the steaks," said Hovan, eyes glinting in the darkness.

"Oh I guarantee you'll like them. We're glad to have you as our guest."

U.S. took a pull of beer, kept his brim low. His bottom lip sucked his mustache.

Hovan said, "So how are those bills coming along?"

The Senator said, "With emergency sessions like these, we typically work pretty quick. Everyone wants to get back to their jobs. We normally only meet for a month or two, starting in January. And of course, our work as legislators is without pay. We do it for the good of New, ah, New Texas. So even though you put a lot on our plates, heh-heh, we'll have them sailing through committee and we'll get them passed right quick."

"Of course, it's simply a formality," grinned Hovan, eyes unsmiling.

"Er, yes, well, anyway U.S., ah Mr. Armstrong, I wanted to thank you for keeping the State Legislature intact. We know this state, and we'll be invaluable to you while you're acting as governor."

"Mr. Armstrong is the active *military* governor, here to oversee the peaceful transition. The Legislature remains intact because we feel comfortable leaving this territory's problems in your hands," said Hovan, taking a sip of his drink to wet his lips.

"That's good. We have some problems here, no denying it, but we'll do our best to address issues vital to our future: drug abuse, economic development, unemployment, DWIs and crime."

Hovan said, "We'll be taking care of economic development, Senator Avery, I assure you. As for the rest, New Texas is definitely going to be completely independent of the Texas Legislature."

"Well that's real good to hear," beamed Senator Avery.

"President says he wants to expand the draft," said U.S., voice deep and dry. "That should take care of your unemployment problem."

"Yes, we do what we can. I'll let you gentlemen enjoy your drinks. And I'm glad you're here to run things proper, Mr. Armstrong. Those appropriations for reconstruction are going to be good for business, good for us, good for all New Texas." Senator Avery pushed himself up, shook hands with them, and made his way to another table.

U.S. watched the Senator drop himself into a chair. "He's thanking *me* for awarding no-bid contracts to my own company. How about that."

Hovan wet his lips with his drink. "He's happy to still have his title of privilege. You've won their hearts and minds, U.S."

"They can keep all that. I just want the water, and the contracts, and the reparations. This ain't got nothing to do with Indochina, neither. No incrementalism. We came to win. We came and we won. It's all over except for the payback."

Mr. White shifted uncomfortably in the seat of honor, untouched tonic water fizzed-out flat. He cleared his throat. "The gentlemen approaching is Representative King. He's the Speaker of the House."

"Sounds venerable," Hovan smirked.

Representative King maneuvered slowly through the crowded chair backs. He was one of the few with a full head of hair, despite his seventy years. It was styled in a pompadour as improbable as his linen-white dentures. His suit properly fit him, at least.

Representative King and the waitress arrived at their table at the same time.

U.S. said, "Young miss, we'll take another round here. And three steaks, rare."

"You got it," she said.

The waitress pulled out a chair, "Here you are, Representative King. Anything for you?"

He sank into the chair. "Yes, Ginger. I'll have another Glenlivet and soda."

The waitress said, "Coming right up."

Representative King looked up their table. "Well, how are you gentlemen? My name is Ron King and I am the Speaker. You must be

Ulysses S. Armstrong. Honored to meet you."

"Likewise," said U.S., wrapping his mitt around Ron's frail fingers.

When the handshake was over Ron returned his hand to his lap limp-grateful. "I want to express the thanks of the Legislature for allowing us to continue to do our job here. And we're glad you stepped in to help us sort things out. Our former Governor ... well he could be a bit pig-headed at times."

Hovan snickered. He rattled the ice in his tumbler.

Ron King turned his head to regard Hovan, who raised his tumbler and said, "Karl Hovan, at your service."

"Yes," said Ron, turning back to search for U.S.'s eyes beneath his hat brim. "We're certainly looking forward to those business ventures you're bringing to the state. Refitting the dams, the new wells and pipelines, all that construction will be good for the economy. These assurances to our business interests will go far to keep them healthy and happy, which provides jobs and stability for everyone."

"Oh it's our pleasure," grinned Hovan.

"Mr. Hovan. Who are you exactly now?"

"Just a policy consultant to Mr. Armstrong. Nobody, really," and again that grin.

Ron looked up as the waitress arrived with their drinks. "Thank you, dear."

"You're welcome," she said, setting the drinks down and removing U.S.'s empty bottle. "The drinks have all been paid for by the table near the mirror."

Ron King half-turned to raise his scotch and soda to the men near the mirror. He turned back to U.S. "One thing does puzzle me, however. We've expanded the budget to accommodate these new expenditures, tax incentives and appropriations. It's just not clear to me where the actual money is going to come from. But it would certainly gladden our hearts, and convince us of your fealty, if Texas were to share its bounty with us, and contribute to our sudden, overwhelming fiscal demands."

"Actually, we're going to need to keep the budgets and tax revenues of Texas and New Texas separate for the time being. New Texas needs to pay its own way for these necessary improvements in its infrastructure," said Hovan, wetting his lips with his drink.

"But, excuse me U.S., the budget was already stretched thin *before* we pushed these expenditures through. How are we going to pay for all this, on top of those reparations in the treaty signed by our Mr. White here?" said Ron King.

Hovan said, "We've got some remedies. There will be levies, fees and contributions asked of the citizens of New Texas. Don't worry, inter-state businesses will be spared. And whatever the remaining shortfall, short-term loans will be available from one of our commercial partners."

A food runner, distinguished by his white shirt and long apron, pushed through the swing doors with a tray aloft and a folding stand hooked over his arm. He dashed open the stand and levered the tray down into place. He looked at the computer ticket and then set the identical plates before Mr. White, Karl and U.S.

"Well I'll let you fellas eat in peace. Goodbye for now," said Ron King. He stood, woodenly erect, and caught the eye of a colleague across the room and crossed to a waiting chair with dignity.

U.S. swallowed his second mouthful of bleeding steak. He grunted, "Not bad."

"Say, White," said Hovan. "Don't you fancy your steak?"

"I'm not really a big steak eater."

U.S. shot his eyes to Mr. White's plate. "If you don't eat it I'll take it home to my dogs. They don't think *they're* too good for it."

"It's not that, Mr. Armstrong, I'm just not very hungry tonight."

Their waitress appeared and smiled, "How is everything guys?"

"Real good. Thank yeh," said U.S.

She said, "Your dinners are being paid for by Senator Avery. Can I get you anything else at this time?"

"We're just fine. Thank yeh," said U.S.

"Say, White," said Hovan, leaning forward until his hair's oil caught a sheen of light. "What are those cards I see these lawmakers collecting from each other?"

Mr. White said, "Cards? What do you mean?"

Hovan said, "I've been watching this little mating dance going from table to table. They arrive, shake hands and sit down. Banter a few moments, then they get to the point. The chief at the table thinks on it a moment, whips out one of these cards. Writes on it with some flourish, caps his pen and hands the card over. The interloper takes the card, adds it to the stack he's got, taps them neat on the table, shakes hands and shoves off to another table to repeat the dance."

"Could be gambling I guess," said Mr. White. "I think they have OTB."

"I don't believe that's it. Watch, two tables over, it's happening now."

U.S. watched under his hat brim, chewing slowly. The scene followed as Hovan had described it: the sit-down, the card, the flourish, the handshakes.

"Curious way of doing business, wouldn't you say? Likely, they're favor cards," said Hovan, pushing away an empty plate that no one saw him eat from. "Pledges of support. Curious way of doing business."

"I suppose," said Mr. White, pushing away his napkin-shrouded plate.

"I wonder when we get *our* favor cards," grinned Hovan. "They're all drinking light beer but it doesn't seem to be working. We're surrounded by the fat cats now, huh U.S.?"

U.S. swallowed his last bite of steak. The fries were untouched. He sucked warm blood from his mustache. Salty. He moved his jaw, readying to speak, and they waited for him. "I tell you what. My older brother, he died in Korea. Somewhere in the winter of '52. Up in them mountains, killed by Chinamen. Cause the politicians didn't allow Macarthur to do his damn job, my brother died holding the line on top of some godforsaken mountain in the goddamn Iron Triangle. He prolly hadn't had a steak in two years. Prolly hadn't gotten no *favors*, neither."

"Well said, U.S." commented Hovan. "You don't suppose any of them legislators are going to be interested in buying us dessert, do you White? It looks like we got another favor-seeker coming our way."

Indeed, a Hispanic man with a mustache and bad suit had stood, straightened his tie and was approaching their table. He stopped once to shake hands with Ron King and continued toward them. He was younger than the previous supplicants, and his brown suit looked worse as he approached. A pin in his lapel caught a splinter of light, briefly.

"Hello," he said, extending his hand. "State Representative Rudy Mondragon."

Hovan shook his hand and said, "Karl Hovan. Have a seat, Rudy."

Rudy took the seat opposite U.S., straightening his brown tie again. He looked over the two faces and the hat brim across the table. Rudy's bottom lip parted from his mustache, rejoined it.

"What can we do for you, Rudy?" asked Hovan.

"Gentlemen, it's a pleasure to meet you. My district is largely agricultural. Most of my constituents are closely tied to farming. Some of this land goes back many generations before we were even a territory of the United States."

"*Very* nice," grinned Hovan.

"They've expressed their concerns to me about some of the aspects of the treaty dealing with the apportionment of water – " Rudy broke off, startled by U.S.'s sudden gesture for the waitress's attention.

Rudy waited as she cleared the table of plates and napkins.

U.S. said, "Young miss, I'll take that leftover steak in a doggie bag."

She nodded, "I'll be right back with that. Everyone ok on their drinks?"

U.S. said, "Thank yeh."

Rudy wobbled his light beer bottle, studying its label.

Hovan said, "Well Rudy it sure was nice talking to you. Thanks for expressing your concern. Good luck now."

"Thanks. But I haven't ... look, sirs, the water allocation in the treaty is not sustainable. It practically *triples* the guaranteed acre-feet for Texas. And if rainfall and snowmelt are below expectations, as they are *this* year ... our groundwater has been pumped dry. There won't be enough water left in my district to raise a single beanfield."

Hovan raised one eyebrow, slightly. All that could be seen of U.S. was his wide-shouldered pearl-button shirt split by a Texas State Guard bolero and the implacable white disk of hat brim.

Rudy continued, "If we don't get enough snow this winter, there simply won't be any water left for New Mexican farmers at all. You can't just void all of the old river compacts like that. With the appropriations for groundwater development that you've proposed, our groundwater will run out on a timetable that you are recklessly accelerating. And yet none of that water will benefit New Mexico's farmers."

Hovan nodded, cupped his hands around his tumbler as if about to make a confession. "Rudy, I assure you, it is our desire to bring things into balance. And please remember, 'New Mexico' is gone. Let's not use that name, it is a reminder of all the laziness, inefficiency and corruption of the old days. Let's all work together to make New Texas the best it can be. Texas is merely recovering water promised it by the old compacts. The new measures merely reflect the need to restore balance, that's all."

Rudy said, "But these new measures won't last forever, right? Without the water my constituents have relied on, they'll all simply ... vanish."

"Rudy, nothing lasts forever," Hovan grinned. He reached into his jacket and removed a thick dark cigar. He put one end in his mouth and snapped his teeth through it. Holding the oil candle, Hovan puffed the cigar to life. Heavy smoke clouded the table. Hovan set the candle down, inspected the cigar's glowing tip. He looked up, cigar poised and smoking. "Rudy, this territory is vast and primitive. There's a little water here, and some investments of time and capital. We must secure these interests so that the territory can prosper and grow."

"I agree," said Rudy, squinting through the smoke. "Though there was some hope that at least a few opportunities would have been made available to local contractors."

Hovan puffed on his cigar, releasing clouds of rich, oppressive smoke. He removed it and said, "There will be plenty of opportunities to be taken advantage of."

Rudy leaned back from the wall of fog rolling over him. "Because right now, it seems that even the laborers are all coming from Texas."

Hovan said, "We find it necessary to manage the resources using the best available workforce, and follow the advice of experts in the field. This is, after all, a free market system, is it not?"

"Which experts advised removing people from their homes to provide housing for your workforce? Armed guards on the waterworks?"

Hovan directed a cone of smoke at Rudy. "The Texas State Guard is committed to protecting the property of Texas. The floodgates must remain open, so that the free flow of water won't be impeded, impaired or otherwise wasted for less than its full market value. The free market demands it. You are *for* free markets, aren't you Rudy?"

Rudy coughed. He blinked watering eyes. "Of course. Free markets. Thanks for your time, gentlemen."

Hovan grinned around his cigar as Rudy pushed away from the table.

U.S. tipped the corner of his hat up, to fix Hovan with a hard blue stare. He held Hovan's eye, then let the brim drop.

Hovan glanced at the retreating form of Rudy. "I understand. It will be done."

"And put out that damn cigar," said U.S. "Smells like tires burning."

Hovan stumped his cigar in the ashtray, let it stand phallic and dormant.

Mr. White said, "Smoking isn't allowed in here."

The waitress arrived with Gray Goose and diet, a Shiner Bock and a tonic water. She set down new cocktail napkins, saying, "These drinks are on Representative King. And sir, here's your take-home box."

"Thank yeh," said U.S., setting the box on the floor beside his chair.

"They sure are generous with the drinks," Hovan grinned at the waitress.

She gave an enigmatic waitress smile in return.

Hovan said, "White, you're awfully quiet. Is there glue in that tonic water?"

"I'm just here to collaborate on any agreements that need to get hammered out. Beyond that, there isn't much for me to add to the ... festivities."

Hovan wet his lips with his drink, "Ah, more festivities are afoot."

Another suit had disengaged from his table. His mass was mounted on short legs, giving him the appearance of a top. Not much hair, string tie. His jowls shook as he nodded at tables in passing.

He had to turn sideways to get past a waitress sliding through, watched her ass as it squeezed by him. He held a glass of red wine. Arriving at their table, he set the wine down and extended his hand to U.S. He shook hands enthusiastically and said, "Howdy. Representative Cisneros, mind if I sit down?"

Cisneros sat next to Hovan, wiggling his stomach under the table. "I just wanted to come by and tell you that I'm real pleased to have you. My district is deep in the south of New Texas and I want to tell you, we've been with y'all from the beginning. Why, I was raised in Texas, and some of my happiest memories are from there. My constituency has a lot of Texas transplants, and frankly we've gotten fed up with the way the Democratic machine has been running things up here in the north. And so we're all real pleased to have y'all 'Get it right'."

"Glad to hear we have your friendship," said Hovan.

"Well that's what 'Texas' means, 'friends' right? So here you can consider us in New Texas as your new friends. We've been with you since the beginning."

"If only everyone were so friendly," smirked Hovan.

"Oh, you mean that horse's ass, Mondragon? It's his first term and he thinks he's a regular FDR. Don't pay him no mind. He's part of the problem up here, a problem we're hoping you help us solve."

U.S. took a swallow of beer, let his eyes rest on the wine-purple lips of Cisneros.

Cisneros continued, "We've got some real barbecue in my home district. We'll have to get y'all down sometime, make you feel right at home. There's been talk about hosting some kind of chili cook-off, you know? Texas and New Texas cooperating in friendly competition, that sort of thing. It would be great if we could all get together."

Hovan said, "That sounds nice."

Gesturing over his shoulder at the other tables, "Some of my *colleagues*, some of these gloom-and-doom liberals, they don't understand the benefits of friendship and are trying to slow some of these bills down. I say hell, we want this emergency session to end before Thanksgiving don't we, let's just 'Get it right'."

Their waitress passed by with a tray of drinks for another table. Cisneros snapped his fingers and raised his wineglass. She nodded.

"Yessir," mused Cisneros, staring at her ass. "It's far wiser to enjoy the benefits. That waitress, she's real sweet. But we're more generous with those who are more generous with their time. Sometimes, after we clear out of here, we take a few of the girls along to a place I know. More of a private club."

Noticing U.S.'s jaw tighten, Hovan let his grin encourage Cisneros who continued, "Yessir, there are benefits to be had. We'd be happy to have you. Maybe we can even rope in your little sweetie."

A cell phone rang – U.S. pulled it off his hip and brought it to his ear, turning away from the conversation.

"They don't usually allow, ah ..." began Mr. White, closing his mouth around his tonic water.

It was Marianne, and she was doing all the talking: "U.S., we've got a big Thanksgiving planned here. We've got the Bells, the Martins, the Kruegers, the Daniels, the Walkers and of course the Nemans, as well as my parents and Fawn of course. I want to make sure you get back here in time to help out, it's *Thanksgiving*. I talked to Fawn and she'll come home from Dallas early, just to see more of you. So do you promise?"

"I do," said U.S. He sheathed his cell phone and turned back to the table.

Cisneros watched him, trying to see past the brim. U.S. tipped his beer empty, placed it firmly away from him.

Hovan clapped his hands together and said, "Well that's going to do it for us tonight. We'll be heading out now. Nice talking to you, Representative Cisneros. Perhaps next time ..."

"Sure, sure, anytime and anywhere, don't worry," said Cisneros, huffing to his feet. He shook hands with Hovan, was ignored by U.S., and waddled to another table.

Mr. White led the way out the swinging doors. U.S. followed but there was a tap on his shoulder – the waitress.

"Don't forget your take-home box sir," she said, handing it to him.

He tipped up his hat brim so that he could look down in her eyes. "Thank yeh."

In the backseat, U.S. said quietly to Hovan, "Go ahead and crush that one fella, Mondragon, get him out of politics. As for that pervert Cisneros. I want him ruined. You got that? Ruined."

"I understand," said Hovan, grinning in the dark interior.

When U.S. got to his temporary residence – formerly the home of a city commissioner – he locked the door behind him, dead-bolted it. He brought the doggie bag with him to a soft chair in front of the wall-mounted TV. He ate the steak with tooth and claw. A few moments after, he was asleep, and snoring.

In the Office of the Governor of New Texas, U.S. had his boots up on the desk. He was leaning back in the swivel chair, hands behind his head. Mr. White had just delivered a stack of bills to the desk.

"This all them?" graveled U.S. "They try to make any changes?"

Mr. White said, "In HR 71, page 2, line 24 they deleted the word 'and' and inserted in lieu thereof '&'. Things of that nature."

Un-lanking his legs from the table, U.S. shook his head in disgust. "What a goddamn waste of ... but that's it right, these bills I'm signing, they're what Seco and the other lawyers wrote up?"

"Yes sir. Now, it's not too late for me to arrange a photo op for the signing."

"No goddamn press. I ain't no Keano Reeve and people don't want to know about all these details and whatnot."

"Well then sir, all you need is this pen to turn these bills into law."

"I got a pen." And with that pen, U.S. signed the nineteen bills: "General U.S. Armstrong, Military Governor of New Texas."

After, he capped the pen and massaged his writing hand.

"Arthritis, sir?"

"No thanks. Already got some. You see Dallas win on Thanksgiving day?"

"Ah, yes sir. Quite a good match, wasn't it?"

"Good match hell. They whupped up on them Eagles."

"Yes sir."

U.S. leaned back in his chair, crossed his boots on the table. "I reckon this'll be your office soon enough, White."

"My own office is acceptable, sir."

"Hell no. After the elections, you'll be the top dog in New Texas. I'll be long gone, out of this godforsaken ... by the way White, speaking of elections, I want the names of everyone who voted against these laws, whether in committee or on the floor."

"Yes sir," said Mr. White, gathering up the stack of legislation.

"Standing in the way of progress is crazier than a cat-humping mouse. We done got'r right now. We got Texas firms making progress using Texas workers, coming out of the ungrateful pockets of New Mexico."

"New Texas, sir?"

"Right, right. New Texas." The phone on his hip rang. U.S. pulled it out and leaned back further in the creaking chair.

It was Hovan: "We got a problem, U.S."

U.S. said, "Where in hell are you?"

"I'm in Dallas."

"What are you doing in Dallas? I been back in Santa Fe two days now."

Hovan said, "I flew here this morning. The problem required my presence."

"And what is the problem?"

There was a pause, a wobble of microwave interference. Hovan's voice cut in, "—volving your daughter."

"What was that? What about Fawn?"

"She's fine, U.S. We've removed her and she's safe and comfortable."

"Hovan, goddammit, what happened to Fawn?"

"Nothing. But it seems that someone ... took some photos of her. Rather candid photographs, I am afraid."

U.S. said nothing. His molars mashed.

Hovan continued, "We're working with her to track that pervert down. I'm on my way to see her again, right now. But I wanted to give you a call to reassure you."

"Reassure me?" U.S. leaned his hat forward until the brim grazed his chest.

Hovan continued, "I've taken the liberty of warning our media people about the value of loyalty. In case there has been some ... distribution of said images."

U.S. sat quiet for a moment, grinding his molars.

"U.S.? You still there?"

U.S. growled, "Find the guy. And cut his dick off."

"I will, U.S. You have nothing to worry about, I'm on top of it," said Hovan but U.S. had already hung up.

"Is everything all right, sir?" asked Mr. White, still holding the stack of laws.

U.S. was silent, heavy, down-hatted.

"Sir? Is everything – "

"Out of my office," growled U.S. "Now."

Sun down, office lights still off. The framed photograph of Fawn and Marianne was again face-down on his desk. U.S. sighed with the gloom. The standing photograph on his desk was of William McKinley, and U.S. could barely look him in the eye.

U.S. flipped the frame upright again. There she was: with her mother, both smiling. San Antonio, the Riverwalk. Some few years ago: Fawn had braces on her big happy smile, and Marianne looked relaxed too. A nice holiday, back when there was time for such things. Fawn was wearing a Spurs hat, a present from their hosts who were part-owners of the storied franchise. Later, after he had snapped the photo, they had gone to a Spurs game, watching from the owner's skybox. She had been on TV, briefly – why, Fawn had been on TV the very day this photograph was taken. Up in the box, above the drunk, screaming crowd, totally invisible and inviolate up there. But the camera found her in the airtight box, stole her and sold her to people's eyes all across Texas, the country, the entire world. They took from her, and she didn't even know it was happening. Just a kid she was, fourteen? They were in the skybox, chatting nicely, glancing at the game every now and then. The televisions were on, showing the game at a seven-second delay. They were so high up that after a play, they had to watch the TV broadcast to see which player did what. And then all of a sudden Fawn was on the TV, she was leaning forward on the glass like kids do and the camera found her, captured her. U.S. took a step for her but she was already off the screen, the camera was looking elsewhere. He was too late, seven seconds too late.

Just like now. Failed to protect her. U.S. turned the frame down again.

The door flew open with a blast of light from the outer offices. Hovan flicked on the light booming, "Why's it so dark in here?"

The lights slapped the room new-born. U.S. lowered his hat against the sudden glare. Hovan was tossing off his jacket, tapping on his PDA. Mr. White followed in, closing the door behind him.

Eyes on the device he was tapping, Hovan said, "Just got in. White was kind enough to pick me up and I've briefed him on the situation already."

U.S. glanced at Mr. White, who looked paler than usual and hovered near the door.

Hovan finished his tapping and holstered the device. He said, "First of all, we've got the situation under control. But there is a mixture of good and not-as-good news. First of all, we caught the perpetrator. Two men, actually. One was the photographer and the other was the web designer. The photographer was the ringleader."

U.S. growled slow, low and distinct: "Did you cut their dicks off?"

"Yes, U.S. We did. And they both bled to death. They are gone, every trace of them is gone. We confiscated their computers, cameras, credit card records and the campus servers. It was a business they had going. It wasn't just Fawn. So it doesn't seem to have any ... political motivation. Be assured, they and their filth are now gone."

"A couple peeping-tom perverts? Crawling around campus on their bellies, taking photos from the bushes? What the hell kinda security is that? You get on that Dean yet, Hovan? For how much I'm paying, I'd like some goddamn campus security."

Hovan said, "Well, actually U.S., they weren't exactly peeping-toms. White, could you elaborate?"

Mr. White blanched. He looked at Karl Hovan full of shock and betrayal. U.S. was watching him. Mr. White coughed once. Took a breath in, let it out. For a moment, no words were available. Then, like a man stepping off a cliff, "Mr. Armstrong, the two gentlemen in question were running a website from the campus they shared with your daughter. They were graduate students. The website was called 'Rude Rudy's Laser Beaver Academy.' It featured about ten girls, including Fawn and her roommate."

Hovan had stepped to the side and sat down. Mr. White took a moment, then continued, "The business was based on direct traffic purchases and feeder sites sharing free teaser pages around the internet, an invitation to join the paysite."

Hovan said, "You should know, U.S., that Fawn's real name does not appear anywhere in connection with the images. She used a ... stage name, didn't she, White?"

Mr. White took a deep, sharp breath, and glared at Hovan. "The name she used was Buttercup. And it seems, ahh, apparent that ... she was not coerced or tricked into being a part of this enterprise. All of the girls seem to have been ... willing partners in the venture. Based on cursory examination of the financial records, it seems they were paid between three and five hundred dollars per photo shoot, and then received commissions based on third-party credit card sales. There was an additional income from affiliate programs. In all, and this is just cursory, but the business seems to have made close to two hundred thousand dollars in its first six months of business."

"Two hundred thousand? Good god almighty, in six months? For doing what?"

Mr. White said, "Well, Mr. Armstrong, the photographs of the girls were oriented toward an adult market."

"Meaning what, exactly?"

Mr. White shifted his weight. "The freely-distributed images were innocuous. Girls in different outfits, with some misspelled text inviting people to join the paysite."

"And *on* the paysite?"

"Uh. More ... graphic images. Nude images, sir. Nude modeling."

U.S. sucked in his breath sharply.

Mr. White plunged ahead, "Many of these, ah, glamour photos are in violation of Texas obscenity laws, if not US 2257 regulations. For example, exotic dancers in Texas are not allowed to have their legs more than six inches apart. And some of the images ... well it seems that the girls must have had gymnastics training, of some sort."

Mr. White stopped to breathe and wipe his palms on his hips. He re-set his glasses. "There were more images, sir. Of the girls posing together. Lasciviously. And engaging in ... adult acts together. With each other. And with the two men, as well. They produced digital movies and hosted a live webcam service. Some of the acts were of a ... depraved nature, I'm sorry to say, with graphic audio. And enhanced extreme close-ups of ... well, the Laser Beaver Academy seems to have been predicated on a body hair removal procedure. That was the theme of the so-called academy."

"Why did she ..." voice small and slow to get out from under his hat brim.

Hovan said, "Money seems to be the motivation, U.S., more than adolescent rebellion. What were those figures, White?"

Mr. White gritted his teeth. "Yes. Karl. The money. Our initial investigation indicates that Fawn received payments totaling over ten thousand dollars."

"Ten thousand dollars! That's ... what's she need that kind of money for?"

Hovan and Mr. White waited in silence. U.S. regained himself, and petitioned, "If she ever needed anything, she could come to me. I never said no to her, not once. My baby angel? What could she need all that money for, that she had to do this?"

They waited for U.S. to continue. He could not. To screen the embarrassing sound of U.S.'s choked breathing, Hovan said, "The good news, U.S., is that no one will ever need to find out about this indiscretion. Obviously, the website is shut down and no more filth will ever emerge from those two. A very strict and harsh blackout has been dropped on this story. Not only your media companies, U.S., but all the local broadcast networks have been instructed, in the strongest possible terms, to ignore the story should it reach them. Texas Air Guardsmen have been allocated to monitor the networks for compliance. We've got tech geeks designing blind links to trap curious perverts, infecting the downloads with a virus. We've got that situation pretty well wrapped up. However, White thinks he has discovered a potential leak in cyberspace."

Mr. White said, "Yes, when *we* ran a search on your daughter's name, there was an item connecting 'Buttercup' to the name 'Fawn'."

U.S. growled, "It was her nickname on the cheerleading squad."

Hovan said, "Nothing to worry about. It will be over soon."

"And if it ain't?" graveled U.S.

"It will, U.S., it will. Come on, let's get out of this office. Go have a drink somewhere private." Hovan picked up his jacket from the couch.

"I need to go back, Christ, what about Marianne, does she know?" With that, U.S. stood up, rising to a full nine feet tall. Then slumping down to a miserable 6'4".

Hovan said, "I believe that it would be most prudent that you not go back, or do anything which might attract any attention to a *situation*. Right now, the less seen and heard, the better. Marianne is fine, she's doing fine. But it seems best that you not contact her. She's relaxed and calm now."

"Goddammit, this is a family matter. I need to talk to my wife and my daughter."

Hovan said, "I'm sorry U.S., but it's more than a family matter. It is a political matter, which means it is an economic matter. Come on now, we've got the car waiting in the underground garage. Let's get out of this tacky building. The cleaning ladies are waiting to get in here. You don't want to put *them* out of work, do you?"

They left. U.S. was corpse-quiet. Hovan and Mr. White did nothing to disturb it.

"Niggers," said U.S.

Hovan and Mr. White were on the veranda with him, nestled up among flowers dying of sunburn in hanging pots. Mr. White cleared his throat and said, "Actually, one was Hispanic, sir."

Hovan stepped to the railing. He looked upon the narrow downtown street. Taking a deep breath of autumn afternoon desert air, he said, "Well it's a lovely day."

Mr. White said, "There is news more significant than the, ah, racial details. In the last twenty hours, the search engine hits connecting Fawn to 'Buttercup' and Rude Rudy have mushroomed exponentially. Hovan's spin machine failed to keep a lid on this."

"It's the internet chatter," said Hovan. "We had the tiger by its tail, but he got loose in the chatter."

Mr. White said, "National media is going to pick this up. They haven't been interested in the New Texas situation in a while, but this is going to bring us right back into the spotlight. It could reach a wide audience."

U.S. still had not moved. Hat down, jaw taut, boots up on the railing. He looked as if he were alone, listening to the birds.

Hovan said, "Aw hell, just don't watch Letterman for a few nights. This'll all blow over soon. So long as no more new images show up, right White?"

White turned to face Hovan, who was still looking down into the shadows of the street below. Mr. White stammered, "Y-You can't make me *do* this."

Hovan stared down into the street. With hellish relish he retched up a loogie, let the glob stretch down from his lips, stretch out long and drop ...

Turning away in disgust, Mr. White found a corner of U.S.'s blue eye cutting under the hat brim. Mr. White said, "Mr. Hovan's unnecessarily graphic illustration is enough for you to understand the ... nature of these newly surfaced images. The girls of Rude Rudy's Laser Beaver Academy were ... humiliated with ... various, uh ... bodily ..."

"That's enough, White," said Hovan. "U.S. doesn't need to hear about all that."

"You *told* me I had to tell him. Mr. Armstrong, this man Hovan here, he is an absolute ... scoundrel. Of the worst sort. If I were you –"

"Relax, White," interrupted Hovan. "You merely mean that I'm effective."

"Well you weren't very effective at averting this disaster!"

Hovan took a deep breath of the blue sky. "The professional thing would be to decide how we can best quiet the storm. Trying to censor the story at this stage might kick up more interest than just letting it die."

White said, "What, you don't want me to dynamite the TV stations for you?"

Hovan said, "So melodramatic, White. Is this your first scandal?"

U.S. growled, "Shut it all down."

"What's that, U.S.?" asked Hovan.

"Shut it all down. TV's not enough. I don't want to wait and see if they violate their loyalty and try to cash in on Fawn. Every newspaper in New Texas, every radio station. Shut down the telephones. Shut em down. I want every computer confiscated from every library, every university. Today. White, call all my unit commanders and tell them they have a new theater of war. I want them all on it, my orders, right now."

"Yes sir," said Mr. White. "Although of course we all rely on cell phones."

"Leave the cell phones," said Hovan. "We can monitor them. All we'll need is more bodies at Carson AFB."

"If that is General Armstrong's wish," said Mr. White.

U.S. nodded, barely.

Hovan said, "Not a cloud in the sky."

U.S. growled low and deep, "Niggers."

One month later, still waiting for snow. U.S. was not in attendance at the Christmas party in his honor at Santa Fe's ski basin. Rather, he was watching a kindling fire snap and spark in the corner of his commandeered bedroom.

A knock at the front door, the sound of it opening. "General Armstrong, sir?"

"Yes Sergeant?" U.S. boomed to reach the hall.

"Mr. White is here to see you, sir."

"Send him in," said U.S. He looked at his socks (boots in the corner) and his white hat on the wall hook. He watched the door as the sound of approaching footsteps echoed in the low adobe halls.

Mr. White appeared in the doorway, momentarily startled by U.S.'s socks and bare head. Unzipping his parka, he said, "Still keeping a guard on duty?"

U.S. sucked in a corner of his mustache. He rumbled, "Well the ban on the media ain't gettin no more popular. He keeps the rabble outside the walls at least."

"Yes sir, I understand. I was just up at the Ski Basin party as you requested, sir. Your absence was regretted by everyone there. However, there was an unpleasant incident. Amid the festivities, it took us a while before anyone noticed that the music playing wasn't just music, but rather a radio station."

"A radio station? We shut down every goddamn station in the goddamn state."

"Yes sir, I know. And, as we listened, it became apparent that it wasn't just a station broadcasting illegally, but an actual pirate station that was inciting riot over the airwaves. Well sir, I cornered the manager and he swore he didn't know anything about it. So we went to his office where the stereo was located. The manager said it was probably one of the ski bums he employs who was responsible. All slacker-types, lift operators and the like. We turned off the radio and there, we found some of these."

Mr. White reached into his back pocket and removed his wallet. He unfolded the wallet and removed a bright yellow business card. U.S. took it between his long fingers.

One side was red text on the yellow background: Radio KAOS.

Flipping the card over, it was the old New Mexican Zia flag, a red sun symbol on a yellow field. But the red sun had been transformed into a red skull, and the red rays were red crossbones. A jolly roger.

U.S. waggled the yellow card. "What the hell is this?"

Mr. White said, "I believe it's being called a Zia Crossbones, sir."

Penetration

Both floors of the condo had filled with smoke before anyone noticed.

"You goddamn idiots," shouted Hormigo, kicking through legs to get to the fireplace. "You didn't open the flue."

"I thought I did," mumbled Half-Tank.

Hormigo opened the flue. The flames stretched up, reaching for the cold oxygen.

Tanya, stretched out on a couch, said drowsily, "Maybe we should open some windows in here."

Lumbres, sitting low on the couch with his beard bushing up over his face, whined, "It's fucking cold outside."

"Open the upstairs windows for a while," growled Hormigo. "Last time we were here, you broke the barbecue grill, now ... this place belongs to *friends* of ours, get it?"

"Sorry Hormigo," said Half-Tank.

Hormigo's head snapped to the TV. "What the fuck is *that* doing on?"

Lani, her blonde hair spilling over Flywheel's lap, volunteered, "Isn't it great, there's satellite here. I wanted to see the ball drop and all. Ain't seen TV in months."

"I thought they was all shut down," said Hormigo.

"Not satellite, just broadcast," said Flywheel, stroking Lani's breast. "And they made it so they can't sell no new systems no more. I hear there's a good black market going on with that, if we can get our hands on some receivers. But anyway, they've had a dish here at this place, shit, since we started coming here."

Hormigo scowled. "What's it saying, anyway? They talk about us?"

"No," said Lani. "Something about the flu."

"The flue? The flue you idiots forgot to open when I was busy upstairs?"

"No boss," said Flywheel. "Some flu, killing chinamen. They ain't saying nothing about Texas or New Mexico or nothin."

Lani said, "No wait, on that one show, they had that thing about that girl, the daughter of the head guy or what-have-ya. Doing pornos."

Ribeye came in from the kitchen with a beer for Hormigo. "They don't show nothing. Gotta go on the internet for that shit, I heard."

"Fuck the internet," said Hormigo, taking a deep pull of cold beer.

Wolfe shrugged. "Without regular telephone, you gotta have like a satellite link to do the internet now too."

"Fuck regular telephones. We got cell phones," said Hormigo. "Are those steaks gonna be ready some day? I'm gonna go check my bike. Ribeye, come with me."

Ribeye followed Hormigo outside; the yellow porch light garishly highlighted Ribeye's scar. The pine trees sparkled with frost. The mountain's air was thin and burned the nose. The bikes were crowded together in the driveway of frozen grit. At the bottom of the driveway, the road twisted steeply up the side of the mountain.

Hormigo said, "You think anyone's gonna be passing by suddenly, going skiing tonight?"

"Nah, not tonight boss. New Year's Eve."

"Help me get this," said Hormigo, taking a screwdriver from his saddlebag.

Ribeye tipped the bike up so Hormigo could get at the pan screwed to the crankcase cover. Hormigo held the pan carefully upright as he stood. Ribeye set the heavy bike down gently.

Hormigo removed cash from inside the chrome pan, setting the bills on his seat. He counted the $100 bills twice and set the cash back into the pan's recess. Again Ribeye hoisted the bike and Hormigo screwed the pan flush.

"How we doing?" asked Ribeye.

Hormigo returned the screwdriver to the saddlebag. He said, "Not bad. With the money in my gas tank and my wallet, and whatever the boys have on them, we'll be able to make the deal in Burque."

"What about all your money in the bank?"

"Tsss. It's still frozen, Ribeye. I can't get *my* money out of *my* fucking account. If I showed up they would probably call the cops on me, you know? But if we make this deal and those idiots in there leave us something to sell, we'll be in good shape for the next deal I got lined up, a bigger one."

"We still ain't got no construction jobs coming up for us? It's been months since I swung a hammer. Not that I miss it, but it was good to have something regular."

"No more jobs at all, Ribeye. And now they got so many guys on the borders and running around, and now Arizona and Colorado put people on their borders, tsss, hard to make a living running this shit."

Ribeye turned his good eye down the road. "Sure our big rig's safe down there?"

Hormigo finished his beer and threw it into the woods. "Got to be. Can't get it up this mountain. And no one's gonna sit in it to guard all night, not tonight."

"Yeah, it should be fine. It's in a good spot. Let's go back inside boss, it's cold."

"I ain't cold," sniffled Hormigo, following his lieutenant in.

After the steaks and the shots and the beers and the lines it turned midnight and the Diablos began to file onto the deck, drawing their sidearms.

"What are you doing?" scowled Hormigo, chopping up lines.

"Outside. You know, to ring in the New Year, like always," said Half-Tank, showing the .38 in his palm.

"That'll get the fucking State Guard here in two minutes!"

"But boss, it's tradition," whined Half-Tank. The Diablos milled around the slid-open glass door.

Hormigo sighed. "Fuck it, let's just go and do it. Letting the heat out anyways."

In toasting a better New Year, Sipapu Ski Valley echoed with gunfire.

Zipping thick leather against the cold-blade air, Hormigo stomped out the front door. "That fucking wedo is never ready. It's starting to piss me off. Let's get a cup of coffee. I ain't waiting in the cold for this wedo. I saw a place up on Central."

The sun was warming but the January wind stole it away. The three Diablos walked up the barren sidewalk to Central and entered the Wayward Sparrow.

"What the hell?" groaned Flywheel.

"Boss, I thought you said it was a coffeeshop," whispered Ribeye.

Two worlds stared at each other from across a gaping, walnut-accented divide. Unexpectedly, Hormigo's hand twitched inside his glove. He approached the coffee bar, where one scruffy customer was sitting. The man had curly hair and was reading some sort of book. He had a mug of coffee and one of those glass push-down coffee pitchers.

Tending the bar was a small, pretty girl. Latina, with a little cleft chin, pretty hair. Hormigo found it easy to smile at her. "I'll take three black coffees. How much?"

The girl said, "Thirteen-fifty please."

"Thirteen-fifty? Everything's so expensive since Texas – it's good coffee, right?"

The girl smiled professionally, "I promise it's the very best."

"Okay then," smiled Hormigo, zipping open his leather jacket and removing his wallet. "Hey, you got water? I could use a bottle of water."

"Yes. But a bottle of water is, unfortunately, four dollars."

"Four dollars? No thanks."

"I don't make anything on bottled water. But I can't lose money on it, can I?"

"No. Hard times to be trying to run a business, huh?" Hormigo lay a twenty.

The curly-haired guy said, "Stuck between a rock and a dry place."

Hormigo chuckled. "You keep the change, sweetheart."

"Thanks. I appreciate it," she beamed, setting three coffee mugs on the counter.

The Diablos shuffled to the back, mincing around the low tables and fat candles pooling in wet wax. They sat on an overstuffed dull-strawberry futon. Reclining comfort from which to survey the Wayward Sparrow: the puffy couches, the little tables and candles, the amber lights glowing up from the floor, ferns, weird shattered mirrors on the brick walls, thick brown shag carpet under their motorcycle boots. The music was some freaky middle-east sounding stuff, but mellow. Not bad really, at least when they weren't singing. The people in the place were all freaks and fairies.

Hormigo finished unzipping his leather jacket and shouldered out of it. His men did the same. Quick cooling of long-set sweat, then the wood-fire warmth of the place – there, not far away, a Franklin stove, bright-faced glass, black pipe racing up the brick wall through the ceiling.

Hormigo shook off the last sleeve of his jacket. Took a drink of coffee from the heavy mug: hot black coffee, barrel-chested and rich. He drank his mug empty. It was work to get to his short legs from the futon. "It's good coffee, no? You want a refill?"

Ribeye drained his and said yes, Flywheel said no, staring at a hippie chick with dreadlocks who was avoiding his eyes. Hormigo was on his way to the bar when he passed two youths on a couch looking at a laptop computer. The screen had some kind of naked girl on it. Hormigo blinked to clear his eyes and stepped closer.

It was a picture of a girl. And she was being fucked, from behind, by a mastiff.

"It *is* real. It's a real picture," said the one whose lap owned the computer.

"But it's not *her*," said the other. "That's her head, but look, the skin tones and the lighting don't match. Look at the angle of her head. Amateur cut and paste job. There's been much better stuff."

Hormigo bent down to whisper, "She's fucking a *dog*?"

The laptop owner turned to face Hormigo – he had a ring through his nose and spiked hair. He said, "Well, someone is being fucked by a dog, and someone put Fawn Armstrong's head on her."

"That's the General's daughter? The Governor or whatnot? This is her porno?"

"Yeah," said the other youth. "But not this jpeg. There's thousands of doctored photos of her now, all over. It's like, a hobby or a contest or something. I've seen some weird shit man. People find the sickest shit and put her face on it and post it all over."

The laptop owner said, "You can still get some of her *real* porno too, but you gotta be careful because a lot of the links are booby-trapped."

"Hey, I told you boys to not download that crap in here," said the barista.

"Sorry Lilah," said the laptop owner, closing the computer. "It's just funny."

Approaching the bar, Hormigo shook his head. "Crazy stuff."

The curly-haired man said, "These kids today."

Hormigo chuckled and set the empty mugs on the counter. "I'll take two refills. So, downloading ... you got like the internet still going on here?"

The barista filled the mugs saying, "No, that would be illegal. But I can't help it if this place happens to be a wireless hotspot. I don't know

155

anything about computers. It was like this when we opened."

"I gotcha," smiled Hormigo. "What if they come down on you?"

"I don't know. They've left me alone so far. Having a hotspot is the only thing keeping me in business, honestly." She set the mugs on the counter.

"Oh, you got good coffee," said Hormigo. "Is this your place?"

"Yes. I have a café in Santa Fe and one called Bitches Brew in Taos."

"Ha, bitch's brew, I get it. How much for the refills?"

"Refills are free," smiled the barista, long eyelashes batting.

"That's cool," said Hormigo. He carried the mugs as carefully as he could, dribbling black coffee nonetheless.

The Diablos passed another quiet half hour in the Wayward Sparrow. It was hushed, relaxing. The Diablos were subdued. The other customers tapped at laptops, read novels and did homework. Hippies, some weirdo goths. Some smart-looking disheveled types. Some cute girls, but not Diablos material.

On the way out, Hormigo brought back the mugs and said to the barista, "That was good coffee. I'd like to see you stay in business. Anyone comes along and fucks with your business, no matter who they are, you give me a call."

Hormigo laid his business card down: red-tipped blue pitchfork with his name, rank and cell phone number.

The barista picked up the card and said, "Thank you."

The Diablos pushed out of the café, into the cold. They zipped up their leather and lit cigarettes against the wind. Hormigo said, "That was a nice place. Now let's do this. He's either ready or we'll kill that wedo and take whatever he's got lying around."

Hormigo led Ribeye and Flywheel in confused loops through the pedestrian mall around the Taos Plaza. Small naked trees huddled in the January mountain air. Cold. Little shops all closed up.

Flywheel complained, "We ain't never gonna find it. Let's get out of here, get some miles up to Colorado before the sun goes down and it's too fucking cold to ride."

"Tsss," warned Hormigo. "While we're here, I want a cup of coffee."

"It's gonna be like the one in Burque," said Flywheel. "All faggots, and no smoking inside."

"You can go back to the tractor trailer and wait with the others," said Ribeye, turning his gnarled face to Flywheel. "Me and Hormigo are gonna check the place out."

"I'm just saying ..." Flywheel trailed off.

"Look, here it is," barked Hormigo. "Bitches Brew, see? Stop whining like a bitch and buy me a cup of coffee. You got money in your pocket now."

The café was tiny. Between the coffee bar, the display of snacks and the one table crammed in the corner, there was barely room for all three Diablos to stand. It was warm and smelled of brewing coffee. The girl behind the counter had dirty blonde dreadlocks. Music was playing, some Bob Marley rasta shit.

"Three cups of black coffee," said Hormigo. "Flywheel, pay the lady, tip her."

Flywheel said nothing, but stepped up to the counter with his money-clip in hand. The reggae song ended and, instead of another song, a man said, "You are listening to Radio KAOS, solar-powered mobile broadcasting from the free soil of New Mexico, the Zia Crossbones coming at you. Although security is paranoid-tight around reservoirs, Radio KAOS sources have estimated that New Mexico's current water reserves are one-quarter of what they were a year ago at this time. It may not feel like it today, but spring is around the corner, and we've got virtually zero snowpack to draw on for the coming year. Texas is draining us dry and there's no hydrological recharge on our horizon. Flushing our water down to Texas, who's topping up their reservoirs as we speak."

Hormigo said, "What is this? Since when is there radio again? Is this satellite?"

The girl behind the counter shrugged nervously. "I don't know. It's on sometimes, now and then I guess. It was on when I came in, so I don't know ..."

Hormigo assured her, "I like it, don't worry."

The radio continued, "And to balance all that with some good news, because we must keep our chins up, plans are back on track for a general strike to be held in every city, town and village of New Mexico. The date and conditions of the strike will be revealed shortly by Dr. X, the mysterious and powerful Dr. X."

"Dr. X," chuckled Hormigo. Flywheel and Ribeye chuckled with him.

"Now let's get back to the music for the people," the radio continued. "And to celebrate a Radio KAOS anniversary – and I'm afraid I'm not allowed to tell you *which* anniversary – here's a little Radio KAOS trivia. Ready? Good. What was the first song ever played on the air by the Zia Crossbones mobile broadcasting network? I'm afraid I can't provide a call-in number for you, but give yourself a turquoise star if you knew that it was 'This Land is Your Land' by Woody Guthrie. Sing along now, if you know it."

The Diablos, creaking leather taking up all the space in the café, sipped their coffee and listened to the song. As the song ended and the announcer started up again, the door opened behind them and a cop walked in. A young bicycle cop, with a goofy helmet. The cop looked over the Diablos and squeezed past them to get to the counter.

"Hey Bekah," said the cop. "I'll have my usual."

"Double latté coming up," she said with brittle enthusiasm. "Any sign of snow?"

The cop said, "Oh no, not tonight I don't think. It's getting – hey, what are you listening to? Is that the radio?"

Bekah left the milk churning around the steam nozzle to reach over the espresso machine and turn off the radio.

The cop said, "That was that pirate radio station again, wasn't it?"

"I don't know, it was just on, I didn't know," she said, spooning out foam.

"It's ok, I'm not gonna ... but I need to call it in that they're broadcasting again from somewhere. I gotta go check and see if they're using the tower at KTAO."

"Why you gotta do that?" Hormigo said sharply.

The cop stiffened and turned around to face the three sneering Diablos. "It's my job, that's why. Better I shut them down, maybe give them a warning, than to have the State Guard come up here to do it, right? I don't make the laws, you know."

"Here's your latté, Jake. I mean, Officer Jimenez."

He turned back to her. "Thanks Bekah. I'm sorry, but I'm going to need to have you – " interrupted by a sizzle*crack* and the cop fell forward, bashing his face on the counter. He lay very still on the floor in a pool of double latté.

"Oh my god! Oh my god what did you do?" she cried.

"Calm down!" barked Hormigo. "He's fine. Just a stun gun. Shut up already."

Bekah squatted down behind the counter and began to cry, to weep.

158

"Let's get out of here," said Ribeye.

"Take his gun," ordered Hormigo. "And cuff him with his plastic cuffs."

The Diablos stepped out of the café and into the brickwork mall. A few strolling tourists. Dog sniffing a bush.

Flywheel said, "Hey Hormigo, this is his bicycle."

Hormigo smiled the very rarest of his smiles.

The Diablos roared through the narrow streets of Taos. The mountain bike dragged behind Ribeye smashed off parked cars, curbs, oncoming traffic. They hit a traffic snarl in the middle of town and took off up a narrow sidewalk with the bicycle spraying shrapnel, running sparks.

By the time they got to the lot where the big rig and the others were waiting, only the handlebars remained attached to the chain from Ribeye's bike. The other Diablos had come out at the sound of motorcycles. Hormgo issued his orders from his bike, shouting over the engine roar: "Jefe, take the truck down to our place in San Velarde. Wolfe, Half-Tank, Lumbres, you get on the backs of our bikes. We ain't done here just yet."

The three motorcycles turned through the dust of the parking lot and opened their throttles to tear back into downtown Taos. The gunners clung through the turns, grasping at cold-stiffened leather. The Diablos swerved through the traffic jam, flashing guns at terrified drivers, until they saw a police truck with lights blazing.

Hormigo led them onto a small side street and down a pine-lined lane. Two Taos Police SUVs followed them, screaming their sirens, as they crossed a bridge and began the steep ascent up to Angel Fire Ski Resort.

The SUVs couldn't climb as fast as the motorcycles and began to fall behind. Hormigo watched in his mirror until the trucks were only visible on the long straight climbs that became shorter and less frequent as they wound up the mountain.

They came to a short road that led down to a parking lot and picnic area. Hormigo raised his fist and turned down the road, bike tires slipping on ice. He led them into formation around the parking lot. Hormigo, with Wolfe riding, stood his bike in the middle of the lot, facing the main road. Flywheel and Ribeye stood their bikes on the flanks, concealed by trees. The shrieking of sirens came closer and closer.

The SUVs nearly passed the lot's entrance. The trucks slammed on their brakes, and backed up. They nosed down the entrance to the Diablos.

Hormigo twisted the throttle and released the brakes. Flywheel and Ribeye roared up along either side of the trucks. Their gunners blasted the trucks with shotguns at point-blank range. The windows exploded and the bikes clawed up to the main road. Hormigo rode his beast up the left side, leaning low into the handlebars. Hormigo made the main road and stopped, shouted, "Tires!"

Wolfe turned all the way around, hand on Hormigo's shoulder to steady, and shot apart the SUVs right rear tire. Hormigo aimed his bike downhill and burned down around the mountain road. They took back roads to San Velarde.

They were drinking in a dark dangerous bar called Cascabel. It was in Tejónes territory, with whom the Diablos had a hesitant truce. Procedure demanded that Hormigo ask permission of their president, Espectro, but none of the Tejónes were around tonight. The Diablos took over the bar, boots on chairs, smoking and drinking and laughing.

They quieted, for Hormigo was about to tell a joke: "So there's two Mexicans who want to cross the border into New Mexico. So they pay a coyote to take them over and he dumps them in the middle of the fucking desert, no food or water. They start stumbling over sand dunes and it's really hot, they're dying of thirst. And then they see up ahead there's a pool of water, and a tree, and growing from the tree is slices of bacon frying in the sun. And Pablo is too weak, so Jose crawls ahead alone. And then: bang! bang! bang! and Jose rolls back over the sand dune full of bullet holes, dying, and Pablo cries out, Jose what happened? And with his dying breath, Jose says, it wasn't a bacon tree bro, it was a ham bush."

They laughed, deep and hearty and a challenge to all in earshot.

"Haha, hambush," laughed Half-Tank. "Like today, when we shot them cops."

"That's why I told that joke," frowned Hormigo.

"Maybe we should keep it down about that," said Ribeye.

"What, in here? Fuck it!" shouted Flywheel.

Hormigo looked around the bar, reddened by the smoke-diffused Budweiser neon. Two vatos by the door, two Indians at the bar. The bartender was talking on his cell phone, smoking a cigarette.

The Indians – one of them looked familiar, flash of silver teeth, but he looked away quickly. Hormigo stared hard, his eyes commanding the head to turn back. Somehow the head resisted. Finally Hormigo stood up, swaggered up to the bar and tapped the Indian on the shoulder.

"Hey," growled Hormigo. "Don't I know you?"

The face looked up: filthy bandana and long filthy hair, hard brown eyes.

Hormigo slammed his fist on the bar. "From Pete's! Right? I seen you in Pete's, way down near the border, out by Hobbes, right?"

"Oh, uh yeah bro, you might've seen me drinkin in there some."

"So how's it going?" shouted Hormigo. He put out his gloved fist. The Indian punched his knuckles.

The Indian said, "It's been better, bro."

"I know what will cheer you up. Barkeep! Shots! Three more shots of tequila, good stuff, not that Cuervo shit."

Part IV Rebellion

The Battle of the Bowl

Jesus bro, how did I end up sitting at their table? I just want to get away from this fucking guy and his fucking maniacs. They do whatever he says. I gotta keep pretending to laugh so they keep buying me more drinks. And I am getting way fucked up bro.

Fuck it, I ain't got nowhere to go. William already drove back to the rez. He told me I couldn't stay with him no more. Said I wasn't allowed on the rez. Because of some fight I didn't even start? That bitch Nancy hit me with a *chair*, bro, and they make *me* leave? Fuck. William said they didn't want no BIA or State Guard to hear about me being there. Bullshit, bro. It's bullshit.

And I don't know where Melody's at. I used to talk to Daniel at Hank's place in Cruces until they shut the phones down. I can't go down to Cruces and try to find *him*, so what am I supposed to do? Hank hung up on me, last time I called for Daniel, before they killed the phones. He's married to my sister-in-law, we're supposed to be family bro. Just like William and all them. They're supposed to be family too. And they fucking throw me out bro? It's all bullshit.

Hormigo and his guys. They're all talking shit about stuff they says they done. Shooting up State Guard. Shooting up Taos coppers. Bullshit. These fucking guys are all talk. All talk, and picking on the oldest and weakest.

We're finishing off another round of beers. Empties rolling all over the table, Hormigo elbows me and says, "How you like that? Old fashioned Indian ambush, huh?"

I say, "Sounds like a good story."

His eyes get narrow, hard, some bad light got turned on in there. I shouldn'ta said it like that. He says, real low so only I can hear, "Maybe you don't believe me?"

"Uh, no bro, I didn't say nothing like that."

Hormigo looks up at the bartender and goes, "Hey! Luis! Turn the radio on!"

Luis shrugs his big shoulders. "Ain't no radio. Jukebox. Dollar for three songs."

"I don't want no *songs*. I want the news."

Luis shrugs again. He pours himself a half-shot of tequila. "Ain't been no radio stations anyway since, I don't know, like Christmas."

"Bullshit," says Hormigo. "What was that one we heard up in Taos? The pirate radio station, that cop said they was coming from some-where close by?"

"We did that cop good," this slick-looking guy named Flywheel says.

"Tsss, shut up," says Hormigo. "What was that station called?"

They all think real hard, or pretend to.

"I bet we're on the news right now," says Hormigo. He turns to me, "Where's your ride? You got a radio in it?"

"Yeah. But like the bartender said, ain't no radio no more, like phones and TV."

Hormigo says, and it's an order, "Come on, let's get in and see if we can hear this shit. Ribeye, come with me."

This is it. I'm dead and they're gonna take my truck. I didn't do nothing to them. But, fuck it. If it's gonna happen, it should happen now, when I'm fucked up. I'm drunk and shit and I ain't got nothing anyway. I got fucking *nothin*, bro, fuck.

I stand up with Hormigo and this other guy gets up too, nasty scar runs from over his eye and *through* it – his eye is fucked up, you can tell – and it runs down his cheek. Real wide and nasty scar, you can tell he never had it stitched up or nothing.

The cold wind outside is a slap in my face. It wakes me up a little but my eyes are watering and my legs get wobblier with each step as we go around back to where I parked the Explorer out of sight. I want to puke.

"Nice Explorer," says Hormigo. "It looks pretty new."

We get in, with Hormigo in the passenger seat and the scarred guy behind me, right where I can't see him. Fuck. I turn the key two stops. The radio is on and there's nothing, not even static. "What's the, the sta-tion?"

"I don't know," he says, next to me in the dark. "Make it scan."

I push the scan button and the numbers whiz by. Nothing out there. And then, at 103.4, it stops. There's some static. Can't hear anything, but there *is* something out there. Unless it's the microwave inside Cascabel's, or fucking aliens or something.

"We're too far away. Drive us up to Taos," orders Hormigo.

"Now?" Gotta be *kidding* me bro.

"Now. Ribeye! Go tell them to wait for us. If Espectro comes, we'll be back."

The other guy, he gets out and Hormigo and I are left alone. Sitting there. He pulls out a flask and all he says is, "You'll see," all the rest is silence and him drinking.

Ribeye gets back in, I start the truck and pull onto the highway. It's about eight o'clock and there's still plenty of traffic driving north with us, and plenty coming south, blinding me with their lights. Gotta blink away my double vision.

Man I should *not* be driving. Not after all those shots. In *this* truck, with *these* guys in it? Even with all the Guard stickers pulled off, and that rack of lights sold off, and changing the tags ... if I get pulled over it might save me from Hormigo, but the Texas fuckers would kill me too. Kill me at *least*, bro. And even if I was in jail, them Texas jails, the Diablos got friends inside. I'm fucked. Fucked and drunk and scared.

No talking. Just the quiet buzz of the radio. All I can do is drive. I've got the .45 under my seat but I could never get both of them. No way. I'd be doing the world a favor if I popped Hormigo though, that might be worth dying for if I gotta die anyway. The static comes in just a little louder each mile.

Around Embudo, it starts coming in better. There's words, but you can't tell what they are. Music it sounds like too, sometimes. Even up through the canyon along the Rio Grande, with the little slice of stars above us. Narrow road, cars coming too close the other way.

Then we come up to that big turn and the radio cuts out completely. They call it the Bowl: the cliff-face road turns around the mesa and then curves down and in, way steep down and then it curves back up sharply. Rockfall cliffs on one side and a long, long way down into the Rio Grande below. I never liked driving this part much. But especially when I'm seeing double, jesus bro.

In the silence without the radio static, Hormigo says, "You know what? This would be a great place for an ambush. A hambush, right Ribeye!"

Ribeye laughs for a long time.

I say, "Yeah, there's nowhere to go but slide down the Bowl into the river."

We make it through the deep part of the Bowl and head up the rise. Hormigo says, "You could make like a roadblock somehow, and make all the rocks come crashing down."

"Yeah," I say, forcing a laugh. "Let's hope no one thinks of doing that to *us*."

We get out of the Bowl, curve around to the end of the mesa and the radio comes back in. Pretty clear now, it's playing a song, some Cuban jazzy song. It would be good to get stoned one last time before they kill me. I'm just drunk, I want a joint. I got plenty in the back but I'm not going to tell these guys that.

The song ends and now we can hear a guy pretty clear, he's saying, "This is Radio KAOS coming at you, roaming up and down your FM dial. Thanks for being with us tonight. We have more about that situation in Taos."

Hormigo punches the glove box. "See? Listen!"

The glove box hangs open, light on, the other .45 sitting right there. But he's listening to the radio and doesn't see. I reach over and close it.

The guy says, "Apparently, the isolated actions of a motorcycle gang is being considered a 'terroristic attack,' if you can believe that. Sources in Albuquerque have been kind enough to inform Dr. X that the State Guard is now mobilizing a massive force to uproot the so-called terrorist uprising here in Taos. This is important, so I repeat it now and I'll repeat it all night: the Texas State Guard is invading Taos tomorrow. The Texas State Guard is invading Taos tomorrow. Get out if you can. We don't know how ruthless and savage they'll be. Expect the worst. Tell your friends, but try to stay off the cell phones because Big Brother is probably listening."

"Holy *shit* bro," I say.

"I told you," growls Hormigo.

"I believed you bro, it's just ... you know, hearing it on the radio and all..." Now I feel like puking again, it would be such a relief to just puke and pass out.

Hormigo says, "They coming up tomorrow? We'll be long gone by then. Here, turn around up here at this picnic spot."

I slow down and turn into the scenic overlook. There's no moon out. So many fucking stars. I get the truck turned around and Hormigo says, "Stop for a minute."

Now I can see back down into the Bowl, the deep scoop out of the mountainside with a razor-thin line of headlights clinging. The Bowl gouges deep into the flank of the mesa. I can feel the truck rocking, it must be windy outside.

The radio has been playing some Beatles song, but now the announcer is back. He's saying, "This is Radio KAOS, the Zia Crossbones coming at ya. We've got a news flash: the Texas State Guard will be invading Taos tomorrow. This is not a joke or a test or a rumor. Their mechanized units are being fueled and serviced in the Armory motor pool as I speak, and militia trucks have been seen leaving Caballo Dam and Elephant Butte Dam, heading north to presumably rendezvous in Albuquerque. Be prepared for violence to your homes, businesses and property. Tell your friends and neighbors but stay off the cell phones because I'd guess that Big Brother is listening. I'll be putting this news out all night: The Texas State Guard is invading Taos tomorrow. Now, how about a little song by Nigeria's great Fela Kuti, he who carried death in his pocket. The military government imprisoned him, tortured him, killed his band members and supporters, raped his wives, killed his ma. And he just kept coming back at them harder. Fela Kuti, martyr and hero to the oppressed peoples of the world, and the founder of Afrobeat music. Get your dance-cheeks ready for one of the most incendiary tracks ever recorded, this is Radio KAOS presenting 'Zombie'."

The song starts but Hormigo reaches over and turns the volume down, his face lit green by the instrument panel. He leans back in the shadow of his seat and says, "That's it? They're not even talking about us no more?"

Ribeye says, "That's fucking disrespectful to the Diablos."

I say, "Yeah, but if the State Guard is coming, the most important thing is to let people know. Those assholes are vicious, bro, take it from me."

Hormigo growls, "Oh, take it from you? You know?"

"Yeah bro, I do. I'll tell you what else, I killed some of them fuckers. Never killed no one before. They were going to kill me, so I killed them. This is their truck."

"Killed them with what?" growls Hormigo.

"Shotgun."

"Oh yeah? Where's the shotgun now?"

I don't give a *fuck* no more. "In the back. Under my sleeping bag."

Hormigo barks, "Ribeye!"

169

I gotta piss real bad. I can hear Ribeye crawling over the back-seat.

He says, "It's in here, boss. Plus some other shit. What is this, weed?"

I say, "They're still looking for me and this truck I'm sure. And they're probably looking for you guys, too. So we should get out of here."

From the back, Ribeye says, "Yeah, what do you think boss?"

Hormigo takes his time. Cars are still going by, and we're out here in the open. Finally Hormigo speaks. "I think ... that we should do something to those fuckers coming up here. Something to stop them. Stop them in their tracks."

"Like what Hormigo?" asks Ribeye.

"The Bowl. Let's do the Bowl," says Hormigo.

I watch the headlights winding through the Bowl, and imagine the mountain coming crashing down on them ... but no, that's crazy. I got to get out of here. Away from these guys. "Wait a minute bro. It's impossible. They got netting all up that to stop rockfalls. Besides it's night already, we got no time."

"We got time. We got all night," says Hormigo.

"Not me bro. I'm drunk. I just want to park somewhere and pass the fuck out."

"Well we can fix *that*," says Hormigo.

"Oh yeah?" I say, the hope and dread in me, I can smell the speed vapor creeping.

"Ribeye!" he orders.

I can't believe I'm out here, I can't believe we're doing this but thank god the moon is just nothing tonight because there's no hiding among these granite rocks. The rocks and boulders are so cool looking, all sharp angles and looking like they're all ready to tumble down if you say the word.

Me and two of them Diablos, we're clipping the nets that stop rock falls. The bolt cutters do a good job, even against these metal wire nets they used. We started by taking down the fence, right on the side of the highway, that was the most dangerous time, best chance to get spot-ted, so we worked fast and got away from the highway.

Then we were cutting the nets up the side of the slope but I was like, hey listen, don't cut *up* the net, cut across it, so all the rocks make it all the way down. It's slow work but it's happening, I'm as sharp and fast as my bolt cutters, I could do this forever but there's not enough time. Man that speed is pretty fierce bro, it cut right through the booze, I can feel it racing around in me, giving me the energy, this ... aliveness. I am going good and strong, bro, I feel good.

Once Hormigo realized they needed me, I knew I'd be safe for a while, he's an ok guy I guess, really. He listened to my ideas, I told them about the construction site where they were deepening the river channel, and all the dynamite they must have locked up there, I said that it would be guarded all night but he said leave that to us, so I did, and I'll just assume that everyone else is doing their job just like I'm doing mine here. A bunch went for the dynamite, the others are rigging up the metal trash cans to aim the blasts, their fucking tractor trailer is a full-on machine shop and garage, bro, they was cutting with torches and shit.

But they need me for the IED. It's really the easiest part of the whole ambush bro, I mean I read about it in a *Popular Mechanics* in the rez library that was like years and years old, it's really simple, I mean if those arab fuckers in Iraq and Iran and Syria and Saudi Arabia can make them, you know *I* can, I can make almost anything, bro, and this is going to be so easy. Tamped dynamite with the cap wired to an electric fuse that's plugged into the ringer on a cell phone, call the phone, it rings and boom.

Now, I ain't never made one before, never tried, but I know it's easy, the rest of it, the big dynamite to start the avalanche, is all hard-wired to one plunger, and all that is up to them, tell the truth, I never worked with much dynamite before.

Thank god the moon isn't out tonight, I feel exposed enough as it is, all someone needs to do is look and they could see me and I think dawn is coming. How long we been out here? My shoulders are sore from this work, each braided wire seems tougher than the last or maybe the bolt cutters are getting dull, but I got the willpower to keep on cutting.

I gave them the idea about the trash cans too, hanging them over the edge like I said, because you can just look at the Bowl and see that no one is going to be able to climb *up* the slope to set the dynamite high enough to bring it all down, it's all steep, sliding rocks, so I told them we could hang the dynamite in the trash cans from above, from up on the mesa, hang them down over the edge and force the blast into the cliff face.

171

I wonder if those guys are ready to set the dynamite yet, dawn is definitely coming, I'm not tired, I don't think I'll ever sleep again bro, but I wish they'd hurry up to get it all done, I want to get out of the Bowl before much longer, because we're about done with the net, I just hope no eighteen-wheeler thunders by or nothing, makes these rocks fall before they're supposed to, because there ain't nothing to even slow them down until they hit the road. They need to get back soon because I need to rig up the IED and set it up in a trash can on the side of the road, right where it climbs out of the Bowl.

The morning sun climbs to the top of the mesa at last, only a couple of gold-faced clouds up there, eating this sweet candy bar, watching the sun come to warm my shivering ass. I'm excited, nervous almost maybe, my hands are sweaty no matter how many times I wipe them, my heart has been pounding, *pounding*, for like twelve hours.

Looking down into the Bowl, still shadowed, me and Hormigo and some of the others, we're standing on the mesa tip south of the Bowl, looking right down into that deep curve, the kill zone, that big scoop with steep cliffs rising all along it, IED hiding down in there, I'm using a juniper on top of the Bowl as my line-of-sight aiming point.

I wish I hadn't pawned my binoculars, from here, if I had my binoculars, I could probably see the men on the mesa above the Bowl, they're waiting with the plunger to bring the cliffs down, we're all just waiting now.

Radio KAOS signed off at about three in the morning, they had said they needed to get out, melt away, to re-form again like quicksilver. Like quicksilver poured through a comb into a cup. I like that, I can *see* it.

From this spot at the south tip of the mesa, we can see down into the Bowl ahead of us but we can also see behind us, back down south to where they're gonna be coming from. Unless ... shit.

"Hormigo?"

He's smoking a cigarette, joking with one of his men, totally relaxed, like he does this all the time, maybe he does, I'm jumpy excited, it's true that they need me, but I couldn't do this by myself, I wouldn't even want to, he shrugs at me, "What?"

"What if they take the high road to Taos, like up past Chimayó?"

Hormigo shakes his head. "They'll come this way. It's the most direct, the best pavement, and besides they ain't expecting no trouble."

"But they gonna get some, right boss?" guffaws a big biker, Lumbres I think.

Hormigo's got an evil little smile and I'm glad it ain't about me, bro.

Just a couple them little clouds up there, the rest is all blue, ain't no snow coming today neither, maybe those little dustings are all we're getting this winter, they been saying the ski season is ruined again any-way, not much snow on the mountains, and here on these exposed mesas it melts away quick, there's a little tucked in dark hollows of the Bowl, where the sun don't ever reach, but it's about to get shaken loose.

Maybe most of Taos has already gone, taken their expensive skis and bottles of wine, gone back to California, I know the Pueblo ain't going nowhere, and the trailer parks and old barrios won't empty out nei-ther, you gotta have money to go somewhere and you gotta have some-where to go to, there's some traffic going north, heading towards Taos, passenger cars, not much heading south to Santa Fe, but a couple here and –

"They're coming!" shouts the scarred guy, Ribeye, looking through his binocs.

Hormigo hurries over to him and takes the binoculars, he says, "It's a long line of trucks, all painted white. I can see the star on the hoods, and the light racks. It's them."

Hormigo hands the binoculars back and goes to his bike, from a saddlebag he pulls a Diablos flag, a blue pitchfork with red tips like blood, it's been hanged on a fishing rod so when Hormigo starts swinging the rod, the flag whips in a big flexing arc, he whips the fuck out of the flag and then picks up the binoculars again, looking across the Bowl to the guys on top of it.

"They're waving back. They know. The next time I wave that flag ... tsss," says Hormigo with that smile.

They're coming, I can see the militia trucks coming, long steady line of them, light glinting off the glass and chrome, they are coming, they are here, passing right underneath us, I hear someone counting them off. All different makes and models, all painted white with the red T, from the smallest Toyota pickup to the biggest GMC Megalith, all white, with that red T over the white star on a blue shield on the hood, some guys are counting them off as they pass us, turning down into the Bowl: "Twenty-three, twenty-four, twenty-five" and so on, and now the lead truck, a white Megalith, is driving into the Bowl. Hormigo puts a cell phone in my hand.

"The numbers is already in it," he says. "All you gotta do is press 'send'."

"Me?"

"It's your gizmo. You gotta make it work." His hand is heavy on my shoulder.

I say, "Ok."

The last of the column is still passing us below, someone says thirty-eight and someone else says forty, I'm just watching that lead truck, working its way through the Bowl, approaching the metal garbage can on the shoulder with the three sticks of dynamite waiting for it, closer ... closer ... there's another car, coming the other way, it's going to be right in the way!

"Hormigo, there's another car coming!"

Hormigo orders, "Do it!"

I have to: I press send.

Nothing happens.

"Do it now!" shouts Hormigo.

I look at the phone in my dirty hands. "It says no signal."

"Fuck!" screams Hormigo, advancing on me. "Do it again!"

I'm scared, I scream back "I don't know the number!"

"Redial, redial motherfucker!"

The lead truck is past the can, and another, they'll be out of the Bowl entirely in a second, I hate these fucking phones, I don't know how they fucking work, I have to use these tiny buttons too small from my fingers, last number dialed, highlight it, press send.

Way down there far away there's a pop of smoke and a white pickup flips over, there's too much smoke to see ... but they've stopped, even the lead Megalith is stopped, five trucks ahead of the burning pickup, there's a lot of smoke, Hormigo is next to me with that fishing pole going, the flag whipping back and forth, I can hear him grunting with how hard he's cranking that thing back and forth.

A wreath of smoke appears around the rim of the Bowl. And then the sound hits us, a crunchy boom that's deeper and muddier than thunder, echoing around the Bowl as the rocks start sliding down, we can hear that now too, like rain on a trailer roof, the cliffs around the Bowl are collapsing in a gray cloud, the cloud speeds down over the highway with the rest of the mountain coming after it, something goes spinning, flashing out into the open air of the gorge – it's about a hundred feet of guardrail, twisting in long flight, glint of sunlight. The entire top of the Bowl has snapped off to join the gray cloud which has poured off the catch of the highway and is still flooding down into the river gorge, still picking up speed.

The sound is fading, that thunder is echoing away. The cloud of smoke is rising too, I can't see what happened, I wish I had my binoculars ... the smoke is thinning, I can see that the entire Bowl has been gashed out, scooped out like by an ice-cream scoop.

Guys are shouting "Holy shit" and stuff and hugging each other, and I can see Hormigo's got his little smile while he's looking through his binoculars, I can't see the road, even with the smoke clearing out, I can see the broken slope of rock fall, the brightness of the fresh-cut granite blocks, but I can't see what happened to the road.

Holy shit.

Now I understand, I can't see the road because it ain't there no more, it ain't there, it's all slid down into the river, holy shit. Holy shit, it *worked*, I find myself with my arms wrapped around some biker and we're just screaming at each other, everyone screaming it worked! It fucking worked!

After we split up, they went north, didn't say where and I wasn't asking. I'm taking this dirt road where it goes along the Taos Pueblo western lands and I'll hook up with the highway again in Pilar. Yeah, I'm going south, figure no one would expect that.

I don't have to worry about my truck looking too nice, the orange dust of this road is taking care of that. But I mean, if I get pulled over, I got those guns and the weed and all the speed the Diablos gave me, and me not having a license or nothing ... and that's before they run the VIN on this truck, and find a way to tie me to what we just did to the Bowl ... but bro, I'm out in the middle of nowhere, big mountains around. I'm all alone, and I'll be fine. No one knows me, no one knows nothing.

This dirt road is fucked. My struts and shocks and cv joints will be done by the time I get to Pilar. This shit is for horses. Going five miles an hour, still bottoming out.

I guess that went pretty good with the Diablos, I guess they like me. I don't like them but I'd rather be on the same side in a fight, you know? Hormigo gave me a card with his cell number on it, said call him if I ever needed him. I didn't have no card to give him, don't even got no cell phone. So I just said thanks, bro.

Hours are passing, the sun is pretty strong through the dirty windshield. Just smoking cigarettes and driving, real slow. Finally get to Pilar, go past the campground and the town. I turn onto 285 and I'm heading south, back towards Santa Fe.

That sound – I lean forward to look up and there's helicopters up there, following the river south just like me. I wonder if they're leaving the scene at the Bowl. Bro, I just want to get to Santa Fe without no one noticing me. I can sell some of this speed off, get some cash to live on and hole up for a little while, plan my next move or something, I think the more I drive around, the sooner I'll get caught. I'm sure I could use a couple days asleep when this shit wears off, *if* it ever wears out.

It feels like ten years since William sat down with me for that farewell drink. Man, I could use a shot and a beer right now. And maybe a shower, after that. Maybe after two shots and two beers, and a joint. Yeah, *then* a shower would be nice. More helicopters heading toward Santa Fe. I hope none of these cops looks at me and thinks something, there's a *lot* of cops around now, getting to the city outskirts. I don't like this.

As I get deeper into the city the traffic gets more snarled up and there's cops all around, what if there's roadblocks? Even a DUI checkpoint? Ok, ok, there's no drunk driver checkpoints at noon on a – what day is this? Jesus bro, I got *no* idea.

I need to get off the road, I could even pull into a big parking lot, ditch the truck. With my fingerprints all over it, and Hormigo's too, they'd love that. No, he always is wearing gloves. But anyway no, I can't do that, I need something to drive, I can't get stuck here in Santa Fuckin-aye. Fuck, let me just get off this fucking road, fucking crazy traffic. Here's a stripmall, there's got to be a bar or something.

I park and get into some bar real quick, glad I've got my sunglasses at least, and not just for that bright winter sun neither. It's dark in the bar, empty, with a pool table and TVs on but the jukebox for sound, cranking out some blues. I go and sit at the bar and say to the guy I want a beer and a shot of tequila.

He says, "I need to see your ID."

He's a young guy, he's kidding, so I laugh and tap out a cigarette.

"Really, I need to see ID. And you can't smoke in here."

"My ID bro? Look at me, I'm almost forty, I could be your dad."

"I need to see everyone's ID. Sorry, it's the law and I'll lose my job."

"I forgot it at home, I wasn't planning on coming this way, I just want a quick drink and I'm gone, no one's here bro, it's ok."

"Sorry, but I can't serve drinks without a valid New Texas ID."

"I haven't had a chance to get my New Texas ID yet, maybe I'll go do that after I get my drink, and then I can come back here and show you. No? Really? All right man, never mind, I got money, but never mind."

I slide off the barstool, now I can really taste that beer, you know, how cold and slippery it would be, with a nice burp to get me going. Just a beer is all I need, don't even need the shot, I turn around to try – what the hell? Since when is there TV on?

"Hey bro," I say to the bartender who wants to ignore me but can't. "What's with the TV? You got like a satellite dish?"

"No, this is regular TV," he says. "Just one channel. Started broadcasting this morning, what with that big attack and all."

"Shit, they *did* attack Taos?"

"No, the terrorists – look."

And on the TV is footage of what's left of the Bowl, just a pile of rocks, guys running around in orange vests and search dogs and bulldozers and shit.

The kid says, "This is all that's on. They're calling it the worst terrorist attack on American soil since 9/11."

"*Terrorist* attack? How can it be terrorists if it's our own –"

"Yeah," he says. "They're calling it 1/27. Doesn't sound as good, you know? It's not as catchy as 9/11."

"No shit, well, I'll see you next time and I'll bring my ID, ok?"

"Sure," he says and I can see how relieved he is that I'm going.

I start the truck. Now what? I know one thing though, I got to get the fuck out of Santa Fe, fuck Santa Fe, I got to get out of this place.

Where? I need to sell some stuff off for some cash. I need to hole up for a while. And I *still* need that shot and a beer. Of course, bro. I'll go to Madrid.

The big male coyote quieted the youngsters with a hard look. His white ruff mane stirred in the wind blowing up from the valley, bringing the smells of wood fire, cars, human food, human garbage ... very few dogs out today. Interesting.

The male was waiting for the sun to set behind him. Waiting for the shadow to start across the valley floor. He knew how fast the darkness would flood the valley, once it started.

The male's shoulders were thin behind his chest ruff; his ribs and flanks were gaunt. The winter had been mild but no water meant no seeds, no seeds meant no rodents, no rodents meant that it had been days since his pack had eaten properly. Which meant they had to risk venturing into the human town again.

The coyote's body cast a short shadow on the rocks. Soon. One of the youngsters gave a yelp in play. The big male growled a low warning but with the wind coming toward them there was no danger of detection.

The shadow stretched over the valley floor, crossing the scar of the arroyo. Almost time. The big male stood off his hindquarters and yawned a soft whine. The yawn traveled around the pack. They were ready.

All that was left of the male was the black streak that his tail tip passed through. His pack poured down into the valley, cloaked by blue-muted dusk.

They parted and reformed around patches of prickly pear. The big male led them past a human dwelling – they surprised and quickly dispatched a cat. Still no smell of dogs around, none of their wretched barking, as the pack spread apart and made ready to dash across a flat open space and into the heart of the human town.

I'm awake. What the fuck? Where the fuck?

I was dreaming. Dreaming about coyotes. I'm in my truck.

I incline my seat: I'm in some little town? Oh right, I drove down to Madrid. What time is it? Sun's pretty much down and – what the fuck is *that*?

A coyote. Two, three. Five. All fanning around my truck, like ghosts I can barely believe I'm seeing them. Then they're gone, melted away. How many were there? Did I really see that? Am I even awake?

What time did I fall asleep? I didn't get enough of it but I'm real hungry and thirsty. I'm gonna go to that bar, the Mineshaft, and see if I can get fixed up.

I needed that sleep. I need more, I could >*yawn*< sleep for about two more days. But I have been waiting too long for that shot and a beer. Now I'm seeing packs of phantom coyotes. I definitely >*yawn*< need a drink.

I'm more than thirsty, feels like I got the flu coming on. Couple drinks will knock it right out. There's a bunch of cars out front of the bar. I climb the stairs up to the porch. There's a bunch of dogs standing around, waiting to see if the big dog is going to leave anything from the plate of cheesefries he's mowing through. I pull open the door and I'm in the dark tavern, a couple dogs follow me in and shoot off under the tables.

I been here before, a few times over the years. It used to be pretty rough. It looks the same as ever. There's a long freestanding bar, must be sixty foot long, with two heavy gauge chains from the old coal mines curled up to frame a space in the middle.

There's some cowboys and some bikers, some punks, vets, hippies. A lot of dogs inside, and some little kids running around barefoot. The smoke is thick, like fog. The lights are low but it seems like there might be some pretty girls at some tables, and there's some good boot-stomping country blues playing out the speakers. The long bar is crowded from end to end so I go to the middle, the space between the chains.

The bartender, a kid with a weird beard, says, "What can I get for you?"

I order a beer and a tequila and the bartender tells me the kitchen's about to close so I order one of their green chile buffalo bacon cheese-burgers. I don't even realize how hungry I am until I say those words – now my empty guts are aching at the thought of food. It's been a day or maybe more since I ate, I figure.

I pull out my wallet to pay and shit, I got almost no cash. I tell the bartender I want to run a tab and give him a credit card from one of them Texans. I'm sure it won't work. There's no seats so I just stand there, hang onto one of them chains and tip that cold beer into my mouth.

Oh yeah bro, that's *good*. That's really fucking good. I drain the bottle, big burp, and order another. I gotta sell some shit off tonight or I won't be able to pay for this. But I'll worry about that later. I light up a cigarette and pick up the shot glass. Jesus bro that's a big shot, trying to kill me?

I get the shot up to my mouth when a hand lands on my shoulder. It's an old cowboy sitting on a barstool, got a dusty hat and Carhartt jacket, he looks at me with been-drinking blue eyes and says, "Ho there pardner, can't let yeh drink alone" and he raises up his shot glass, looks like whiskey.

The bartender says, "Is it that time again already? Hold on, let me get mine" and he pours himself a big shot of tequila. We're holding our glasses up to toast when a raspy voice behind me says, "Where's mine?"

I nod at the guy while his tequila is being poured, he's got a leather jacket and a goatee, old White Zombie t-shirt. He's got a dog leash around his neck and a loose pitbull at his feet – two loose pitbulls at his feet.

Now we finally hold up the shots, and the cowboy says "Here's to getting rid of that fucking dog catcher" and we clink the glasses, I tap it on the bar like they do and send the tequila down my throat.

Christ that was a big shot for an empty stomach. Least the beer slowed it down before it hit my stomach full-speed, like someone diving into an empty pool. I set my glass upside down like they did and wipe away some tequila from my chin.

The guy with the pitbulls says, "What dog catcher?" as this Ted Nugent-looking guy with a crazy mustache and long crazy hair coming out of his Eagles hat comes up on his long legs and says, "You didn't hear about that shit Steve?"

Steve, the guy with the pitbulls, shrugs and takes a deep drink out of a big coke. If I did that my teeth would be killing me, from the sweetness *and* the ice. The guy with the long hair sets his pint of beer down and says, "Shit man, the dogcatcher was here all day, trying to round up town dogs. I saw him nab Queenie and Dr. Potatohead right in front of the coffee shop."

"Why the fuck was the dogcatcher here?" asks Steve, chewing ice.

"Not sure," says the long-haired guy. "Probably because of that Texas lady who got bit on the ass yesterday."

We all laugh and the guy says, "Seriously, some lady straight from Texas, wearing a fucking matching Texas flag outfit, the pants and the shirt, married to some mucky-muck of the Texans, down here with a bunch of people doing the tourist thing and shopping and Mack was sleeping under a bench on the boardwalk and she stepped on his tail. So he up and bit her on the ass. Tore the lone star right off her."

We all laugh again and Steve says, "Mack doesn't even have any teeth anymore."

The long-haired guy laughs, "I know, and he'd probably still be asleep right now if she hadn't stepped on him. All I know is, the dog-catcher was here all day. You should have seem him trying to put that lasso thing on Amber down in the ballpark. There was a bunch of us smoking up top, just watching this idiot get her into a corner, get the noose around her neck ... and then Amber took off, dragged the dude through stands of cholla *this* high," and he knocks his pint of beer all over the bar, "Aw shit man!"

The bartender shows up with a rag and mops up the beer. The glass was nearly full so he has to wring the rag out a few times, and he says, "Damn, that's the first beer that's ever been spilled on this bar."

He refills the pint glass and the long-haired guy says thanks man and then he looks at me and says, "I remember you, you been in here before."

I say, "Yeah, I come around every once in a while. I ain't no dog-catcher though."

Then the bartender shows up with my burger and fries on a plate and I go blind and deaf to everything else. I take my plate and my beer and sit down at a table. I hit it all with ketchup and pick up the burger. Cheese and green chile and burger juice all running out the sides perfect. I lean in and take a big bite.

Oh fuck yeah. *Food.* I forgot all about food for a while, about how *good* it is. I eat and eat, each bite making me hungrier for the next. Then the long-haired guy drops down into a chair at my table and says, "Hey we're about to go burn one."

I'm still chewing. I swallow and say, "Later, definitely bro. I got some to twist up too. I'm looking to sell some too, maybe."

"Well whaddya got?"

"Some good weed, homegrown, and some real good speed."

The guy looks up at the ceiling, taps his temple. He says, "Ok, let me burn one and talk to some people. I'll be back in a bit."

He leaves, and I'm alone with my burger and fries again at last.

Hours must have gone by and I don't know how many shots. I can barely keep my eyes open but it feels good, good to be fucked up and don't give a shit. We're sitting in the dark corner, half hid by the fireplace.

I paid my bill with some of my wad of cash and now I'm buying drinks for everybody with it, and everybody's buying drinks for me. I can't remember the names of all the people here, they're all crazy fucked-up people and it's cool. Telling jokes and stories. I almost already told them it was me that did the Bowl, they was all talking about it. They was saying the cops and State Guard hardly ever come to Madrid if they can help it. That's good. Someone has a bindle and we pass it around under the table. Their shit burns. I'll be able to sell off this Diablos stuff no problem.

Then the door opens and a guy walks in, wearing some kind of uniform. Everyone stops talking. It's the dogcatcher and it looks like he just crawled through barbed wire and manure. He looks at all the dogs staring at him from under the tables, looks around at all the people staring at him over their drinks. It's totally quiet except for the music playing some funky song.

The dogcatcher, he's got scratches down his face, his uniform is torn down one sleeve, and his pants are coal-dusty. His glasses are cracked, or it might be the light. He points at sprawled dogs and says, "Do these animals have owners present?"

No one says nothing.

He says, "I have to take all the unlicensed dogs to the Santa Fe Shelter."

No one says nothing.

He's got a metal bar with a loop at the end, and he starts approaching a fat brown dog sleeping between tables.

"That's my dog!" someone shouts.

"Well it ain't got no tag so it's coming with me," dogcatcher taking another step.

The sqeak of a chair being kicked back, and a big guy is standing up with his cowboy hat and he says, "You ain't taking *my* dog nowhere."

The dogcatcher takes a step back, turns and sees a small yellow dog watching him from under a chair leg. He raises the metal bar, getting the noose near the dog's head.

The guy with the raspy voice, Steve, gets up from our table and jumps onto another table with a big noise, then stomps across the tops of tables – people grab up their drinks – until he gets to the dogcatcher. He jumps down and his two pitbulls are at his boot heels. Steve says, "You're gonna have some trouble taking any of these dogs."

The dogcatcher blinks and says, "They're a public nuisance, and dangerous, so back off and let me do my job. Are – are those pitbulls?"

Steve looks down at his dogs and says, "Them? No. They're pure-bred trouble."

The dogcatcher shakes his head and says, "Pitbulls are banned in

New Texas. I have to take those dogs to be destroyed. I have to take them, and all these stray dogs."

Steve stares the dogcatcher down.

Some guy yells, "You're not taking any Madrid dogs!"

"I already have. Now back off bro, or I'll have you arrested. Don't piss me off."

Steve steps closer but says loud, "First off, it would take the cops half an hour to get here at best, and by then you'll be at the bottom of an abandoned mineshaft. Second, you're not taking *any* dogs with you. Why don't you check your truck?"

The dogcatcher turns around and goes onto the porch to look at his truck, and we can hear him swearing. He storms back into the bar, pointing his finger at everyone and says, "Whoever let those animals loose is facing *serious* criminal prosecution."

Steve says, "We got two dozen witnesses say when you parked here, your rear door was hanging open and empty."

The dogcatcher looks around the room. I'm just sitting here fucked up bro, trying not to laugh. It's real tense and shit.

The dogcatcher turns around and leaves, smacking the metal bar real hard against the door. A couple people trail out onto the porch to laugh at him driving away. We're settling back to our drinks and some-one buys a new round. How many shots did I have? A lot. By the way everything is double unless I close one eye, a lot.

Then we're out the side door, smoking a joint. I can taste that it's my weed and that makes me happy cause I didn't roll it, which means someone bought my weed and now they're getting me high with it, it's like a perfect circle bro. The joint goes around and around and around and then there's a new one and someone says "The joint got bigger" and we all laugh and laugh and bro I am fucking *wasted*.

Then someone says in that toke-holding voice, "Look out, Crazy Ken's coming."

We all look to see this old guy coming down the street, he's got a cane but he's not really using it. He gets closer and in the light his clothes are a crazy mismatch of stained plaid and his gray hair is long and ratty like his beard. He looks around our circle with crazy Manson eyes and smiles some really fucking bad teeth – the few that are still there are bad to look at. The joint comes to him and continues around the circle.

All of a sudden, the Crazy Ken guy – I can smell him from over here, and I know *I* ain't smelling good – he says, "Well I just got the con-firmation about this so-called invasion and the complicity of the Great

Authority. Blows the lid right off it."

He waits until someone says what is it and he says, "I'll tell you exactly what it is, but if anyone asks you didn't hear it from me, you've never heard me talk about it and as far as you know I'm a deaf mute most of the time. I'm just a conduit, a conduit of intel and it ain't up to the conduit what it's got flowing through it, a pipe can carry chocolate or a pipe can carry sewage, it don't matter none to the pipe unless it *ruptures*, right?"

Right someone says and the joint comes around and Crazy Ken takes a hit and starts up again, "Out on Darby's land where he was getting set to sink a well even though me and Shaman Jim told him there wasn't no water for three hundred feet and no good water for five hundred feet, well, you wouldn't believe what they dug up."

Someone says, "I didn't hear about Darby digging a well."

Crazy Ken says, "They found a perfect unmarred *metal* arrowhead that conforms exactly to the design of a Clovis head. Cast, not chiseled."

Someone says, "What kind of metal?"

"I don't know, I didn't get my hands on it but that ain't the point. The point is that the so-called Anasazi, the people who left, actually had the ability to smelt ores and make castings, probably just before their ascension back through the Sipapu. It proves that they had help, right, help from *above*, whether you call that God or UFO's. We regular folks are ants to them. That's how they were able to ascend generations before Columbus and Cortes were even born. They made it to the home planet, and that's what this invasion is about. This area is more ready for an ascension than at any other time in the last four thousand years and they *know* it. That's what happened to the Mayans, to the Easter Islanders, to the Atlanteans, to the Anasazi. It *was* going to happen in Panama, which is why the United States invaded. All these droughts and floods and hurricanes and tidal waves, they've always preceded ascensions on a grand scale. I'm not talking about one Buddha at a time. I'm talking about the Knights Templar all at once, the Jews who ascended while their bodies were being herded into the showers at Dachau, all those ships supposedly 'lost at sea.' Nonsense. No one gets *lost* at sea. We *came* from the sea, give me a hit of that roach."

He hits the roach. Some of the people are chuckling but I am really fucked up and some of what he's saying could be true, shit bro I don't know nothing. Crazy Ken goes on, "There are sacred portals, entrances, called Sipapu through which ascension is possible. And it's Someone's idea of a joke to put them always in the most inhospitable regions. The Bermuda Triangle, Everest and Denali, both Poles, Afghanistan and, surprise surprise, our chunk of mountainous desert here, this dry broken tail of the Rockies. Evidence? This is the land of turquoise and rattlesnake and skinwalker. That's why the Texans are here, they want to prevent the final steps of our imminent ascension. They are the lizard creed, of course, they're from lizards and monkeys mating."

He just keeps going on and on, I can't follow it any more. The joints are done and we shuffle back inside. I fall into my seat at the table in the corner, in the dark, feel the wall against my back. Nothing can get up behind me or surprise me. That's good because I am fucked up, spinning bro.

The bar is pretty empty now. There's just some of us in the corner, some at the bar. The music is slow, low. My eyes are so fucking *heavy* bro. I want to tell them about the Bowl but I can't talk no more.

"Billy," someone says.

"What?"

"No one said nothing," says someone.

I try to look at him, all blurry. "Someone said my name."

They look at each other and one says, "Sounds like they're fucking with you."

"Who's fucking with me?"

"Spirits in this place. If *any* place in the world is haunted, it would be this bar."

"Oh yeah," I say, half-grinning.

"Lot of people have died in here, or from here. And especially this corner. Why do you think it's table thirteen, why do you think it's called Dead Man's Corner?"

"Whatever bro, I don't believe in that shit. I'm gonna take a leak." I stand up and *bang*! my knee into the corner, "Ow, goddammit!"

They bust up laughing. "Careful what you say about the spirits."

I rub my knee. It really hurts.

"It's about time to clear out of here. Where you staying, Billy?"

"In my truck. I'm parked over there." Still rubbing my knee.

"Well if you want, I got an empty Airstream on my property, all the way up Pyschobitch. You can crash there if you want. I got some beers at my house. We're gonna cruise up there."

I don't even remember this guy's name but fuck it, I'm wasted and tired. "Sure bro, that would be good. Let me take a leak and I'll follow you there."

185

I walk the length of the room to the pisser. The bartender is there, wiping things down, I say thanks bro and he says see you next time. His girlfriend is there, talking to him, waiting for him to get off work. His girlfriend is hot, with big tits and a sweet ass.

I start pissing and I think about that girl's ass and my dick gives a jump, splashing out of the urinal. I get it back on track. I shouldn't be thinking about no girls. I need to get Melody back. I need to get her back, I miss her, I love her and I need to get her back.

Jesus bro, I'm almost crying. Thank god I'm alone in here. Shit. Can't be crying and shit.

But I miss her. I'm so alone bro, so fucking alone, I don't have Daniel or Melody or nobody. And all those people I helped kill today. I mean, they deserved it and all, but they're people and ... fuck, I don't know, I don't know. Let me wipe off these fucking tears and get out of this stinking bathroom, get up to the dude's trailer and just sleep for two fucking years bro.

Terrorism

So we gotta take the long way, on account of them terrorist niggers shutting down the regular highway. All the pussies were scared of another ambush. We almost there, ain't been nothing on this *scenic* route.

Bobby Earl Valentine's Massacrers is at the head of the convoy, rolling into Taos with over a hundred vehicles behind us and not just militia but up-armored Humvees too, for real. And then after them, we got flatbeds bringing bulldozers and shit and all the supply trucks with empty-handed Captains coming up the rear.

Huh, coming up the rear. That's something they know about in Taos. And they about to get it Longhorn Style. The rules is, can't touch no banks or churches or pueblos or them places like McDonalds, Walmart and whatnot. The rest of that town of cowards and murderers is fair game, like a passed-out girl.

I got Mayles riding shotgun and Davis is folded up in the crew cab. My rig is bustin to get up in there, ridin heavy cause of the armor plating I had them install when I got my new stripe. I ain't paying for no armor for my passenger-side, dumbfuck that Mayles is. My mean old .50 cal is shrouded in the bed, just begging to pop up and start knocking dicks in the dirt.

This is about fucking respect, and justice. Right is right. They *started* it, we gonna finish it. We come in here, run their corrupt governor out for them, and the fucking thanks we get is cold-blooded murder? Like fucking arabs, killing the people who are *trying* to protect them. Well, protection is over. They done riled the wrong rattlesnake this time.

There's mountains around us, off on the horizon. There's a little snow all the way on the tops. That's prolly where them terrorist homos are hiding, stuck in the snow. Like penguin shit.

Buncha penguin shit cowards. That could have been me that day, could have been us instead of the 24th and 36th going up to hunt down that motorcycle gang. Instead, we sat around the Caballo Dam. But they could have sent *us* up instead.

They showed on the news what the cliff and road looked like after. It looked like when you kick over part of them big ant hills. Caved down on one side, like it was stepped on, the rest of it still standing but just begging to be kicked in the rest of the way, and all the ants scurrying all over it, looking for survivors that wasn't there.

All the shooting was supposed to be over with. They told me I was gonna rotate out, get paid finally. And then some fucks set off a landslide ... well shit, you want it the hard way, you gonna get it the hard way. We *all* gonna fuck you now, like that bitch on top of that pinball machine in that movie.

Look at fucking Mayles sitting there, watching out the window like some booger man is gonna jump out. He's got his little sister's shitty SKS on his lap, all ready. He'd be a pussy if he wasn't such a faggot.

Time to put in another dip. This one's wore out like a pair of jumper cables at a New Mexican wedding. Some music would be good, been driving the scenic route for hours, scaring the shit out mouseshit towns. But the twats running this Op say no radio. Too bad, Rebel Yell Radio's finally back on the air. To go with that one channel of TV, fucking lame bullshit, rerun sitcoms and TV preachers, home shopping late at night.

It's all real postcard pretty out the window, real Brokebutt Mountain pretty. Our formation is spread, but I keep my rig *bang* on the line. I'm Sergeant Taylor Jon Bridges, motherfuck. Valentine's Massacrers. Gonna fist you right off the bed.

Like that freak in the tattoo parlor, with his face all pierced like he fell face-first into a tackle box. I bet there's fishing in that lake we passed ... shit, I ain't thinking about that shit, got to stay in formation, I ain't going out on no goddamn ... lake.

That freak, trying to tell me I gotta pay *cash*. For a fucking Get'r Right tat they said was free if you want it. Tells me it's extra cause I got the barb wire band around my arm, and I gotta pay cash and the Guard will reimburse me. I go, reimburse *this* when he tries to muscle me, huh. Stare down the barrel, bitch, there's a hollow point in the chamber for you. Ain't got your name on it – no, it's addressed to *any* dumbfuck will do.

Tat came out looking pretty rugged, barb wire running over my scar. Looks rugged, the long streak where that bullet burned along my shoulder. Hurt like taking a camel cock in the pooper. Doc said I was lucky, another inch and it woulda hit my joint and I'd be all fucked up. Woulda been sent back to Texas though. Instead they stick a lollipop up my ass and tell me to suck it up.

I never thought I'd miss being bored. Sitting in the truck, waiting at the entrance of some dam or whatnot, checking IDs. Like a bouncer at a strip club, but instead of strippers it's our river we guarding. I'd rather have strippers. Tell you what, I'm horny enough to fuck that canyon crack. Then I'll show you a goddamn flood. All over your little sister's braces, huh.

Still, waiting for the days to pass, staring out at that fucking boring-ass desert, not even clouds in the fucking sky to imagine like big titties or nigger heads exploding or whatnot, still, bored's better than driving in towards some sneak attack cause they too scared for a real fight.

But I don't care, I'm gonna put my boot so far up their ass they gonna have to yawn to get me a polish. How much farther before we get there?

"Mayles!"

Huh huh, faggot jumped like a hot hard-boiled egg got shoved up his pussy.

"Mayles, look at the fucking map, tell me how much farther we got to go. And dump out this spit cup."

He takes the spit cup, lowers the window.

"Hurry up goddammit, I got a mouthful right now. And if you spill one drop on my truck I will staple your balls to your neck."

I let the window down a bit, get some fresh air in here. These guys are stinking up my rig with their shit breath. Air's cold but I like it, wakes me up and I ain't gonna have no time to smoke a wake-up when we get there. Behind me, Davis starts whining about the cold. Mayles says he can't read the map with the wind flapping it. So I definitely gotta leave it open for a while.

Shit all right, we're finally getting there. Thought I'd died and gone to nowhere. We connect with the highway at last and now all the gas stations and Days Inns all done up in that diarrhea-color adobe, looks like someone took a perfectly good building and hershey-squirted all over it. There's some stripmalls and shit, with a few cars in the lots. But that's some other unit's deal, someone at the rear of the column. Valentine's Massacrers are going through to the north end of town, block off 64 and gun down any terrorists show their shitbrown face while the bulldozers are doing their thing.

Well fuck me running. Even McDonald's done up like an apache outhouse. What do they serve there, Faggot McNuggets?

Shit, *this* is Taos? This is where the flower power tortilla terrorists is at? Buncha fucking t-shirt stores, all closed up. That's all I see. This fucking mud village ain't even got a proper stoplight. It turns red and we keep cruising through, light racks blazing hot white in the middle of the day. We own this fucking road, just like we own everything in this miserable litterbox, New Texas.

There's a park to the right with some people agitating in it. The 14th turns off there so now it's just us heading to the north end to close it off. Me and Bobby Earl and our ten other trucks, rolling through these abandoned streets. We're the baddest fucking unit in Major Bishop's Battalion, baddest fucking unit in the fucking State Guard.

Almost there I reckon, yup, there's the fork in the road ahead. Bobby Earl stops and he's out of his truck, pointing us off to how he wants us, pistol tucked in his belt looking like the bearded lady on her day off, I mean fella's gonna have to lose some weight or ol' Bobby Earl's gonna have to pay someone to scratch his balls for him. And it ain't gonna be me.

It's the regular drill, I park sideways on the flank. I tell Davis to go on up and light flares ahead so anyone coming down from north is gonna know to turn the fuck around. Me and Mayles uncover and load the .50 cal, my baby, and I cock it. It's the best after-market bolt-on in Valentine's Massacrers. Others got their gunwales built up high with diamond plate, some uparmored like Mad Max, some gots recoilless rifles and shit, but if you want some offensive iron, some intimidation, let me swing this heavy fucker on you. I can't wait to fire her again.

But we *are* waiting. Been waiting an hour, helmets on like retards at a bus stop. My fucking stomach is growling. Our flatbed with our bulldozers finally gets here, and they finally back them off it, and we're still fucking sitting here, waiting for them to get to work or for them tortilla terrorists to show up, *some*thing. And I'm fucking hungry. So hungry I could eat some a them Faggot McNuggets, huh.

Finally they figure out how to remove their heads from their own assholes and they get the bulldozers going and they caterpillar off, one on each side of the street. The one on our side has to cross a big lawn to get to a museum or whatnot over there. It knocks over some stupid 'Noble Redskin' sculpture they had out in the lawn, trucks right over it. The building is low and wide and will probably take a while.

The other D-9 has crossed the street and it goes up to the front door of some little house and politely knocks on it with 474 horsepower. Caves the house right the fuck in and we all cheer. Yeah, fucking take *that* you fucking cowards. We'll huff and puff and plow your house in. The bulldozer backs up and turns to the next mud hut, looks like a restaurant oh! looks like it *used* to be a restaurant. Now it's dirt, bitch.

On our side of the street, the bulldozer is having some kind of problem, he's backing up over a statue of a coyote or something. Oh I see, a fire started inside the museum, maybe a gas line or something. Good, fuck it, let the fire do the work for us. Sooner we knock all this fancy crap down, sooner we go home. Let's just get'r right and get the fuck out of here.

A truck, like a delivery truck, is coming down the left fork at us, and it don't stop at the flares. Bobby Earl shouts for us to take aim when the fucking idiot finally stops, he's close enough to see him waving his arms, scared shitless, apologizing for being born, he backs the fuck up, turns around and goes back the way he come.

Someone shouts, "Hey! We got looters!"

Coming out the side of the museum, the part what ain't burning so bad, there's these people running out with like paintings and pottery and rugs in their arms.

Bobby Earl shouts for warning shots and they fire some rounds but *fuck* warning shots, that line of people starts scattering and from fifty yards away I lean into the spade handles and chug! chug! chug! chug! chug! chug! dust flying up and they disappear in it. The fire's spreading fast now, smoke coming out the windows and the last ones run for it and we all open up on them.

Is that the last of them? Fucking typical beaners, looting their own museum. We gonna take down this fucking town, burn it down to the ground, and ain't no fucking terrorists gonna crawl out of here to pull shit no more.

Now *this* is a motherfucking waste of time. Bobby Earl comes walking down our line and I lean out my window to tell him what a waste of time this is. He takes the cigarette out of his mouth and flicks it, just like we ain't supposed to.

He says, "We're just making sure these here negotiations go smooth."

I let a big ol goob of dip spit stretch down to the dirt next to his boot, to show what I think. "What the fuck are a buncha drunk Indians gonna do about it?"

Bobby Earl shrugs. He needs to wash his uniform, christ even I can see that. He says, "Orders is orders. And it's better to show force and not use it then the other way around."

"What're they gonna do, a rain dance?"

"You know, there was a rebellion out of this Pueblo, back in the real old days. They came down to Taos and killed every white person they could find. Beheaded the governor, murdered his family. Held off the Spanish army for like ten years. I reckon we're just trying to make *this* situation clear."

I'm working up a mouthful but it ain't quite ready yet. There. I let it drop next to his boot. "I hope these fuckers *do* try something. That would make this shit go a lot faster. Faster than them lawyers smoking some peace pipe with Chief Cheesy Cunt. Let's just burn down their fucking casino and call it a day. Go get some waffles."

"First of all TJ, they ain't got a casino here."

"Then what the fuck they need water for anyway? They're all so old-timey, let them get their water the old fashioned way. Collecting dew drops and whatnot. Why we gotta ask, with sugar on top?"

"Well, back in the day, all the reservations got real sweet water deals from the Feds. We're renegotiating those deals, get'r right this time round. Them with the casinos, we got the bargaining chip right there. This Pueblo is holding out, don't want to make the deal more fair. So we here to keep them at the bargaining table."

"Keep em from being Indian givers you mean?"

Bobby Earl nods. "Mind you boys stay in your truck unless I call you up. This is still their land. We all hoping to get this done real friendly-like. Shouldn't be more'n a couple hours here. We'll go to

Santer Dominger next, if there's time."

He walks off. I look over at Mayles, his pointy nose. I say, "Shit, they coulda seen the smoke of Taos from here. *That* should be our fucking negotiation."

Mayles says, "I guess, Sarge. I'm hungry. Why don't they come out and sell us some tamales or something?"

"Fucking tamales. Get worms, you eat that shit. They don't wash their hands."

Mayles just shrugs like the dumb shit he is. Why am I stuck with the retards? Parked on some dirty rez?

"Fucking buffalo niggers. We should just *take* the fucking water. In the old days they just took what they wanted and that worked out fine."

"Not for Custer it didn't," says Davis from the back.

"Shut the fuck up, Rain Man." I lean out and drop another gob of spit on their sacred dirt.

There's a little Indian kid out there, about twenty yards away, squatting by a rusty pump. Just watching us. Fuck it. I wave at him.

He don't wave back, just stays squatted down and watching. I pull out my flask, take a quick look to make sure Bobby Earl ain't around. I show the kid the flask and call out, "Hey Tonto, want some firewater?"

The kid turns and runs off. Well you rude little fucker. Try to be nice and they just spit on ya. Fuck them and the donkey they rode in on. Just get me outta here, away from these mud walls, these mountains, this stupid fucking desert. Only people stupid enough to live out here are redskins, beaners and hippies. Buncha fucking weirdos. We should just burn it all down, start over.

I can't fucking believe them mother*fucks* did it again. That's all everybody's saying to each other in our hotel lobby, gearing up. I can't fucking believe them motherfucks did it again.

They didn't learn? I seriously can't believe it. It's like that fight with my celly, way back when I was in the joint. The junior joint, JD. Some faggot, liked to start fires or some shit. Little guy. I beat him down, broke his fucking jaw. And he kept getting up. He looked like a zombie, like in that movie, face all bloody and kinda walking all Frankensteiny at me. It freaked me out a bit, and by then my knuckles were all chunked up from knocking his teeth out. So I kicked his knee in, and kicked his knee while he was on the ground until he couldn't get up no more. And I reckon that's what we're gonna have to do to these fucking cowardly motherfucks.

I can't believe them mother*fucks* did it again.

They haven't put it all together yet, Bobby Earl is telling us, don't go watching the TV and believing everything you hear. All we know is, at a Texas State Guard recruiting office – brand new – in some fucking stripmall in the mexighetto, some of these terrorist fucks ... well shit, like Bobby Earl said, stick with what we know.

So what we know is that when a State Guard patrol drove by ten at night and saw the lights still on, he checked it out. And found the two dumb bastards dead in their seats, naked, and the whole place ripped off. Buncha those flag stickers over everything, the walls. He called it in, and then saw a bunch of people watching him from a pickup truck. They took off and he chased. That's all we know.

They found him at the end of a culdy sack, naked. Broken glass and shell casings, no sign of his truck. And none of them neighbors heard nothing. Like fucking hell they didn't. They was probably in on it.

Shit, those recruitment guys wasn't even armed, not even really Guardsmen, just some retired fucks clocking in for twenty bucks an hour. And what kind of fucking pervert leaves a man naked? Took the uniforms, even the underwear. Very fucked up.

So here we are gearing up at four in the fucking morning. We're supposed to be *off* for a week now. Our hotel – it's better than the last one, and those fucking *barracks* we started in, fuck a duck, I seen Mexicans sleeping less people to a room. They're working outside our hotel right now, pushing them concrete road dividers into place around the entrance. What're they specting, suicide bombers? I wouldn't put it past these motherfucks, not no more. Desecratin bodies and just ... they're fucking animals, fucking coward faggot tortilla terrorists.

You think Taos got it bad? When we get these bitches, they gonna *wish* they only got what Taos got. And I'll tell you who are a bunch of fucking useless sombrero niggers, the fucking police around here. So we gotta take care of this shit ourselves. I guarantee some serious shit is about to go down.

Shit man, we been driving patrol around in circles so long, the fucking sun is coming up. I ain't had a wake-me-up since I woke up. But I'll be fucked before I let some dumbshit like Mayles drive my rig.

Bobby Earl comes on the radio and I turn down Rebel Yell, playing crap anyway. He says we been ordered back to the culdy sack again. We follow in a long line, ain't nobody else on the road. We follow Bobby Earl through the mexighetto, buncha poor people with shit all over their yards. Not specting no ambush from these lazy spics.

We get there and there's already a truck, like a paddy wagon, waiting there and one State Guard pickup. Major Bishop gets out and talks with Bobby Earl who is all yessir yessir, kissing his ass.

Then Bobby Earl gets on the horn and tells us how we gonna split up and arrest all them liars said they didn't hear *nothing* when a Guardsman was ambushed and murdered while performing his duty. So me and Mayles and Davis get out and go up to a little house. One story, piece of shit.

Good morning, fuckass. I can hear the others knocking on doors already so I tell Davis to hurry the fuck up and knock. He knocks. Nothing happens. He tries the knob but it's locked. So he knocks again.

Behind me, Mayles says, "A light came on in the back, Sarge."

"All right, get your weapons up." I can hear people leaving their houses, all scared, whinnying like horses. Like cows to slaughter.

A little voice comes through the door, some little old spic, all "Who eez eet?"

I say, "Texas State Guard, motherfuck, open up."

The little guy is saying, "I already talk to theem, we dint hear notheen" and I hear the dead bolt slide and Davis shoves open the door, raises his .45 yelling "Get the fuck back! Get your fucking hands up!" at this tiny little guy shitting his pj's.

Good stuff. The guy is blubbering something about his sick wife as we shove him inside. I send Mayles to get her. Old guy says there's no one else. Mayles comes out pushing this old lady who's even smaller than the guy, but her mustache is about as thick.

I say, "Take these two out and stick them in the paddy wagon with the rest."

Davis and Mayles shove them out and they're all "Where we going? We didn't do nothing! I need my pills!" and I take a look around.

What a shitbox. I've farted better-looking furniture. The kitchen is tiny. At least the place is pretty clean. The others are prolly waist-deep in cucarachas and cat shit. Photos on the tiny fridge, grandkids and whatnot. One's of a girl, kinda hot, school picture in her cheerleader uniform. I take it for later.

Inside the fridge ... nothing. No food, just tomatoes and shit. I open a drawer and man, even their silverware's old and crappy and tiny. Mayles and Davis walk back in through the open front door.

Mayles says, "What are you doing?"

"Having a look around. Ain't nothing here."

"Major Bishop said not to touch nothing."

In about two steps I'm at the door with them. "Fucking relax, ain't nothin here to touch. Fucking other beaners be over soon as we leave, picking over their shit anyway. I mean, you talking about people that loot their own *museums*, right?"

"I guess," says Mayles.

"Bet your ass. Let's get out of this shitbox, go take care of the rest of these fuckin terrorist lovers. What're they doing with them all?"

Mayles says, "Deportation. Sending 'em to Texas, some prison over there."

"Ok. Break's over," I say, shoving them out the door.

This is the time for this. Late night. Alone. Breathe in, breathe out. Yup.

That workout room's a fucking joke, just them faggot combo machines and stationary bikes. It's all about the steam room for me, god-damn right. Breathe in, breathe out. Tastes like soup.

It's about the only thing that feels good. Fill up the lungs with some *steam*. Get a sweat on. Feels like summer, growing up. Fucking Houston. If I was there I'd be bitching about the heat, prolly lie on the couch with the AC on, eating a box of popsicles. But after being out here, breathing this sandpaper air ... fucking steam room's real nice. Nice to have the sweat rolling off me, it never does that out here. You sweat but it doesn't run off, you know, like carry the poisons away. Cause this dry-ass desert is really fucking up my skin. Better when the sweat rolls off, it carries the poison away. I got zits going real bad. I got zits on zits. I got zits growing on my ass from sitting in my rig all day and night. My zits are as bad as when I was fifteen, shit.

Fuck it. I'll just sit in this little steam room. Breathe in, breathe out. Whatever they paying me ain't worth it. And I *still* ain't got no cash in my hand. They say all this bullshit economic shit, New Texas slow paying its bill and shit. I don't care. Just gimme my fucking money. Least the Guard Card works most everywhere.

Door opens, light comes blasting in. *Shit.* Guy standing there, surprised too. "Well, don't let the steam out," I say. I slide down the wall away and he comes in, sits by the door. This room's too small for two people unless they're gay. Least we're both wearing towels. Shit, that's fucked up.

"Late night," he says, stretching his head back, looking at the ceiling. "Thought I'd be the only one up."

"Well, y'ain't."

He yawns. I think I recognize him – think he was up at Taos, too. "Say, was you up in Taos for that?"

"Yep," he says, eyes closed.

"Who you with?"

"Bisby's Rangers."

"Oh yeah. I'm with Bobby Earl Valentine. You know, Valentine's Massacrers."

"Right," he says.

I say, "Hear we ain't allowed to go to strip clubs no more? How about *that* shit."

"I don't give a turtlefart. What *I* like," he says, opening his eyes and leaning forward, hands cupping out in front of him, "are big ol' Texas titties. I'm talking big, big titties. Not these little dried-up raisins they grow out here, smell like burriters."

"You said it."

"S'yer name?"

"Taylor Jon. You?"

"Bo."

We reach out through the steam, shake hands – he's pretty built. He's got short red hair and wide shoulders, pretty built. But I could take him.

He says, "You play ball?"

"Me? Nah."

"Oh. Thought maybe you had. I miss playing ball. Not as much as I miss big titties but ... I thought this shit was gonna be fun like that. Bustin heads. But it's just sitting around, waitin for something to happen, a bomb blows up and we rush over and ... they gone. Never know when it's your time and the bomb blows up next to you."

"Aw bullshit." I can see the red light from the exit sign picking up the shine on his skin. He's sweating now too. Man I could melt into the floor, this steam is just melting me. Hard to think even.

Bo says, "You never know."

"Hell man I already been through the shit. See this? Caught a bullet up at the Battle of Las Vegas."

"You was in that?"

"Yup," I say, leaning back. "Fucked some shit *up*, too."

"Right on," he nods. "Anyway, alls I'm saying is, I'm looking forward to when my tour is up and I can get the fuck out of here."

"Shit, they already extended mine. You'll get the same."

"No shit? That's fucked. How long you been in?"

"Since last ... hell I can't remember that shit. Feels like forever."

Bo says, "Least now they raised our health care benefits and the death pay."

"What the fuck is death pay?"

He leans forward, grinning in that swirl of steam smoke, "That's what they pays your mama when you dies."

"Well, whatever." But ... death pay? That's fucked up. "How they gonna pay death pay when they ain't even paid me my cash money yet?"

"Hell I don't know. They'll just squeeze these New Texas fuckers for it. Buncha fucking terrorist injun B.O.-having cowards."

I laugh at that. "Shit man, Indians can't fight no more. They all drunk, eating that government cheese."

"Yeah, but I mean ... it's been a month since that landslide and all this shit started happening all over. And so far we ain't done shit. I mean, we've fucked shit up, but we ain't caught no one. Ain't stopped nothing in the act."

"Hell man, we fucking burned Taos to the fucking ground. And I musta sent a hundred people to be deported my own self."

"Yeah but who knows if any of them was even in on it, you know? Ain't slowing nothing down. Hell, there was another kidnapping tonight."

"No shit," I say. I could use a breath of cool air, but ...

"Yeah, some executive in charge of something out here. All night we was running from one end of Albuquerque to the other, chasing that radio station back and forth across the basin. Waiting for the nerd to tri-angulate or whatever. Either it was mobile, or they had more than one ... fuck I don't know, but they bragged about that kidnapping while we was chasing them."

198

"They announced it on the *pirate* radio?"

"Yeah, all this shit about this Dr. X guy. They was probably fucking watching us drive back and forth across the city. Fucking fucks."

Sweat is dripping in my eyes. I say, "Man I could use a dry towel but they ain't none in the thing out there."

"Cause they're fucking lazy," says Bo. "They barely got any maids left here, and the ones they got are the fucking laziest of the lazy."

"Can't trust them, that much I know."

"Yup. All right, Taylor Jon, I think that's about alls I can take of this steam."

"I gotta enjoy this now while I can. We moving up to Santa Fe next."

Bo says, "It'll be the same as here. Fucking stupid. But I'm done with this steam. I'm finished, like a Mexican condom on Friday night."

I laugh, "That's nasty."

"Yeah cause the whole village shares it. I'm gonna go jump in the pool. You ever do that? Cold plunge?" Bo stands up, nearly drops his towel.

"No."

"Aw, you kiddin? Come on, ya gotta try it. Sounds crazy but man it's a rush, hit that cold water and you go *snap*. Come on."

"Naw."

"Come on now, just try it once and you'll be hooked. Cold plunge, man."

"Naw. I don't want to."

"I ain't asking you to finger a fat chick, I'm saying cold plunge, you'll like it."

"I said no."

"All right man, but you're missing out. Later."

I wait until the door is closed shut behind him, heavy, before I breathe out. Breathe in, breathe out. It's like soup, like chicken noodle soup. Campbell's.

It's too much, I want to get out. Breathing's just too hard. Need some fresh air. But if I go now I'll go past Bo in the pool and he'll see me, or in the locker room. I'll just stay in here a little while longer yet.

Yeemotherfuckinghaw! This is what I'm talking bout!

Hansen's Megalith loses control on the turn and I cut off some faggot coming the other way and now I'm only four back from Bobby Earl. I'm right on Chandler's tail, holding my rig hard on the line, jam it into third as we hit this hill. Engine's roaring, I'm roaring, Davis in the back is roaring, bouncing around in the crew cab, whoopin and hollerin. Our lights are scorching the dark narrow streets, you can run but you can't hide motherfuck! Hard turn up a narrow switchback, Bobby Earl slows to take it and we bunch up, long line of follow the leader, I punch the wheel, c'mon *move* motherfucker! We running again now, brown mud walls on both sides, anyone coming the other way is fucked. Can't see the terrorists, I just stay locked on Chandler's tail. My heart's pounding, sometimes it's too much, I gotta swallow and breathe and stay on target.

We're twisting and turning, following the tortilla terrorists who are driving one of our *own* trucks, believe that shit, wearing *our* uniforms, shot *our* fucking General Armstrong! We're in a long line, each truck chasing the one in front, all chasing, we all want blood. He's running scared, up and down back roads of Santa Fe. We got these faggots in our lights though, they won't – Watch it Fucker! Fucking little gangbanger almost made me plow into his Honda, come back for you later. I get back on Chandler's tail – it bounces oh shit speed bumps and Boof! everything inside jumps up in the air, crashes back down.

Shit! yells Davis from the back, in the rearview I see one leg sticking up. Mayles is holding the side of his face where he hit it on the window. Boof! Jesus how many speed bumps they got here? Hitting them at fifty is Boof! Fuck man this is bullshit, my rig ain't wanting to be Boof! catching air every ten feet, I can feel the body crashing down into the wheel mounts and Boof! and Chandler's truck all sudden steers straight into a wall, I cut the wheel away and Boof!

Shit! Recover it, now I'm second back from Bobby Earl.

Mayles yells, "Broke his front axle!"

In the rearview they look all fucked up, Chandler is stuck half in the wall and no one's following me, they all stopped. Go around another turn and now I can't see any of their lights behind me. Fuck it, here we go, we've gone around in some big circle and we're back in town, cars going both ways and the terrorist cuts across traffic ...

Shit, he made it. C'mon Bobby Earl, just Go!

He does, traffic skidding and crashing into each other, we gun across the intersection, make that hard left and everything in my rig flies to the right, I'm hanging onto the wheel, feel her trip up on two tires, then settle back and I floor it.

But then he whips another hard left across oncoming traffic and we follow up another narrow street, dead branches clawing both sides of my rig, can't see nothing but the back of Avery's pickup. Mayles got the CB turned up all the way but it's just squawking noises, if there's orders in that squawking I can't hear it. Still no lights behind me, hope we ain't lost the unit in this maze of stupid streets.

We climb steep, my rig is shaking in its armor, gears grind but my rig has big balls. Terrorists turn onto a dirt road, oh shit we got you now motherfuckers! We bounce after him, banging inside the cab, everything shaking, banging, my ass taking a pounding but we *on* these motherfucks!

Davis in the back, he's yelling, "We on TV again! We on it!"

Mayles yells back, "Whutz say?"

Davis holding his little TV, bouncing around in the back. He hollers, "They didn't kill General Armstrong, they missed him. He's fine!"

Mayles yells, "What else?"

"That's it, they got it back on that reality show, the new one."

Mayles yells, "Oh yeah? What's happening?"

"Shut the fuck up both of yous! I'm trying to fucking drive! Shut the fuck up!"

The dirt road is long and straight, I can see the terrorists driving *our* truck up ahead, Bobby Earl's on his ass, or close anyway. No one behind me. They'll never find us out here, wherever the fuck we are, wherever the fuck we're going. Mind I don't drop the tranny, blow a flat, banging hard down this shitty road, rocks slamming off the underbelly. Avery's truck fishtails, I slide around it. His lights stick out in the darkness behind. It's just me and Bobby Earl and Jed, and those running cowards. If only we could get a shot off at this fucker.

Shit!

Spun out a bit there but I got it back. I can see Bobby Earl trying to put a move on to go around but the road's too narrow, steep rocks on both sides and thick bushes. We start up a bunch of switchbacks. Terrorists crossing back just above us, I can see the State Guard insignia on the fucker. You don't drive one of our trucks, you don't wear our uniforms. We got the fresh desert camo, they had shitty old green fatigues. Don't be sneaking – fuck, where the fuck'd he go?

I see him there, he pulled a 180 and his lights are out but I see him, I stomp down the brake and cut the wheel hard, we tip and I can feel us going over, Mayles screams but we settle and the low white glow of the terrorist drives out of my lights. I drop her into gear, tires spin the loose rocks and we roaring after him.

Where's Jed and Bobby Ear? There's squawks coming from the radio, Mayles is screaming useless shit into it. I hope they can follow my lights because I can't slow down to wait for them, it's just me and the terrorists now, clawing up this rock road, cracking my ass on the seat and my helmet on the ceiling but I got you, you can run but you can't hide motherfucker!

He makes a hard turn and I gotta hit the brakes to make it, he gets out ahead of my lights but I'm after him, pick up the tingle of his dark tail lights. Ain't even a road no more, blasting through cactus and sagebrush. My lightbar picks them up and we blast right through them. Long shadows ahead, makes it seem twice as dark and I'm straining to see the outline of the truck through the dusty windshield, dust rising from his tires.

He don't know what he's doing, we're going up the side of a goddamn mountain. I can feel my rig slipping on the loose shit, but if he can do it so can I. Climbing steep, pressed back in my seat, clawing up the steep dune of rocks and sand.

My lights pick him up going over the top and he disappears over the other side. My lights are firing off into the sky useless, finally get to the top and scrape going over, almost high-center, drop the nose down the other side of the ridge and ... where the fuck he'd go? Start skidding down, I'm falling forward through the seat belt, trying to hold it straight and FUCK!

For a minute there's nothing but the sound of the radio, Bobby Earl calling out for everybody. And something still running in the engine. I unbuckle and fall onto the dashboard. I try the door but it's jammed. Hold myself up and kick the door open. It keeps swinging back to close on me while I'm getting out.

Good to be standing on solid ground. Shit-smeared Jesus, look at my rig! It is fucked. It is well and truly fucked. Front end piled up in this here ditch. There's tumbleweeds and shit all struck in the wheel wells. The rack of lights are staring stupidly down at the ground. Lucky we didn't puncture the gas tank.

It's cold out here in the middle of fucking nowhere. Dark all around but the stars and the blob of blinding light from the lightbar. How the fuck we gonna get a tow truck out *here*? How the fuck did they disappear like that? They dropped over the ridge and fucking disappeared. I dropped over the ridge and crashed into this ditch at the bottom, lucky to be alive.

Mayles is trying to crawl out, I can see his blonde hair.

"Mayles! Get on the fucking horn and tell Bobby Earl where we're at."

Mayles says, "Davis looks pretty fucked up Sarge."

"Hurry up goddammit, we're losing them!"

"Sarge, we lost them. And I think Davis is pretty fucked up. He ain't waking up, there's blood all over. My arm's busted, help me get him out."

"The mission comes first." I walk in the tracks we made, back up the ridge we fell over. Where the fuck did they go?

I can see lights coming across the plain, must be Bobby Earl. Looks like two trucks, maybe. Pull my flashlight off my belt and shine it for them. I can't believe we're letting these murdering, assassination-attempting cowards get away.

With my rig smashed in some ditch. And somewhere out there, those fucks are getting away. Prolly fucking laughing. Can't stand and fight like men. Makes me sick. And I can't do nothing about it cept waggle this fucking flashlight, wait to get picked up.

I take a deep breath and scream loud enough for their deaf boyfriends to hear it, "You can run motherfuckers but you can't hide!"

It's all quiet afterwards, not even an echo. Just the dark hills. Fuck this stupid fucking empty desert.

Surprise

News Noose: Independent Online Journalism
Newsnoose.org>archive>interviews>DrX

Shewolfhound: Today, March 26, I am being joined by the leader of the insurgency in the territory of New Texas, the infamous Dr. X. Thank you for joining me on this internetwork, Dr. X.

321DrX: It's my pleasure. It seems ages since someone from outside our indentured borders took an interest in this occupation.

Shewolfhound: As our readers across the planet know, News Noose is committed to gathering the Truth that often lies buried.

321DrX: There has been plenty of veritas buried, *requiescat in pace*.

Shewolfhound: To begin, what can you offer as proof that you are truly the Dr. X responsible for the organized resistance to the established territory of New Texas?

321DrX: Proof? Such as my social security number?

Shewolfhound: No, of course not. But some operational or personal details could persuade our readers. As you may know, many "Dr. X's" have protested this scheduled interview, literally flooding our message boards. Our preliminary contact, which as we agreed will remain undisclosed, has convinced our editors that you very well might be Dr. X. But right now, we don't even know if you're a man or woman.

321DrX: I'd guess from your appellation that you are a woman, and commendably sensitive to the issues of identity politics. However, in this particular case, my burka of anonymity illustrates the universalism of our movement. Which is why I offer no proof of my identity and commend the others – even the wiley agents of Texas – who continue their mongering. We're all Dr. X, and we will fight to the death.

Shewolfhound: What is the official name of your movement?

321DrX: We never got around to deciding on one. We are of course symbolized by the Zia Crossbones flag.

Shewolfhound: Are these the stickers that are reportedly showing up all over New Texas? Your calling card, as it were?

321DrX: Yes, it's the new flag of the new state of New Mexico. The Zia Pueblo sun symbol incorporating the Jolly Roger, which indicates that no quarter will be given. The ubiquitous stickers have been freely distributed to demonstrate the widespread support of the New Mexican population.

Shewolfhound: You refer to New Mexico, but that state officially ceased to exist at the stroke of midnight on January the First of this year. Your own representatives signed the treaty which was immediately ratified by the U.S. Congress. What, then, is your political program? And to follow that up, what personal role do you expect to play in the territory's future, should you prove successful?

321DrX: Personally, my interest is in reform, not power. Once we have succeeded in expelling the occupying force – our sole political program – I will return to the more passive anonymity of my former life.

Shewolfhound: What was that former personal life?

321DrX: Sorry. You know I can't answer that. I was something between a hunger artist and a professional walnut cracker.

Shewolfhound: Going back to the idea of popular support of your resistance movement ... public opinion polls show an overwhelming disfavor with your activities. 85% of New Texas citizens polled say that your resistance movement is causing more harm than good. 99% say they prefer peace and calm to terrorism. How do you respond to the statistical evidence that your movement is unpopular with New Texans?

321DrX: When Mark Twain wrote, "There are lies, damn lies, and then there are statistics," he wasn't just calling out a sounding. Assuming these polls even took place, which is doubtful, the essential elements of *who* is asking *what* questions to *whom* has to be considered. Everyone prefers peace to violence. That isn't the right question.

Shewolfhound: Nevertheless, there is a public perception which, influenced by the media or not, regards your actions as isolated banditry or anarchy, causing deliberate violence to impede the progress of the government of New Texas to restore peace and prosperity.

321DrX: What are you doing, reading directly from their press releases?

Shewolfhound: You need to respond to your critics at home and abroad. This is your first published interview, soon to be available throughout the planet. I would like you to address the disconnect between your insurgency and the will of the people. And incidentally yes, I was quoting a press release by Governor Burton of Texas.

321DrX: First of all, "disconnect" is a verb, "disconnection" is the noun. And I would disagree with the media's portrayal of the events and sentiments here. There are no independent journalists on the ground here, and everything reported has been thoroughly manipulated by the Machine. Except for News Noose, of course, dear Shewolfhound, and a few others attempting to circumvent the media blackout. There are no reports about the atrocities committed by the Texas State Guard, only about our reprisals. There are no reports about the economic rape of New Mexico and its reduction to a colonial territory, only about some new flu they want everybody to be afraid of.

Shewolfhound: You hate Texas – is that your justification for fatal violence against them?

321DrX: We'll hate them less once they go home. Until then, we resist.

Shewolfhound: By resist, do you mean the Battle of the Bowl, where several hundred Guardsmen were killed in a triggered landslide?

321DrX: I am unable to comment on specific operations. However, that ambush is what gave the resistance its angel wings. It proved that we weren't powerless. It was the reaction of the Texas State Guard, in razing the city of Taos and murdering those who could not leave, which filled our ranks. With each act of Texan barbarity, more freedom fighters join us. By the cruelties inflicted by an illegal, hostile force on our own soil, they have ensured a hatred that generations will not dilute.

Shewolfhound: Was Taos the headquarters for the resistance movement? Did its destruction hamper your movement?

321DrX: On the contrary. We live in New Mexico. This is our headquarters.

Shewolfhound: In contrast to your military operations, your calls for civil disobedience have failed. There was a general strike called for February 14, Valentine's Day. It was announced on Radio KAOS and its sister website. Yet across the territory only a handful of people stayed home from work. Those who participated have all been arrested and deported to Texas. Does that, again, point to the disconnect between your movement and the wishes of the people?

321DrX: It only points to the connection between poor people and their wish to eat. Unemployment is higher than it was during the Great Depression. Food has doubled in price, water has gone up 1000% in some areas. There will be virtually no agriculture this year, which means even higher food prices. People can't even grow gardens. It is hard to be brave on an empty stomach. Even if the people of New Mexico believe in the rightness of the strikes, it is too much to risk the little wage they draw. You have to remember, New Mexicans have such an inborn skepticism that they regard the very concept of "truth" with cynicism. This, I think, is the great casualty of our era.

Shewolfhound: A decidedly post-modern lens to look through. Returning to the question, besides apathy, do you think the particular violence of your actions is frightening off would-be supporters?

321DrX: The "particular violence" of Texas is what precipitated our movement. Like Mao wrote, "the population is the sea in which the guerilla fish swim."

Shewolfhound: Can you give us an idea as to the size of your movement? Which social classes fill its ranks and support you the most?

```
[5 minutes idle]
```

Shewolfhound: Dr. X? You are still logged on with us. Are we still conducting this interview?

321DrX: I agreed to this interview after we checked out your site and past columns and interviews. And yet I distinctly get the feeling that you are trying to entrap me.

Shewolfhound: I am a journalist, and my search for Truth sometimes forces me to ask penetrating and probing questions. I am as objective as I can be (within my particular socio-economic, gendered, sexually oriented etc paradigm) and I am neither your friend nor your enemy.

321DrX: Very well, Shewolfhound. I am in favor of probing and penetrating, especially if it's the truth you're after. However, please no more questions that, as we previously discussed, I am not able to answer.

Shewolfhound: To give the readers of this a better idea of what your movement has accomplished, could you describe the operations you have undertaken, without discussing specific operations themselves?

321DrX: I am all for publicity of our rampant successes, I just can't tell you which bale of hay I'm sleeping in tonight. A comfortable bed, by the way. So far our campaign is responsible for theft, homicide, kidnapping, bombing, sedition and, of course, conspiracy. All of which are justified by the Geneva Convention and U.S. Rules of Occupation as legitimate reprisals for the illegal conduct of the enemy.

Shewolfhound: The governing authority accuses you of illegal conduct.

321DrX: Deportation is illegal conduct, as is economic depredation, confiscation of property immaterial to war, arson and using deadly force against unarmed civilians. All forbidden by both customary and conventional law.

Shewolfhound: Can you speak to the critics of your actions, among them a large number of noted humanitarians such as Bono, who condemn the violence of your campaign irregardless of political justifications?

321DrX: In theory, you don't need the bullet when you've got the ballot. But the elections have been postponed, and if I may quote Carlos Marighella, "It is a farce to vote in any elections which have as their sole objective the survival of the dictatorship and covering up of its crimes."

Shewolfhound: The elections re-scheduled for March have been postponed ostensibly because of the actions of your insurgency. Would you stop your crusade of homeland terrorism if elections were held?

321DrX: They are stealing and deporting and killing. It's too late for elections now. Doesn't Bono care about that? Isn't our blood innocent as well?

Shewolfhound: There has been an effort to portray you as a cult leader, and your followers as backwoods militia-types. Oklahoma City and Waco are mentioned frequently. Does this bother you?

321DrX: There was even one, can't remember which online rag, brought up the Unabomber. No, it doesn't bother me. If Texas claims that we're a cult, so be it. That's pretty transparent though, don't you think?

Shewolfhound: Are you critical of Federal policy as regards New Texas?

321DrX: What policy? The time to act was before it got too late.

Shewolfhound: Do you mean before the invasion, or before your insurgency began its campaign?

321DrX: I mean before we sucked all the water out of this desert to feed sprawling cities and golf courses. Like Edward Abbey wrote, "There is no lack of water here, unless you try to establish a city where no city should be."

Shewolfhound: What could the President or Congress do to hasten peace in New Texas?

321DrX: With all U.S. military overseas, all we can hope for now is economic pressure on Texas to quit its claim for New Mexico. The federal government was so intent on getting their nuclear facilities back – Kirtland, White Sands, Sandia Labs and LANL – that they gave us up in the bargain.

Shewolfhound: When will you lay down your arms?

321DrX: When Texas leaves. Once you begin a guerilla war, only victory or death are the possible outcomes.

Shewolfhound: Do you acknowledge that, by your own actions in this "guerilla war," innocent U.S. civilians have been killed?

321DrX: I acknowledge that innocent people fall every day, as unremarked upon as ants. That some might die as martyrs is likely no consolation to their loved ones.

Shewolfhound: Finally, Dr. X. Are you a terrorist or a patriot?

321DrX: As always, that depends on who is telling the tale.

Shewolfhound: Thank you for participating in this exclusive News Noose interview. Do you have a closing statement?

321DrX: Yes, words of warning from two guerilla leaders. The first is:

> "I will march your troops until their legs become the size of their bodies. You will not have a blade of grass, nor a drop of water: I shall hear you every time your drum beats, but you shall not know where I am."

The second is:

> "These mountains are the basis of my plan ... they are full of natural fonts where one man for defense will be equal to one hundred for attack; they are full also of good hiding places, where large numbers of brave men could be concealed, and baffle and elude pursuit for a long time."

Shewolfhound: Interesting. Who are those quotes from?

321DrX: One quotation is from John Brown, the other is from Hyder Ali.

Shewolfhound: Who is Hyder Ali?

321DrX: For more information, visit your local library. They're all closed here. Remember, learning is fun because knowledge is power.

The attic was sunny, cozily half-finished. Hands suddenly covered his eyes – small hands, clean and light: Lilah's.

"Surprise!" Her voice. Other, heavier footsteps up the stairs. Birds outside.

Her palms were cupped over his closed eyes and his other senses took in her touch, the sound of her voice, her smell. She said. "Guess who."

"Um. Madame Bovary?"

"Nooo," breath on the back of his neck.

"Frida?"

Laughing, her hands were gone. Cool air on his eyelids suddenly red from the window's sunlight.

"Look," she said.

Eddie opened his eyes. Stuart stood there, holding a white t-shirt with a Zia Crossbones blazoned on the front.

"What the hell is that?" Eddie heeled himself forward on the chair's wheels.

"Show him the back," said Lilah. She wore her rarest, most unguarded smile. The part in her hair was a razor line of clean brown skin, dark liquid curls diverging like the night ocean splitting over a reef. Her eyes of anticipatory glee.

Stuart flipped the t-shirt over. It read: "Once you begin a guerilla war, only victory or death are the possible outcomes." – Dr. X.

"What the hell?" asked Eddie, eyes quickly running up Lilah's tailored pants.

Stuart said, "You can buy them all over town. I think they started selling them in Santa Fe, but now they're everywhere."

"I don't understand. Did we ...?"

"No," said Lilah. "We don't have anyone doing this for us. Someone else is just making them. There's other ones, too."

"Poorer quality," sniffed Stuart. "Bad designs, poorly executed. But *this* is nice. Good screens, well-printed – that's a commitment to excellence. This one is yours."

Eddie caught the t-shirt and spread it across his knees.

"Happy birthday," said Lilah.

Eddie looked up sharp. "How did you know it's my birthday?"

"Because she is a *genius* sneak," said Stuart. "Look Li, he's blushing."

Lilah said, "That News Noose interview and the last few months of Radio KAOS have made you an icon. Sorry – they've made Dr. X an icon."

"This is ridiculous," said Eddie, reading his quoted words on the back of the shirt. "I was just paraphrasing Che, you know."

Clomping of heavy soles ascending the stairs.

"Lesbianism's answer to Nijinsky," said Stuart.

"I heard that, sissy," said Joanna, reaching the top of the stairs. She had a newspaper under her arm. "You guys didn't lock the door. Anyone could've walked up here."

"Oh, we kept an eye on the thing," dismissed Stuart, waving his hand at the security monitor: in grainy black and white it showed the front half of the Wayward Sparrow. "The fright buzzer never went off. We knew it was you."

"It coulda been a surprise raid. Keep the goddamn door locked."

Eddie said, "Is that a newspaper?"

"Yeah," said Joanna. "It started today, just this one, the *New Texas News*. Buncha crap, but look at the headline, Li."

Lilah took the newspaper and unfolded it. She read aloud, "Terrorist Ambush in Tijeras Leaves Two Officers Dead, One Wounded."

"No shit," said Eddie.

"We don't have any cells in Tijeras. Who did this?" said Joanna.

"If y'all gonna talk about your gangsta shit, I'm going downstairs to give Jonas a hand," said Stuart.

"Give Jonas a hand with his *penis*," said Eddie.

Stuart's cackle echoed in the stairwell.

"Lock the fucking door!" Joanna called after him.

Lilah looked up from the article, her perfect little glasses reflecting the sunlight through the window. "It says they have one in custody. A 'Tortilla Terrorist.' Damn that's offensive. Can they really write that?"

"Tsss." hissed Joanna, settling her weight into a chair. "What I'm worried about is, what if they make him talk?"

"Relax," said Eddie. "That's *why* they're in cells. They don't know any of the others, or from where their orders come. It's an internet blind drop. Radio KAOS gives them the information to access an online account and read emails saved as drafts. Interception systems to monitor traffic are useless because the emails are never sent."

"He's not one of ours. That order did not come from us," said Lilah, shaking her curls over her trim shoulders.

"Well we're getting blamed for it," said Joanna.

"We're getting the *credit* for it," stressed Eddie. "This is good. Every little thing helps to make it seem like we're everywhere. An insurgency is armed theater."

"No," said Joanna. "It makes us look like psychos. Somebody shoots up some cops and they blame us. It's gonna bring heat from the cops. They've stayed out of our way mostly. That'll be over now. Just getting pulled over for speeding could ..."

"The police just enforce the law. They don't make it," said Lilah.

"Same as soldiers, Guardsmen, whatever," said Joanna, seductively pulling a chocolate bar our of her jeans pocket.

"No," said Lilah. "The Guardsmen are enforcing an illegal occupation. The police enforce the laws that keep society from tearing itself apart."

"It *is* torn apart. Shit, it was never together. You're only saying that because your cousin is a cop," said Joanna, tearing the wrapper with her teeth.

"No, because it's true." Lilah pinched a wine bottle in her arm, wiggling at the half-tucked cork. "Is that glass clean, Eddie?"

"Um, well ... I used it for orange juice. Yesterday."

Lilah took the glass and open bottle to the attic's tiny bathroom. Leaving the door open, she washed the glass and filled it with wine.

Joanna bellowed, "It's a little early to start drinking, don't you think, Li?"

She glanced at them through the mirror and took a defiant mouthful. She poured another glass and returned to her leather armchair on little pink toes.

"Whatever," sighed Joanna, biting into chocolate. "But I'm worried about our internal security. All the publicity is good for recruitment, but with this extra heat ... I'm always thinking someone is following me. You know?"

"Yes. Recruiting moles is a danger. But your girls – sorry, womyn – are doing well at sifting the applicants. They are an excellent litmus test of fealty."

"You can always trust a stripper," said Lilah. "No one reads a man better. That's why they're perfect interrogators for recruits."

Eddie said, "Security is something we should be concerned with always, but the worst they could do is rupture one of our cells. As far as we are concerned – as far as Dr. X is concerned – nobody can make a connection to another cell."

"Unless they come *here*, and search this place," said Joanna.

Lilah bolted her entire glass of wine.

Eddie pretended to not notice. "Even if they did, everything is written in code. One bottle house wine means one explosive device, Brazilian Santos means Radio KAOS MP3's and all that. With everything stored in internet blind drops, they could seize the computers and find nothing to imply that this is anything but a lovely café."

Joanna said, "But you're building bombs and planting them in public. Someone will see you, sometime. And then they'll follow you here. Right?"

In the deep-backed leather armchair, Lilah crossed one leg over her knee, revealing a slim smooth ankle celebrated by a gold chain. A bit dreamily she said, "Where's your friend Gordon?"

"I don't think he's coming to any more meetings. He was paranoid before all this started, so you can imagine how he is now. He's happier doing the DJ stuff and the computer work for Radio KAOS by himself in the dark."

"Suits me," said Joanna.

"Does he know that today's your birthday?" asked Lilah.

"No. I don't really ... go in for all that."

"Is it your birthday?" asked Joanna.

"It is," said Lilah. "Maybe we should all go out? It's been ages since I had any fun. Now we have an excuse. And Eddie's going out in the field tomorrow."

"We have to get through this meeting first," said Joanna. "Running this whole Dr. X thing is getting hairier and hairier. We shouldn't be seen in public together."

"The News Noose website claims half a million hits on that interview," said Eddie. "They want to do another."

"Half a mil? In a month?" Joanna whistled low.

"Practically a household name. Among New Mexican households with satellite internet, anyway," said Eddie.

"Well maybe this time," said Joanna, shifting her thighs, "you should do it better, and listen to us before you type in shit that's going to be seen by half a million people."

"It was good," said Lilah.

"It was ok. But he went off on his own with some of that. Like, what the fuck was up with correcting her English all the time, and showing off with those big words? And you didn't talk about half the shit we had planned."

"I was in the moment," grinned Eddie. "I was *feeling* the Dr. X."

Joanna said, "Everyone knows Dr. X is a man from that. A woman could tell."

"I'm not sure we can trust that interviewer. Too ... I don't know," said Lilah.

Eddie said, "Yeah, but even if it's bulletproof General Armstrong himself, even if the number of hits is cooked up, the results are indisputable. People are printing up Dr. X *t-shirts*, for fuck's sake."

"And making attacks on local police in his name," said Lilah from deep down in her chair. She tipped her glass, tongue to the last drop.

"Maybe we should get to what we came here to talk about. The problem with money. As in, we don't have any," said Joanna.

"We could kidnap another executive," said Eddie.

Joanna said, "It's too dangerous. The phone calls and the drop-off. You said they almost got busted last time."

Eddie scratched his scruffy neck. "I could plan it out better, this time."

"All the cafés are doing well, considering," said Lilah.

Joanna shook her head. "You're bleeding your businesses dry."

"I could always sell my house in La Cienaga," said Lilah.

"No you couldn't. Real estate ain't worth shit these days," said Joanna.

Lilah's hand fished the floor for the wine bottle and found the neck. "It's got all that water though."

"Joanna's right," said Eddie. "You'd be better to keep drawing the steady monthly rent off that, rather than negotiate a depressed market."

"Speaking of steady monthlies," said Lilah, pouring herself more wine. "I feel like crap."

"Really? You're early. We're not on until the twenty-first," said Joanna.

"Tell my stomach muscles that," Lilah said, setting the bottle down. She took a big mouthful of wine. "Mm. Go find some glasses, someone, and join me. We can toast Eddie's birthday."

"We could always sell drugs," said Eddie.

"That crack you make? No thanks," Joanna scowled.

"Look, it isn't crack. It's more like ... weaponized adrenalin," said Eddie.

"That's a great selling point. We can put that on the chalkboard, just below the soup du jour," said Lilah.

"Which is, today, beer-cheese soup. And it is delicious. Sara is serving it with bread from le Petit Bebé bakery." Eddie licked his lips in remembrance. "Anyway, we could use inactive cells to distribute the product."

"No, no, no. They'd get arrested and blow our cover," Joanna said.

"It needlessly complicates everything," said Lilah. "And you need to be doing your thing, not cooking up speed in your hovel."

"We'll just have to keep our belts drawn tightly then," said Eddie. "Like Che Guevara said, 'My slogan is little baggage, strong legs and a *fakir*'s stomach'."

"What about the bees? Are you still drawing that one up?" sneered Joanna.

"Well. An *Apis* bomb is a lot more elegant than poisoning bottled water," said Eddie. "That's so razor-blades-in-apples-on-Halloween."

Joanna said, "But going after the drinking water that they're importing ... it gets right to the issue. It's artistic, because it will make people think."

"It will make them think we *are* a doomsday cult or al Qaeda or whatever," said Eddie. "It's indiscriminate. It could easily hurt the wrong people."

Relaxing into her wine-warm limbs, Lilah said, "We can't be the bad guys. I don't want, like, my grandmother to be scared of *us*."

"You read the paper," said Joanna. "We already *are* the bad guys. If we're gonna get blamed every time some flat-Earth survivalist shoots a sheriff – if we're gonna be called terrorists, we might as well *do* some terrorizing. You want terror? Make people think their water is poisoned. That's terror."

Eddie said, "Aside from ethical quandries, we don't have the capability to do that on the scale you're talking about. The danger of arrest is too high."

Lilah said, "What will they do if they catch one of us, somehow?"

No one said anything.

"Nevermind. Sorry," said Lilah, leaning for the wine bottle. The frown of her wine-rich lips ... trembled?

"Well," sighed Eddie. "PATRIOT V legalized torture for interrogating terrorists, so we should assume the worst. Deny everything. Admit nothing. Pretend to faint. Hunger is supposed to help you withstand torture better. I read that, but I hope it remains in the realm of the theoretical for me."

Joanna awkwardly patted Lilah's arm. "Li, they're not going to catch any of us."

Lilah said, "If we had to escape, what would we do? Stay together? Split up? The businesses are in my name. I would lose them, wouldn't I?"

Eddie said, "We could probably get into Colorado, maybe."

"And then what?" pressed Lilah.

"I don't know. Gordon told me there's word that the old New Mexico Defense Force is re-forming somewhere in southern Colorado with the help of local militias."

Joanna snorted. "Under that same idiot? Camby? Leading a bunch of kooks?"

Lilah said, "But is that it? Just keep fighting? What if they never leave?"

"They'll leave. We'll make them leave," soothed Joanna.

"It's starting to work," said Eddie. "I've got a brand new t-shirt that proves it."

Lilah smiled.

Eddie said, "We just need to be cautious and clever. 'Know thyself and know thy enemy, and in a thousand battles ye shall be victorious.' Sun Tzu."

Lilah said, "But there's more Guardsmen around then ever."

"If a guerilla force is surviving, it is winning. Time is our weapon. Like the mujahideen say, 'The Americans may own all the watches, but we own all the time.' The more they spread themselves out, the easier it is to surprise a weak link. These Guardsmen out here, most wouldn't graduate from the police academy. They're weekend warriors, you know? Bi-monthly bullies. They want to go home. All we really have to do is make life unbearable for them. They'll start to desert."

"And until then we have to live like this? The stress is eating me up." "We haven't slowed them down at all. We're talking about people that took Karma and killed her, just because she's a pit bull. They're raping New Mexico, and you're all proud of your coded phone numbers," said Joanna, passion flaring. "Our main problem isn't going to go away. We're running out of money."

Eddie said, "I'll talk to Gordon about raising online donations, like the jihadis."

Lilah sighed pointedly. She tipped her glass back, swallowed. They waited for her to speak. She pulled on her socks and one boot, then the other. Finally she said, "Sorry, but I'm not feeling well. All this ... stuff is giving me a headache. Can we call it quits for tonight?"

"We haven't decided on anything yet, honey," said Joanna.

"There's nothing to decide, not yet," said Eddie. "I'm going out in the field tomorrow morning. I'll do some thinking out there, maybe come up with something. A kidnapping maybe, if I planned it better ..."

Lilah stood up, stopped to steady herself on the chair's arm. The glass fell from her hand and smashed on the floor. "Shit."

"I'll get it," said Eddie, rooting under the desk for the dust pan.

Joanna helped Lilah to the stairs, firing a hard look at Eddie that he blinked away. She soothed, "Come on Li, let's get you home."

Eddie brushed up the glass as they descended the stairs. Lilah's voice echoed up, "Eddie, happy birthday."

"Thanks," Eddie called back. He emptied the dust pan into the trash. Then he sat for a while in his chair, smoothing out the folds of his Dr. X t-shirt.

He put himself in bed early that night. But he could not sleep. He tried to jerk off thinking about anyone but Lilah. But he failed, and it was into her phantom body he detonated. And wrapping himself around her phantom body, he fell asleep.

Too late, Eddie realized that the traffic jam wasn't caused by construction or an accident: a Texas State Guard checkpoint. It wasn't the March sun that brought sweat to his palms. Time to think – the string of trucks and cars were being thoroughly examined. Nowhere to run – concrete dividers hemmed the lanes.

Most of the guns have already gone up. They're going to wonder about all the water and dried food though, and that might inspire them to look deeper in the bed to find fertilizer, jellied ethanol and my notebooks. But it's ok. It's ok. You're bad bad Eddie Brown, the baddest man in this whole town.

The brown earth was hard and dry. Desiccated cheat grass buzzed, stiff in the wind. Eddie sneezed. Twice. Moaning, he pulled a length of toilet paper from the roll on the dashboard. He blew his nose: running clear. He muttered, "Fucking juniper."

Ahead, vehicles crawled through the checkpoint one at a time. The occupants had to stand outside, blasted by the wind. Semi-automatic weapons whispered panic, run away. The Guardsmen searched thoroughly, as if looking for something specific.

Something specifically like the contents under the camper shell of this truck.

"No, it's ok," Eddie said aloud, "I can talk my way through this."

Even with the wind, car exhaust was piling up on the road, leaking through the vents. Eddie turned on the capricious air conditioner to recirculate what little fresh air he had. Between the exhaust and the juniper, *his asthma was just starting to squeeze. Come on, now's not a good time. Just breathe Eddie, nice and easy. You're just sitting patiently in your truck, not running a marathon. Just breathe, nice and easy.*

He idled ahead as cars were passed through the cattle pen of concrete barriers. Only one truck ahead now, a green SUV. He ran one last mental check on the contents of his truck. The Guard didn't seem to have dogs which was good, very good.

Edddie coughed up a gluey gallon of merc. Where to spit? Out the window? No good. Liberating to let the gob drop between his boots and mix with the dirt on the floor.

The SUV was waved ahead through the chute. A Guardsman in desert camo waved Eddie forward. Eddie pulled up, turned his truck off and opened the door. There was a gun barrel in his face. He stood with his hands up, blue wallet aloft. One Guardsman read the ID to a lieutenant named Springs, another walked around Eddie's truck with a telescopic mirror. The gun barrel remained twelve inches from Eddie's face.

Two more Guardsmen descended on Eddie's truck. One opened the cab, the other opened the tailgate with some difficulty. At last, Lt. Springs addressed Eddie directly: "Sir, do you have any weapons, explosives or radio transmitters in your vehicle?"

"No."

"Are you certain, sir? If my men find anything, I'll be mighty sore."

Eddie said, "No, there's nothing. I work for the New Mexico Zoological Park. They need me to go out and do some field research."

"What kind of research? Sir?"

"Ants."

"Ants?" The puzzlement was typed onto the lieutenant's face.

"Ants," said Eddie. "Specifically, *Solenopsis invicta.* The imported fire ant."

"Shit," said Lt. Springs. "You mean them little red ones come up from South America? The killer ants that eats babies that falls on their hive?"

"Yes," said Eddie. "Exactly. I'm going to bring a colony back to the zoo and put them on display. So that the children may learn."

"Who the hell wants to learn about killer ants?"

A Guardsman pulled Eddie's temporary parking pass from his blue wallet. "It checks out sir, this is from the zoo."

Eddie said, "Ants can be fascinating. For example, there's a type of army ant that is actually able to build bridges out of – "

"Sir!" came a shout from the Guardsman heels-deep in the pickup's bed.

"What is it Corporal?" said Lt. Springs, jaw hardening.

The Guardsman shimmied out of the truck and saluted the officer. "Sir, there's a lot of water containers in there, as well as some fertilizer and other chemicals, and some sort of chemistry equipment."

Lt. Springs stared down hard into Eddie's eyes.

Eddie said, "I need that for my research."

"Fertilizer, sir? You're not planning on building any bombs now, are you?"

"No, no," chuckled Eddie. "That's for transporting the ant colony safely back to the zoo. The nitrogen-rich soil acts as a natural narcotic sedative on the ants. I mean, you don't think I want them killer ants getting *loose*, do you?"

Lt. Springs stared down hard into Eddie's eyes. Then he looked past Eddie to the endlessly long line of cars stretching back down the highway.

"Ants," Lt. Springs said, shaking his head. "All right, get on."

Eddie took back his wallet and climbed into his truck. He started it. Lt. Springs was saying, "Heads up on this one boys, looks like we got a lot of spics in the backseat" as Eddie drove through the chute and out onto a wide-open road.

After passing through the village of Villanueva, Eddie took the dirt road that ran through BLM land. This home stretch always took longer than he expected and was hell on the pickup. The Pecos cut its deep canyon through layered rock. Eddie took it slow, watching for trouble. The junipers were thick and pollen stuck to his windshield. Eddie was sneezing and blowing his nose, banging down the road at fifteen miles an hour.

At last he came to the turn-off that would take him down to the river. There didn't seem to be any fresh tire marks. Eddie chewed his lip, rumbling slowly towards the stand of cottonwoods ahead. Eddie stopped the pickup in the cool shade and listened for a moment: birds. High flying airplane or the sound of the river? Wind in the trees and grass. Birds.

He got out, stretched. Around the back he dragged two five-gallon water jugs onto the lowered gate. He removed the camouflage tarpaulin that had been under the jugs, unfolding and tossing it over his pickup. Eddie slipped his backpack onto his shoulders, grabbed the jug handles and heaved off. He bore the weight in his calves and forearms as he began his ascent through the cottonwoods. Immediately his lungs started burning.

Fuck.

Eddie forced his feet to climb the narrow path. Each breath was shorter and tighter than the last, his eyesight began to tunnel so he set the jugs down and took two blasts from his inhaler. He turned around to measure his progress. About twenty feet. "This is gonna take me until the Rapture," Eddie said. From his slight increase in altitude he could see the river's surface through the tree trunks. The far canyon wall was barren naked like a geography textbook.

A sudden dog came barking, crashing through the undergrowth – Eddie dropped his inhaler. The dog stopped at the top of a boulder, black face bisected by a white blaze, showing its teeth. High dry growl.

"It's me, Roscoe. Come say hi."

The dog closed his mouth but continued to stare with intent rigidity. Then his ears pricked and rotated back. The dog scrambled down the backside of the boulder and appeared on the path, grinning and ramming his nose into Eddie's crotch.

"Oof. Ok, that's a good boy Roscoe. Oof, that's a good dog."

A form disengaged from the deep shadows at the edge of the tree line. It was Jimbo. He waved a green kerchief towards the cave up above, then stepped down the path towards Eddie.

Roscoe leapt away from Eddie and raced up the path to Jimbo, wagging his scimitar tail. Jimbo wore hunter's camo, slung rifle. He was smiling. Stepping heavily down the path he said, "Roscoe heard you way up the road. I sat right there, watched you come in. Waited til you was close before I released Roscoe. You know, practice."

"It worked," said Eddie, bending down to slip the inhaler into his pocket. "I nearly crapped myself."

Jimbo laughed, stuck out a big hand for Eddie to shake. "That's good. Called him off with this," lifting a silver dog whistle off his necklace.

"He takes whistle commands, huh? Smart dog."

Jimbo patted tongue-lolling Roscoe on the head. "Border collie. Smartest goddamn dog ever made. Smarter'n most people you meet. The other guys are coming down to get the stuff from the truck. You all good, Dr. X?"

"Yeah. There was a checkpoint on the highway but they let me through."

"Shit, that's no good. What if you'd been popped?"

"Never," said Eddie. "I just told them these weren't the droids they were looking for. Having Roscoe come roaring down on me was a lot more intimidating."

Carlos and Freddy were highly visible against the sun-bleached sandstone, hiking the narrow rock path from the cave's dark mouth. Eddie felt the tension in his chest easing by the time they finally attained the edge of the woods. They marched down the steep dark path; Roscoe joyously ran to welcome them. They shook hands with Eddie, commented on the fair weather.

Carlos said, "How's the war going?"

"It's going well. We're winning. They just don't know it yet," said Eddie.

Freddy smiled – was he blushing? Or just the heat? Eddie found himself staring at the geometry of Freddy's cheekbones so he said, "There's two loads for us to get up into the cave and then that's it, this cache is fully stocked. I'll wait for you at the edge of the trees up there, and then we'll run across that open stretch of cliff all together."

Freddy said, "We're pretty safe I think. Haven't seen nobody in a week."

"Except them rafters," corrected Carlos.

"Yeah, but they really *was* rafters. They were too busy paddling over the rocks, with the river so low, to be looking up," said Freddy.

Eddie said, "By all rights we should be doing this last load at night, like we did the others. But it's too dangerous, not being able to see. Long fall to the river."

"Probably lose some speed against the bigger rocks and cholla," said Jimbo. "Likely lose some mass on the way, too."

Eddie smiled. "Plus, you boys have been in a hard week alone out here and I know you want to get back to your homes as soon as possible. Take a bath, screw your wife. Or somebody else's wife. So let's get this over with."

Eddie exhausted himself, carrying the jugs up the path to the edge of the woods. He was grateful for the chance to regain his breath while they caught up with him. The rest of the way was going to be a bitch. A narrow foot path scrambled steeply up the cliff face to the cave. The mouth was shadowed by the mesa's overhang. Not only would they be completely exposed performing some very suspicious activity, the path was cut with dangerous footing. Carlos had nearly gone down the cliff on the night of the first load. He would have taken their only two AR-15s with him, and two hundred dollars worth of ammunition.

The others made it to Eddie's position. They stopped to wipe sweat off their foreheads. Freddy said, "Sweat like pigs in the day, freeze at night."

"It ain't the Ritz, that's for sure," said Eddie.

"Ritz hell," said Carlos. "You haven't smelled these two all week. Plus the dog."

"Dogs don't sweat, man," said Jimbo.

"Actually they do, but they only have functional sweat glands on their nose, toes and anus," said Eddie. "And on that note, let's get going."

The first load was water. They huffed and swore the entire steep hundred yards, with eighty pounds swinging at the ends of their arms. Eddie's lungs cauterized shut but he fought on, wheezing and kicking rocks ahead of him. When he looked up, the cave mouth was no closer. The pain was hot and sharp, his forearms burned, his fingers were cramped claws, the loose footing set him stumbling dangerously.

But he made it to the mouth and lugged the jugs inside. Three feet into the cave, the temperature dropped. The others arrived one at a time in the overhang's shadow, backlit by the sun. They pushed the jugs deeper into the cave to make room for the next load.

It took them over an hour to finish. Deep in the cave, where it finally narrowed to an evil crease, they organized the cache. Their sweat had cooled so they returned to the mouth: crawling, stooping, finally able to stand.

"You've done a real good job," said Eddie. "Everything is secure, the cave is spotless and this cache could support a team for weeks."

"It's a good spot," nodded Carlos. "Even if they do find out where we're at, ain't no one gonna get up that cliff. One man with a rifle could hold off all of Texas."

"That's the idea. Good job, Jimbo, telling me about this place. How many people around here know about it?"

"Most, I'd guess. When we was kids we sometimes came here to drink and try to screw girls," said Jimbo. "But this fella named Manly Stanley, he got bit on the ass by a rattler one night. The girl he was with ran away screaming so he had to get back to town by himself with an ass the size of a couch. After that he told everyone who would listen that he was gonna dynamite the whole rattlesnake den. We talked him out of that, on account it's probably some old Indian haunt and such, but no one comes here any more."

"You didn't tell me we was sleeping in a rattlesnake den," said Freddy.

"You didn't get bit, did you?" grinned Jimbo, rubbing Roscoe's dirty belly.

"Easy for you to say, you was sleeping down at the lookout point in the trees."

"It's too early for rattlesnakes at this altitude," said Eddie. "Soon, though."

They sat watching from the cave's mouth: down the steep-broke slope to the dark Pecos below, the far canyon wall ribboned in pink and brown, the mesa table lands, the distant range of mountains. Deep clear blue sky beyond.

Finally Eddie said, "All right gentlemen, you are discharged from your duties. I'll spend a couple nights here to make sure it's still secure. After that, no one is to come anywhere near here, until Radio KAOS contacts you by name. Your name is the Rattlesnakes, and this camp is going to be called Rattlesnake Den. How you fellas getting back to civilization?"

Freddy said, "There's a good place for crossing about a half mile downstream from here. Me and Carlos got my truck on the other side."

"Pretty good. Don't be seen leaving, right?"

"No problem, Dr. X," said Carlos, shaking Eddie's hand. "My grandmother was half-Apache."

"An honor to help out, Dr. X," said Freddy, lingering handshake. Then they hiked down across the cliff face and into the cottonwood stand, disappeared.

Eddie said, "What about you Jimbo? How are you getting home from here?"

"Well, actually, I wanted to talk to you about that. See those boys are younger, got family and friends and whatnot. But me – well it's just me and Roscoe. I ain't got no work I'm missing, I'm on Disability. Being out here is a helluva lot nicer than killing time in the trailer park, drinking my ass to death outta boredom. Roscoe likes it up here too, don't you Roscoe," looking down into Roscoe's upturned warm brown eyes. Jimbo shrugged his shoulders, still talking to his dog's eyes. "Being on guard duty – well, a dog with a job is a happy dog. And me too, I guess. I mean, I want those Texas fuckers out, they deported my stepson and he didn't *do* nothin, my ex said she can't write him or visit him at the jail in Texas. But also, shit, I'm just happy to have something to *do*. You know, something important. Something more important than me. Roscoe too. He knows this is what he's been training his whole life for."

"I know the feeling. So you want to stay out here on permanent guard duty? Because you would be stuck here, there'd be no coming and going."

Jimbo's eyes stayed linked with Roscoe's. "Well if that's ok with you Dr. X, yeah. Because it would be a shame if someone somehow stumbled onto our cache. And then it wouldn't be here when we needed it. I won't eat much of the food or water, and I already got plenty dog food for Roscoe."

"I think that's fine. I guess I'll swing back to resupply you when I can. Just make sure no one ever knows you're here. During daylight you need to be either inside the cave or in the cover of the trees. You can't let your trash or biological waste betray your presence. No fires of course, that has to remain in effect. And Roscoe can't bark."

"He don't bark unless I tell him to," said Jimbo. "Right, Roscoe?"

Roscoe thumped his white-tipped black scimitar tail against the cave floor.

"Well," said Eddie. "That's a good dog."

They watched the sun set from the cave's mouth, sitting cross-legged. For dinner they ate canned pasta, canned spinach, beef jerky and canned peaches for desert. Coyotes began howling on a mesa. Roscoe pricked his ears but didn't respond to the provocation.

In the quiet fading light, Jimbo said, "Don't feel like wartime here. River and trees don't care. When I left the service, I swore I'd never shoot at anything ever again, not even a bird. You knew I was in the service, right?"

Eddie said, "We talked about it when we met for the first time in O'Bryan's, for that rally against the deportations. But just a little bit."

Jimbo rubbed his dog's head. "Rangers. I parachuted into Panama City, Rio Hato Airport, December of '89. Operation Just Cause."

"Just Cause. That's a pretty cynical code name," Eddie said.

"Yup. Course, we didn't know it at the time. They said our Canal personnel was endangered, said this drug kingpin had stolen the election. Had to restore democracy, safeguard liberty, defend the hemisphere and all that. No one never said nothing about how our control of the Canal was expiring in *ten* days. They left that out of the briefings. Even newspapers left that, uh, motivating factor slip through unmentioned."

Eddie said, "And the fact that the drug kingpin had graduated from the School of the Americas at Fort Benning and was on the CIA's payroll."

"Yup, all that. And once we got over there ... they had us going through these slums, looking for remnants of the PDF, their little army. We had armor rolling through. Rumble alone knocked down their shacks. And then, if we made contact ... with our ordinance, it was like killing kittens with a rototiller. Rounds went *through* the sheet metal shacks and come out the other side not even slowed down. A lot of friendly fire casualties happened that way. And the people living in them slums, the poor people what didn't have nothing ... yeah, it was bad. It was real bad."

Eddie let the moment sit. Then, "You thought you were defending your country."

Jimbo rubbed his scratchy beard, dog hair catching in his bristles. "Yeah. It didn't make no sense, once we were on the ground. We killed a lot of people we never even saw. Not PDF, just people in the way. After my discharge, I swore I'd never ... but this is different. Isn't it? This is more like we're the Panamanians, or the Iraqis or Irish or whatever. And they're the bullies, you know? Backed up by lies."

"The Brazilian revolutionary Carlos Marighella wrote, 'this moral superiority is what sustains the urban guerilla'."

Roscoe nudged Jimbo for more petting. "How's it really going out there?"

Eddie brushed dirt from his palms. "Following the brutal tutelage of Mao Tse Tung: 'When they advance, we retreat. When they stop, we harry them. When they retreat, we advance.' Slowly but surely we're eroding their willpower, corrupting their supply lines. Out here, supply lines are more important than battles. Do you know what happened during the Civil War out here in New Mexico?"

"Nope. Didn't know they fought the war this far out here."

"It was the westernmost front of the war. Confederate Texas invaded the Territory of New Mexico to turn us into a slave state and to get access to California's ports on the Pacific. Most of our army was lost when, retreating from Mesilla, soldiers filled their canteens with whiskey rather than water."

Jimbo said, "That's smart."

Eddie continued, "They beat us decisively in every battle from Mesilla into Santa Fe. We were outnumbered, poorly equipped and incompetently led. But at the Battle of Glorieta Pass, even as exhausted Union forces were withdrawing, Major Chivington of the Colorado Volunteers led a small force in a flanking maneuver over the largest mesa in the Territory. They surprised the Texas wagon train and destroyed it. The Texans had to withdraw to Santa Fe, already exhausted of supplies. From there they withdrew to Albuquerque. There was no food or water left anywhere so they just kept withdrawing until they left the Territory altogether. They won every battle and lost the war for thirst."

Jimbo grunted. Then he said, "So how we gonna make that happen again?"

"I'm working on it. I'm working on it."

"Say, you got any more of them Radio KAOS MP3's? They really help pass the time, you know. I try to spare my batteries, and I don't listen when I'm on post, but..."

"I've got some in my truck. They're old, you know, from last week."

Jimbo said, "Don't matter to me. It's still news. And I like some of the music. It makes me feel connected to it, you know? And since you probably don't want me setting up no satellite dish right here..."

"Right," chuckled Eddie. "I'll make that part of the resupply, next time."

In the period of darkness before the moon rose, they carried their trash down the path. Eddie hiked back up into the cottonwoods, leaving Roscoe and Jimbo at their lookout in the trees: a pup tent on a flat mossy rock. Eddie took his time getting up the steep path to the cave but still needed a blast from his inhaler once he got there.

Lungs relaxing, the moon rose. Eddie bedded down on the cave floor. It *was* cold, and his nose stung. Moonlight in the canyon. River sound. It was so beautiful.

Eddie unlocked the front door and stepped in. The room had been avalanched with male-pattern debris. Beer, cola and water bottles castellated the coffee table. Pizza boxes were piled in the kitchen. The air smelled of cheese and perhaps old socks. Eddie tripped through heaps of computer magazines lining in the hallway. The bedroom door was locked. Good.

He could hear Gordon talking inside. Words were indistinct, but the voice rumbled and rose in pitch, then tipped back down into the rumble. The voice stopped for a moment and Eddie knocked three times. Inside, the squeak of chair wheels.

Eddie said, "It's me."

The lock clicked and the door was pulled inward. Gordon stood there, white belly hanging over boxer shorts, legs scaly with eczema. The wrinkles in his forehead smoothed out and he smiled, ushering Eddie in.

The humid bedroom was in worse shape than the living room. The computer desk was a ruin of CD piles, cookie boxes, and crumpled tissues. An army of energy drink cans had fallen out of rank and were lolling at ease on the floor. Eddie smiled at Gordon and waited until his friend turned away to glance at the open closet (dirty laundry on the floor, Gordon's one suit hanging).

"Sit down, Eddie. I need to get back to this," said Gordon. He sat into his wheeled chair and pulled himself up to the computer.

Eddie pushed a pile of dirty socks and frozen burrito wrappers off the folding chair and sat next to Gordon. His pale naked shoulders and back were splotched, with pimples puckering the skin. Eddie took as shallow breaths as he dared and focused his attention on Gordon's computer screen. The pointer flew among the layers of windows, highlighting and dragging.

"How far have you – " began Eddie but Gordon raised a "wait" finger. Eddie's eyebrows went up like drawn crossbows, but Gordon wasn't watching.

He was leaning into the microphone and then the *voice*: "Hey now, this is Radio KAOS coming at you, the shoutbox for the Zia Crossbones network. We hope you enjoyed that speech by the late, great Hugo Chavez as we continue today's theme of great martyrs. Here's some serious Afrobeat to make you groove, grieve and grow righteous. Fela Kuti performing 'Coffin for Head of State' on Radio KAOS, where music is the weapon."

Gordon leaned back, clicking through windows. He turned to Eddie. "I have to get this song off my zip, so I can give you a sec – hey, your chair leg is on my set list."

Eddie looked down and indeed his chair leg was tearing a hole in a piece of handwritten paper. He pulled it out and handed it to Gordon, who filed the paper neatly beneath his keyboard.

"So what's the rumpus, Dr. X?" rumbled Gordon.

"Are you going to use that voice to talk to me?"

"Sorry," said Gordon, voice flattening out nasally. "I want to stay in character."

"Even Wolfman Jack relaxed the lycanthropy after hours. I'm here because I need to send a message: Catamounts assemble at Crossburning, Orange Hour. Got it? Do it for seven days. Post a bulletin on the sites, too."

"Sure, I haven't uploaded this KAOS set. The message will make tonight's webcast. So, thy will be done," said Gordon dramatically.

"Can I take some hard copies?" pointing to a bakery-fresh stack of MP3s.

"Well you *can*, but I wish you wouldn't. I mean, if you've can-celled the mobile radio teams, it doesn't seem any safer to be carrying around hard copies of Radio KAOS. I just mean, with you being" *il sotto* "Dr. X and all."

"Safety first, my fur-bearing mammal. But I have some friends without internet access who are inspired by the great work you're doing here."

"I'm not going to argue with you. I have to get back to work to get this done in time for tonight. I'll paste that message throughout the set. See you tomorrow?"

"Yes, tomorrow. I'll bring breakfast or dinner, whichever it may be. Green chile on the side?"

Eddie let himself out of Gordon's apartment. He drove cir-cuitously to Nob Hill, parked on a side street and walked to the Wayward Sparrow, making certain no one was following him. The air smelled of Spring – from what Eddie could absorb through his allergy-clogged nose.

Inside the Wayward Sparrow, the sound of traffic was muted. *Astral Weeks* was playing softly. Joanna was behind the counter. The ring under her septum trembled when she sneered her greeting.

"One pressekönnu of Icelandic Roast, please," said Eddie, handing her a ten.

"Fine," said Joanna. She rang him up, slapped the change on the counter. She filled the french press with coarse grounds, boiling water. Eddie discreetly tipped her jar.

Picking up the mug and coffee press in one hand, Eddie asked, "Any sugar?"

"Cream and sugar are waiting. Above the counter. You're late."

Eddie poured a little pitcher of cream for himself, pinky hooking it level to the mug. He weaved through the café. The thick carpet gave way to warped hardwood at the kitchen doors. Eddie unlocked an unpainted door and slipped in, locking it behind him. He walked slowly up the stairs to keep the cream from spilling. At the top of the stairs he smiled his entrance at Stuart and Lilah, seated at the computer desk.

"Hello cream and sugar. Lids is here," said Eddie.

"You're late, lids," Lilah said.

"I know, and cups reminded me. She's doing a very convincing job of treating me like a manager she hates."

"She puts the 'bull' in bulldyke," quipped Stuart.

"That's an old one, Stuart. Sit down Eddie, we need to get started," said Lilah.

Eddie set his coffee clutch on the floor and arranged himself cross-legged behind it. "How's the sugar, sugar?"

Lilah said, "Sugar is kind of stressed at the moment."

"What's the matter?" Eddie plunged down the coffee press and poured the mug.

"Nothing with our thing. But we turned on the swamp cooler for the first time. It put out a smell like rotten underpants. We need a new one before Summer."

"And she doesn't have the money," finished Stuart.

"It's just that the accounting is confusing, between the three busi-nesses and all the black hole budgeting. I'm not sure what's real any-more. If I get audited this year..."

Stuart said, "They wouldn't dare trifle with you, a lipstick lez. However, it is my contention that 'bisexuality' is simply greed. Wouldn't you all agree?"

Eddie said, "Sexual omnivorousness is just good math. She sticks with the vagitarians, you're with the cockovores. Whereas I, at the top of the food chain, enjoy all the meats in the great genital cook-off."

Lilah rubbed her temples.

Eddie said, "Seriously Lilah, when this mission is completed you'll have enough money for ten swamp coolers, each one more power-ful than the last."

Stuart said, "No talk about your gangsta shit while I'm here, remember?"

"All that is required of you, cabrón, is to disguise Eddie," said Lilah.

"It's a costume, not a disguise," sniffed Stuart. He walked to the closet and paused for effect before opening the closet door. He reached in, producing ... khaki pants. "Ta-*da*. These are convertible pants, with zip-off legs."

"I already have a pair of those," said Eddie.

"Of course you do," said Stuart, returning the pants to the closet.

Lilah snickered and, unaccountably, Eddie felt his neck and cheeks blush tinglingly. Stuart was squatting low and produced "a pair of leather sandals to be worn with white socks."

"Hm," said Eddie.

Stuart was busy behind the closet door.

"What's taking so long? This is where 'closet' jokes come from," said Eddie.

"Now, accessories," said Stuart, first pointing each out in turn, "gold wedding band, ugly gold watch, *de rigeur* fanny pack, big cheap belt buckle, shapeless sun hat with a Kokopelli-motif brim, dark sunglasses and a digital camera around your neck in a bright turquoise soft case."

"Is that my digital camera?" Lilah asked, pink tongue at the floor of her mouth.

"He doesn't have one Li, and I need mine for work. You want I should blow my meager costume budget on a new camera?"

Lilah said, "Yeah, but ... it's got pictures on it already, I need to erase them. In case, you know ... well if it gets lost at the scene, or something."

"There's a brand new card in it. Your card is at my place for safekeeping. I enjoyed the slideshow, mind. You're quite the petite athletique, I had no idea."

"Shut up Stuart," said Lilah, sipping from a glass of wine no one saw her pour. "He isn't serious, Eddie."

"Ha, look at his face! Now the – attention *please*, thank you ... and now, *le mot juste*," said Stuart, reaching into the closet...

"There is absolutely no clown-fucking way I'm wearing that shirt. Not for a disguise, not for a costume. No."

Stuart spokesmodeled the shirt. "But it is *so* hideously perfect. It boldly announces: I like chile peppers, and I like people *knowing* that I like chile peppers."

"Abso-fucking-lutely not," said Eddie gravely.

Stuart said, "Please? Look at how it incorporates the theme of chile peppers into the buttons ... *hmmm*?"

Lilah said, "I told you he wouldn't wear it. Show him the other one. It's better. More discrete, anyway."

Stuart made a face and tossed the offending shirt into the closet. He unfolded a khaki t-shirt that read, "Lonestar Mortgage of El Paso

BBQ Rib Cook-Off, 2003."

"Isn't that perfect?" asked Lilah.

"It's brilliant," said Eddie. "Absolutely brilliant. Where'd you find it?"

"In the racks at the secondhand stores, just like all this stuff," said Stuart. "You just have to have the *eye* to ... anyway, I love the other shirt like I love my mother's butch girlfriend, but I must admit the khaki-on-khaki is a strong effect. Just make sure you wash it, iron it as if your own was wife doing it, and make sure it's tucked in. Keep those pants riding high and tight. Show off those socks. And you know what else? Li, if he won't wear the shirt, he at least has to wear the pin. Right? You think?"

"What pin?" asked Eddie.

"This," said Stuart, holding up a jalapeño pin.

"Uhhh," stalled Eddie, looking to Lilah. She was biting her wineglass in smile at him. "Ok, it's a deal. I'll wear the pin."

"Uh oh," said Stuart, alarm rising in his voice. "Lookit, the red light is on!"

Eddie and Lilah turned: the red light was burning red. In the security monitor, a police officer was at the counter. Joanna was shaking her head no at him.

"I knew breaking those mirrors would be bad luck," said Stuart.

"Shh, quiet down, it's ok. Shush now," said Eddie.

Stuart shut the closet door and covered it with his body.

"Stop banging around Stuart, just sit down where you are," said Eddie. "We are simply in the middle of a normal business meeting. You two just keep an eye on the monitor. I'm going to check the back window."

Eddie stepped lightly on the creaking attic floorboards.

Lilah said, "Joanna just gave him a cup of coffee."

"Good," said Eddie, sneaking up on the window frame. Keeping himself in shadow, he peeped down alley behind the Sparrow. "There's no one in the back. I don't think this is a raid."

Stuart said, "He's reaching for – what's he doing?"

Lilah said, "Relax, he's paying. There, see? He's leaving. Joanna turned the light off. All right? He just wanted a cup of coffee."

"You do have good coffee," said Eddie, returning to his spot on the floor.

Stuart brushed lint from his tight corduroy pants. "I don't like being involved in these ... stakeouts or whatever. Look at me, I'm sweating. I don't want to get picked up by the fuzz. Now, I know Lilah likes to get picked up by the fuzz ... and twirled around. I've seen the pictures."

"Ok, we get it," said Lilah. "Enough."

"If my wit isn't going to be appreciated then I shall take it wit me," said Stuart. "I have a dinner date with some respectable company, you see."

"I've got to get working on my taxes," said Lilah wearily. "It never ends. I finally recovered from last year, and now I've got the Sparrow too, and the complicated New Texas new taxes ..."

"I guess I ought to head out for my rendezvous ... with destiny," said Eddie.

"Don't be dramatic. And don't put yourself in any danger, I mean it."

"Relax Lilah, they'll never see it coming. And soon all your financial woes will be vanished, poof."

"Good luck with your what-have-you," said Stuart.

Eddie picked up his empty French press, mug and cream pitcher. He looked back at Lilah: her toe-ring toes like candy buttons, her quick brown eyes that believed in him. He swallowed. He said, "Bye."

When they knocked, Eddie sprang out of bed and turned off the porn. He fidgeted down his erection before letting them in.

"Are you certain no one saw you?" he asked, closing the door behind them.

"Yeah, bro. This motel is empty," said Ray, coffee-skinned kid whose wife-beater exposed the elaborate black tattoos across his muscular back. His hair was short and jelled upright. Pencil-thin mustache and an emerald in his left ear.

"Let me clear some space for you," said Eddie, shoving dirty clothes and taco bags off the bed. "I didn't know when to expect you, if you were even coming at all."

Benny shrugged, easy smile, "Javi didn't get the message until today."

Javi, the smallest and youngest, scowled his fuzz dust mustache. He kept his eyes on his construction boots as he said, "I couldn't get it until today. I can't do it from my house, and then the servers –"

"It's all right," said Eddie. "I've only been here a couple of days.

I'm glad you got the message, because our mission is in two days."

The Catamounts smiled.

Eddie sat in a chair and gestured at the bed. Ray loped around the dresser and sat down, eyes running the room. Benny stepped around the bed corner and free-dropped his weight, "Nice springs." Javi took a corner of the bed, fussed with his jeans to straighten the seams.

Eddie said, "Dr. X has commissioned me to lead you. This mission is his top priority in this region. Do you all understand how important this is?"

Ray said, "You know Dr. X? Like, you seen him?"

"I think I met him once," said Eddie. "But I'm not sure. He's kind of ... everywhere and nowhere, know what I mean?"

"Where's the mission at?" asked Ray. "We gettin guns?"

"No guns to spare. It's a chili cook-off in Artesia. We will be in disguise. You, Javi, will be dressed like you're on the cleanup crew. Get an apron, hairnet maybe."

"Yeah, I can get that stuff at work tomorrow."

"Perfect. Now, Ray and Benny, you are going to look like secret-service type security. Do you have dark suits and sunglasses?"

"I got sunglasses, but no suit, bro," said Ray.

Benny shook his head no, amused by the thought.

"That's ok," said Eddie. "There has to be a discount men's store around here."

Benny said, "Yeah, Hernan's, down highway 74. Cheap shit, though."

"What are you, fucking fashion guy all a sudden?" laughed Ray. He stopped laughing when Eddie pulled a bankroll out of his pocket and counted out ten twenties.

"Tomorrow get yourselves two cheap black suits, white shirts and black ties. If they ask, it's for your cousin's funeral."

"My cousin *did* just die," said Ray, watching the bankroll be pocketed.

"I'm very sorry to hear that. But this is to protect your identity. It's acting."

Ray nodded.

"Put on long-sleeve shirts when you go to the store. Don't let them see your tattoos or your earrings."

Ray pointed to the back of his neck, "My cross comes up higher than my collar."

"Wear a turtleneck."

"A what?"

"Never mind, just cover what you can. After you buy your cheap black suits, shave your mustaches, all of you."

"Why?" said Javi, finger on his upper lip.

"We need to protect your identity, because we're going to do something bad," said Eddie. He lowered his voice to continue ...

Eddie tossed aside his fourth tiny paper cup of chili. In the parking lot, Ray and Benny were sitting in the Oldsmobile. Javi had actually been put to work, emptying garbage cans. The Catamounts awaited his signal. But the target had not yet arrived.

Eddie had invented a walk for his character and practiced it from booth to booth. He tried another cup of the Artesia Volunteer Fire Department's Five-Alarm Chili. The event was smaller than he had expected, with only about twenty booths. He killed time at a vendor selling chili cookbooks, chili-cooking aprons, chile pepper magnets, chile pepper posters and hundreds of bottles of hot sauce that had the word "ass" in their name.

Eddie found a pair of high-cut jogging shorts with a chile pepper on each cheek and decided to buy them for Stuart. At the last minute he remembered that all of the money – almost the last of the petty cash– was in a suspicious bankroll. With a (hopefully) enigmatic smile he moved on, remembering his new walk. He felt the first squawk from his duodenum. At that moment, the PA squealed into life.

A lanky cowboy-type was on the stage at the head of the three columns of booths. He bent down to the microphone and boomed his Texas voice over the dusty lot: "Ladies and gentlemen and y'all in between, welcome to the First Annual Texas-New Texas Friendship Chili Cook-Off Classic of Artesia! Our celebrity judge, your own Representative Carson Cisneros, wants to say a few words to get us started."

There was a spasm of applause. Eddie wandered closer to the stage, zapping pictures with his digital camera like the rest of the hundred-strong crowd. He stole a glance towards the parking area to see that the Oldsmobile was now empty. Good: target acquired. Javi was in position, smoking a cigarette near the portable toilets, a short distance from the post holding one end of the "First Annual Texas-New Texas

Friendship Chili Cook-Off Classic of Artesia" banner that stretched above the stage.

Cisneros got a helping hand from the cowboy-type to ascend the stage. He waved, waddling across the stage to the microphone beaming a plausible politician's smile. Short and fat in a brown suit, his comb-over was sweat-stuck. He was built like a top, and his jowls rattled as he began, "Howdy folks! Thanks for helping us inaugurate a great new tradition, starting right here in the great city of Artesia, which I am so proud to represent in the State Legislature. This great city, home of clean cold water and rich thick oil, points the way to a future of friendship between the peoples of Texas and New Texas. A friendship based on cooperation, free enterprise ... and great chili!"

Cisneros paused for their cheers before continuing, "I am very gratified to be invited by the Chamber of Commerce to be a judge at this friendly competition. Remember there are no losers here – except for vegetarians!"

Laughter. Eddie began shuffling through the crowd with his new walk, excusing himself as he went. He became trapped behind an obese family and couldn't see.

Cisneros said, "All kidding aside, I think this is a great day for the beautiful city of Artesia, a great backdrop for this historic event. As many of you may know, this city had the very first underground school, a shelter for the Soviet attack that thankfully never came. Today, we break ground in the name of peace, a brotherhood – and *sister*hood – of full bellies. Please enjoy the First Annual Texas-New Texas Friendship Chili Cook-Off Classic of Artesia with me, your representative in the New Texas State Legislature, Carson Cisneros. I hear some stomachs growling – let's get eating that good chili!"

The crowd applauded him off the stage. Eddie felt his throat tightening. *No, not now. It's the dust, or the chili, not ...* Eddie willed himself to breathe calmly. The inhaler was in his pocket. *No, not necessary. Don't let them see you use it.* He took a rattling breath and walked pigeon-toed to a booth promising "Arbenz Family Venison Chili."

He showed his wristband and received his sample cup and tiny spoon. He took a bite and made a yummy noise for the benefit of the Arbenz family. His stomach flipped over and gurgled when the chili dropped into it. The crowd had dispersed from the stage and was spreading out to the booths. A blues band was lugging their equipment onto the stage.

Eddie walked to the "signal" trash can. He saw Javi in his peripheral vision, smoking another cigarette. Eddie tossed his cup into the can and walked away.

He wore his character's expression of baffled inanity as he shuffled to observe the abduction. Right now, Javi should be stealing up to the banner's post which he should have already soaked with Ecogel, a jellied ethanol firestarter the same green color and consistency as dish soap. Javi should be dropping his lit cigarette into the oozing pile of Ecogel and going behind the portable toilets, lighting strings of long-fused Chinese fire crackers. And the fire should get someone's attention right ... about...

"Fire! Fire! The banner's on fire!"

Everyone turned to look at the stage. A gust of wind flipped the flaming banner up onto the stage's awning. Molten nylon rained on the blues band who leapt out from under the furiously-widening hole in the awning.

Herd-fear washed through the crowd. Cisneros and his aide were looking back in the direction of the fire. Edddie saw Bennie and Ray step out from behind a booth. Then the first string of fire crackers went off.

Vendors dove to the bottom of their booths, women ran, men squatted and covered their heads. Eddie moved closer. Ray and Benny intercepted the startled Cisneros, catching him behind his elbows and rushing him to the parking lot. The aide followed, grabbing at Benny's shoulder, "Hey, hey, what are you doing?"

Ray and Benny shoved Cisneros along. Ray said, "We're moving the governor to safety. S'okay, we're security."

"Who? Who?" asked Cisneros, feet barely touching the ground.

The aide continued grabbing at Benny's shoulder. A few people were turning their heads when another string of fire crackers went off. Someone was screaming about an attack. Another string of fire crackers exploded and the wind shifted to blanket the lot with the smoke of gunpowder and burning plastic. The crowd broke into a full-sprint panic for the parking lot.

The abductors were almost to the Oldsmobile but the aide was still with them. Eddie ran, arms flailing, into the kidnapping. Ray and Benny looked startled to see him but the aide never saw him at all. They crashed and Eddie goonily tangled his legs up with the aide. The crowd stampeded around them. The aide finally kicked free, stood up to locate Representative Cisneros. Eddie bumbled into the aide again.

The aide grabbed Eddie by the fanny pack and threatened, "Who are *you*?"

Eddie threw back his head and wailed, "Fire! Fire! They made it too spicy!"

He broke free and ran with the crowd into the parking lot. Engines started, horns blared, bumpers crashed. Eddie jumped into his truck and joined the flight of vehicles. Eddie eased onto the highway as fire engines came roaring. Only then did he look back: three rows of burning booths, the aide running from truck to truck, tie wildly askew.

Fear-sweat cooling, highway rolling under his wheels. He laughed to hear the sound of it. "Ha! 'They made it too spicy.' That was funny. That was good. But oh *man* have I got some bad gas."

Part V Liberation

Operation Zero Tolerance

U.S. Armstrong

"Well it's a pretty big territory, U.S. Sparsely populated. They could have taken him most anywheres," said Hovan, sipping on his Gray Goose and diet.

U.S. dropped his hat brim lower, staring at Hovan's crossed ankles. The julep was melting in its glass. "And how much do they want?"

"Half."

U.S. snorted. "And this fella, this Cisneros, ain't he the one I told you to ..."

Hovan shrugged his sharkskin shoulders. "The wheels of Justice turn slow but they do turn fine."

U.S. looked around the second rate lounge. New but ugly carpet. Uncomfortable furniture. Some weird Indian shit all over everything. Some smell in the place. Not many golfers about in the heat of noon.

U.S. baritoned, "This place has all the charm of a circus tent. They think someplace has class just because they exceeded their budget, building it. And this is the worst julep I ever ... whoever heard of a julep served in a Collins glass?"

Hovan shrugged, lips glistening.

U.S. growled, "This should be just paperwork, another hostile takeover. Why are we having trouble squashing bugs? They took a pot shot at me. At *me*, Hovan."

"I know it, U.S. That was before we appreciated the necessity of security. How were we supposed to know this territory was filled with terrorists?"

U.S. rubbed down his mustache. "Seems they're taking care of *your* business for you, kidnapping that Cisneros fellow. Let them shove their demands up their ass and set fire to it. We ain't paying. They can chop him up into cow feed."

"I agree on principle," said Hovan, wetting his lips with his drink. "But the publicity makes things more complicated. If they kill him, it looks like we can't protect our own toolbox. If we pay, it encourages them to do it again. If we get into an extended hostage deal, it keeps the storyline going. Keeps the Tortilla Terrorists in the news. Publicity helps them. Only way out of this jam is to nail the bastards."

"Well I do assume someone outside this room is working on it."

"Our investigation is using all of the resources at our disposal. However, there are resources currently beyond our regulatory and financial reach. We would be able to unearth these kidnappers, break up these terrorists, wrap up this venture and get the hell out of this third-rate territory, if we had the means."

U.S. raised his brim to read Hovan's placid expression with both blue eyes. He said, "Hovan, what are you on about?"

"I'm saying it's time to really declare war on these terrorists."

U.S. dropped his brim. He chewed his mustache invisible. Hovan blew his nose on a cocktail napkin, examined the contents with a look of derision, and tossed the crumpled napkin onto another table.

U.S. raised his eyes to meet Hovan's and said, "Like you said, if there wasn't no publicity, there'd be no problem. One goddamn TV channel and you can't squash it. I never should've let you talk me into letting them start broadcasting again."

Hovan shrugged, "There was a crew there, filming that insipid cook-off. The network went with it before anyone contacted my office. A lot of heads will roll, sure. But overall, having that channel has been a tremendous boon."

U.S. watched the last pebbles of ice tap together in his glass.

Hovan continued, "TV is a great way to get our message out, whatever it might be. It holds people's attention. And with only one channel, we're able to charge whatever the market will bear for advertising. We're making a lot of money keeping people at home where they belong. Two birds, U.S."

"Keeping them watching the most vulgar ... what happened to them shows before? Family stuff. Now it's all garbage, just like any regular TV channel."

"It's a small compromise. The content reflects the lowbrow interests of this territory. And that's what brings in the money. I mean, last Friday's episode of 'So You Want To Be A Ho' brought in more than Cisneros's entire ransom."

"We ain't paying that, we ain't negotiating with terrorists."

"Absolutely, U.S. But what I'm saying is – "

U.S. interrupted, "And all this vulgar stuff on TV, it's pushing all the wrong buttons. Teaches lack of respect, insolence. There's still stuff about Fawn all over that goddamned internet. You couldn't shut that down either, could you?"

"That will blow over soon. Don't worry yourself over that."

"Don't worry myself over that?" U.S. raised his brim enough to nail Hovan with one blue eye. "That's my goddamn *daughter* they're on about. Don't worry myself? She's talking about changing her name when she gets out of rehab. Moving away somewhere, starting all over. That's *my* name she's talking about changing, Hovan."

"I'm sure the trauma will fade ..." Hovan trailed off under the stab of blue eye.

"And I can't get a decent goddamn julep to save my life. This is the most pathetic golf course, country club, whatever, I ever seen. Even the *greens* are dead-dirt brown ugly out here. Ugly and dry and I'm tired of it. Soldier! Get me a Lonestar."

One of the Guardsmen snapped to attention, saluted, and marched to the bar.

Hovan said, "I'm glad you accepted a full complement of body guards. You're stubborn as a mule in mud sometimes. Even after the assassination attempt you'd be driving yourself, if it were up to you."

"Seems like not much is 'up to me' anymore. Things were going fine, doing it my way. It's less secure than ever, and now we got problems with the *Mexicans*?"

"That's very minor, just resolving some old border issues. Once we get that wall finished, it'll be easier to keep them from aiding the terrorists over here."

"It never stops. Goddamn agitators. If Border Patrol and the Minutemen and the National Guard can't stop it, I'll have to put Guardsmen down there. Keep the Old Mexicans out of Old New Mexico. What a goddamn waste of money and manpower."

"It's an old problem U.S. We'll solve this – hold on, my phone's ringing," said Hovan, turning away to flip it open.

The Guardsman returned with a Bud.

"I said Lonestar."

"Yes General Armstrong sir, but the bartender said they ain't got any. Bud's ok?"

U.S. took the beer and tipped it up. He brought the bottle down, swallowed, and sucked the bottom of his mustache. "Least ya coulda brought me a cold one."

Hovan snapped his phone shut and turned back to the table. "I think we got something on the kidnappers, U.S. Because of the reward, my people been fielding a lot of crank calls. They don't tell me unless they checked into it. So there's these two cousins live in this slum down in Alamagordo. Gang-bangers, speed dealer types. The neighbors think Cisneros is in that crack house. We need to send the Guard in, with full media support. Not a live feed, of course."

"Maybe we ought to let the local sheriffs or whatnot handle this."

Hovan wet his lips with his drink. "We have an opportunity to blow this insurgency out of its boots. The publicity will scare the sympathizers, get them back to doing what they ought: having too many children. If we get this Mr. X, we've got the lunatics by their scrotums. We can't lose this opportunity because of some due process bullshit, technicalities and warrants and all that. This is terrorism we're fighting. War is all they understand. These crack dealers, they probably got some firepower. We ought to go in with overwhelming force."

U.S. grunted, took a swallow of beer. "I reckon Roswell can spare the 45th. That should be plenty to stomp these road apples."

"That's right, U.S., you got it. It's time to go to *war*. Make it public, get the terrorists in a panic. Jack up the rewards, get them fingering each other. Let's enlarge the arsenal at our disposal. Expand your emergency powers. Give this war an operation name, make it territory-wide. Something like ..." Hovan paused to think. He grinned, string of saliva connecting his canines. "How about 'Operation Zero Tolerance'?"

U.S. grunted and pulled out his cell phone.

Billy Ortiz

Bro, my Explorer has just about had it. A couple few months up this road, a tank would be on retreads too. Two miles of Psychobitch – that's Seco Basto but no one calls it that – from the highway out to the land. Bounce over rocks, ruts and juniper. This road is a rough dry one, but the last two miles is what makes it "Psychobitch."

It's a clear, cool night. Warm today, nice May weather. The dust clouds up in my headlights. In the mirror I see my red tail lights in the cloud behind me. Otherwise it's black. There's stars out. Sometimes see the lights of I-25, across the basin.

Damn! That rock almost came through the floor. I've driven Psychobitch enough to know where's the bad places, which side of the ruts to run, every rollover marked with descansos. But there just ain't no easy going up this road. Stone wedges stand on their ends for the oil pan, bottomless holes slam the suspension, exposed rocks look to blow out a sidewall. Even the beginning, where it actually got graded a few years back, now it's nothing but a washboard that jiggles your teeth loose inside your head. Still, like they say, bad roads makes good neighbors.

Sound of the engine and the banging of the truck, rocks slamming off the trannie. CDs won't play on this road and there ain't no radio but that Texas bullshit. What ever happened to that Radio KAOS?

Up ahead is where Lesbian Kim's dogs always set their ambush. One of these days, one of them dogs is gonna end up under my tire. And it won't be my fault.

Right on cue. Bro, if my truck wasn't already fucked I'd have to repaint it every week, the way they scratch the doors. They're barking, snarling, sound like they ready to murder. I came through once, smoking a cigarette with my arm hanging out the window and one of them, looked like a chow, took my cigarette right out of my hand. Almost took my hand with it, too.

They chew on my tires for a quarter mile, then run back to set a new ambush. With dogs like that, who needs shotguns? Well you know what bro, I guess I do. She's right here on the seat with me, nice and oiled and loaded. Just in case, you know?

Dogs and guns. I love them but they sure can get you in trouble. What went down at Chemo Carl's place is just one example. But that made waves around here, means we gotta be extra careful. I mean shit bro, Carl shouldn'ta had his dogs running loose, but maybe Carmen shoulda built a sturdier chicken coop, you know? And then after, Chemo Carl really shouldn'ta pulled a gun on Carmen. I mean I know Carl is sick and all, but Carmen's about four foot tall, bro. But after that, she shouldn'ta called the State Guard. I mean, the police would be bad enough. But the fucking State Guard?

They were everywhere. I mean, helicopters, army trucks, guys on ATVs all over the back roads. Just because Carmen lost some chickens and said that Chemo Carl was Dr. X himself. They was setting road blocks. We got buzzed by helicopters. They was everywhere from Golden to Lone Butte. We was a little worried, up at our place. But they'd never come all the way up Psychobitch. Heard they got shot at when they went up Owl's Perch Road, which is almost as bad as Pyschobitch. Almost.

I hate this part here, there's never enough clearance. A monster truck wouldn't have enough clearance. But it means I'm almost home. *Damn*, that sounded bad.

They kept the militia trucks out of the upper end of Owl's Perch, I heard, but then army APC's came, so the people split. The Texans knocked over a bunch of trailers, shot up some abandoned cars. Then they left because there was nothing out there.

Here's the driveway, at last. I get out and dial the combination on the gate's lock. Push the gate back, kick a rock to keep it from swinging shut. It's a quiet night, under the sound of the engine. They are coming, barking. I get back in the truck and roll forward, get out again and the dogs are barking happy, now they know it's my truck. Their eyes flash green in the headlights. I swing the gate closed and they're on me.

"Ok, hi guys, hi. Hi Dorado, hi Chaco, hi Reina, hi dogs." I pat them each and close the lock. Reina tries to jump into the truck with me like usual but I keep her out. I drive up to Mary and Joseph's, dogs pacing my tires. The driveway is so smooth compared to Psychobitch that I could roll a joint. But I'll wait until I'm inside. I park next to Joseph's Scout. The dogs are already ahead of me, banging through the trailer's dog door. I grab my stuff and my shotgun and go up the steps into the double wide.

Pretty big mess in the living room still. Smells good, like spaghetti sauce cooking. I set my shotgun in the rack with the others – Mary's rule, only she can pack in her trailer. Mary's chopping something on the kitchen island. She looks up and says in her raspy voice, "Hey there Billy, just in time for dinner. What a surprise."

"It smelled so good I just followed my nose the whole way," I say, opening the fridge for a cold beer.

I can hear Joseph's muffled shouting from another room. Mary points with her basil-chopping knife, "Joseph was taking a bath. The dogs knocked through the door and ... well you can probably figure the rest."

I laugh and take a seat on one of the kitchen island chairs. This way I don't have to look at the mess behind me in the living room area. It looks like the heap on the coffee table has attacked the couch and is starting to claim the floor. I watch Mary cooking, trying to read what the old blue tattoos on her arms use to say.

Joseph came out, long hair down and wet, tying the towel around his skinny waist. "Mary, your goddamn dogs broke the door and filthied up the bathroom and Chaco stepped on my balls in the bathtub."

Mary and I laugh.

"Shut up Billy, you're the one that got them all riled up," says Joseph.

From the bathroom comes the sound of three dogs playing in a small tub of water.

"I'm not cleaning up the mess they're making. All that water was wasted. We can't afford to empty our water tank for this shit," said Joseph, tightening his towel and walking away to the bedroom.

I sit with Mary, joking about Joseph's bad mood. She's making a big salad. The dogs come out of the bathroom dripping wet and pretty happy about it. They shake themselves and then run outside to roll around in rabbit shit, if they can find it. Joseph comes out and gets a beer from the fridge. Mary serves up the spaghetti and sauce and salad on paper plates and we dig in with plastic forks. Eating, I realize that I forgot to pick up bread while I was making my delivery today. I hope Mary don't remember.

The food is good. Mary only does simple stuff, what she can chew. I mean, it's spaghetti three or four nights a week but it comes out good. No idea I was this hungry. We eat in silence, just wolfing it down. The dogs come back inside, all dirty and smelling bad, to beg under the table. Mary kicks them out with the steel toe of her boot.

We finish, toss our plates into the contractor's bag on the floor. Step out the trailer into the cool night. Lean back in the plastic lawn furniture, smoking and digesting, looking up at the stars. The dogs are wrestling over something next to my truck.

"It's nice out," says Mary. That's all anyone says for a while.

Finally Joseph sighs, tosses his butt and slaps his hands on the arms of his lounge chair. "Guess I better clean up then."

Mary is lighting another 120 from her first and rasps, "Make up a plate for Lester and put it in the fridge."

Joseph grunts "I know" and the screen slaps behind him.

My beer's empty. "Hey, sorry I forgot the bread, you know."

"Billy, you know you don't owe me nothing for – oh you mean the garlic bread. Ha. Would have been nice but we didn't need it."

"Maybe tomorrow." I close my eyes. My belly's full, the air is the perfect temperature, I have a perfect combo of weed, beer and nicotine in my blood. Just sitting here alive makes me happy.

I maybe must've dozed off because I don't hear the dogs or Boss clomping in, only when I hear the jangle of Boss's tack do I look up and see Lester getting off.

"Evenin y'all," says Lester.

"Evening, Lester," says Mary. "There's some supper in the fridge for you."

"Is there? Don't mind if I do." Lester marches off towards the trailer. Boss makes a little sound behind me, nose buried in his oats.

I call after him, "Hey Lester, you gonna tie up your horse or what?"

Lester chuckles, opening the screen door. "I'm sure he'll be right by you, Billy."

I look over my shoulder. Boss makes a noise. I get on with horses ok, but ever since that time Boss bit me, I don't trust him. And Lester, he just laughed. It fucking hurt, got the whole part from my neck to my shoulder. Big bruise. Lester kicks out the screen door, comes and sets with us. He gets the paper plate up to his face – it's pretty soggy now, sits in his hand like a wet tortilla – and he's shoveling it in as fast as he can.

"Does it need to be warmed up?" asks Mary.

"No'm," he says, not even slowing down.

Mary lights another cigarette. "What's happening in town?"

He finishes, swallows and his tongue works at the food in his bushy beard. He smacks his lips and sets his plate down for Reina. He burps. "There's stuff going on."

"And?" says Mary, shaking out the match.

"Hey I almost forgot," reaching inside his vest. "I brought you this."

Mary takes the hip flask of SoCo and cracks it open. "Black label. Hundred proof. I thank you very much. But quit making me wait. What happened in town?"

"Oh yeah, all that," teases Lester.

"This clown," rasps Mary, hitting the flask. She shakes it at me. "Billy?"

Bleh, I can smell it from here. "No thanks. I can smell it from here."

"All right," and she hits it again. "Now. Lester."

He chuckles. Between his big dirty blondish beard and glasses and the brim of his hat, you can't ever see his face. I think he might have brown eyes but I'm not sure. Lester says, "Well it seems some fella was in the Mineshaft Tavern this afternoon. Pretty crowded, band playing, locals drinking on the porch. And this fella starts hanging around, not drinking much but sure seems to be listening a lot. Well. Then he kinda starts talkin to people, and he always steers the conversation to 'the Resistance.' That's what he kept calling it. Said he was looking to join up."

"The 'Resistance?' What in hell's that? If you're talking about folks saying get the fuck off my porch and here's a .357 to tell you *why* ... that's a different story."

"You don't have to tell me, Mary," says Lester. "But he was calling it 'the Resistance' and asking if anybody knew anybody. And he was asking about the Diablos, did they ride through town recently. Said his uncle was a Diablo, some shit."

"Diablos, huh?" In my mind I can see that wreath of smoke around the rim of the Bowl, and then the crunchy boom hitting me, and then the whole face of the mountain sliding down the Bowl into the Rio Grande. And that guardrail flying out into the air, like a strip of foil. I still got Hormigo's card, somewhere. Maybe I should warn him.

"So what happened?" asks Mary, waving a moth away with her cigarette. "Hey, Reina! Quick, she's taking the plate, it'll blow all over my land."

"Got it," I say, pulling the paper plate out of the dog's mouth as she tries to slip past. It comes apart and we each get half. She runs off, trailed by Dorado and Chaco.

Lester says, "Well. No one would talk to him, except Morris the Hun."

"That drunky could talk to a fencepost for an hour. Until the fencepost up and leaves," Mary chuckles hoarsely.

"But what happened?" I ask.

"He left when the night time band started to play. I guess that was eight or nine. Driving a late model Ford Explorer. Looked a lot like Billy's, actually."

"Didn't have no State Guard insignia or nothing, did it?"

"No Billy, they ain't quite that stupid. I also heard they picked up Gomez today."

"Who, police or State Guard?" asks Mary.

"Haven't heard. Which means it's probably State Guard." Lester turns to look over at the trailer. "There's the man, Mr. Clean."

Joseph comes down the steps. "Damn girl, you sure can make a mess."

"We doing all right on drinking water?" Mary asks.

"We'll need more. Don't know what I'm going to pay for it with."

"Well Joseph, if you didn't use our drinking water for your god-damn baths ..."

"What do you want me to use, Mary? Graywater? Or how about I just take a bath in the composting toilet?"

"I hear that's good for the complexion," says Lester.

"You would know, wouldn't you? So what are y'all talking about?" Joseph sets himself down in a chair next to Mary.

"Oh," says Mary, wiggling the flask. "Some fella trying to be a secret agent and infiltrate 'the Resistance.' And Gomez got arrested."

"They come to arrest me, they gonna get some of this in the face," says Joseph, aiming something at the road.

"Joseph! You do not *dare* fire that pistol, the dogs are out there," scolded Mary.

Joseph drops his aim and smiles. "It's the light bulb, calm down."

"Well someone around here is finally talking sense," says Mary.

We get high, passing the light bulb around. And now I've got another addition to the perfect combo in my blood. Then we all hear it, and stop talking all at once.

"That would be Pissed's bike," says Joseph.

We all listen as the sound of the dirtbike gets closer. Boss tosses his head, makes a jingly noise. Then the engine cuts out and Pissed steps into the weak glow of the porch light. Shirtless and all tattooed, with motor cross pants on for the cholla.

"Hey Pissed," says Mary. "We're smoking a little pick-me-up. You want some?"

"No thanks, those days are long gone."

I haven't figured Pissed out yet. He's a young guy, all punk rock. Got enough metal stuck in him to swing a compass. Used to be hard, he says, but he got himself a wife and a couple little girls, got some land.

"Maybe that's why you're pissed all the time," says Joseph, laughing at his joke.

"No, I already told you," Pissed says seriously. "It's from the scene when I was drinking a lot. It's how they say drunk in England."

"So what's up young man? Grab a seat," says Mary. "There's some spaghetti left, right Joseph?"

"I got to get back home, it's almost bedtime for Skylaña and Francessica. But, you know, we were talking about doing stuff. And I gotta not do it. So don't, like, talk about doing anything in front of me because I don't want to know about it. I mean if they come up into my canyon, I got my blind set up to give Ashley time to get the girls away. But I'm not gonna do anything to make them want to come up on my land, you know?"

"Sure man, it's cool," I say.

"There was a fella in town today, asking questions," says Lester.

"I heard that. I heard there was a bunch of undercover guys in town," says Pissed.

Lester says, "There was only one. I was there."

Pissed says, "And they picked up Gomez, who's got all those kids."

"That's true," says Lester.

Pissed looks around the dark land. His forehead is wrinkled up, serious. "I got a bunch of starts and I'm gonna need to put them in the ground soon. Water police is bad enough. I don't need the Guard looking over my property."

"I know it," says Joseph. "We're out here totally off the grid. No land lines, no water, no trashman, no mail, no electric lines, no plumbing, no cable, no propane deliveries. And the Man still comes to harass us. How far away do we need to go?"

"Yeah, well. Bye," says Pissed. He steps out of our light, kick starts his dirt bike and whines off like a mosquito.

"I guess he's out," I say.

"That's fine. He's got his family to think about," says Mary. She chucks the empty flask at the dead Omni. It smashes on the door. "Hooyah!"

"If he's worried about it, it's better for him to get out now," says Joseph.

"I ought to ride on, get bedded down for the night," says Lester, getting up. He tips the brim of his hat with his finger. "Thanks for the grub, always."

"You want some more to take with you?" asks Mary.

"You're welcome to bed down anywhere on our land you like, you know that," says Joseph.

"Thank yeh, no. Me and Boss are gonna cut across country, get up on high land. I got some flake and water stashed up there. Good practice anyway. Be seeing yeh."

Lester gets up on Boss and turns him, and Boss clops off into the darkness.

"Least he don't gotta take Psychobitch," says Joseph.

"Yeah. I think I lost another filling on the way down tonight," I say.

"Lester the Molester's the only one whose life ain't changed," says Mary.

"Now Mary, he only got that nickname cause it rhymes," Joseph says.

"All I know for sure," says Mary, pushing up from her chair, "is that I wants to get molested. Right now."

She gets up and straddles Joseph. He grabs her around the ass and says, "Reckon it's about time to put out the lights, save the solar. Have a good night, Billy."

"Night guys. I'll see you in the morning."

"Rise and shine!" Mary cackles, wrapped around Joseph's waist as he stands up.

There's a bit of moon but I know the way to the Airstream in the dark by now anyways. Past the goat pen, past the chicken coop. Killing that rooster was the smartest thing I ever done. Goddamn I hated that fucker. Here it is, home sweet home. I open it up. Darkness and the smell of trapped heat spill out. I'd sleep with the door open tonight but the dogs would find me and lick my feet all night. I find the box of kitchen matches in the dark and light the oil lamp. It's all yellow and shadows inside now. I close the door and feel that closed-in feeling. Sit on the bed to get my boots and socks off. Pfew, I need some new socks here pretty soon.

.45 under my pillow? Check. Strongbox covered with the Zia Crossbones stickers Mary got in town? Check. I unlock it, add today's cash, lock it again.

All right. I'm ready to sleep. I blow out the lamp and fall into bed, pull the sheets over me. There's a little breeze coming through the window slats. It's nice. I got it pretty good here. I got it pretty good.

All right. I'm ready to sleep.

Pissed said that he's got starts. It's already that time of year. That was some great set-up I had, when I tapped into the irrigation line back – how many years ago? Sucks to lose that operation, it was cherry, bro. It feels like fifty years ago. It feels like a million years. I wonder what happened to our trailer, and all my trucks and tools and shit. I miss having my own place, my own stuff.

All right, forget about it. I'm ready to sleep.

I wonder where Melody is at. I miss her combing her long hair.

I miss her in our bed. Getting all wrapped up in her warm skin. Her hair all over the pillows. That perfume she sometimes wore. What was it? Smelled like flowers I guess. I wonder how Daniel is doing. Hank said that they was gonna put him in school in Cruces. But that was a long time ago, since I talked to any of them.

All right. Enough of all that. I'm ready to sleep.

Maybe I should have one last cigarette. Then I'll be ready to sleep.

Taylor Jon Bridges

I don't need your fucking disciplinary procedures, I need my fucking rig back. *My* motherfucking truck. Don't offer me no fucking Nissan. Don't threaten me, you gonna hit me with no Article 15. And don't stick me in the crew cab of some fuckin *mor*on. Back here there's some dried blood, looks they couldn't get out, looks like a black girl's been here on prom night.

Hope it was a miscarriage.

I been out here from the very fucking beginning. I stood on the border, the beaner barrier. I was part of the invasion force, a combat veteran and wounded in battle at the Battle of Las Vegas, one con*firm*ed badass, and they got me out here. Sitting in the crew cab. Guarding ... pumps. Next week it will be some lake.

Why the fuck – who's gonna steal a fucking lake? Or we back down on the border with Mexico, like I was back in the fucking Minutemen. Or if we do something cool, like raiding that kidnapper's house, there ain't no hostage there, never was. I don't think the singing pissflaps running this show know what the fuck they doin. Bobby Earl's an idiot and that Major Bishop, Major Bitch-up I call him, he's an idiot too. But they're chicken-fried retards *all* the way up.

Good waste of my day, thanks. Guarding a couple dozen shiny new well pumps. I ain't got my dick wet since I been in this stupid fucking dry desert. Sure ain't getting laid hanging out with a bucktoothed Opie like McDowell. The wind's always blowing. Some nasty shit in the air is making my nose run all fucking day and night, eyes itching.

Fucking hotel room stinks like bloody queefs. No maids nowhere to be found. And last night, jackin off, I felt something weird. Like one of my balls was bigger than the other one. Probably nothing. I'd still rather be sitting in my hotel room growing an extra ball than being stuffed in the crew cab of this shitty truck. With these two assblasters who barely outrank me.

When they gonna fix my rig? They don't say. When the fuck do I get out of here? They don't say. When do I get paid my cash? They don't say. They just say, sorry Taylor Jon, the taxes are all fucked up, we'll get it all sorted out just as soon as Zero Tolerance is finished. In the mean time, some terrorists just blew up some pumps in one of our new water fields, go out and sit in the desert with a couple drooling tards and see how much sand you can collect in the crack of your ass.

Fucking terrorist nigger faggot cowards. If those pussies would just for once crawl out of their little hidey holes and fight like men, this shit would be over faster than a lapdance. But they don't. They come sneaking around at night, or pull some fucked up Indian shit, leave you dead and naked. I heard they cut some dude's dick off but I know that's bullshit. They ain't got hedge clippers big enough for me, no how.

About the only fun, like the only *payback*, was what we done to Taos. I think we ain't done enough of that kinda shit. Knock over all them hippie ranches and rotten buildings and beaner trailers. Step on their nuts – fuck *you* – and leave. Instead we're stuck in this endless lit-terbox, guarding some fucking pumps and a fucking pipeline. It's no wonder I had to let off some steam. Threaten disciplinary procedures on *me*?

May I remind you I lost my fucking rig, and all the equipment that I put on my Guard Card, in the line of action? It's been, what, two months? More? I lose track of the days, every one is the same. Except at least it ain't yesterday, stuck in Pierson's rig, when his crew all had the flu or whatnot. Probably had the 24-hour AIDS. Pierson only listens to the Christian station. No music, just preachin and asking for donations. I'm pretty sick of Rebel Yell, they play the same shit over and over but at least it's music.

That time we was up north, a while ago. Still real cold. That pirate radio station was coming in loud and clear. And it was, like, kinda fucked up. Eerie. Fella was talking about some helicopter crash hap-pened that morning out by some place called Pie City. Too bad it ain't Hair Pie City, they'd make me the goddamn mayor. Anyway, guy was bragging two Air Guard choppers collided, and a bunch of Guard they was carrying died too. Fucked up, to die in some accident, when you're supposed to be fighting a war.

The radio guy, he was *happy* those men got killed. Gloating, you know? Tell you what, if these beaners respected their sister as much – ah shit, here comes Bobby Earl.

Newton and McDowell are asleep in the front, passed out in the air conditioning. I'm in the back, wide awake. Bobby Earl's coming over and he's gonna catch them asleep, I love it.

I wait until he's looking through the window and then I say "Howdy Bobby Earl!" real loud so's they jump. And I do my best not to laugh. McDowell sends the window down and catches a bitching-out from Bobby Earl that would make my drunk old man's eardrums burn. I reckon Bobby Earl can still get it up when he wants, just like the old days. He tears them a new pussy, then sends us out to run the perimeter.

At first I thought he meant, you know, *run* the perimeter. Thank fucking god. Once we're out, driving along the fence line, Newton turns around to me and says, "Dammit TJ, why dint you wake us up when you saw him comin?"

"Bullshit, man, I only woke up when he was standing right there. Not my fault you dint wake yourself up like I did."

He turns back around. Him and McDowell look at each other. I know what they're thinking. Well fuck the *both* of yous with a two by six. What was that one thing Bobby Earl called them? Oh yeah, "fingernail-shitting faggots." I like that.

Just watching the fence roll on past. Brand new, shiny. Razor wire along the top. Great, cept they just cut through it. They was probably gone before the splosion.

Patrolling a fence in the middle of fucking nowhere is pretty gay. Dirt and dead plants on one side, dirt and dead plants on the other. All a fence says is, hey nigger nigger nigger, inside this fence is some stuff worth stealing.

Oh, but the fucked up thing about hearing about the chopper crash on the pirate radio is that it wasn't on Rebel Yell at all, and the TV didn't say nothing. I figured it was bullshit but I saw Bo and he said it was true, Blanchett's lost twelve, he knew some of them. He's getting as fed up too. He said recruitment is down, even with the new inducements and shit they never offered *me*.

McDowell's driving so fast I can't keep the binoculars steady. Prolly in a hurry to get back and finish his nap. Finish his dream about being Santa Claus and all the little kids sitting on his lap. You fingernail-shitting faggot, huh!

There's – what is that? "Stop the truck a second!"

McDowell stops the truck. I'm looking at the far hill – thought I saw a flash of light, like metal. Or a pair of binoculars looking back at me.

"What is it?" asks Newton, looking through his.

"Thought I saw a flash of something out there, flash of light."

We sit for a minute, looking. I can't remember exactly where it was, but I'm pretty sure I saw something.

Newton says, "I don't know. I don't see nothing."

Shit. It looks like the same old regular dry dirt hill with scrubby bushes, same as all the fucking rest. The wind's blowing hot dust in through the open window.

I shrug and say, "Fuck it. Prolly nothin."

"At least some of these folks figured out what was smart," says Mayles, turned around in the front seat to bother me. He's real friendly, now that we're the same rank.

Fuck. I lose my temper a little bit and they bust me down to junior shit sniffer like Mayles here.

Pierson says, "How's that, Corporal?"

"Well, I mean going for the rewards. Realizing that the sooner we get rid of these terrorists for them, the better. I mean, *look* at this place."

Out the window it's the usual brown wasteland. Rocks, hills, mountains, sky. Dead plants. Dead desert of rusted cars and garbage blowin all over.

"I say, they want to live like niggers, let them."

"Hey now TJ, what did I tell you about that kind of talk?" Pierson says all stern.

"Yeah, sorry Lieutenant," I mumble, just so he don't put the radio preacher on.

Mayles don't know when to shut up. "I mean, we got rid of their corrupt politicians, got them headed in the right direction. Showed them what a little hard work can accomplish. Only thing in the way is a handful of ni – I mean terrorists. Right?"

Pierson nods like that old Pope. He says, "Right, Corporal. They call us in to uproot the weeds, so the garden can grow like General Armstrong said. And they get themselves a nice little reward to boot."

Listen to these two fingernail-shitting faggots. My guts are cramped up, and each bounce of this road makes them uncoil like some big snake. Some big diarrhea snake.

Bobby Earl squawks out the radio, "Hold position. We're waiting on a helo."

Great. Waiting on some dirt mountain that I can *feel* crumbling under our tires. The sun is fucking brutal, as always. Thank god air conditioning ain't no sin, or we'd be frying out here like fake titties in a microwave. I got to fart but I'm afraid of, you know, a blowout. Just gotta work it easy, be ready to clamp if ... ok, that was ok. Hot and silent into Pierson's churchy upholstery.

Least he's got something to have upholstery in. Tell me my vehicle is totaled, and I go, where's my new truck then? And they say that's up to my insurance. What fucking insurance? So naturally I had to express how I felt about being treated like an altar boy at Michael Jackson's house. Is that the chopper?

I can hear it, the whole mountain can hear it. What the fuck kinda surprise do we get now? Don't matter. We're moving now, jamming fast up the loose road. The two old-school M113 APC's at the head of the column disappear around the outcropping, squealing clatter of their treads. The helicopter is hovering just off the edge of the ridge.

Bobby Earl's squawking about taking fire. Over the sound of the radio and trucks and helicopters, yeah, I can hear rifle shots. Now I can hear automatics responding like fast zippers, the M113's chain guns going chunk! chunk! chunk! chunk!

We've crawled up to the flat top of the mountain. There's a bunch of smoke and the radio is squawking "Cease fire! Cease fire!"

Shit man. Come all the way up here and don't even get to shoot nobody? Pierson drives around the jam of trucks and we park on some busted chicken coop. We get out and there's white feathers everywhere, starting to fly around in the chopper's wash.

Pierson steps over the rotten lumber without even glancing at it and says, "Come on, let's see what's going on."

We walk over to a group gathered around this round circular thing – I guess it's a house. Getting closer, it looks like its walls are just canvas. Living on top of some rock covered in chicken shit in a canvas house, crapping in a bucket like a caveman. This is what they're fighting for? Unfuckingbe*lie*vable. There's two piles of clothes which turn out to be two bodies, male and female. The female, even face-down, you can tell she ain't too hot but would probably do if you was stuck on top of some rock. Pair of old bolt-action rifles next to them. What the fuck were they thinking? Against APC's?

"Any wounded?" asks Pierson.

"Nope," says Sergeant Caldwell. You can tell he don't like Pierson neither. "Just them two and their dogs."

259

"Where's Bobby Earl at?" asks Pierson, trying to be in charge.

Caldwell jerks his thumb over his shoulder. "In the yurt."

I laugh, I can't help it. "What in the high-holy fuck is a *yurt*?"

Caldwell don't smile much. "That round thing there. Wood frame and canvas. It's one big room inside."

Pierson goes over to the yurt, huh, gets himself through the flap. I'd like to yurt inside some bitch's flaps. It's quiet suddenly – the helicopter's buzzed off and everyone is half-deaf from it, not saying much. Just look around the sorry scab of land these folks chose to die on. Little garden with a little fence around it, things growing in rows. The wind is blowing strong, even without the chopper. There's a hawk or whatnot circling, some kind of bird, making circles high up.

Bobby Earl comes out the yurt, talking on a big satellite phone, followed by Pierson, Newton and some others. We all quiet to hear Bobby Earl talking to whoever, maybe Major Bitch-up. Bobby Earl says, "They offered resistance and we had no choice but to use overwhelming force. But listen, I don't care what your informer told you, if these folks were with Dr. X then I'm a chinaman. Listen sir, there ain't nothing here to indicate ... well yes, some rifles. M-1's I think. Well yeah, you can call it a weapons cache if you want to. But hell Major, they ain't got no computer here, don't even got no proper lectric, toilet, nothin ... Well I don't know sir, maybe your informant had some old beef with them. Right, we'll bring it all in – what little there is. Yes sir. Out."

He hands the phone to Pierson who's just standing there like an eager beaver. Bobby Earl says, "All right, we're gonna load up those books and papers, and the rifles. Let's get off this windy tit."

Pierson says, "Sir? What are we gonna do with the bodies?"

Bobby Earl squints up at the sky. He's looking at that bird circling – now there's two. He says, "Leave em be. Vultures gotta eat, same as the worms."

Hormigo

The Diablos roared through Alamosa Estates, a golf course community on the outskirts of Rio Rancho. Car alarms whooped a chorus as they passed. They stopped at one particular driveway and stood their bikes, leaving Wolfe to watch them.

Hormigo knocked. He said, "Hey Ribeye, did you see the color of their golf course? Looks like even the rich folks can't water their lawns no more."

Ribeye chuckled, "Yeah boss."

The door cracked open to reveal a slice of a wedito in white bathrobe and slippers. He looked shocked. "Hormigo. What are you ... what's going on?"

"Aren't you gonna invite me in, Ritchie? I don't like the way your neighbors are looking at me. Undressing me with their eyes," Hormigo said, smiling.

"Ok, but why – I mean, you're not supposed to – oh, hello, hello, ok," said Ritchie as Ribeye, Flywheel and Lumbres followed Hormigo through the door.

Hormigo looked around the foyer: vaulted ceiling, marble, chandelier. All clean and white. "Nice place Ritchie. Very white. It matches your bathrobe."

"I'm sorry Hormigo, but you and your friends ... aren't the cops looking for you? You can't be here, man."

"Ritchie," said Hormigo, spreading his arms. "We *are* here."

"Hormigo, this is my home. I mean Christ, Nina took the kids to school twenty minutes ago. I have a strict rule, no business out of my house. Sorry, but you need – "

"*You*," interrupted Hormigo, "are doing too much talking. What kind of hospitality is that? You don't even offer my men nothing to drink?"

Pale Ritchie, dark hair thinning except where revealed by his bathrobe, looked at the dark Diablos in their creaking, dust-stiff leathers. He swallowed and said, "Can I get you something to drink?"

"No, they're not thirsty, but thanks for asking," said Hormigo, admiring the chandelier again. "See Ritchie, I came to ask you a question."

"Look Hormigo, I know we do good business together, and I'm speaking with respect to you, but I don't have anything here. I keep it away from my kids."

"You're a good role model," sniffed Hormigo. He broke his stare from the chandelier and applied it to Ritchie's wavering brown eyes.

Ritchie looked away.

Hormigo said, "Me and you have made a lot of money for each other. Me and you have always been straight, right?"

"Yeah Hormigo, always. You and I have always been good."

"So why do I hear these bad things about your business? I thought you were trying to be a role model?" Hormigo's stare darkened.

"I don't know what rumors you heard, Hormigo. You and I always been good."

Homigo's eyes opened in uncovered anger, "You been selling to the State Guard, haven't you? You been selling to *them*."

"I ... uh yeah, a little bit. I mean, business is business, right? And if it wasn't me it would just be someone else, right?"

"Do they know about our deal? If they turned on you, would you tell them? To save your house and your chandelier and your kids? Role model?"

"No, of course not Hormigo, no, never," said Ritchie.

Hormigo's burn cooled slightly. "We have to change how you do business."

"Change? Hormigo, listen. I don't have anything here. No cash, no drugs."

"We're going to your place of business right now. Lumbres!" ordered Hormigo.

Lumbres stepped forward and put his heavy paw on Ritchie's shoulder.

"Wait, Hormigo, I'm still in my bathrobe," pleaded Ritchie.

Hormigo said, "You're riding with Lumbres. Hang on tight, he goes fast."

The Diablos growled past the crumbling remains of the Truth or Consequences Spaceport. They turned the corner at the never-opened Spaceport Café and Souvenir Shop and soon entered the quiet verdure of the El Cid Spa and Hot Springs Resort. They took their rooms and had already been partying for an hour before the girls arrived. It was a debauchery of triumph and immortality. And then someone drags Hormigo out of a perfect mineral bath with two naked ladies to put him in front of the TV?

"What the hell is this?" he barked, penis retracting beneath his towel.

"Look," said Ribeye.

The news reporter was behind his desk, and he was saying that it was confirmed, the Texas State Guard had captured the notorious fugitive terrorist Dr. X and associates in the Nob Hill area of Albuquerque earlier that evening. Words too fast to read ran along the bottom of the screen.

"No shit," said Hormigo as the reporter continued to rattle off details about the fine men who had finally arrested the most dangerous –

and Hormigo turned it off.

His Diablos, drinks in hand, stared at the floor.

"Well, fuck it, right?" said Hormigo. "No one can capture us, right? Come on, we're celebrating. It's a party. Come on!"

"Yeah boss," said Ribeye.

"Let's drink to that motherfucker. Dr. X, he did pretty good," said Flywheel.

"I ain't drinking to that faggot. He got caught? Fuck him! Diablos!"

"Boss," said Ribeye, handing Hormigo a shot of tequila.

"Shit. Fine," said Hormigo, raising the glass. "To Dr. X, RIP."

"Dr. X," they toasted and shot.

Hormigo threw his shot glass at the wall – it dented the plaster but did not break. He grunted and left to rejoin his naked ladies. The rest of the Diablos stood around, not saying a thing.

Watershed

U.S. Armstrong

"I hate being stuck in here. It's like a prison."

Hovan leaned back into the white leather chair. "Come now U.S., this is one of the finest domiciles in all New Texas. Luxurious. And any time you want to go out, you've got about twenty comp steak dinners waiting for you at the Bullring."

"If I gots to go out, dragging a bunch of bodyguards, I don't want it to be *there*. Surrounded by all them ... sychophants."

"The legislature is not in session. It will be empty."

U.S. tipped his Lonestar back.

Hovan continued, "Here we are, finally able to wrap up this venture in a nice little package. Their homegrown Osama bin Laden is currently being, ahem, interviewed by special investigators. The terrorists will collapse into their power vacuum. Groundwater exploration is completed and our drilling operation is Herculean in its scope. Revenues from New Texas are creating a boom for the Texas economy, making it one of the very richest *nations* in the world. And yet, with peace, tranquility and prosperity at last, Mr. White and I have never seen you look so blue. Isn't that so, Mr. White?"

"The Governor's mood is his personal business. But professionally, sir, I agree with Mr. Hovan. It may well be time to un-postpone those elections, to assure goodwill and to ease the burden on the current administration."

U.S. tipped his Lonestar back. He sucked foam from his mustache and said, "They cancelled my hot air balloon ride."

Mr. White said, "Tomorrow's trip, with the bankers? They've already spent a fortune promoting it."

"Exactly. Claimed it was a security risk, ain't that right Hovan?"

Hovan pushed himself further into the white leather. "Officially, it will be cancelled because of high winds."

U.S. growled, "It would be nice to get out of this stinking place. Feel like I'm in an underground burrow. Get up into the clean air. I never been on a balloon ride. Marianne is scared of heights so ... I think I must've always wanted to."

Hovan made a sympathetic noise. "There will be plenty of balloon rides to look forward to. But both the banks and my people feel that, as symbolic as you are for all New Texas, that might encourage some desperate scoundrel at this time."

U.S. shot Hovan a hard eye from under his hat brim. "What are you, the blue balls of happiness? My command is spread out all over the map. I got men tied down the entire two hundred miles of the Mexican border, and now I gotta worry about the Texas border with Mexico too. I can't bring my wife over, or even go take myself for a walk. And back in El Paso, my CEO has gone AWOL."

Hovan said, "We're looking for Geldman, don't you worry. In the meantime the Armstrong Corporation will be fine under Vince. And you know that we'll sort out the scuffle with Mexico soon enough. They just got a strange idea about how many acre feet of the Rio Grande they deserve."

U.S. snorted. "Here we go again. What in hell's *wrong* with people?"

"They'll de-head their own asses eventually, U.S. In the meantime, they're at the *end* of the river, and there ain't much they can do about anything. And if they get any fancy ideas, flashing around their surplus U.S. Army gear, we can let Border Patrol and the Feds take care of things. It is, after all, a national boundary."

U.S. said, "You know, all the Texas State Guard is equipped with Army surplus."

Hovan said, "Sure U.S., what's your point?"

U.S. shrugged, finished his beer. He belched and blew it out. "Surplus has dried up. Regular Army and National Guard say they need it all overseas. Running out of spare parts. And here, recruitment has bottomed out, even in the poorest counties."

Mr. White, "I think it's a mistake to rely on the Federal Government to deal with Mexico. You recall to what little degree they influenced events here in New Texas. With the current world crisis, they might not risk offending one of our top trade partners."

Hovan said, "Twaddle. The Feds endorsed our corrective measures, after the fact. It's almost six. We need to watch the news at six."

"Do you know something we don't?" said Mr. White acidly.

Hovan grinned wet lips over white teeth.

Mr. White said, "I think we ought to reschedule elections. It will make the people feel invested in the future of New Texas."

"You are just chomping on that bit, aren't you Mr. White? Don't worry, you'll be Governor soon enough. We want to keep our friends close." Hovan demonstrated by crossing his hands over his heart.

"The sooner we have elections, the sooner people will forget about this Dr. X nonsense," pressed Mr. White. "We need to give them something else to believe in."

Hovan licked his lips. "I think they'll be forgetting Dr. X soon enough. U.S., we need to watch the news."

U.S. grunted and zapped the flatscreen into life. It was a truck commercial and U.S. muted it. Hovan commented, "That's a premium ad spot right there. The lead-in to the news? I would say it was priceless, but there's definitely a price."

"I hate commercials," said U.S.

"So do I," said Mr. White.

Hovan said, "Mr. White, why don't you hush down, the news is starting."

Montage of fire, flood and frenzy; U.S. hit the mute again and a booming voiceover announced, "Action News of New Texas at Six, with Hank Godbody and Debbie Ramirez, and the Stormologist Triplets Dori, Cori and Lori." The montage exploded in a fireball to reveal the news spokespeople waiting earnestly on their set.

"Good evening, I'm Debbie Ramirez."

"And I'm Hank Godbody. The Homegrown Osama bin Laden, the self-proclaimed 'Dr. X,' died by suicide today while in State Guard custody. Dr. X's lawyer was not available for comment, not even about the revelations that Dr. X had not filed an income tax return for the past eight years. The news about the suicide of the Tortilla Terrorists' leader sparked a demonstration in the Plaza."

Cut to a sleepy-looking Hispanic man in his forties, scraggle beard. Into the microphone he said, "I can't believe Dr. X would give *up* like that. People around here have hard lives too but, tsss, we don't give up like that."

Cut back to Hank Godbody. "Once again, the infamous Dr. X committed suicide today, just one week short of the grand jury that would have seen newly uncovered evidence of Dr. X's ties to both Al Qaeda and MS-13. Debbie?"

"Thanks Hank. In tonight's special report, there is a new crisis lurking in your homes, your children's schools, even in your recreational facilities and hospitals. Colorless, odorless and tasteless, this compound is capable of dissolving any substance it comes in contact with: metal, stone and even *human* flesh. Inhalation of as little as one teaspoon can be fatal. One single drop can destroy computers, cell phones and other sensitive, essential electronic equipment. If heated it can cause third-degree burns. If allowed to freeze it can cause millions of dollars in damage to pipes, roadways and even the foundation of your home. We'll have a complete report on the potentially deadly compound Dihydogen Oxide later, but first here's the Sportsnut, Harry Bottoms, with – " the TV winked out.

U.S. kept his face inscrutable under his hat.

Hovan grinned with real pleasure. "That man-on-the-street was great, I wonder where they dug him up?"

"When did you know about this?" said Mr. White.

"Ah Mr. White, you don't need to run everything in New Texas all by yourself. Being as my office is involved in the investigation, naturally I've been kept abreast of the situation. Blow by blow, if you will. And rest assured, we squeezed every last drop of information on Dr. X's organization before, ah, allowing the investigation to terminate."

U.S. growled, "Why am I learning about this over the damn TV?"

"Hell U.S., you know I'm not a good storyteller. I figured I'd let the professionals announce the good news. It is your station, after all."

"Any other surprises to look forward to, Mr. Hovan?" Mr. White asked.

Hovan sighed. "You see, White, problems get solved. You have to trust your Uncle Karl. We'll use Dr. X's information for one last flurry of arrests and this Territory will be secure. No more assassination attempts, U.S. And balloon rides every day you want one. Sounds pretty good, don't it?"

"What are you gonna do with the body?"

"Already taken care of, U.S. For all the faults of these people, their crematoriums can be swift, accommodating and very discrete."

Mr. White sighed. "No autopsy."

"And no grave for laying flowers. Dr. X is well ... dispersed," quipped Hovan.

268

Billy Ortiz

Me and Joseph are sitting under the shade of the awning, sharing a joint, when we see Mary's Brat flying up Psychobitch faster than I've ever seen anyone take it, jumping and slamming back down. Dust trail hanging back, probably clear to the highway.

"This looks like bad news," says Joseph in a squeaky voice, handing me the joint.

"I don't think she's in such a big hurry just to keep the beer cold." I hit the joint as Mary catches air and bounces off a juniper. The Brat is making some terrible sounds as it comes, metal-on-metal in a mistimed engine in a garbage compactor. Joseph runs to unlock the gate. Mary makes the turn and Joseph hauls the gate open.

Her tires spatter to a stop – there's fluid pouring out and the right front tire is flat. The dogs are jumping all over and Joseph is locking the gate and Mary's yelling, "They're here! They're coming right now!"

Mary's out of the Brat and running to the trailer in her motorcycle boots. Stomps up the stairs, yanks the whole gun rack off the wall and brings it outside. She squats down, starts filling her vest with shells. Joseph comes running over to us. She's all tweakin, babbling about the Guard coming up Psychobitch and how she had to turn around and haul ass back.

"Well now they know to come *here* you dumb broad," says Joseph, looking pale against his dark hair.

"Shut the fuck up and start loading," rasps Mary.

"We got to get the fuck outta here," says Joseph looking down Psychobitch.

"They was just finishing up with Bad Gregg's place, they fucked it *up*, I could see from the road, they was all over it."

Joseph runs his hand over his long hair and says, "Yeah, and now they're gonna fuck up our place cause you led them right to us."

Mary feeds the fifth shell into the twelve gauge and pumps it. "This is *my* place."

Fuck bro, I left my truck over at Pissed's yesterday. I was bringing him some soil, and afterwards we got fucked up and I walked home, oh shit.

"Billy! Git yisself ready, they comin!" Mary looks fierce, vest bulging with shells, pistols tucked into her cutoff jeans, fuzzed-out tattoos like war paint.

269

I run to my trailer and I can still hear them arguing. Past the goats and chickens, into my Airstream. Ok. Done this before. I grab my backpack, toss in the heavy strongbox, the pistol from under my pillow, a box of shells, the shotgun off the floor, my hat ... what else? *Come on, Billy, come on!* My canteen! I pull it out from under my bed, feels about half-full, and run back to Mary and Joseph.

"They're here!" shouts Joseph, pointing.

In a tunnel of dust coming up Psychobitch, I can see the lead truck. It ain't a pickup truck, it's a real fuckin army tank on treads, all armored and shit, carrying Guardsmen.

Mary gets behind the junked Studebaker, sets the Mini-30 against her shoulder, snaps back the bolt and starts shooting. The sound echoes off the mesa behind us. I grab the .308 from the rack and get on one knee beside Mary, set the barrel steady on the hood. The army tank is coming fast and there's militia trucks behind it.

Mary is reloading next to me. I aim for the treads of the army tank and pull the trigger. The kickback jolts me into what I'm doing.

"This is crazy Mary! We can't stop them!" I scream over the thunder of her rifle.

Joseph is with us, grabbing Mary by the shoulders, "We gotta go now baby."

Some of the Guard has split off, crashing through the fence and bouncing over Mary's open acreage. The Studebaker steel cracks and sings – they're shooting at us!

More Guard trucks pour through the hole in the fence, the rest are following the army tank right up to our front gate.

"They'll surround us Mary, we got to go!" Joseph yanks on her, finally gets her on her feet and running with him to his Scout on the other side of the trailer.

I sling the .308 over my shoulder, then the shotgun, and run after them yelling, "I gotta get my truck! I'm gonna cut across the land to Pissed's!"

"Good luck Billy!" as the army trucks converge on the Studebaker.

I run past the trailer and I can hear the screech of the tank treads and guns firing, a lot of guns firing. I stay low, try to keep the trailer between me and the action until I get to the dirt bike path. The path is dry sand, I stumble as I run, backpack bouncing and guns slipping off my shoulder. I got a big open space to cross before I get to the edge of the mesa and the path to Pissed's and my legs are already burning. I crouch down behind a juniper and look back. There's a dozen trucks and two tanks and they're all moving up on the trailer. Joseph and Mary are on the other side, he's trying to start the Scout. I run for the arroyo that separates the mesas. I stay low as I can, low enough to cut my face on a yucca, low enough to cut my face on a prickly pear. I can hear gun shots. The canteen is banging hard from my hip to my kidney and back. Stumble over a patch of dead twisted piñon, keep on going. I'm breathing hard, sweating, I feel sick. I can't feel my legs, it's my beating heart that's moving me to the hole in the fence straight ahead. Another thirty yards but I got to zig zag between junipers. My breakfast gulps up into my mouth and I swallow it back down, my mouth has an awful eggy taste now. The hole in the fence bounces closer and closer, all I can hear is my own breathing like I'm having a heart attack. I get to it, through the other side, and drop into the rocky arroyo. No vehicle can follow me – ugd, my stomach pukes up my breakfast and this time I let it out, scrambled eggs all over my own boots. I spit and spit to get it all out.

I hear myself whimper. I force myself to crawl up the other side of the arroyo – they might be following me on foot. Fuck I am so fucking out of shape. But I push myself ahead, following the single-track dirt bike trail. The curve of the trail puts the edge of the hill between me and the Guard – they can't see me no more. I might be home free, if I can just cut across the country quick enough to get to Pissed's, get in my truck and drive out. But I got to go *faster*. I can hear trucks and tanks and gun shots but I can't tell where they're at, the sound is bouncing around the mountains.

My knees feel forty years old for a *reason*, bro. But I push myself on, staying in the narrow rut. The hill falls away sharply to the left and I gotta go around the big rocks tumbled down from the mesa above. It's too narrow for trucks with these boulders, even if they've gotten across the arroyo. But I won't be safe until I get to Pissed's.

But jesus christ bro, I gotta stop. A second. I lean against a boulder, the little shade it gives. My shins are tore up and bleeding down into my socks. My mouth is eggy and I can't catch my breath. What's the goddamn elevation here?

I unscrew the canteen and put it to my mouth. Warm water comes out, tastes funky but it stops the burning. I choke on it like it's a mouthful of cobwebs and waste a bunch spitting it out, coughing so hard I gag up bile. Feels like something stabbing me in the side. I just need to rest for a minute, just one minute.

I hear rocks being kicked and I spin around, trying to get the .308 off my shoulder. It's a man on a horse, blocking out the sun for one blessed moment. It's Lester and Boss. His beard lifts a little and I think he's smiling, hat low over his glasses. Boss is looking at me, wiggling his lips around.

"Looks like you could use a lift," he says.

"State Guard – Mary and Joseph's," is all I can pant out.

"I saw them APC's but couldn't get there fast enough. Did they get away?"

"Don't know," I pant.

"Where you headed? Fixing to run to Burque like that?"

"Pissed's. My truck."

"Well then we gotta hurry, I saw Guard heading up to his place too. Come on, get up on Boss, you'll never make it on foot."

Lester takes his boot out of the stirrup and holds out a hand. I get up to Boss, who puts his head up, dances around a little bit but I get my foot in the stirrup. Lester hauls me up behind him. My legs only have a second to relax because Boss starts off and I'm bouncing my ass on the bedroll, gripping Boss's flanks with my thighs as tight as I can.

I got to hold onto Lester to keep from falling off. Try to not think about the fact that my dick and his ass are bouncing together. Boss is moving fast, we're just cruising up the path. He picks his way between boulders and never slows down, never gets tired. Lester was right, I never would have made it, and here we are, almost at Pissed's.

Boss carries us up the steep loose track above Pissed's canyon. My truck is down by his house – I hear a noise.

He pulls the reins and Boss stops moving. Lester says, "Helicopter. You better get off here, Billy."

And a white helicopter floats over a mesa, heading right for us. I slip and fall off Boss. I say thanks but Lester is watching the helicopter as he gets Boss turned around.

"Good luck Billy!" he shouts as Boss gallops back down the way we came.

I run down into the canyon – Pissed is already outside, AR-15 in his hands, looking up at the helicopter. I run down to his level ground.

"What did you do?" he screams.

"They came to Mary and Joseph's. Lester brought me here, for my truck."

"You brought them *here*?" and Pissed has his assault rifle aimed at my face.

"Whoa, just let me get my truck and get out of here bro," I say, trying to sound calm looking down the black hole of his AR-15.

"You fucking brought them *here* Billy! You fucking brought them here!"

"Listen bro, they're all over Psychobitch, they coming for everybody. Let me get in my truck, they coming up Psychobitch right now for us!"

"What," screams Pissed, "about *that*!" pointing at the helicopter hovering at the mouth of his little canyon, watching us.

"Fuck that thing," I say, raising the .308. I can feel Pissed staring at me, his gun still aimed at me. I put the shaking red dot on the cockpit of the helicopter and start squeezing the trigger.

The helicopter backs out of the canyon until it's too small for me to hit except by luck. Pissed spins around to run back to his little cabin where his wife is on the porch holding his littlest kid who's crying, crying, crying. He runs with his AR-15 in one hand screaming, "Ashley! Ashley! It's happening! Get the girls on your bike!"

I turn and run to my truck. Keys, keys, where are my keys? Here, and I'm about to climb in when I see the first truck, a Hummer, start driving up the canyon. I hear a dirt bike start and Ashley is fighting to get up the steep wash out the back end of the canyon with the kids crammed in a sidecar. Pissed comes running out of the cabin with an ammo box and he flops down with his gun behind a wall of rocks he made for just this purpose.

Pissed yells for me and then he starts firing. I run to him, past their homemade hot tub and vegetable garden and solar panels and slide into the dirt next to Pissed.

He's got his barrel through a chink in the rock wall and he's shooting bursts of three at the trucks. I set the .308 in a perfect groove for it. I'm safe behind the wall, I'm safe behind the wall, hold the red dot steady and wait for the tire – bang!

I got the tire, I saw it explode! Pissed is switching out magazines, he snaps the bolt and starts firing through his chink at the line of trucks coming. He's wasting bullets. I know I ain't got many 7.62's left so I take my time. It's easy to hit the other tire now that the truck ain't barely moving – bang!

They're firing back but it's flying over our heads. We're up above them and now they're stuck on a narrow dirt road with their lead truck not moving. We're shooting down at them and they are stuck.

I have to reload and Pissed yells, "They're getting out!"

273

I roll back over but I'm too late to get a shot at the guys scurrying out of the lead Hummer. Something big and heavy starts blasting our hill, the rock wall sends dirt and fragments into our eyes. We both get down low, waiting for it to stop but it don't, slugs keep smashing into the hill, our wall, his cabin, the hot tub which is pouring out water.

Pissed looks through his chink and yells, "They're pushing it out of the way!"

The big bullets are exploding all around us. I get my barrel through its slot. Through the scope I can see the second Hummer nudging the disabled one forward and it goes tumbling down into the canyon. The Guard starts creeping up again, our rock wall is breaking up under the heavy barrage.

I aim for the tires. Squeeze the trigger and miss I think, keep firing but I can't connect, the heavy slugs are dialed in to us, shaking the wall and my scope. I fire until the hammer falls on an empty chamber.

"Reloading!" I yell but Pissed is too, thumbing NATO rounds into a clip. The trucks are crawling to us, I can't reload fast enough and my pocket of bullets is almost empty. Our rock wall is coming apart, chips are raining on us.

I slide the .308 into the groove, drop the red dot on the right front tire, squeeze the trigger – miss. Why is it harder to hit, now that they're closer? Fire again, miss. Pissed is bursting *dakdakdak! dakdakdak!*

I try to slow my heart, get that red dot in a spot and wait for ... Bang! I think I hit it. But the army truck keeps on coming.

Pissed shouts at me, "We can't hold them! You cover me so I can get to my bike! You take your truck and head out the back way! I'll block the road on them!"

Pissed fires until he's empty, then he scrambles away. I move to his chink which gives a better angle – the army trucks are closing in. I fire until I'm out. Fish around in my pocket, thumb in one, two, three rounds. Reach back in for more and there ain't nothing. Fuck, I'm *out*. I turn and Pissed is crawling under the cabin's supports.

I try to put the dot right on the windshield. Boom! our wall's collapsing on me. The machine guns are tearing up the hill, shredding everything, I can't stop them. I drop the .308, pick up the shotgun and crawl under the cabin as fast as I can.

All I can hear is gunshots coming for me. I crawl through the cool underneath of the cabin, come out the other side. Pissed is chainsawing up the steep wash on his bike. Fuck, my truck will never make it up *that*.

But it's all I got bro. They're hitting the cabin hard now, pieces of it are landing all over the place. I cross myself, which I ain't done in like thirty years, and run for my truck. Get in throwing my shotgun and back-pack ahead of me. In the rearview, their trucks are lurching over pot-holes, not twenty yards behind. My truck jumps into gear and I race for the back of the canyon. Then my rear window explodes.

"Shit!" fishtailing a bit but I get it straight before hitting the steep climb. The engine is straining to haul me up the grade, tires slipping. Loud popping sounds and my truck starts shaking but keeps climbing. In the rearview the trucks are swarming the cabin. They all have a shot at me. All I can do is keep it floored and going straight.

The Explorer is begging for mercy but we get to the top, peppered in the ass the whole way. I'm out the canyon and about to start down the back side when I see Pissed, shoving one of them big cable spools to the edge of the rim. He gives it a heave and it tumbles down the wash and wedges itself under the Hummer that was trying to crawl up. Pissed drags a fencepost trailing four strands of barbed wire across the path.

His bike is standing next to me, still running. He looks over the edge down the wash, then hurries to his bike. Through my deafness I can still hear him yell, "What are you doing? Get the fuck out of here!"

"Where?"

"You follow me down Miner's Gulch Road, then we split up! I don't care where you go, just don't go south! Ashley and the girls are going south!" And he drops the goggles over his eyes and is ripping away, spattering me with dust.

The Explorer lets out a curse but takes me forward, down what definitely ain't a road. Too narrow for this truck, the junipers rake the sides with a sound like fingernails on a chalkboard. I keep checking the rear view. It's so bright without the glass, but so far nothing's come out the canyon. We grind down the trail, sounds like my truck is tearing itself apart. We pass the old mine. Be a good hiding spot if it wasn't filled in. I check again: still nothing behind us.

I can see the end of Miner's Gulch Road. Then I hear it: a heli-copter is right on top of us, where the fuck did it come from? Pissed whips his bike down the right fork, which I think takes him east. Which means I go left at the fork – west? North? Piece of shit compass in this truck never worked.

The helicopter hovers higher as we split up. Watching us both. And then it decides to follow Pissed. I drive way fucking fast, bottoming out and slamming into junipers. I think this takes me out to 401, and then maybe I can get to the casino. I'll be safe there, it's Pueblo land. If this truck can make it, I'll get there. I tip the canteen up to my mouth and finish what little is left, down to the last drop.

The truck didn't make it. It threw a rod with about a half mile to the casino. Explosion under the hood and it totally seized, couldn't even move it out of sight. Not that there's any cover out here anyway. Now I'm running, backpack bouncing, twelve gauge heavy in my hands. It's all so heavy, weighing me down, makes me want to stop just for a minute, drink some water but I'm out, I got to keep running, I can't stop or they'll find me and kill me.

I make it to where they dug out the hill on the backside of the casino. I can't go no farther than this embankment here. I crawl under a juniper, hot dust choking my throat. Just breathe, breathe. My legs are shaking. I'm going to be sick again.

Ugh god, and nothing comes out, whole body squeezing, can't breathe, dry heave and like mercy some bile drips out and I can suck air back into my lungs. I dig my hands into the dirt and just breathe.

Finally, finally, I can look where I am. The backside of the casino ain't like the front, with all the lights. Afternoon shade makes it seem dark and forbidden, just dumpsters, doors that only open from the inside ... and two trucks idling, facing each other and talking through the driver's windows. Just like cops do. Yeah, the truck on my side has the State Guard symbol. Fuck. Are they waiting for me? Are the others coming up behind me, followed my tracks even when I cut across the land? I spin around and there's nothing, just the dirt road across a cattle guard leading back through the desert to the mountains I just escaped from.

But I can't just stay here under this juniper in the dirt. I've got the shotgun and the .45. No good from this distance. Could I rush the Guard trucks? Not the way I feel right now, fuck. Fuck I am thirsty, I can't even *think*.

The near truck suddenly screeches off, speeding away around the corner to the front parking lot. The other truck ain't State Guard, it's

Tribal Police. He gets out of his truck, starts walking towards my embankment. Shit. I don't want to do this. But I slide the shotgun forward in the dirt, push the safety forward.

Then I hear the faint sound ... he's pissing. Jesus, he's only pissing. I take off my hat to wipe my face and that sends a bunch of rocks tumbling down at him. He takes a step back, dick still hanging out, and he yells, "You there! Get down from there, this is Indian land!"

I croak like a frog, "That's ok, I'm an Indian."

"Get down from there! That hill's all rattlesnakes! They feed on the dumpster rats!" He puts his dick away, reaches for his walkie-talkie.

"Ok bro, I'm coming down!" My voice gives out. I stand up with my hands up. He jumps and I realize I'm still holding the shotgun, shit. I sling it over my shoulder and keep my hands up. Start walking – skidding – down the embankment.

This is a mistake, but I can't run no more. I just can't run no more. I'll die if I stay out here another minute, twenty yards from water fountains and an all-you-can-eat buffet. Maybe if this guy takes me, he'll lock me up on the Pueblo, won't kill me.

He keeps his hand on the walkie-talkie as he watches me slide down. My clothes are torn off me, black blood dried on my legs. I jump off the retaining wall and stand in front of him. He's pretty tall, late twenties. Looks like he's in good shape. I don't have the energy to fight no more anyway.

"You ok?" he asks.

"State Guard started shooting everybody up. We didn't *do* nothing," I croak. All dizzy, and the next thing I know he's helping me sit down on the pavement.

"I know the State Guard. You wait right here. Don't point that gun at me."

I nod, trying to keep from falling backwards. He comes with a big bottle of water and hands it to me. He motions for me to drink and I do. I tip the bottle up and suck on it, don't give a shit for nothing. Delicious cold water fills my insides, I keep gulping and gulping against a thirst I'll never quench, gulping and then there's no more.

I'm breathing hard, drooling spit. Hand him the empty bottle, gasp, "Sorry."

"That's all right. What's the Guard after you for?"

I burp. Shake my head. "Not me. Everybody. Specially if you ain't white."

The cop watches me. He doesn't reveal nothing in his face. He's just watching. I try to stand up, but can't quite.

He says, "Yeah. I know the State Guard. They don't think much of tribal land these days. If they saw you looking like this, with a twelve gauge in your hand ..."

"I know. I know, bro. You gotta help me. Get me to my rez."

He raises his eyebrows.

"Please bro. I'll die out here. And I didn't do *nothing*."

"What's your name?"

"Billy Standing Elk." Hope it's ok to use William's name. This is life or death.

"Well, Billy Standing Elk, the Texas State Guard has just given me very specific orders for what I'm supposed to do for the next eight hours." He smiles. "But since I do not recognize their jurisdiction, they can go fuck themselves. I'll give you a ride. But you can't have that shotgun up front."

I'm sitting, looking up at him. "What?"

He says, "It's got to be racked until we get there."

The ride up north, the cop – his name is Bernie – tells me about all the shit that's been happening. About how they was saying the Nations was hording water and couldn't take care of our own people. About how the rez's are nothing but a place for outlaws to hide in, and run drugs from, and aid the terrorists out of. And how they have a duty to solve this problem by terminating the reservation system at long last, and, like they say, get'r right. But, of course, still keep them casinos running.

All this Bernie was saying, and something about how Dr. X was really a woman and part Navajo and it wasn't no suicide, not even. And that Texas was getting ready to do to Mexico what they did to us. Already had the Guard massed on the border. And more, and more he keeps talking. I can't keep my eyes open. Nodding out against the window as we drive north, sun setting out his window.

I caught a couple minutes sleep I guess, because now we're past Santa Fe and I can feel we're higher in altitude. My stomach reminds me that the only food I've had is now sitting in an arroyo a hundred miles south. The moon is out, full, and the stars too.

He says, "I haven't been up here in a while. You have to tell me the way."

I direct Bernie up the back way to the rez. Good to avoid the main roads, we agree. I can smell myself and I smell bad. I'm so tired I can't move. We come up on the old horse trade path. Instead of the welcome sign there's a metal gate across the path and two men standing there, shining a flashlight on us. They see that it's a Tribal Police truck but don't do anything to open the gate.

Bernie says, "You're on your own from here. Good luck, Billy Standing Elk."

"Thanks Bernie. You really did me good."

He smiles and says something I don't understand, I can't speak Tewa or whatever he speaks, I just nod and smile back. He pops the rear for me and I get my shotgun and then he turns around, headlights in the dwarf cottonwoods.

I walk up to the gate, dragging the shotgun behind me, and I say real relaxed and friendly, "Hey bro, what's happening? Open the gate so I don't gotta climb over it?"

They have their flashlights in my face. One says something in Tiwa or whatever to me. I let them see me drop the shotgun in the dirt. "Sorry bro, I'm no good with the home tongue. But this place is my home and I really need to get in, real bad."

"No one's getting in. Who are you supposed to be?"

"Billy Ortiz. I grew up here bro. My aunt is Lisa Marie White Cloud."

The other one says, "Lisa Marie White Cloud has been dead for years."

"*Look*," I say, and the panic in my voice makes them step back, reach for their hips. "Look, I'm not one of them. I'm one of you. Call William Standing Elk, he'll tell you. He's my cousin. Call him, you got a radio right?"

One of them grunts something to the other, and walks to his pickup. The other one keeps the light on my face.

"Can't you take that light out of my face? I've had a pretty rough day, bro."

"Nope."

The other one comes back and says, "William is coming."

It's all I can do to keep standing upright. Exhaustion makes my fingers shake when I try to light a cigarette. Seems like hours before I see the headlights of William's truck. He pulls up to the metal gate.

"William!" I shout, forgetting what's going on, I'm so happy to see him.

"Billy." He climbs over the gate, stands in front of me.

I try to put my arms around him but he steps back. I say, "William, I need your help. I need to get in."

"That's what you said last time, Billy."

"They'll get me out here. I ain't eaten all day, I run for miles. They'll kill me."

"You said that too. Except the part about running. You had a stolen truck last time, didn't you?"

"From the fucking State Guard! Come on, let me in William."

"You can't come in Billy. No outsiders can come in."

"I'm not an outsider, I'm one of you!"

William makes a face. "No you're not. You're a half-breed and a criminal."

What the fuck?

He says, "They are trying to take away our land. Again. The Elders, including me, have decided to say no, and we are barring all outsiders from our land."

"William, we're *blood*. I won't make it through the night on my own."

"I didn't tell you to come here."

"Look William, I've got a shotgun and a .45. I can help you defend our land."

William holds up his hands to wave me away. "We don't want your guns, Billy."

"I've got a little money too, hold on," and I struggle out of my backpack, to get at the strongbox.

William shakes his head. "We don't want your money. You need to go away."

I stare at him, and tears are in my eyes. I blink and they runs down my cheeks. "William? How can you turn your back on family? How can you do this to me?"

"You turned your back on us first, Billy," he says. Then he turns, climbs over the gate. Gets in his truck without looking back once.

And there's nothing for me to do but pull on my backpack, pick up my shotgun and walk away.

Dr. X

Lilah's profile emerged from her curls when she shifted, then was subsumed in them. In that brief moment, sunglass-serene, the grip of her jaw was apparent in the thin press of her lips. Her silver Mazda flitted through the interstate traffic.

The small back seat was stacked to the ceiling with boxes. The air conditioner was at max power: her diamond nose stud was ice bright, her nipples poked her silk blouse. She had her shoes off to drive, piled in her lap – the only free space. The chain around her ankle ragdoll-wobbled as she punished the pedals. The engine humming at her command was the only sound. Then, breaking the glacial silence:

"I'm sorry, I didn't mean anything bad by that. Just ... trying to stay on the light side," said Eddie, like a moose breaking cover. "It's a terrible, tragic thing. But if we let ourselves be consumed with grief or rage ... "

Lilah flashed the Mazda through a narrowing gap and into the passing lane, speeding into the open road ahead. She passed a truck and mellowed into the middle lane. Quietly, as if to herself, "No, forget it. I'm just ... you know."

"You're frightened. That's ok. I am too." Eddie dared put a hand on her slim smooth silk shoulder, lightly, just for a moment of conference. "But we'll be fine. This sort of thing, we knew it could happen. It does not mean we've lost."

"I don't care about losing. They took her and – do you think they tortured her?"

Eddie sighed to give himself time to see down the paths of his possible answers, to see where they led. "They would have to, to get anything out of her. She was a heroically stubborn woman. After they turned the café upside down they let you walk away, which means she didn't tell them anything Which means that they probably didn't, ah, torture her."

"They probably raped her. If they knew she was gay, they'd rape her. Just to – you know, you know that mentality. That's *exactly* what they would do."

"Lilah, you don't know that. Resist the urge to make it as bad as you can, to make it hurt more. All we know for sure is that," taking a sip of his lukewarm coffee, "she's gone now, and it's probably best for us to be far away from Albuquerque and anything that associates her with us."

"She was my best friend. And they killed her. Because of this ... shit we started. It's our fault she's dead."

"Don't start thinking that. You know she was willing to make that sacrifice, to fight for what we know is true. She's a martyr."

"I don't want a martyr. I want my friend."

"You know, I also lost my best friend to them."

"Yeah, I know. That's why he ratted on Joanna instead of *you*. Dr. X."

Eddie watched the sun fissure through the pass ahead as they drove into its blinding morning cascade. "We can't turn against each other. Not now."

"And Stuart's gone, I think he went to California. He won't answer my calls. He blames me for Joanna too."

"I didn't think they even liked each other."

"They *loved* each other. And now she's dead, and it's all my fault."

"Lilah, it is *not* your fault. If you want to blame, blame Texas. They invaded us, they forced us to fight back or be destroyed forever. *They* murdered her."

Lilah's response was to pass a landscaping truck at ninety-eight miles an hour. They jetted through a wide turn, sending Eddie into the door. When the roadway straightened out, Eddie pushed himself back into his seat and said, "Whatever you need to do is fine but please don't kill me. Now that my life finally has meaning."

Her sunglasses flicked to him through her arras of curls. And she slowed down. A bit. Silence until they reached exit 275 and started up State Highway 14.

"I need a drink." Her voice was small.

Don't say it's only eight in the morning. Don't say it's only eight in the morning. Don't say – "It's only ... it's ok. Whatever you need."

Pause. "I don't know what I need. Are there really less police on this road?"

"Usually, but ... you might want to slow down. Especially through Cedar Crest."

Lilah slowed down. Her knuckles gripped white.

Eddie said, "We'll feel better once we're in Santa Fe, planning our next move."

Lilah did not respond. She pulled into the right lane to allow a sheriff to pass.

"Jesus, where'd he come from?" said Eddie.

Lilah shrugged. She said, "I'll feel better when we get to my place and I can get out of these clothes and into my bed."

Completely unbidden, Eddie's cock nudged him in the thigh and he was suddenly aware of the car's vibrations jiggling his balls. He said, "Thanks for taking me with you. With my truck up in Santa Fe, I couldn't have gotten out on my own. I wouldn't have known that they had questioned you, ransacked the Sparrow ..."

"Fuck the Sparrow!"

Is – is she crying?

"Sorry," she sniffled. "It's because you're the only one here, the only one left."

"We'll get through this. And if you want out, you can quit. And trust that I'll revenge Joanna and Gordon for you."

"It's too bad about your friend. I'm sorry about that too. About what I said."

Eddie said solemnly, "Gordon had a great mind. But his common sense was sometimes ... I told him to be more careful, a thousand times. He was so confident in his successive layers of zombies when he webcast Radio KAOS ..."

"Is that what you think happened? They got him through the computer?"

"That's what I figure. Once they closed down his department at the U, he never left his casita. He never talked to anyone or had anyone over, except me. I don't think his neighbors knew his name."

"And then they did whatever it is they do. And he told them Joanna was Dr. X."

Eddie said, "I wish we hadn't stashed the ransom Cisneros's family paid at Gordon's house. That was probably the nail in his ... anyway, we're poor again."

"Poor but not destitute. I have one café left and it's the most profitable one. And the catering is still going. I can rebuild."

"It's a crime that they can destroy your business just because Joanna worked there part-time. But at least they didn't arrest you."

Lilah maneuvered the car through the East Mountains and across a broad mesa. Finally she said, "I just don't understand how most people can be so ... apathetic about this. Some people do everything they can to not know what's happening around them. While other people are dying for what's right."

"That's human nature. People don't want their bubble popped. But when the tipping point comes, when we hit the watershed, they'll rally."

"I don't think we're heading towards a watershed."

283

Eddie said, "Then call it the hundredth monkey, or critical mass, or a sea change."

"I mean, nothing we've done has mattered. No one cares."

"We've forced them to spread out all over the state. We sabotage their pipelines, spread fear among their soldiers. Blow up their trucks. And what about all the people who are fighting back in ones and twos all over the state?"

"All those psychos and survivalists, they don't care. It's just an excuse to dig up the supplies they put aside for World War III or Y2K or whatever."

Eddie tried to grab the trail of his indignation before it escaped into his voice. "We're not the only ones who have reasons to fight. We're not the only ones who have lost loved ones to this."

Lilah took a hand off the wheel and patted his bare knee. The sensation went to his lap. She said, "Oh, I love this little town. I haven't been this way in ages."

The Mazda crawled through Madrid, mindful of the dogs.

"It looks like a strong wind could knock these buildings over," said Eddie.

"We could stop for some coffee?"

"We should get to your place," said Eddie. He felt his erection in his voice.

The town was quickly behind them and the Mazda picked up speed, riding the S curves hard. Looking over the Cerrillos hills, Eddie said, "I'm going to keep fighting."

Lilah took her hand off the gearshift and ran it through her curls, revealing the dimple of her chin for one instant moment. They rode in silence through the sunburnt sea floor of antiquity. Miles later, slowing down to avoid a jackrabbit, Lilah said, "What if I raid the petty cash from Cesar's Cup and we go have a fabulous dinner somewhere tonight? And talk about *any*thing besides fighting, and revenge, and martyrs?"

"I think that is a perfect idea," said Eddie, hoping she was too busy driving to notice the goose bumps on his arm.

Lilah somehow found a parking spot in downtown Santa Fe. The morning sun defeated their sunglasses, leaving Eddie blind when they entered the dark of Cesar's Cup.

It was a small place with a crowded patio of hipsters, dogs and freaks. The dreadlocked and pierced woman behind the counter gave Lilah an enthusiastic hug. Lilah said "I'd like you to met my pal Eddie. Eddie, this is Cesar's steadfast manager, Z."

Z gave Eddie a manful handshake. They began talking about some business details and Eddie drifted away, careful to not trip over the twin-bearing stroller which had been pushed up behind him by a pregnant woman. He drifted to the bulletin board.

Handwritten ads elbowed each other for position on the cork: Self-Actualization, with advanced courses in Applied Selfishness. Geriatric Rolfing. Aromatherapy for dogs. Acupressure for cats. Pilates for infants. Colonics for houseplants.

"Ready to go?" asked Lilah.

"All done here? That was fast."

"Unless you want a coffee or chai or something. Me, I'm ready for a nap."

"I know, you haven't slept yet. I ought to go softly into that good nap myself."

Lilah parked on a quiet side street in northwest Santa Fe. "This is my little hovel, in the back here. I rent out the front."

Eddie followed her down the driveway to a casita in the back. Sunlit, overgrown with grape vines. *Apis mellifera* buzzed the tiny white flowers.

She opened the door. It was cool inside, and larger than it looked from the driveway. "Sorry for the mess. It's kind of stuffy in here."

There was no mess, nor was it stuffy. Saltillo tile floor for the attached living room and kitchen. Some bookshelves, two closed doors.

"How often do you stay here?" asked Eddie, closing the door to the sunlight.

"Not much, since I opened the Sparrow. Z has Cesar's pretty well in hand. All my managers are good."

"That's because they love you," said Eddie, dropping his dusty pack behind a reading chair.

"No, it's because I know how to pick the right people," she said, flash of alabaster armpit as she removed her earrings. "I'm going to take a shower before my long nap."

Eddie sat on the futon, flipping through an old Adbusters. The sound of shower water reached him through the bathroom door. Eddie could hear the pattern change as she moved beneath the spray. Like sonar he could sense the shape of her naked body. Her naked, coffee colored, smooth female body, with Lilah alive inside it.

He woke up, startled by the sound of the bathroom door opening. Lilah was wearing a short white bathrobe, rubbing at her wet empire of back curls with a big pink towel. She smiled at Eddie and padded on bare feet to a kitchen cupboard.

"Join me for one glass to usher in the good dreams," she said, wine bottle in hand.

Eddie's mouth was clumping cat litter but he said yes.

They toasted wordlessly. They sat across the Scandinavian coffee table from each other. Her hair was up in the pink towel. Her legs were tucked underneath her robe.

"Mmm," she said, sipping. "You can take a shower too, if you'd like. Actually, I'd recommend it, sweaty bear. I'll make a reservation for us before I sleep. The phone's in my bedroom."

Eddie's neck prickled pink. "I didn't have time to pack any clothes to wear to a fancy restaurant."

"What was all that stuff we hauled up here then?"

"Things I might need."

"Things you might need more than clothes? Tss. Boys. Well, we can stop at a consignment shop on the way to the restaurant. My treat, po boy."

"Thanks," Eddie said into his wine.

Wine finished, she brushed her teeth and padded into her bedroom. Eddie showered, acutely aware of how recently she had shaped a space under the very same spray. He resisted the bugle call of his boner and dried off, looking into the mirror.

He pulled on the same dirty boxers he had been wearing and curled up on the futon. Sleep came like a long-postponed prayer.

Dinner at the fancy restaurant. Not only was she clean, lovely in a summer-light dress, she had found an outfit that almost looked good on him. She had ordered the wine and it was delicious. As was the second bottle.

Through the meal of lamb carpaccio, dandelion-green salad, elk tenderloin and rosemary flan, the conversation swung on its own momentum from childhood fears (him: tidal wave, her: the dark) to places they wished to travel most (him: the Amazon, her: India) to favorite films (him: *Delicatessen*, her: *Harold and Maude*) to favorite books (him: all 730 pages of *The Ants* by E.O. Wilson, her: Anaïs Nin's diaries) to favorite musician (him: Gustav Mahler, her: Ani diFranco) to how their parents met (him: unrepeated encounter after a Jethro Tull concert, her: high school sweethearts) to professional goals (him: "the respect of those I admire", her: "creating a foundation to help women start their own businesses") to first loves (him: Jerome from Cocoa Beach, her: Genevieve, her professor) to worst heartbreak (him: Lisa the dolphin researcher, her:

Genevieve) to wildest place for sex (him: in the DJ booth of a club in Key West called "The Boom Boom Room" with a boy and a girl and ten hits of ecstasy between them, her: in the university library's elevator with Genevieve) to favorite sexual position (him: "all of them", her: "me with a strap-on, my lover doggy-style and handcuffed to the wrought iron headboard") and he choked on his wine.

It was only while she was counting cash for the sizeable bill that any mention of the present occurred (him: "Maybe I can call that bike gang leader, see if he can help distribute my chemical alchemics", her: "We're not talking about any of that, remember?"). They bumped hips, walking to the car. The smell of her. Warm on wine, she drove home with the windows open to summer night, dress furling across her knees.

A mildly hilarious interval trying to find the proper key on her ring of thousands. Another bottle of wine opened, Antonio Carlos Jobim playing on the stereo, dusty candles summoning and banishing shadows. An accidental brush with her arm and she looked up at him with a liquid mouth open to the quickening of a smile.

Eddie said, "It's just you and me."

He placed his palms on the smoothness below her cheek bones and kissed her.

She pulled her face out of his hands and punched him in the mouth.

Lilah locked herself in the bedroom, weeping with unquenchable grief while he scratched the door, begging her name. He finished the bottle of wine and sat with his face in his hands against the sound of her crying long after she'd stopped, tongue swelling to fill his mouth until he stumbled to the cupboard for another bottle. He poked the cork into the bottle and drank straight from the neck until he fell to the kitchen sink and vomited in tears.

He awoke with his face cemented to the floor with vomit. He pulled himself to his feet, weak and nauseous and desperate for water. Relieved to discover the kitchen sink was in front of him, less so when he looked into it. He ran the faucet to get most of it at least moving, then sucked cold water straight from the tap.

In the end it was too much water and he puke-burped some back into the sink. He stumbled to the bathroom to relive the dangerous pressures within him. It was only when he saw his split, swollen lip that it all came back.

Eddie's bronchial tubes stiffened and shrank, a throat of thorns. Wheezing, he fought with the lock until he was outside in the cold threshold of dawn, shoes in one hand and inhaler in the other. He sat on the hood of her car until he could breathe again. Tears prismatic, he walked away.

Morning rush traffic was legion by the time he walked to his truck parked in the lower lot at the Chavez Center. There had been a long time to think, a hammer for the chisels of his headache. Black funnel funereal spiral of his thoughts. There were too many people about so he had to lie in the dark bed of his pickup to make his preparations, fighting with gravity and encumbrances.

Growling his mantra to himself, "You want a martyr? I'll give you a fucking martyr." He spat it over and over as he finished his work, zipped his coat over it, slid out of the bed of his truck and climbed into the cab.

Eddie drove in traffic to the State Capitol and parked illegally. He walked across the busy street to the main entrance. He kept his left arm around his waist to hold the belt of dynamite in place; his right hand gripped the plunger in greasy sweat. A line of people waited to go through security. There was a pair of Guardsmen and a metal detector.

Eddie waited, sweat running fiercely now. Breathing was hard work. Grinding his teeth, *You want a martyr? I'll give you a fucking martyr*.

"Please state your name, sir."

"My name is Dr. X!" as he thumbed the plunger all the way down.

U.S. Armstrong

"White. Is this my goddamn office?"

"Yes," said Mr. White, hanging his head, glasses sliding down his nose.

"Are you currently the Governor of this Territory?"

"No sir."

"Then why is *my* goddamn office filling up with all this ... hokum?"

"I thought your office, and the rest of the Governor's Gallery, would be improved if the pilfered artworks were replaced with – "

Hovan interrupted, "I do believe it was a rhetorical question, White."

The Governor's Office was in silence.

Hovan said, "More pressing business, U.S. We have tracked Geldman down."

"Yeah?" U.S. looked up fully, exposing the bags under his blue eyes, the shocked white of his mustache. His skin was loose, papery.

"Geldman is in Mexico City."

"Mexico City? Why in the hell?"

"We don't know U.S. All we know for sure is that last month he passed through Mexican Customs on a flight from Oklahoma City with two bags containing clothes, toiletries and a laptop computer, with the stated purpose 'por negocios.' On business."

"We don't have any goddamn business in Mexico no more. Not with them sending sabotagers and agitators and weapons and drugs across my border. No one in his entire office knows why? Not even his secretary Janet?"

Hovan said, "Nobody in the office knew that he was going to Mexico. He didn't buy a ticket with his corporate account. Perhaps if you would allow me to politely query the Geldman family?"

U.S. dismissed the notion with his hand. "He's got no family left, cept his son out climbing the Himalayas or feedin the lepers or some shit. I'm all the family he's got."

U.S. let his hat brim lower to his chest. Mr. White sat solemnly. Hovan drummed his fingers on the arms of his chair.

Hovan said, "Did you tell him about the arrests?"

Mr. White said, "No not yet. We're naturally hoping to avoid a major confrontation, U.S., but the police chief in Albuquerque confirms that he has three Texas State Guardsmen in custody. He refuses to release them, tell me their names or their alleged offense. Under the provisions of Operation Zero Tolerance, the writ of *habeas corpus* is suspended for all law enforcement. However, the terms of the occupation specifically grant Guardsmen immunity from arrest. What do you want me to do?"

From under his hat, U.S. growled, "Fire the dumb son of a bitch."

"That ... could be a problem sir," said Mr. White. "I've received informal reports that he has a large force of police officers, uh, occupying City Hall where his office is located."

"We got the damn police turning traitor now? What *is* it with these people?" His voice was low and slow from under his hat.

Hovan cleared his throat. "U.S., this is as good a time as any to discuss a new direction here. This piss-poor territory is becoming a financial ... cadaver. Their coffers are empty, with an expected budget shortfall – even with the tax hikes – of two billion dollars. Now, the vast majority of that has been properly channeled into our – I mean, Texas's – intelligent design. Over half of the new water fields have already been pumped dry. Reservoirs are so low an ant could walk across them. It is perhaps time to consider our economic withdrawal."

"Economic withdrawal?" said U.S., hat tipping up slightly. "You mean retreat?"

"We knew the day would come. Our efficiency in gathering the spoils of war has surpassed even our most optimistic economic models. New Texas has been fully ... realized. And, truthfully, there wasn't much here to begin with."

U.S. growled, "We ain't retreatin. This job ain't done. White couldn't handle this population on his own, you kiddin? There's Mexicans running amok, Indians doing the goddamn war dance, gangs and cult leaders arming their followers. Next you gonna tell me Fawn is still all over that goddamned internet."

"Um," blanched Hovan. "We're making excellent progress."

U.S. snorted. "Progress. That's what the rehab shrink says about my baby girl. Locked up on suicide watch. On account of her meds making her gain so much water weight. Huh. *Water* weight. *Progress.* Shit."

Hovan ran his palms on his shining pant legs. "It probably won't amount to nothing, U.S., but the first word from our people in Colorado is that old coward Camby really *has* assembled a handful of forces and is hooked up with some of those militias they got around Durango. Puking a lot of talk about liberating New Texas. We don't know yet where their funding is coming from but we'll squeeze it off, soon as we do. Now, they don't have enough strength to liberate a taco stand, but with our troops fully allocated to Operation Zero Tolerance, we may – "

"Shit!" exploded U.S., slamming his palms on the desk. "*This* I can put an end to right goddamn now. I'm calling the Colorado Governor and I'm telling him if he don't bust up them agitators right goddamn now then the Texas State Guard will do it for him."

U.S. picked up the telephone and barked, "Grace? Get me Governor Drummond of Colorado on the line."

At that moment there was a massive concussion that rattled the entire building, followed by the tinkling of broken glass. They jumped to their feet.

"What was that?" said Mr. White.

"It sounded like a bomb," said Hovan, nervously straightening his tie.

U.S. shouted into the phone, "Grace! Get security up here! And will someone please tell me what in the goddamn hell is going on?"

The Outcome

Dr. X

Eddie had a running head start before the Guardsmen reacted to his failed mission. He shoved through the glass doors, unzipping his jacket as he ran. The zipper stuck and he tried to pull the jacket over his head. He tripped over the median, stumbled into traffic, hands asprawl – into the path of a GMC Megalith.

The Megalith swerved into the other lane and collided heavily with a civilian Hummer. Momentum carried the Hummer into a glazier truck parked on the corner. The explosion of plate glass was deafening but immediately overwhelmed by the chaos of traffic crashing into the pile-up. Insistent horns and the glazier truck's alarm.

Eddie pushed himself off the pavement, looked at the wreckage in awe. Then he heard the shouts of the Guardsmen running out of the Capitol. Eddie sprinted, feeling a terrifying pinch in his trachea. He got into his truck and started it. Through swerving rubber-neckers and spastic drivers, Eddie chanced a look in the side-view mirror: the Guardsmen were picking their way through the pile-up, the locked fenders, the screaming injured; they had their pistols drawn but dared not shoot.

Eddie whipped down a narrow street, shuttled through a rich neighborhood of old adobe walls, and shot up an old highway. Nothing behind him. Stop sign ahead – nice and easy now.

What? The Fuck? Did you just try *to do?*

Eddie let out a sigh of such lugubrious self-pity that the wind-shield's cracks spread. He followed his escape route unconsciously, will-fully ignoring the past and future. It was enough to finally get rid of his jacket, get out of the dynamite belt and fling them out the window. Hit the inhaler that he thought he would never have to use again.

He was through Villanueva when he realized that there was a helicopter following him. He took the dirt BLM road fast, bounced and jarred in his seat. To his left, the Pecos cut through layers of rock to carve its canyon. The junipers were thick here, and wildflowers had risen. The helicopter was a hunting wasp.

Finally the stand of cottonwoods was in sight. They were in full green beckoning. Eddie floored the gas and the pickup leapt into the cottonwoods in four bounces, stopped by a web of blackberry branches. The helicopter circled around the grove, its *whupwhupwhupwhup* echoing around the canyon.

Backpack snug on his sweat-stuck shirt, Eddie started up the path. The helicopter was somewhere above the tree canopy. The leaves patched over the sky but the turbulence loosened the stitching. Sand and sound came from all directions in fury. He stayed low to the soil. Breathing was hard. Breathing was very hard.

Eddie found himself crawling on his hands and knees. The helicopter was everywhere and nowhere. It was like breathing through a folded towel. But slowly, slowly, he made it to the edge of the cottonwoods. The sun-blinding canyon was before him, one hundred yards of treacherous narrow ledge at steep ascent. The cave was a distant cool mouth. Where was the helicopter? Everywhere, nowhere.

Eddie tightened the waist belt on his backpack, took as deep a breath as he dared, and sprinted into the sunlight. Loose rocks skittered under his feet. Arms out and low for balance, Eddie charged up the path.

The warble of the helicopter changed, it was moving: it had seen him. Eddie felt fingers around his throat. He tripped and went down, palms split open on rocks.

Gunshot. More, following insistently. Eddie willed himself forward. Muzzle flash from the cave's mouth. Body choking on sour lactic acid, he stumbled up, up.

The sound of the helicopter flattened to a buzz saw. Eddie looked and it was peeling away, up out of the canyon. Eddie turned to face the cave but it was just a foreshortened crease from his angle.

Jimbo's voice fell down over the rock face, "Hurry Dr. X!"

Eddie hauled himself up the path, dust clotting his bloody palms. The last echoes of the helicopter were fading. Was that the river or the pulse of blood in his ears? Eddie climbed the last jagged stone buttresses and a brawny tanned forearm came down to haul him up. Eddie tumbled into the cave. *Breathe. Breathe. Just breathe. Just breathe.*

A dog was licking his face.

"That'll do, Roscoe," Jimbo's voice. The hot tongue was gone. "He's just happy to see you. Taste someone else's sweat for a change."

Eddie couldn't talk. Couldn't breathe, even with his legs up on the cave wall.

"Sorry I chased off your friends. Sniper was fixed on you. You – you ok?"

Wheezing as shallow as a drum skin, he could hear the sounds he was making.

"Jesus, Dr. X, what's the matter?"

Eddie couldn't see Jimbo, couldn't talk. He yanked an arm to point at his backpack as his vision tunneled gray.

"In there? What is it?" Jimbo started zipping open the pockets.

Airless tomb, jackrabbit heartbeat wasting the little oxygenated blood left. Trying to breathe with boulders piled on his chest. Python strength. Darkness came like mercy.

"The syringe? You need the syringe?"

What's a syringe? *Yes!* All willpower went into nodding his head once.

A prick somewhere in the far distance. The pain was somehow attached to him ... by his arm. His arm came back to him, then air ripped into his ragged lungs. He heard an inhuman sound that came from his throat. *Breathing. You're breathing.*

Eddie was lying on his back on the floor of a cave. A black dog with a white streak from his crown to his nose was watching him, sharing a look of concern with the man far up above. Frightened – they looked frightened. Jimbo still held the syringe.

Breaths came. Like river waves. Slowly dissolving his fear.

"I'm ok," said Eddie weakly. He struggled to sit up. Jimbo tossed the syringe away and helped pull Eddie into a sitting position against the cave wall.

Jimbo said, "Did they poison you? Tear gas?"

Eddie shook his head. He was drenched in sweat and shivered, the cave was cold.

"What was that stuff I shot you up with? Adrenaline or something?"

"It's like adrenaline, except ... whoa, give me a minute. Ohhh. Ok."

"Are you sure that was enough? There's more syringes in there."

Eddie shook his head. "The comedown is a bitch. With subcutaneous. Injections. But thank you. For giving it to me. Jimbo. You saved my life."

Jimbo beamed. "Happy to help. Though, for the record, that was the second time I saved your life in the last five minutes. There was a sniper in that helo and you made yourself a real easy target, trying to climb the ledge. I had to reveal my position by opening fire, but I figured you wouldn't mind. Under the circumstances."

Eddie smiled feebly.

"How bout some water?"

Eddie nodded. Jimbo ripped the top off a bottle and Eddie glugged it empty.

Jimbo was looking out the cave. "Are the other Rattlesnakes on their way?"

Eddie shook his head. "No time. Unplanned visit."

Regarding Dr. X with a squint, "You got the asthma or some-thing?"

Eddie said, "Yeah. Listen, we ought to get out of here. They'll be coming."

Jimbo said, "If we run, they'll nail us in the open on any of these slow roads. We should stay here."

"Here?"

Jimbo nodded. "That's what we're set up for, ain't it? We got a line of sight on every approach. Overhang protects us from above. Enough food and water for a couple weeks. We'll wait right here for them."

Eddie started to crush the empty bottle in his hand, looking for a trash bag.

"Whoa, don't do that Dr. X," said Jimbo, taking the empty bottle and popping it out. "We got a use for these. You know that Ecojel stuff for lighting barbecues and whatnot we got? Jellied ethanol. Makes some real nifty Molotov Cocktails and it's stable enough to be kept in plastic. I call them Roscoe Cocktails. Burns long and sticks like napalm. I tried it out. I know, against regulations, but I had to make sure they was gonna work. They do – that green shit is something else."

Eddie said, "I never thought of using it like that."

A big smile on Jimbo. "You would have eventually."

Eddie slid his back up the wall and stood, wobbling.

"You just relax, Dr. X. Roscoe gave me good warning so I got everything set. Rifles and the AR-15's if they get too close, cooler filled with Roscoe Cocktails. And, if they really piss me off, I got my daddy's Kalashnikov he brought back from Vietnam."

"All right," said Eddie. "I guess we'll wait for them."

"Time is our ally, right? Just like the man on Radio KAOS always says. Hey, you bring any more to listen to? I listened to all them others a bunch of times through."

"Sorry, Jimbo. Radio KAOS is ..." began Eddie. He dropped his eyes to his boots. "I didn't have time to get the MP3's."

"That's ok. What were you running from in such a hurry? Checkpoint?"

"No, it was ... something stupid."

"I don't believe that. Now, if you need to use the latrine there's a bucket back in the cave. Makes it easier to slop down the shaft I cleared."

"I'm glad you used your time out here so well."

"Normally I use the great outdoors but I reckoned we'd need an option if we couldn't leave the cave for a while. And I expect the rattlesnakes down there won't mind getting dumped on a little bit, seeing as it's special circumstances and all."

They were sitting on the food lockers enjoying an early supper of canned soup when Roscoe looked up from his bowl, ears pricked and whiskers trembling. He trotted to the mouth of the cave and cocked his head.

Jimbo shot Eddie a look and wiped his mouth on his sleeve. Roscoe started growling low and serious. Setting down his can of soup, Jimbo said, "They're here. That'll do Roscoe, good dog. Go lie down. Dr. X, it's showtime."

Eddie stood and brushed Roscoe's tail as it swung by. "What should we do?"

Jimbo stalked up to the mouth. "There they are, coming up the road. APC's, bunch of pickup trucks. Maybe two dozen in all. I reckon they'll deploy under cover of them cottonwoods. Find your truck and figure they got us where they want us. We'll be able to shoot straight down that ledge path into the woods, pick em off one at a time."

Jimbo handed Eddie a pair of ear plugs as the column of Guard trucks disappeared behind the cottonwoods. Sounds of doors slamming, babble of men over the river. From the back of the cave Roscoe raised a growl and Jimbo said, "That'll do."

They lay prone at the cave entrance on coarse blankets. Ammo box between them. Jimbo was looking down the ledge into the trees. He whispered, "They can't even see us from where they're assembling. Stupid bastards, trying so late in the day. Sun'll be in their eyes when they begin their assault."

Eddie swallowed a mouthful of dust. "I've never shot at anybody before."

Jimbo moved his finger to the trigger guard. Quietly, "You'll get used to it. Remember to aim low, they're below us."

Eddie looked through the scope. Cottonwood silver bark, some branches bobbing in and out of focus. He flicked the safety forward.

"Keep up continuous fire. I'll call out when I need to change magazines, you pick up fire," whispered Jimbo.

"Ok," breathed Eddie.

The sound of the river. The wind in the cottonwoods. Heat bouncing off the stones. Heartbeat bouncing through the blanket and off the rocks underneath.

The *crack* from Jimbo's rifle penetrated Eddie like a broken spear. *Crack! Crack!* Eddie tried to hold the crosshairs steady – what was Jimbo shooting at?

"Reloading," Jimbo said sternly, feeding rounds into the internal magazine.

Eddie pulled the trigger and felt the god-power of the powder. He sent bullets blindly into the trees. The rifle kicked hard, spoiling his aiming at the darkness.

Jimbo snapped the bolt and said, "You reload now."

Edie pulled the trigger once more and it clicked weakly. He rolled onto his side and began feeding rounds into the breech. Jimbo fired steady and patient, *Crack! Crack!* and said "Reloading" while Eddie was still fumbling bullets.

Eddie pulled the bolt back and released it. They were shooting back, bright flashes from the woods and a chaos of reports. Eddie swung the crosshairs at the bright flashes. *They're trying to kill you!*

The crosshairs trembled around the muzzle flashes. Eddie fired five times as fast as he could. While he reloaded, Jimbo continued the fire. Eddie brought the rifle up, looking for muzzle flashes. He found them low in the cottonwoods and pulled the trigger, leaning his shoulder into the painful kick.

Empty, Eddie dug into the ammo box. Jimbo was ready, eye to the scope but he wasn't firing. It was quiet, thunderously quiet. Eddie whispered, "What's up?"

Jimbo whispered, "They pulled back into the woods where we can't see them."

"Look!" said Eddie. Guardsmen dashed from the bottom of the cottonwood stand, scurrying along the rocky river bank, dipping behind boulders. Jimbo swiveled and fired down at the minute running figures. Eddie held his crosshairs on the clearing they had to pass through, waiting for someone to – *Crack! Crack!*

"I got that guy!" whooped Eddie.

"Settle down, don't get cocky," said Jimbo, waiting for his shot.

"How many made it to those boulders?"

"Don't know," said Jimbo, stretching out his hand against his hip. "Dozen. They're gonna try to climb up your side, flank us, get us in a crossfire."

"My ears are ringing," said Eddie.

"Imagine if you wasn't wearing plugs."

"I want to hear for a second," said Eddie, pulling one plug out. The river was a wall of cottony white noise. But through that he could hear men shouting for each other, angry and in pain and tiny-harmless.

They lay there, loaded and watchful, as the slow sun passed. A sharp shadow crossed the canyon and muted the colors.

"Why aren't they doing anything?" asked Eddie.

"Reckon they're gonna wait for nightfall and try again. We'll be ready. Got some energy bars and water bottles in that locker by your feet."

"I could use some water," said Eddie. They both drank.

"You're ok there Roscoe, that's a good dog. You stay," Jimbo called softly into the cave. To Eddie he confided, "Gunshots, thunder, fireworks, mountain lions ... they don't bother him. Plug in a vacuum cleaner, he runs like he's French."

Evening became night in a stately purpling of the sky. No sounds or movement from below. Just the soothing slough of the Pecos.

Jimbo whispered, "If it comes to it, we can sleep in shifts. No reason for two of us to be uncomfortable out here, waiting for them to try again."

Eddie whispered, "Actually, we don't need to sleep. Dr. X has just the thing."

Eddie crawled into the dark cave and found his backpack. He crawled back to Jimbo with two capped syringes. Eddie whispered, "Popping works in an emergency but for the best effect I'll find a vein.

299

Scared of needles?"

"Nope," said Jimbo, eyeing the syringe. "What is that stuff?"

"All natural. No preservatives. Homemade, world-class sleep repellant. I'm gonna inject behind your knee."

"Ok," whispered Jimbo, swiveling the scope smoothly between the entrance to the copse and the boulders on the riverbank.

Eddie rolled Jimbo's pant leg up to his knee and pushed the gathered material over. He uncapped the syringe, stretched the skin and poked the needle into Jimbo's saphenous vein. Drew back a red ribbon of blood and pressed the plunger.

"Ohhh god. Oh god, what is that stuff? Jesus, Dr. X, I ain't had anything like that in – hoo doggy, oh *man*."

"You're ready for the night," said Eddie, uncapping a syringe for himself.

Small stars came out shyly, emboldened by their peers. Eddie was about to point out a constellation when Jimbo said, "They're coming, right now they're coming. I got the woods, you got the boulders."

Eddie trained the scope into the darkness of the riverbank. He said, "I can't see them," but Jimbo had started firing down the ledge path. With his naked eyes straining to discern movement in the dark, Eddie felt the exposure of wind on his face. Then the sandstone bump he was looking over shattered, filling his eyes with dust. He dropped the rifle and grabbed his scorpion-stung face, rubbing at his burning blind eyes.

Jimbo was rolled on his side, reloading, "Don't let them climb up the side there, don't let them get height and flank us!"

"I can't see," said Eddie, feeling the corneal scratches under his lids.

The Guardsmen lay down a heavy cover fire as they advanced out of the woods. Some broke up the steep treachery of the path. Jimbo sent them rolling down to the river.

Reloading, he said, "You got to stop them climbing up that side! If they get in position they'll have us in a crossfire!"

Eddie blinked through the scope. It was too dark. He fired once, turned back to Jimbo. "It's too dark, I can't even see them. How can they see to climb?"

Jimbo snapped the bolt and said, "They must got the night vision goggles. Quick Dr. X, grab the cooler of Roscoe Cocktails, there's a Zippo in there with them."

Eddie left his rifle and scrambled into the cave. Bullets cracked off the rocks, fragments scattering. He dragged the cooler up to their redoubt and opened it. Two dozen plastic bottles filled with green jelly, dry fabric wick poking out the top. As Jimbo had instructed, Eddie pulled the wick out by its dry end, turned it over and poked it into the bottle leaving the gloppy end exposed.

Eddie flicked open the Zippo and snapped it alive. He touched the flame to the wick. It ignited, melting down into the bottle.

"Throw it!" shouted Jimbo over the crack of bullets.

Eddie dropped his arm, then flung the flaming bottle. It fell and a rising flame plumed on the rocks. The gunfire stopped from that flank; the sound of men screaming reached up to them. They stumbled out blind from behind their cover, arms over their eyes and Jimbo dropped them one at a time.

"Eye for an eye," said Eddie, lighting another Roscoe Cocktail. He heaved this one further – it smashed on rocks and spread fire down the flank.

"Reloading!" shouted Jimbo. "Get one down my side."

Eddie turned the wick around, lit the wet end and chucked the bottle in a high arc. The flame left a streak in the sky. The bottle came down on the path, bounced rubberly and fireballed into the woods.

Jimbo swiveled and fired as their positions were revealed by the long-burning orange flames. "More! On your side! Up there! They got too close!"

Bullets began to strike accurately around them. Eddie heaved a Roscoe Cocktail at his flank. Jimbo rolled over with his father's AK-47 up to his chest. "Get down!"

Jimbo fired staccato bursts at the men exposed by the chemical fire, hot casings bouncing jingly on the sandstone. Eddie readied another cocktail. He looked for a target but the flanking group had been dispersed.

Now Jimbo was firing down at the river bank boulders. Eddie heaved a Roscoe Cocktail out into the canyon. It splattered fire on the boulders, illuminating.

"We got them trapped," said Jimbo, reloading the banana clip. "Grab an AR-15. Wait for them to try and withdraw to the trees."

"Do you hear that?" said Eddie. "What are they yelling?"

Taylor Jon Bridges

Fuckin hiding behind a fuckin pile of rocks with a bunch of stupid fucking niggers! Another firebomb hits and they relax on me for a second – I go back for more, scream into Bobby Earl's fat red face, "IT'S ALL YOUR FAULT!"

McDonnell and Mayles are holding me back, telling me to keep my head down. I knock them away. Bullets crack off the top of the boulder – we all drop onto the sand.

"Stay the fuck *down* TJ, don't lose your head," says Bobby Earl. "Ain't nothin to do but just wait em out, wait til the sun comes up and our boys can spring us."

"Who, them faggots hiding in the woods? They're not the ones that got all shot and burned up trying to climb straight up some fucking *cliff*. Only reason I made it back is cause I never got night vision like I was s'posed to."

"TJ, it's fucked up, I know. But you gotta calm down, don't lose your head," says Mayles, my good buddy, fucking nigger.

"It's fucking Taylor Jon, fucking goddammit."

I give *up*. The river is noise in the dark, this noise like it wants to suck you into its darkness. My fucking hands. I poke a black, bubble-burned finger into the damp sand to feel the cool.

I saw Bo take it. I was following him cause he could see cause he had them goggles. We was climbing the hardest, steepest part, getting an angle on that cave. And then this little burning string came flying down like a joke and it turned into an exploding star. The star hit and the fire was burning Bo, I heard him screaming and he's ripping his goggles off and stands up, and I go to pull him down and he got hit and fell over backwards on top of me, still burning. I rolled him off and beat at the fire with my hands and the fire got on my hands too, and it wouldn't go out, and the flames were coming up my sleeves and I ran down the hill, the only light was from the fires that was blowing up behind me and my own burning hands. I ran into the river. It still burned underwater, for a while. My hands now ... that smell ain't fadin. Fingers look like burnt sausage links, makes me sick to look at, makes me puke and I puke on the sand, stringy and sour. Gotta keep my hands out of the dirty puke.

"Jesus," one a them says.

Someone puts a hand on my shoulder. All sudden, I'm too weak to knock it away. And it feels ok actually, if it has to be there.

The hand belongs to Mayles and he's saying, "Maybe we got a boat they'll send up the river to get us."

McDonnell says, "There's no *boats* Mayles, ya fucking moron."

Bobby Earl says, "Wouldn't matter if we did. River's too low to float a turd."

Mayles says, "Can we get across it you think?"

"Reckon it's still deep and swift enough to kill ya. Not to mention being an easy shot for those snipers up there."

"Specially as long as those fires are burning. I think that's the grass and shit burning now. Maybe it will smoke them outta the cave," says McDonnell.

"What if the guys in the woods leave us behind?" says Mayles.

"Shut the fuck up, Mayles," says McDonnell. "Go take care of your boyfriend."

I look up from where I'm on my knees. They're all peeking between the rocks, watching the grassfires burning. I take my .45 from its holster. Sits heavy in my black, sticky fingers. I quietly chamber a round. "It's all your fault, Bobby Earl."

Bobby Earl don't even turn around: "Two squads is all they give me for this. Now quit *ridin* me TJ or I'll bust your pimpled ass all the way down to private!"

I go, "It's Taylor Jon fucking god*damn*it!" and shoot Bobby Earl in the back of his fat head, McDonnell is turning around and I blow the side of his head open like meatballs and spaghetti. Mayles is looking at me and I shoot him in the face.

It's quiet at fucking last except for the fucking river and the crackle of the fires up the hill. Then I can hear them in the woods calling out what happened? What happened? Like ghosts. Fuck em.

I holster my .45 and crawl on my hands and knees to the river. I'll just get in, then wade across, even float if I have to. I can take my time, let it carry me away from here. Get to the other side and ditch this uniform, get out of here. Get out of this desert, this war. Get out, get some real drugs and kidnap a stripper, yeah, and fuck her day and night. Day and fucking night.

The water's cold on my hands, it *hurts*. Fuck it. I crawl into the river. I can walk across the bottom, and the water will hide me and no one will be able to see me.

Shit –

I'm off my feet, the water's pulling me, can't touch the bottom, can't ugk! keep my head up, I feel my boots fillin with water.

Slam off a rock, it hurts and I'm being pulled down, water fucks my mouth and comes down my throat! Dennys at the lake, this must be what he felt! FUCK!

 Oh. It's ok.

 It's ok ...

U.S. Armstrong

 "Well, the good news is that Camby waited for the Mexican Army to take Albuquerque. Gave us enough time to tie down some loose ends before leaving Santa Fe," said Hovan, spinning his recliner with his shoes' pointed toes. The Learjet's engines whited-out some of Hovan's voice but not enough.

 "14th cut to pieces too. Guard was too spread out. They went like dominoes."

 "Relax," grinned Hovan. He tapped himself left, right on his toes. "None of that matters."

 U.S. raised his hat brim. Fired a torpedo blue eye. Growled, "How in hell can you say that? Territory's overrun with the entire Mexican Army. The *Mexican* Army. Prolly in Santa Fe by now."

 "Probably. Unless Camby's ragtag militia got there first." Hovan stopped spinning to wet his lips with a Gray Goose and diet.

 "That's *right*. Plus you got bike gangs and El Salvadoran gangs and cultists and al Qaeda and Indians running amok. State Guard is scattered to tiny pieces. How long you think they're gonna last, split up and cut off?"

 "About as long as White, I imagine," said Hovan.

 "Jokes? All New Texas is lost. My chair'll still be warm when some Mexican sits down on it. You gonna tell me none of that matters?"

 "That's right, U.S.," said Hovan. He set his drink down and started tapping himself back and forth again. "Let them fight over the scraps that fell under the table. What was worth taking from that dried-up wasteland, we took. Wait until we get back home, and you see what a killing we made. Wait until you see."

 U.S. snatched the phone from the molded plastic table. He turned to the window, dark night land of Texas below. He saw his eyes in the reflection and dropped his hat brim down low. He dialed a number.

 Moment of static.

 "Marianne," he said. "It's U.S. I reckon I'm coming home."

Hormigo

"Shit Hormigo," said Flywheel when the last bike went silent. "Why we stopping at this shitty Tejónes bar? The party's in Albuquerque, bro."

"I know where the party is, motherfucker," said Hormigo. He raised a gloved finger to Flywheel's attention. "The Diablos keep their word of honor. Always."

A Mexican flag hung over Cascabel's door.

"That should be a Zia Crossbones, like I got tattooed," he said, opening the door.

The Diablos filled in after Hormigo. There were a couple of Tejónes in a booth next to the door. Hormigo walked up to them and put out his glove hand, "Hey bro, Espectro is my boy. We're cool in here. Just meeting a friend. I'm Hormigo. Diablos."

The grizzly bearded Tejóne reluctantly shook Hormigo's hand. "Grizz."

Hormigo said, "You guys want shots? Hey we're celebrating, right bro? Got rid of them Texas fuckers, once and for all!"

Grizz rumbled, "Now we just get a bunch of different fuckers instead."

"Come on now," Hormigo laughed good-naturedly. "Let's celebrate one thing at a time, right bro? I'll get some shots coming."

Hormigo shouldered through the crowded room. The jukebox was loudly playing a Mexican chart-topper. He turned to whichever Diablo was behind him and said, "I hate that music, it sounds like my aunt's at Christmas. Haha, fuck it, right?"

Whichever Diablo was behind him snickered. Hormigo made his way to the bar and elbowed himself a space next to three hard-looking bikers. Independents? Ah, fuck it. He got the bartender's attention with a crisp hundred dollar bill. "Shots of tequila. Good stuff, not that Cuervo shit. Me, Ribeye, Flywheel, Lumbres, Wolfe, that Tejónes guy Grizz and his buddy. And hey, shots for these three guys too."

The three looked hard at Hormigo. He looked hard back. Then he smiled. "It's a party, right guys? A fiesta. Texas is going home."

One of them nodded thanks.

Hormigo said, "Okay, so how many is that? Oh shit, hey Billy! Almost forgot you and you're the reason we're *here*. What are you doing sitting at this bar by yourself? Hey barkeep, one for Billy here, ok? How many is that now?"

The bartender said, "Ten ... eleven."

Hormigo set the stiff bill onto the bar. "Round of beers too. Keep the change."

Hormigo put his arm around Billy's limp shoulders. Billy looked up, eyes rolling wide like a flounder, bad sheen on his face. "Jesus Billy, you look like shit bro."

"Sup, migo?" slurred Billy.

The shot glasses arrived, each wavering its meniscus. Hormigo gestured across the room at the Tejónes. "Hey we got our shots bro!"

Grizz looked away.

"Fuck them," said Hormigo. He raised his shot glass. "To getting rid of Texas!"

The Diablos put up a roar and they clinked glasses, shot the tequila.

"So Billy," said Hormigo, leaning on the bar. "What's the matter?"

"Huh?" Billy's scraggly hair looked like he'd been sleeping in kivas. His mouth was slack, blubbery.

"Billy," chuckled Hormigo. "You called me, remember? Said it was an emergency, I had to meet you here. You remember?"

"Yeah. Yeah, Hormigo."

"So what's up?" Hormigo gave Billy's shoulder a firm squeeze.

"Yeah, I need help bro. Got no one I can, I can turn to, bro."

"You got my help Billy – whoa, watch my beer. Tell me what the problem is."

"Melody."

"Huh?"

"Melody and Daniel," said Billy, looking up with tears in his slit red eyes.

"What's that?"

"My wife. My wife and my kid."

"Where they at?"

Billy pointed a finger in no direction. "Out there. Gotta find them bro."

"So do it. What do you need from me? Money?"

Billy nodded. "Yeah. And my truck's gone."

Hormigo smiled. "Why didn't you just say so, instead of all this carrying on? Billy, you remember when me and you was sitting at that table over there? And I got the idea to do the Bowl? And we did it bro, us together, and you wired up those things and it worked? Fuckinaye did it work. I always got your back bro. You got a cell phone? No? Ok.

306

Barkeep! Gimme a pen and a napkin. All right. Here Billy, take this number. Ok, I'll put it in your pocket. You don't look so good. Listen to what I say. Across the parking lot is a motel. Go over there, get a room. Get some sleep. When you wake up, call that number and tell him that Hormigo sent you. He'll bring you a car. Here's some gas money," tucking a folded wad into Billy's shirt pocket.

"Thanks bro," said Billy.

"Go sleep it off. Good luck, Billy," said Hormigo, pushing Billy towards the door. "Diablos! Let's do one more victory shot before we head down south. We run New Mexico now, let's celebrate! Barkeep! Five shots of tequila!"

Their glasses were filled. The Diablos gathered around Hormigo and held them up, spilling drips.

Hormigo said, "To the Diablos!"

"To the Diablos!" and they clinked the glasses, shot the tequila.

Billy

Where the fuck am I?

I can hear cars on a highway. I'm in a motel. I'm in the motel next to Cascabel, in San Valerde. Why am I here?

My stomach feels bad. My mouth is so dry ... how much did I drink last night? What *happened* last night? What time is it?

I roll off the hard bed and hit the floor. Doesn't hurt. I think I'm still drunk.

I gotta piss so bad but I'm so thirsty I'm gonna die. Fall into the bathroom. Turn on the sink, cold water comes out and I'm sucking it out the hollow of my hands but the *sound* is making me piss, I'm so thirsty I can't stop drinking so I grab my dong and aim for the toilet, still sucking water with one hand.

Well, I pissed all over the wall, forever. Fuck it. I feel better anyway.

I can remember parts of last night. Hormigo I remember. He gave me a phone number. I stumble in the dark, feel in my jeans. Nothing. I find my shirt and there's stuff in the pocket. A napkin, and a bunch of twenties. From him? Shit, man ...

I can't remember for sure. I just remember Hormigo writing that number for me. And leaving, I remember bumping into those other bikers outside. One, big bearded one, saying how they had friends on the way over to take care of them Diablos.

Really? Did I dream that maybe? My brain is so fucking

smashed up I don't know. Fucking booze and speed and shit, my brain is cold menudo. I got to cut that shit out. Gotta get straight, get Melody back. Then we'll get Daniel back, together.

I call the number. A guy answers. I say, "This is Billy Ortiz."

"Who?"

"I'm a friend of Hormigo's. He gave me this number. I need a car."

"Where are you?"

"I'm at the motel next to Cascabel in San Valerde."

A moment's static. "It'll be there in an hour."

"Thanks," but the line was already dead. So. One hour and then I'm going to get Melody back. I sit on the bed and accidentally catch myself in the mirror.

Jesus bro. I look like shit. Melody won't take me back, looking like this. There's a drugstore in the stripmall across the highway. The guy said one hour. I got time.

I dress and walk out of my room. The sun is bright, like morning. Lots of traffic. I get halfway across the highway and have to wait, dizzy. Inside the drugstore they got the air conditioner blasting. Feels good but makes me shiver.

Back in my room. I forgot, there's my own cold piss all over the bathroom floor. I mop it up with half a roll of toilet paper. Then I shave in the cracked mirror over the sink. Then I cut the worst ends of my hair off. Then I take a long shower in the hot, hot water. I'm going to get Melody back. I'm going to get Melody back, and we'll get Daniel back, together.

Eddie Brown

He had rehearsed it over and over in his mind but still couldn't get it straight. So he wrote it down on a piece of paper. Edited it. Rewrote it. It was as good as it was ever going to get. Eddie took a deep breath.

Read it once more. So it doesn't sound rehearsed on her machine. Because you know she won't answer when she sees the call's from you, right?

Eddie read aloud in a voice that sounded very alien to him: "Hello Lilah, it's ~~Eddie it's me it's me again~~ Eddie again. Um. I couldn't help noticing you haven't answered any of my phone calls for a few weeks. I hope that it's because you're not talking to me, and not because of any difficulties you might be experiencing. Um. I just had to try one last time. See, this grant I applied for a long time back – before the war, before I met you and everything – well, I *got* it. I'm as surprised as ~~you are~~ anyone. I'm flying to Brazil in a few days. It's a grant to study army ants, *Eciton burchelli*. I'm excited about it. I would send you a postcard but I don't know where to send it ~~now~~. So you need to call me back soon, or you won't get any postcards. Um. I can only apologize for my actions, Lilah, but not for my heart. Looking back, I realize that my passion for what we were accomplishing – and we did accomplish something great that you and I and all New Mexico and all the people everywhere should be proud of – well I was doing it because of you. Because I wanted to share something with you. And we did. Don't let my ~~stupidity lust stupidity lust~~ stupidity invalidate all that. Please, Lilah. Don't abandon me. ~~I loved you~~ I love you."

Eddie choked himself up by the end. He wiped his eye with a finger. He cleared his clogged throat. "Ok. Here goes."

Eddie picked up the phone. He dialed her number. It rang once.

"We're sorry, but the number you have dialed is no longer in service."

Eddie looked around the boxes nestling the detritus of his life. It would all fit in his pickup truck and most of it was junk. Eddie unplugged the phone and dropped it into a half-full box of the last random items.

She knows you're a liar. She knows there's no grant.

"Could be," Eddie said aloud. "But I'm still driving to Brazil."

A fleck of movement caught his eye. Two female *Lycosidae* spiders were maneuvering around each other on the ceiling, legs arched. Eddie watched the agonistic combat, mouth open in wonder, following their every feint and thrust.

Governor Armeño

Governor Armeño raised a glass of New Mexican sparkling wine and warmly crinkled his Conciliation Eyes. "Gentleman. And lady. Thank you for coming together as we pick up the pieces of New Mexico. We have a unique opportunity to remake history. So let us toast New Mexico, and to getting things back to the way they used to be. Here's ... to the way things used to be."

The assembled interests raised their glasses and sipped. The moment was as sweetly piquant as the sparkling wine. They swallowed, lingering aftertaste.

"To the way things used to be," added Josephine Partridge of Davenport & Partridge Real Estate. "Before the Texas corporations killed the market by driving inflation through the roof and making development impossible."

"To the way things used to be," added Juan Mondragon of the New Mexico Farmer's Alliance. "Before the developers stole all our irrigation water for golf courses, and made it impossible to grow a single beanfield."

"To the way things used to be," said Brandon Titus of the Titus Ranches. "Before farmers started digging ditches and damming up pastureland and hording their water behind barbed wire, and made it impossible to raise cattle except in Mad Cow feed lots."

"To the way things used to be," said General Manuel Alvarez of the Mexican Army. "Before el Norte was stolen by the Americans and our people were forced to drink the impossible filthy trickle that drips downstream to us."

"To the way things used to be," said William Standing Elk of the United Pueblo Council. "Before the white man came, and tried to do the impossible. Gather all the waters in his hand, and call the waters his own."

Governor Armeño turned to Mr. White. "I think we're going to be here for a while."

Mr. White said, "I expect we are."

HO

One particular water molecule twisted along with its compadres in the great ocean abundance. Loose associations allowed the molecule to sink into the cool depths. With the others, the molecule carried a cumbersome burden of compounds. At one moment, the molecule was swept into the beating gills of a fish. The oxygen and dioxin molecules were wrenched out of its grasp.

The one particular water molecule was dumped back into the general rabble of the milling millions on trillions of compadres. A rising chain captured the water molecule's fated progress down towards deepest gravity. They climbed up to the aroused surface, where sun pierced the naked open ocean. The molecule absorbed the sun's energy. Electrons humming with potential, it broke free from its compadres and spun into the air.

Free and light again, at last.